MW01659515

Golden Nuggets

Golden Nuggets

Frits Forrer

Holland's Glory PO Box 488, Gulf Breeze, FL 32562

This is a work of fiction. Names, characters, places, and incidents either are the product of the author's imagination or are used fictitiously. Any resemblance to actual events or persons, living or dead, is entirely coincidental.

Copyright © 2009 by Frits Forrer

All rights reserved. No part of this book may be reproduced or transmitted in any form or by any means, electronic or mechanical, including photocopying, recording, or by any information storage and retrieval system, without permission in writing from the author.

This edition was prepared for printing by
Ghost River Images
5350 East Fourth Street
Tucson, Arizona 85711
ghostriverimages.com

Cover illustration by Betty Shoopman
bcshoop@bellsouth.net

Contact the author at:
fforrer@bellsouth.net or
www.fritsforrer.net
850-916-7566
Fax 850—916 1861

ISBN 978-0-9822207-1-9

Library of Congress Control Number: 2009937137

Printed in the United States of America

October, 2009

10 9 8 7 6 5 4 3 2 1

Contents

AUTHOR'S NOTE

This is a work of FICTION, pure and simple. Exciting, but simple.

Many thanks to my number one spelling genius, my Katy.

Also, thanks to the dedicated members of the West Florida Literary Federation that make up the *Writers Anonymous*, Joe Hefti, Jack Beverly, Andrea Walker, Jeanie Zokar, Lynn Huber, Dr. Joe and Marilyn Howard.. My *English* improved daily under their watchful eyes.

The critique from my buddies in the *Belles & Beaux* was very helpful and inspiring. True buddies, Kay, Selma, Fred, true buddies indeed.

Special thanks to Art Giberson for his beautiful critical review.

Again, many thanks,

Frits.

Dedicated to

The memory of my old flying buddy Jan “Katjang” Wildbergh

And

Jan Pronk
Who taught me to love Colorado

GOLDEN NUGGETS,
(BIG ONES)

Chapter One

The robbery,

Saturday Morning

The robbery had gone well. Surprisingly well. There was no one around and apparently there was no security system in the old mining company building and museum north of Granby. The guard let them in the backdoor, so they walked in, pulled the glass cases forward, unscrewed the back board and took whatever they wanted. It had taken only ten minutes to empty the pouches, fill them with rocks and bolt the cases to the rear wall. Everything looked as if they hadn't been moved in fifty years.

Randy had taken the time to clean all doorknobs and sliding door handles.At 9:30 on Saturday morning, nobody passed by the old mining company building in Rand and the museum attracted very few people nowadays. Half the building was still being used as an office and the other half displayed all the old mining equipment. To most of the employees it was just junk, but the owners cherished the memories of the old miners who had pioneered the gold industry in Colorado.

What the present staff was unaware of was that the pouches, displayed in the glass cases had actual nuggets in them, worth thousands of dollars. For nearly fifty years, no one had even considered the thought that real gold was on display. No one, except Randy, who worked on the ceiling in the museum room for two days as a plasterer for a Boulder, Colorado company.

When they had to move the display cases in order to finish the cracked ceiling, it took just minutes to unscrew twenty bolts to get them off the back wall of the building. While the tall units were standing in the middle of the room, it seemed like an open invitation, to remove the rear boards and take a look at the display items. Especially the pouches. To their surprise, the old cracked leather bags held real nuggets. Real old-fashioned gold nuggets. Twelve innocent looking weather beaten sacks, loaded with gold.

Jack wanted to pocket a few immediately, but Randy's cooler head prevailed.

"We're coming back on Saturday with a load of gravel. We'll tell'em on Friday that we need just a couple more hours to finish up and the security man will let us in. There won't be nobody around, so we empty out all the little pouches and fill'em with gravel. Put them back right where they were and nobody will ever know for another fifty years."

"Can't I just take one? Maybe a few?"

"No, don't be stupid. On Saturday we'll take'em all and nobody will ever know."

That's how it went. They carefully dumped the nuggets in a five gallon plaster can, refilled the pouches with fine gravel and placed them back in the identical spot from which they had been removed. They worked with latex gloves and only a very close examination would have shown that the leather sacks had less dust on them than the rest of the items on display. They finished the final touch-ups on the ceiling and around the display, loaded the truck, stashed the ladders and scaffolds and left.

Randy's 1990 Ford pickup hummed its way down the mountain and not until they passed Granby on the Fraser River did he slow down to slide into a rest area, lined with picnic tables. Jack's Harley still rested in the same shady spot where he had left it. None of the five picnic tables had any visitors yet, so the two conspirators had plenty of privacy. The cooler in the truck produced two *Miller-Lite* bottles and they made themselves comfortable on one of the benches.

"I'd as soon take my half, get on my bike and ride into the sunset. Reno, here I come."

"What will I tell Johnson when you don't show up for your check on Monday?"

"Tell'em you'll hand it to me when you see me. Tell'em I probably got drunk on Sunday. Tell'em anything you want. You cash that lousy check and if I'm ever broke again, I'll come and find you, so to me it's like money in the bank. How do we split the stuff? Count them out?"

"We could, but let's just take an empty can, fill it up and the first one goes into your saddlebag and the second one in my truck and so on. How's that sound?"

"You got an empty can?"

"In a minute." Randy returned to the truck and came back with an empty *Bush* can. "See if you can get that top off."

"Leave it to an old Navy man. Nuttin' to it."

With the open aluminum can in hand they moved to the back of the truck, took the tarpaulin off the five gallon buckets and pulled the one with the gold to the edge of the bed. Jack reached in first, filled the *Bush* can to the brim and emptied it in his left saddlebag on the rear of his motorcycle.

Randy's turn was next. He grabbed an empty plastic Wal-Mart bag and filled that with a matching load. Twice more, a full can found its way to the bike and the bag and then it became a matter of counting the remainder.

"Why don't we make it easy. You select the biggest nut you see and put it in the can. Then I pick the largest one I can find and put it in my bag and so on till they're all gone. Make sense, Jack?"

"Makes sense to me. Here I go"

Minutes later, the loot had been divided and Randy deposited his share under his front seat, while Jack kicked life into the Harley Davidson.

"Well Jack, you have my address and number, let me know how you make out. I might need an address of a good dealer out West someday. Have a safe trip. Don't let some blonde chick con you out of your money!"

Laughingly, they shook hands and Jack roared out of the lot, back onto the road leading toward Utah.

At forty-five, Randy didn't share the foolish notion that taking gold to a gambling town would make him rich. He had already learned some hard lessons. Lost his first wife to a good friend while he was spending time in prison for dealing drugs. Then, when he got back on his feet, she sued him for back-child-support and the judge ruled in her favor, so now he lived with a garnishee on his paycheck, keeping him working six days a week, just to get by. His boss, J.B. Johnson knew about his background and stood by him all the way, giving him as much over-time as they could muster. Randy knew, he couldn't blow that solid relationship, so he would keep right on working, while he cashed in the nuggets, one by one. His present girlfriend, a widow with three children, was having a positive influence on him and he felt his life was finally back on track. His dirty blond hair was thinning rapidly, so he grew a goatee and a mustache and felt that his physical image and his looks were improving right along with his positive attitude.

He was feeling good. Hugging the speed limit, the miles crunched away.

In the opposite direction, the miles flew by much faster. In Sulphur Springs, Jack stopped to buy a six-pack and on straight stretches, he calmly sipped his beer, while in the many turns, he kept both hands on the handlebars while the sun played hide and seek on his back and neck. He didn't have a map of Colorado, but he knew he had to head South to intersect I-70, so when the road swung to the North after passing though Kremmlin, he realized that he should turn somewhere in order to stay on course. The sign that read *STEAMBOAT SPRINGS 50M* didn't appeal to him at all, so the next road that turned off to the West: *134 to Gore Pass*, was his obvious choice. He had not intended to cross over a 9,000 foot mountain range, but that couldn't be helped. The weather was beautiful with patchy clouds circling the mountain tops. Luck was with him weather-wise. There he was, twenty six years young, in good physical shape and reasonably good looking, he felt he had the world by the tail. How much the gold would bring, he couldn't even fathom, but it had to be at least $100,000. That would get him well on his way to riches, he was sure. He'd gamble some, but the rest he would put into real estate, property, land and stores, maybe a small motel.

The air got thinner and the temperature dropped three degrees for every 1,000 foot he climbed. There were no rest-stops or buildings, so he stopped on the shoulder of the road to get his leather jacket out. That was better. Up and up! There seemed no end to the climb and every so often, the clouds would hang over the road. Jack slowed down to a crawl and took off his sunglasses. They were fogging up anyway. Just as suddenly as the fog had appeared, it dissipated and he could speed up again. Nice going. The view was spectacular from this altitude, but that did not hold his attention very long, as he was cursing the height of the pass. He was dying to let down again into Central Colorado and I-70 with its four-lane highway.

A sign saying *"Gore Pass" One Mile* was the blessing he had been waiting for.

One more sharp turn! One more cloud! He slowed even more as the fog got thicker between the canyon walls but out of nowhere, a truck appeared before him, maybe climbing at five miles an hour. Jack hit his brakes hard, but skidded sideways, crashed into the rear of the truck and while trying to correct, he slid into the grass, hit a rock and tumbled head over heels down the slope. His Harley crashed into him briefly as it rolled out of control down the mountain, spraying golden nuggets into the foggy ravine.

Jack's head was crushed immediately and his neck nearly severed from his spine, only holding on by some bloody neck muscles.

"Did you hear something?" The truck driver turned to his wife.

"It sounded like something hit the back of the trailer."

"That's what I thought. I better check." He stopped the vehicle, turned on the flashers and walked to rear of the trailer. Indeed, it looked like a black object had left paint scrapes on his back bumper. "They weren't here this morning." He said to himself. "I better walk back some and see what happened."

Indeed, some 150 feet back, there were tire marks on the macadam, skid marks into the grass and tracks spilling down the mountainside. "Holy shit. That must have been a motorcycle. What am I gonna do? I can't go down there. God knows how far down he went. I see no flames, no smoke, no explosion. No nothin'!"

He looked back at his truck. He could barely see it. "I better get it the hell outta here before someone else clobbers into it." He jogged back, jumped in and put the machine in gear.

"What happened?" His wife noticed how pale he looked.

"Some motor cycle hit us and went over the side. Get on the cell and start calling 911 and the State Troopers. I think that's Star CHP. Keep dialing till you get somebody. The location is one mile East of Gore Pass. Keep trying. They gotta get some rescuers up there. I couldn..." He glanced over... "Keep trying. In a minute we'll clear the ridge and we outta be able to get through. Keep trying."

Golden Nuggets
II
The rescue

Saturday afternoon

Within the hour, troopers, fire trucks, ambulances and dozens of rescue workers were on the scene. The fog remained a hindrance, but the sun came through from time to time as the little clouds continued to drift to the East along the mountain tops. From the edge of the canyon, there was nothing to be seen on the slope, only a bit of a trail through the grass and the shrub, indicating that something or somebody had slid down there. With long ropes attached to their belts, two ESU workers rappelled down the mountain until they came upon a lifeless body. From there they called on their walkie-talkies for a stretcher to be lowered down. While tying the remains to the canvas, one young worker, Brad Phillips, spotted a shiny little rock and picked it up. He didn't have any time to really admire his find, so he put it in his left pocket and lifted one of the metal bars that made up the stretcher and called into his mike, "Bring her up!"

Keeping the body balanced on their shoulders with one hand and grabbing at bushes with the other, they inched their way up to the road. Every so often they had to holler; "Slow down!" because their footing wasn't very solid going up, while strong hands on top kept pulling up the gurney. Twice more, Brad thought he saw something glistening, but there was no time to bend over and retrieve it.

The decision was made that the motorcycle was too far down in the canyon to risk a recovery attempt and that it was not needed for any kind of identification, so the long parade of vehicles returned to their original locations, with Jack's body strapped in an ambulance.

Once the remains had been searched, the only relative or acquaintance that could be identified was his boss, Mr. Johnson in Boulder. A hearse was dispatched to transport him there for a proper interment.

***

Sunday morning.

Randy had spent a pleasant evening with his girl friend and the three children and was staggered with a surprise on Sunday morning, when he found a note on his door from his boss, Mr. Johnson, to call immediately.

"I can't believe it, I can't believe it." He sobbed on the phone. "We finished the job, Jack got on his bike and I came home in my truck. I can't believe it. What the hell was he doing up there in that canyon?"

His boss had no answers and asked him to come over and help with the final arrangements and wanted to know more about immediate family and close friends that needed to be notified. Randy knew he could be of some assistance and was anxious to know if there had been any report of gold nuggets, so he rushed to the funeral home. The police and ESU reports were very sketchy and only listed known details and speculations that he had collided with a truck. "Dumb bastard!" was all Randy could think of, but he wondered, "What happened to the gold? Could it have gone all the way down to the bottom of the canyon with the nuggets securely in the saddle bags?"

He knew if they were discovered, he would be implicated immediately, so he felt he should recover them as soon as possible. It was too late on Sunday to even consider a trip out there and during the week, he couldn't get off work long enough to think about it either. All he could do was wait till next weekend and meanwhile hide his share of the gold in such a way that nobody could find it. Just one solution came to mind: bury them in the park.

The Wal-Mart bag with his treasure disappeared into a gunnysack, then in a five gallon paint bucket under some heavy rocks. The lid was sealed and taped securely and a stainless steel cable attached to the handle. Toward dusk, he drove north to Loveland, to the *Boyd Lake State Park* and parked between the trees along the lake. Nobody was in sight, so he took his bucket and walked along the shore till he found a rocky spot, where he lowered his loot slowly till it hit bottom. The cable was wrapped around a young sapling and additional stones were put on top of it, so none of the shiny rope was visible.

For additional security, he hauled additional rocks and stones from along the shore and finally stepped back and looked at his art work. It looked absolutely natural. Satisfied, he paced the distance from his fortune to his truck and from there to the parking lot. He was sure he could find it again.

***

Saturday night, in the only bar in McCoy, Brad Phillips contemplated whether he should keep the gold discovery to himself, or share it with his best buddy, Scott Pierce. Scott was a carpenter in the off-season and a ski instructor at Breckenridge in the winter. At home after the rescue, Brad had shined up the nugget and was convinced that he had discovered a trace of a goldmine, because he had seen some other glittering stones on the way up. The biggest question was: was it legal to keep his find, did it belong to the property owner or could he go back and gather up all he could find?

Going down the mountain by himself was a dangerous undertaking. Like mountain climbing, you should never do it alone. A second beer convinced him, he should consult Scott. He ordered another beer. Prospecting for gold and staking out claims were things that hadn't happened since he was born and he was not sure at all if he could get in trouble with the law or maybe already was since he picked up that one nugget. He felt he could even use some legal advice that was beyond the scope of Scott's knowledge and intelligence. He was also dying to find out how much that rock in his left pocket was worth. He had no idea whether he was walking around with a ten dollar item or a fortune. He did have visions though, of being worth millions if they could work it out and discover and own a real gold mine in the Rockies.

Scott was late. Maybe he had to work late and was still getting dolled up for their regular dancing date in Frisco. There was a nice club and especially during the ski season, the place crawled with good looking ski bunnies. The only problem was always, driving back after dancing and boozing all night. Sometimes they got lucky and spent the night in some condo with another bunch of lusty youngsters, but tonight, Brad had more glorious thoughts on his brain.

Where was Scott? Time for another beer. It was already getting dark. Maybe they should just sit and discuss their golden future and not go struttin' tonight. Three beers before getting on the road was probably a plenty already. Going home was no problem, he lived within a block from the joint and could even walk there if necessary. He didn't have a cell phone and just when he considered borrowing one, Scott strolled in, dressed to kill, hair slicked back and cowboy boots with silver tips.

"Com'on boy! We're running late." He wasn't even gonna have one beer.

"Wait Scott, wait. Grab a cold one and join me there." He pointed to an empty booth along the wall. I got something to tell you." The two were as different as day and night. Scott was over six foot with dark curly hair and Brad was squat, just five feet, eight with a blond crewcut.

In spite of twenty interruptions by Scott and beer deliveries, in ten minutes Brad got his whole story out, including his opinions on prospecting and getting rich.

"Holy smokes! You got it with you? Can I see it?"

"Make sure nobody sees it." With that he slipped his hand in his pocket and passed the nugget on to Scott, who cupped it in his hands and angled them toward the light. The barroom was dimly lit, but there was no question about the glow of the gold piece.

"Wow!" Scott handed it back. "And you saw more of them? Out in the open? Just like that?" His eyes had opened wide. "Just lying there for people to grab?" He shook his head. "I guess nobody has been smart enough or stupid enough to work himself down that slope."

Brad nodded. "You're right. If you ain't got no business down there like we did today, what's the point in risking your neck? There's nothin' there, just rocks and shrubs." He finished his last beer. ""'How can we find out if we can lay a legitimate claim on the stuff and who actually owns the property. I think the State owns it or maybe the county. It's not in a National Park, is it?" Brad wasn't sure.

"What time is it? I have a cousin in Denver who works in the courthouse. She might know somethin'. Let's go to my place and call her. Your folks are home, right? Yeah, let's go to my place. Get a couple of six-packs before we leave. Take your truck. We're not dancing tonight."

Scott's Cousin Pauline was no expert and no lawyer, but did have a certain amount of answers and also a lot of questions that the boys were not prepared to answer, like: "Where is that ravine? What County? What jurisdiction, State? Sheriff? Local Police?"

Her general opinion was to lay low until she could get more answers on Monday morning.

"Don't you know a lawyer you could call?"

"On Saturday night? At home? Are you insane?" She was adamant. "No, no, Scott. Whatever is there will be there on Monday as well, so don't do anything stupid, like trespassing or stealing, you hear?"

They heard, but weren't happy with the answers. "Let me get my atlas out of my car, that way we can find out more details." Scott disappeared.

With the atlas and a map on the table, Brad showed exactly where the accident had taken place and to their inexperienced eyes, the whole area was in the *ARAPAHO NATIONAL FOREST.*

"Aye! What does that mean? Can we get permission from Washington to explore if we do no damage and construct no mines or buildings?" Brad was stunned.

"Don't know, I don't know. Are we now stealing from the government?"

"Moses on a horse! What are we gonna do?"

"I say, the parks belong to the people and are there for the taxpayers to enjoy and we are taxpayers and I'm about to go and enjoy it. Let's go out there tomorrow and gather up as much gold as we can find and we'll ask questions again on Monday. The worst that can happen is that we may have to give it back, right?" Scott had made up his mind. "Go home, you can't go mountain climbing in that outfit and tomorrow morning I pick you up, get a bunch of ropes and we're off. Have one last beer and by the way, buddy, thanks for sharing that with me. I haven't been this excited since I was in bed with three girls."

Golden Nuggets
III
Sliding from nugget to nugget

Sunday morning.

It wasn't hard to locate the spot where the body had been pulled up the day before.

Tire tracks from two fire trucks were still obvious on the shoulders of the road and there was a distinct path down the slope, where the body had tumbled down and been brought back up. Brad and Scott surveyed the area and decided to park their pickup about two hundred feet down from the point of impact and returned with ropes and spikes. Their first job was to find a solid trunk or rock, from which they could suspend themselves without the rope being visible from the road.

Brad descended first, one hand sliding down the rope, the other one from shrub to shrub. "Hold on tight. This is steep, brother."

"I got it wound around my waist. Just go down easy, so you won't pull me down after you." Scott braced himself by digging his heels into the dirt.

"Alright. alright! I see a good size tree that will support the both of us. Just hang on a minute. I'll wrap the other rope around it and then you work your way down, easy like."

"Who's gonna stay up here and hold a rope while I come down?"

"Just take it slow. Hold on to each rock and shrub as you inch down. Nuttun' to it. I do this for a living."

"Then how come you went down first with me bracing you from up here?"

"For God's sake Scott. Stop bitchin' and get your ass down here."

"Here I come. Is this the steepest damn canyon in Colorado? Couldn't you find some place with a gentler slope?"

"You're doin' okay. Move over to your right a little bit. Just a foot or two." Brad reached up. "See? I've got your right leg. Now lower yourself onto that limb. Good boy. Now we're in. See, this way nobody from the road can tell we're here and we can explore all we want. This tree is solid and it should support the both of us as we go down. Tie this around your waist." He handed Scott a belt with a huge stainless steel snap and hooked a rope through it while attaching the other end to a small tree and looping around the rock that already held his own rope.

"Put your gloves on, so you won't get rope burn."

"My gloves? I don't have gloves!"

"Com'on. I gave you a pair of gloves...."

"I left them in the truck on the roadside, I don't know."

"Oh shit. Just don't let the rope slide through your hands. Go down easy, hand over hand. We're about twenty feet above the spot where I thought I saw another nugget. So, rappel down easy like... ."

"Do what?"

"Rappel... Never mind. Just go down slowly. You can see the trail where we dragged up the body. Just stay with that and look around."

Little by little, inches at a time, they let themselves farther down into the canyon.

"There it is!" Brad shouted as he eased over to his left and picked up another nugget.

"I told you, I told you. There's gotta be a goldmine here somewhere. Let's spread out a little and go slow. Look to your left and right constantly. When something glitters, grab it. We ain't in no hurry. The sun is gonna swing around the mountain in an hour or two and give us even more light."

"How much rope have we got?"

"That's the only problem. I can go another 150 or 200 feet and that's it. If it's too steep from there on down, then we quit for the day and rethink our plans, okay?"

"Whatever you say, boss. You're the mountain climber. I'm just a skier and a lover, so let's go for it."

They worked their way back and forth while inching down slowly for about twenty minutes. Sometimes they lost sight of one another, but they always came back to the centerline of their descent. Scott found two nuggets and was ecstatic. "You're right, old buddy! There's gold in them thar hills. How do we figure out how much this is worth?"

They had come to the end of their rope, literally, and were sitting on a ledge staring down into an ever steepening slope.

"I don't know and I don't know how to find out, but I know one thing: that's a hell of a ravine down there. We may have to find us a map and figure on a different way to get in there. Usually at the bottom there's a creek and little paths or roads always follow the creek or the river. Let's stop by the Ranger Station and ask for a map and buy a year's pass or somethin' so we look like serious campers or fishermen and they won't wonder what we're up to."

"Good thinkin' man. By now I wish I had strung a six-pack on my belt. This was a hell of a climb."

Brad corrected him. "This was not a climb buddy. This was a descent, the climb comes next. This is how we're gonna do it. In order not to put too much strain on that tree up there, you climb for five minutes and stop. Take the pressure off the rope and find a place to rest. Then I climb for five minutes and so on, because if both our weights are on that tree at the same time and it uproots, we'll both end up in the bottom of the ravine."

"Where do you get all that wisdom, man?" Scott was impressed.

"I see a lot of dead people who didn't use their head and ended up in the morgue. I'm not about to be one of them."

"Okay! Am I first?"

"Yep. Go for it." Brad watched as his friend climbed steadily, working his way from rock to rock and shrub to shrub. He was obviously in prime physical condition.

After five minutes Brad got into action and after three minutes he could already see Scott's outline against the blue sky.

"I found another one!" Scott nearly screamed in spite of the quiet environment. "This one's even bigger."

"Let me see, let me see." Brad edged closer. "Wow. We better keep looking around as we go. You're up next for the next five minutes. You holdin' up alright?"

"I'm fine, but I still wish I had some beer with me. Next time let's prepare a little better."

"Alright man. I'm counting."

It took them forty minutes to get back up to the road and Scott had to admit that it had been as strenuous as walking up on a ski-slope.

"You do this crap for a livin'?"

"Like I said, nuttin' to it."

Nobody was in sight as they coiled their ropes and hid them behind a rock before returning to their truck. After making a U-turn, they stopped long enough to recover the ropes and once over the crest, at a scenic rest stop, the beer came out.

Scott took a long swig and started, "You know buddy, something don't make sense. How could there be a goldmine that drops an occasional nugget here and there down the mountain slope? Why isn't there some gold dust mingled in along the way? Why…?

"Because the rain washed away the dust?"

"That don't make no sense. Think about it. If there was lode…"

"A what?"

"I think they call it a lode or a vein in which there was gold, then that lode should be right at the top of the ridge, because otherwise, there wouldn't be little nuggets floating down the slope, right? They don't float upward, that's for damn sure."

"What are you saying Scott? The real treasure should be high up along the edge of canyon?"

"Have you ever seen anything jump up the slope?"

"Hahahaha! No I can't say I ever have, other than a frog."

"So, what I'm saying is, either there is a mother-lode along the edge or even on the other side of the road in the cliff or somebody tossed little nuggets down the slope like Hansel and Gretel, luring us down."

"You're crazy. Who would throw real gold down a canyon slope?"

"Who was the guy that got killed? Did he have gold in his pockets?"

"Gold in his pockets? I don't think so, I didn't hear about it. We found his ID and we called Boulder to come get his body, but there was nothing unusual about his possessions, I don't remember."

"You said he rode a motorcycle, right?"

"Has there been anything in the news about a robbery anywhere that involved gold?"

"I don't know. I don't watch the news that much."

"Give me another beer. You know what I'm thinkin'?"

"What, Scott. What?"

"I'm thinkin', we should find a way to the bottom of the canyon and then figure a straight line down from the top and see if we can find a broken bike that carried little nuggets."

"Oh, come on! That's too farfetched. Scott, that would make for a good fairytale, but things like that don't happen in real life."

"Okay. Tell me then, how nice little golden nuggets jump down a trail, or maybe even up a trail in a pretty straight line and none to the left or the right of that trail? Did some great Indian Manitou arrange that for his Braves? Or maybe a volcano spewed some gold in a straight line up the mountain, exactly where a guy went overboard and killed himself? Com'on, Brad. There's got to be some logic behind this."

"Alright. Maybe you're right. What are we gonna do?"

"Let's find some good maps of the area. Find out how we can get farther down below without making it a four day camping trip and then start searching the area, quadrant by quadrant, like we do when we're looking for survivors after an avalanche until we find the bike and then we take it from there."

"Damn! I thought it would be simple to find a gold mine."

"Just remember ol' buddy; nothin' worthwhile is simple. Give me another beer and let's go find a map of the area."

Golden Nuggets
IV
Gold on the market?

Monday, 3:15 PM.

"Sheriff Cobalt?"

"Just a minute. Who can I say is calling?"

"Chuck McGuire."

"Just a moment, Mr. McGuire."

"Thank you," he said to a dead phone.

"Chuck, Ronald here. Do we have a problem? You don't call me on the job very often."

"No, you know, not really, although I'm checking to see if there might be one."

"What gives?"

"Just a question. Has there been any report of a gold find or a gold robbery in the area lately?"

"Not that I know of. Why do you ask?"

"I had this young fella in my shop a while ago, asking me for the price of gold nowadays and how to weigh a nugget and tell how much it's worth."

"Did he have an actual nugget?"

"At first he said 'no' and then he said 'yes' and produced the cutest little nugget I've seen in years and that's why I'm callin' ya Ronald, he seemed extremely nervous and he wouldn't tell me where he got it. He told me some cockamamie story how a friend wanted to sell it to him for twenty bucks and he's not sure whether it's a good deal or not."

"Who's the boy?"

"You may know him Ronald, he's Scott Carpenter, I mean, Scott Pierce. He's a carpenter I mean..."

"Oh, I know him. He's a good guy most of the time. Loves to party, but what the hell, I would too if I were that age. What made you decide to call me about him, Chuck?"

"I don't know. He seemed so nervous, you know and wouldn't give me straight answers and I think he's got more of them. Have you heard anything about a new prospect or a heist anywhere that I don't know about?"

"No, I haven't gotten any word from anyone. Did you weigh the rock and how much did you think it was worth?"

"Well, I told him it was just over an ounce and that he could get at least $500 for it because gold is worth over nine hundred an ounce on the stock market."

"What'd he say?'

"I thought he was gonna have hiccups, you know. He stuttered and stammered and then he started to leave, you know and he turned around, you know and he asked me if I would pay that much for it or was there a place that buys that stuff, like a wholesaler, you know. I told him his best bet would be a jewelry maker in Denver, you know and I gave him the name, because you know, they need that to melt it into jewelry designs you know..."

"Was he happy with that answer?"

"He seemed to be, you know 'cause he left and I thought the whole thing was kinda suspicious, you know and that's when I called you."

"Why don't you call that firm in Denver and ask them if there's been anything unusual in the gold market and ask them to keep you posted if something develops. Meanwhile I'll keep an eye open and keep you updated, okay Chuck?"

"Yeah, thanks Ron."

The sheriff shook his head and moved over to his computer to check and see if any news had come in about a gold heist or discovery. He said to himself: 'you never know.'

When he saw that nothing earthshaking had happened in that field, he went back to his paper work.

***

Scott left a message with Brad's mother to call him or drop in on him after work. She said she would pass it along.

He could hardly contain himself. They now had a total of five nuggets and that would amount to at least $3,000.

"Wow! A few more and I buy a new truck!" He thought. It seemed urgent that he'd call Cousin Pauline at work and finally, after about five minutes got her on the horn.

"Pauline? We found out that we were talking about the *Arapaho National Forest,* what does that mean to us, you know what I'm saying?"

"For one thing it means: stay the hell away from taking anything because it is Federal Property and everything in it and on it belongs to the government."

"But it belongs to the people, we can hunt and fish there and we..."

"No you can't. Go to the nearest entrance and you'll see a sign, 'No hunting, No fishing. Camping only in designated areas.' Anything on that property belongs to Uncle Sam and..."

"What are we gonna do?"

"What have you done so far? How many laws have you broken already Cousin Scott?"

"Well... I mean..., nothing serious..."

"How serious?

"Pauline, all we did was, we found a gold nugget and we think there may be more there, so what can we do?"

"I'll find out and..."

"Don't use the name *Arapaho t*o anyone. There'll be a million gold diggers out here before the weekend. Use *Routt Forest*, okay?"

"Good thinking, Cousin. You're right, but is Routt Forest also a Federal State Park, so I'll be comparing apples with apples?"

"I'm pretty sure but I'll check. If it ain't, I'll call you back and..., thanks Pauline."

"Just remember Scott-baby, keep your nose clean."

"Sure."

By the time Brad dropped by, Pauline had already called back and told him that with a lot of paperwork, anything might be exploited in due time, but she advised him to go by the County offices and find the spot on the aerial photographs of that section and ask for a copy when he'd located it.

"They have photographs of that area?" he'd asked in amazement.

"Every inch of it. Just don't arouse suspicion."

***

"Brad baby, I've got some good news and I got some good news..."

"No bad news?"

"Grab a beer and listen. Gold is worth 900 dollars an ounce on the stock market..."

"Jeez..."

"The nuggets probably will bring five hundred dollars an ounce and each of them weighs at least an ounce..."

"Holy Moses!"

"No... you should say; 'Holy Moses on a horse', it's that important to you..."

"You're not kiddin'!"

"Just one problem..."

"You said there was no bad news..."

"There isn't. Really! Nothing can be taken from the Federal Parks without a lot of paper work and permits and stuff..."

"Jeez!"

"But my reasoning is, if the nuggets were really in the motorcycle bags, they didn't belong to the Parks Department in the first place, so we don't have to worry about that. All we have to worry about is when somebody is owner or part-owner of the gold in the bike, they're liable to come after it and then we may have to arm-wrestle them over the little treasure."

"Arm-wrestle? They may shoot us!"

"Come on! You worry too much. Meanwhile, do you know that the county has photographs of every inch of this county and that we can have any copy we want? All we have to do is ask."

"You're shittin' me."

"No, you work for the county and you should have no problem finding the right spot and the right maps and they'll think it's part of your job."

"How do you know that?"

"Cousin Pauline. It comes in handy sometimes to have relatives in high places."

"High places? For God's sake, she's a secretary..."

"Yeah buddy, but in a high place. I need another beer."

"Me too. Bring me one. How'd you find out about the gold? Also from Cousin Pauline?"

"No, I went to the jewelry store and had it weighed."

"Here in town?"

"Yep."

"Was that smart?"

"Why not? Anyone can have a gold nugget, right?"

"I don't know, I don't know. I don't like it."

"You worry too much. Here's your beer."

Golden Nuggets
V
Indian Angle

Wednesday afternoon

"Mr. Samandran, please."

"Who's calling?"

"Mrs. McGuire at the County Office."

"I don't know if Mr. Samandran is available. Is it important?"

"Mr. Samandran must decide that for himself. Just tell him I'm on the line."

"Can I tell him what it is all about?"

"For crying out loud, have him call me!" She slammed the phone down. "Those Indian bitches with their clipped British accents drive me crazy." She was addressing the secretary at the other desk. "Here I'm doing him a favor and this bitch in her sari is giving me a third degree. Screw'em. I got more important things to do."

It didn't take but a few minutes before the intercom sounded in the county office. "A Mr. Salamander or something returning a call. Pick up on five."

Sue McGuire picked up the phone. "Mrs. McGuire speaking."

"Ah, Mrs. McGuire, you called. Anything important?"

"Not according to your secretary, it isn't. Is she the boss around there or are you the owner? She's got the damnest…"

"She's only doing her job, controlling the incoming calls. You know how it is. Every other call is somebody begging for money. Anyway, you called, what's happening with the county?" He sounded very British, but pleasant.

"It may be a coincidence, but remember the property at Gore Canyon that you petitioned for three years ago?"

"I do. I got it approved, no?"

"Yes, years ago, but you never did anything with it."

"Well, I thought of building a restaurant/hotel/casino combination because of its exquisite view down the valley, but with the turndown in tourism and such, I decided to hold off on it. I'm losing money in nearly every venture I have and..."

"I know, we're all bleeding for you while your stock has doubled in the last six months. Anyway, the reason I called; you and your wife have been good clients of my husband's jewelry store and I thought it might be decent on my behalf to tell you what's going on."

"Well, that's nice. What *is* going on?"

"I'm not sure, but a few things happened in the last coupla days. Two different people have requested maps and photographs of the canyon, one from Boulder, one from McCoy..."

"Is that so unusual?"

"Not in itself, Mr. Samandran, but someone walked into my husband's store with a gold nugget that he wanted evaluated and I think that there are too many coincidences here. Also, right at the Pass, a motorcycle rider went over the cliff and his body has been returned to Boulder. Did I tell you that one of the map requests was from Boulder?"

"Yes, you did. What are you trying to say, Mrs. McGuire?"

"You might want to check out your options and exercise your rights to the properties around there, in case you still want to build a hotel or something."

"Yes! Yes! I see what you mean. I'll check it out. Thanks for the call."

"Anytime, sir, any time."

***

"Keith? Samandran here. Do you remember the property at Gore Pass where we were going to build?..." He listened for a minute... "Yes, that's the one. Without making waves or arousing suspicion, find out who else has an interest in that area, maybe even a gold discovery…" Again a pause… "Don't arouse any suspicion. Drive by, take some pictures. Don't ask any questions, okay?" As he stared at the dead phone after hanging up on his number one security man, he murmured, "Well, you never know."

***

Friday night.

Bending over the 36x36 aerial photograph that Brad had bought for five dollars from the County Zoning office, they planned their next strategy.

"See here Brad… Federal Road 217 turns off 134 to the right and then loops around to the south and back to the highway, but it looks like here on the eastern end, it also runs to the north, but it ain't very clear on this photograph. How come these are all in blue and white? Why ain't they in color?"

"I don't know Scott, that's the way they come and that's the way they print them out. Not bad for five bucks a piece, is it?"

"No. So what we'll have to do is find that road and then go down it and figure out exactly at what point we are directly under the glide path of the bike…"

"Glide path?"

"Well, you know what I mean. The path that motorbike must have took as it tumbled down the mountain. And the cliff ain't as steep farther down. It looks like there's like a shelf, a platform. I bet that's where it finally landed. It never burned, did it?"

"We never saw no smoke and we were there an hour after it went down and…"

"So how do we pinpoint that spot?"

"Scott, if we draw a line from here… where the guy went down… straight down… then what is there that we would recognize if we're down below it?"

"Let me see."

With rulers and pencils, the twosome figured out what their destination was going to be on Saturday. They couldn't wait. Cousin Pauline had already advised them against taking guns because it was out of hunting season and even if it were, they would have to apply for regular permits and tags.

"What if we meet a mountain lion or a bear?"

"Well, don't worry. After they eat you, they'll be so stuffed that they'll leave me alone."

"Thanks a lot buddy. I'm bringing the biggest hunting knife I got."

"You do that."

***

Boulder, Wednesday night.

Randy had called for a map or a photograph of the area, but because he had no credit cards, he had to send a check and wait for delivery. The library proved more helpful. On their computer, a young whippersnapper had brought up the map of the area and Randy had studied the Gore Pass area for a while, but he had no idea on what side of the road Jack had taken his dive. According to the map, the pass was just ahead of the point of impact, so Jack could have tumbled down on either the north or the south side of the road. He assumed that his partner was driving in the right lane, hit a truck in the same lane and consequently went down the mountain on the right side of the road, the north side. Seemed logical. He could only hope that there would still be tracks on the shoulder showing where he went overboard.

It was hard to tell how steep it was and how far the Harley went down. It might have tumbled down much farther than where the body was found. As a sympathetic friend and working buddy, the police had readily let him read the ESU report and at least he had something to start with.

He had taken Saturday off and would make the drive, and if necessary, sleep in his truck and finish searching on Sunday. His girlfriend was disappointed because she and her girls were looking forward to a weekend with Randy, but she understood.

He'd like to have taken a gun, but as an ex-convict, he wasn't allowed to have one and if he were stopped for any reason, having a gun on him would send him right back to the pokey. A hunting knife would have to do.

The newspaper carried the stock-market report every day and for the first time in his life, Randy learned to read the trade sheets. Gold hovered around nine hundred an ounce, and he guessed that each beer can with nuggets had to be over a pound, so he had at least fifty ounces in that bucket in the water of Boyd Lake Park. "Wow!" He exclaimed. "On the retail market, I should have at least forty thousand and if I can find Jack's share, I'll have double that amount. Wow!"

The papers had not reported a gold robbery and as far as Randy was concerned, it shouldn't come out in the next hundred years. He made up his mind, he'd continue to be very cagey and not get carried away. The most important thing was: to get to Jack's nugget before anyone else did, because they might trace it to his last job, the gold mine company, and that would link him to Randy, who had worked there with him. No! He couldn't let that happen. He had to find the bike before anyone else did.

Saturday was it. He needed some luck, but he never even thought about a rope or other mountain climbing equipment. He was from Kansas. Never spent any time in the mountain wilderness of Colorado. It would come back to haunt him.

***

Scott had a four-wheel drive that was loaded with extra lengths of rope and both the young explorers went out and found spiked boots at an antique shop. The twosome was ready to tackle any mountain. A larger, sturdier beer cooler was found at Wal-Mart, plus a pair of huge flashlights that hooked to their belts and they felt as prepared as they were ever going to be.

"Scott, did you get to call that gold dealer in Denver about how much they'd pay for rough gold?"

"Whaddaya mean, rough?"

"You know, never melted down, just in nugget or powder form?"

"No, I wasn't about to call them myself, but Pauline said she make some inside inquiries, whatever that means."

"Do you suppose that clown was driving around with saddlebags full of gold? Where the hell did he think he was going?"

"What's more important, Brad, where did he get it? How much trouble could we get into if we're caught?"

"Wanna stay home?"

"Hell no!"

Golden Nuggets
VI
Gore Pass

Saturday Morning, 8:20 AM

Keith Brannon had his first opportunity to drive through the Gore Pass since he received his boss' call three days ago. After all, there was nothing urgent about the trip. The mountains were still the mountains and the cliffs were still the same cliffs. What could have changed?

He drove slowly through the pass, coming from the west but the only thing unusual was a pick-up truck with Denver plates, parked on the east side of the peak, just where the descent toward the other slope started. Nobody in it.

Nothing else moved, but the sheriff's car coming from the other side was also moving slowly, although there was no fog, nothing but clear sunshine. Was that odd? Could a Sheriff's patrol be on the look-out for something? Keith shrugged and kept cruising.

***

The sheriff's deputy stopped behind the parked truck and ran the license plate on his computer. Came up clean. Owner registered in Boulder. No outstanding tickets. "Wonder what he might be doing here?" He was talking to himself as he got out and walked along the shoulder. "Here's where the guy went over last week. The tracks are still obvious. There's no fishing down there, so what could he find? The body's been recovered and buried. I'll park around the bend and see how long he stays."

***

Scott and Brad had passed the truck at the pass and wondered who could possibly have an interest in the exact location of last week's spill, but decided not to interfere and follow their own plan. They moseyed on down to the obvious turn-off to Forest Road 217, but turned left instead of right, bouncing along a crude little dirt track. It couldn't be called a road because there wasn't any, nor could it be called a path and after a little more than a mile, they had no choice but to stop. They consulted their aerial photograph and concluded, that was it! That was as far as they could go by truck, four-wheel drive or not.

"Damn. That's gonna be a long haul. What do you think Brad? A mile? Mile and a half?"

"At least. But we knew that. That's why we got up early. Let's take some spikes and a hammer. Enough rope, not to wear us down and a few beers in our pouches. It's gonna be a doozy."

"You're not kiddin' brother. How are we gonna figure the distance we've travelled?"

"We stay on this trail, otherwise we may never find our truck again and we estimate the distance from point to point and write it down. For instance, how far is it to that big pine?"

"I don't know. Two hundred feet?"

"Okay. Write that down. Big pine, two hundred feet. So when we work our way back, we'll reverse it and we'll find our beer cooler again."

"Where'd you learn all that shit? Boy Scouts or something?"

"I'm in the ESU, remember. We do this every day."

"Every day?"

"Okay, maybe once a month. Let's go."

***

The Sheriff's Deputy saw a man emerging from the brush and put his car in gear. Swinging to the opposite side of the road, he stopped in front of Randy's vehicle and got out while Randy was cranking his window down.

"Hello there! Out hunting early?"

Randy was startled but kept his cool. "No sir. Not hunting season yet."

"May I see you driver's license and registration, please?"

"Sure, Officer. What's the problem?"

"No problem. Just hand them over and stay in the car."

After five minutes, the deputy reappeared at Randy's driver side window and handed back the documents. "What brings you all the way out here?"

"A buddy of mine went over the cliff here last week and got killed and I just couldn't believe it. Why would he run into a truck? Was it parked? Was my buddy drunk? He couldn't have been. It was early in the day, wasn't it? I..."

"Sorry sir, I don't know anything but the report I seen and it seems it was real foggy. That's all I know."

"Officer, do you know if they hauled up his motorcycle as well as his body last week?"

"I don't know, but I don't think so. It gets real steep down there and unless there were other people involved, like a passenger, the ESU wouldn't have any reason to go after a car wreck or a motorcycle that was probably crunched to hell on the way down. No sir. There are probably dozens of wrecks down there after all these years. What's your interest?"

"Well, we work for the same company... I mean we did work for the same company and he had a little sweetheart who liked to ride the bike with him and I just wanted to satisfy her and my curiosity, that's all."

"Well, did you find anything of interest?" The deputy remained inquisitive.

"No. Is there another road down there where I could get a closer look?"

"I don't think so. It's all ravine and woods down there."

"Alright. Thanks for your help. I can make a U-turn here, can't I?"

"I don't see why not."

"I mean the double yellow line and everything?"

"Don't worry about it. Nobody's coming from either direction. Drive safe!"

"Thanks, Officer."

***

Keith cruised by the pair of vehicles stopped by the roadside. A sheriff's car in front of the pickup truck. Normally, not even a mule or a chicken would be seen on this road at this altitude. He couldn't understand why his boss had considered this spot for a hotel. At 9,000 feet? You could hardly breathe up here and there were no ski slopes nearby. Why then? He never did understand what motivated his Indian boss, but he always managed to make money and Keith was paid regularly, so who was he to question?"

***

Initially, Randy was shaking in his boots. He wondered if the cop had checked his prison record or only his license and registration? He could be in deep trouble. Under the terms of his probation he wasn't even allowed to leave the county of his residence unless he had written permission from his gorgeous probation officer, which he obtained every time he had to work out of town. This wasn't work and this was a hundred miles out of town. He could have landed in jail without bond for violation of probation, so he decided not to push his luck and headed for home. When he passed the narrow turn-off to his left, he hit the brakes, backed up and turned into the narrow pass that Brad and Scott had negotiated an hour earlier. Just as he decided that the trail really was impassible, he noticed a white pick-up in front of him.

He braked to a stop, checked his hunting knife on his belt and walked slowly toward the parked vehicle. Moving from tree to tree, from bush to brush, he snuck up to the rear and hesitated. No one was in sight. Not inside or anywhere around it. Randy checked the truck bed and noticed coils of ropes, pegs, pins and heavy duty gloves.

"Mountain climbers?" he asked himself, "or searchers for a lost motor cycle? Damn!"

He couldn't imagine who else could possibly have an interest in Jack's bike and his first intuition was to slash their tires and that way discourage them or him from coming back here again.

That thought didn't linger very long. What would it accomplish? What if they had found the motorcycle and the gold? Then what? He decided to follow along the trail, estimate the distance to the track that the falling bike had created and maybe meet up with the owners of the other truck. As he hiked along, he regretted not parking his own vehicle in such a way that the others could pass in case they came out of the woods before he did.

Well, too late now. Besides, he had a gut feeling that they were after the same goal: gold nuggets. What didn't make sense to him, who else could possibly know about this? Had Jack made a phone call along the way? Had he told somebody before the Saturday morning robbery?

"Cripes. I never considered any of those things." He muttered to himself as he worked his way up and down the narrow trail. "Hell, if they find it, but don't link it to me, I'm scot free, but if anyone figures out whom Jack worked for and learns that we worked together that last morning of his life, I'm in deep shit."

Suddenly there were voices. Male voices! Someone yelling at somebody else, just up ahead and a little up the slope. Randy stopped, but couldn't see anything through the dense shrubs between the trees. Quietly, very quietly, he moved one cautious step at a time, careful not to step on dead branches or kicking over rocks. After about twenty-five paces, he caught a glimpse of blue clothing. They were about sixty feet ahead of him and slightly higher up the slope.

"They must've found the location or the track. I wonder how they did that?" He talked to himself and decided to climb straight up, so he would parallel the path of the other climbers and stopped whenever the other team hollered back and forth at one another. It was impossible to understand the conversation between the men, but the higher pitch convinced him they were on to something.

He changed direction and climbed diagonally up the slope, clinging to bushes and trees and cursing the lack of solid footing that had him dangling in mid-air half the time. It took him ten minutes to get level with the couple of young guys that were bent over a twisted motorcycle frame and undoing the straps of the saddle bag underneath the wreck.

"Fellows, you're fooling with my property!"

Golden Nuggets
VII
Ouch!

"What the hell is this?" Scott said, jumping up. "Who the hell are you?" Reaching for his hunting knife, he realized it was in his truck. He ran behind a tree, scared like a rabbit.

Brad remained where he was, kneeling in front of the crunched up bike, but the look on his face was worth a prize: utterly dumbfounded.

"Leave that stuff alone and get out of here!" Randy's voice sounded threatening, but he had nothing to back it up with, no rifle, no pistol and no impressive uniform.

"Hold it a minute!" Scott had regained his nerve. "We found this and this is a National Park, so it belongs to the government and we aim to give it back to them."

"Give'em back what?" Randy took two steps forward. "What have you found?"

"That's none of your business and..."

"Oh yes it is. That bike belonged to my buddy Jack and I'm gonna take it back to his family."

"All by yourself? Who are you shittin?" Scott stepped next to the bike again as if that proved 'possession'. Brad just sat there, looking from one to the other.

"I'm telling you one last time: *SCRAM!*" Randy yelled as loud as he could, but he might as well have saved his breath. He was as tall as Scott and outweighed him by at least sixty pounds, but he was up against two guys. For a moment there was complete silence and then Brad spoke up, "Can't we talk about this? He may be right, Scott. He may have rights here too. We found it, so we can claim possession under the law and he may be able to prove that he has some right to it as well, so..."

"What are you? A law professor now?" Scott was flabbergasted.

"Can't we just talk a minute? I don't know who you are, but my name is Brad and I work for the county and last week I drug up your buddy from down here and now I'm following up. By the way," he pointed at his friend , "That's Scott. What is your name?"

Randy was taken aback by the turn of events and stammered.... "I'm Randy... uh... yeah, Randy."

"Well, Randy. Let's look at this. Here's a bike that tumbled all the way down here from the road overhead and every time it was flying upside down, it seemed to drop a little gold nugget and the strap never broke, so the rest of the gold must still be in there and we should decide who gets what." He pointed toward the bottom of the bike where the saddle bag was weighted down by the frame on top of it and continued, "Like Scott was saying, this is Federal property, so maybe we can't get a dime out of this, but on the other hand, the government doesn't even know it's here, so why don't we say it belongs to the three of us?"

He smiled up at Scott and added, "Whaddayasay, buddy? There may be plenty for all of us. Let's look at it."

"No need to. I know what's in there."

"You do? How much and how do you know?"

"I told you I'm his partner... uh... I *WAS* his partner. There's approximately fifty ounces of gold in there and it's actually all mine, but I'm willing to listen. Can the Feds really claim possession, even though they don't know it's here?"

"I know and the county knows," Brad was bluffing, "but they have no concept of the amount involved. How do you know there's fifty ounces in there?"

"I put it there and my friend was takin'it to Reno to cash it in and that's how I know it's mine." Randy was becoming more sure of himself.

"Well? Scott? Whaddaya think?"

"How'd you get it? You don't look like no prospector."

"That's my business, ain't it?" He straightened up, looking defiant. "Let's talk about it. You guys have gone through a lot of trouble, so what do you say we split it evenly, I take one half and you guys get the other half and we don't say a word about it to nobody?"

Scott wasn't so sure. Fifty ounces was nearly fifty thousand dollars! That was a lot of dough. "How about 1/3-1/3-1/3?"

"No, no, no!" Randy bent over and waved both hands from left to right. "You guys had no idea how much was here and all of a sudden you want two thirds of the loot. That ain't right." Randy waved his right hand as if he were scolding a kid. "Who else knows about this? Your whole county office?"

"No, I haven't told anybody specifically, but they provided maps and photos so we could approach this thing from below." Brad pointed at the valley below him.

"So they know you're here, but they don't know about the gold, that's it?"

"Kinda."

"Then why don't we do this? We divide it three ways upon condition that you tell nobody else about it and never mention my name or my presence here. What do you say?"

"Like we never saw you?" Scott was apprehensive.

"Yep! Whaddaya say?"

"Okay by me, Scott"

"Alright, let's do it. I think the easiest thing would be to just cut the saddlebags apart, lift the bike and whammo, there's the half with the gold. You see, we already discovered there's nothing here in the topside bag. Make sense? You got a knife?"

"Yep." Randy produced his hunting knife and took the ten steps that separated him from the wreck, bent over it and started slashing at the leather. It was tougher than he anticipated, but after some serious sawing, the top bag came off and all six hands reached out to pull up the rear of the busted motorcycle. Two hands could have done it, but four held it up, so Randy could cut the final strap that held it to the framework.

"There you go!" He pulled it from underneath the wreck and triumphantly raised the bag as if it were a trophy. "How do we figure it into three equal parts?"

"I don't know. Spread it all out on a handkerchief or a shirt and separate it into three little heaps?" Brad thought his was a good idea.

Scott concurred. "Okay by me. Let's move to that level spot over there."

"Alright. I'm taking my shirt off. Let's pour out the whole heap here in the middle and use my knife as a dividin' tool, like they do in a pharmacy."

"Okay." The older of the three was handling the saddle-bag and undid the straps that hadn't been broken or cut and slowly poured the gleaming contents onto his shirt.

"Wow!" Was all Scott could utter.

"Holy Moses, wow!" was all Brad could add. None of them had ever seen a glittering heap of gold before and it was indeed hypnotic. It was like a scene from an Indiana Jones movie.

"No wonder these gold-rushes started all over these mountains." Randy whispered, "How do we measure this up?"

"Make three little heaps?" Randy's right hand already started to divide the little mound into three equal little bumps of gold nuggets, some dull, some shiny.

"Just make them kinda equal." Scott was skeptical.

"I'll tell you what. If you don't like the way I divide'em, you take the first pick. That way you may end up with the largest, okay?"

Scott, slightly embarrassed, "Okay, okay. I'm sorry. I've never seen that much money before."

Randy became condescending, "Neither have I buddy, but let's keep our cool."

With his hunting knife, he separated the nuggets, big and small, into three fairly equal looking little heaps.

"Look alright, gentlemen?" He looked at both their faces. "Scott, you pick first. What are you gonna put them in?"

"I'll put them in my handkerchief."

"Go ahead."

Scott put his big red linen cloth next to the tallest little heap and reached for Randy's knife to ease the nuggets onto his red kerchief and even scraped the dust off the shirt with the help of his finger. The corners were carefully folded over and tied together, tightened up some more and knotted into a little ball. The bundle disappeared into his jeans pocket and he stood up triumphantly, like Caesar after a major victory.

"How about you Brad?" Randy had taken control.

"Who? Me? Okay!" On his knees he moved closer to the shirt with all the glitter and pulled out a napkin. A McDonalds napkin. Large enough, but sturdy enough?

"Go for it." Being at least ten years older than his co-conspirators, Randy felt his confidence rising by the minute. His only worry was, would these guys ever talk? Would they be able to connect him to the robbery and his probation? So far so good. He rolled up his shirt with the remainder of the loot and stuffed it in the saddle-bag.

"Now guys! Not a word to anyone about this gold and you never saw me in your life, right?" He stood up and faced the two friends, holding thousands of dollars in their hands. "I'm blocking you in with my car, so I leave first. Stay here for fifteen more minutes before you leave. You'll never see me again and my name is really George. So enjoy the money. Don't follow me. I'll be gone by the time you get back there. Enjoy, gentlemen, enjoy."

Randy started to back up to ease his way down the slope, but hesitated behind a tree while the twosome waited.

"You okay, Scott?"

"I've got more money than I've had in my life, but I don't feel good about the whole deal. Who was he and are we now part of a real big crime? One that might even have involved murders and hold-ups and killings of LEO's and things?

"LEO's?"

"Yeah, you know. Law Enforcement Officers."

"Whaddaya wanna do? Give back the gold?"

"Not really. But how are we gonna hide it and more important, how are we gonna get rid of it?"

Golden Nuggets
VIII
From theft to murder

Randy was on pins and needles. All seemed to go well and the other boys seemed very agreeable, but one thing kept bugging him. If these boys ever talked and involved him, he would automatically go to jail without bond. His probation officer would immediately hit him with *violation of probation* for being out of the county without permission and that would mean instant arrest and serving out the rest of his sentence. He had been in prison for a year and a half and had no intention of ever going back. If they could then also pin a gold robbery on him, he might as well kiss the rest of his life good-bye. He felt he had no choice. These two guys had to go! Somehow!

While Scott was busy re-folding his red handkerchief and neatly tying the ends together, Randy stepped behind him and stabbed the young man right beneath his left shoulder blade. With a scream, Scott collapsed and Brad jumped up and turned to see what caused that outcry.

"What the hell are you doing? You ass!" He grabbed a rock and raised it just in time, because Randy was on him like a panther ready to plunge again, but the rock deflected the hunting knife. The force of the attack slammed Brad backward into a tree, probably saving his life. He remained upright, smashing the rock into Randy's face, who reeled back, giving Brad a chance to duck and sidestep into the open. In two seconds he was out of Randy's reach and he dashed up the slope, putting ten yards between them.

"Hold it there! Hold it!" Randy hollered, but he had nothing but a knife to back up his threat. Brad ran up another five yards and stopped again.

"Why did you do that? Why'd you kill him?" Scott had not moved an inch. The blade must have punctured his heart. "Why did you do that? You ass! You want all the gold for yourself? Well, you can have all of it, you bastard. I hope it kills you."

Brad ran east, back toward the truck. He had to get help and get away from that maniac. He was in excellent shape, so he could easily outrun the older Randy, but Randy wasn't worried. He had their truck blocked in. He gathered up all the gold, wrapped the handkerchief and the napkin into his shirt, tied it into a neat bundle, stuck it in the saddle bag and started running as well.

The young ESU worker was hundreds of yards ahead by then and made it to the trucks within twenty minutes.

He realized he had just two problems: The keys were in Scott's pocket and the pickup was locked and besides, Randy's vehicle had him blocked in anyway.

"Oh, shit!" Brad moved up the slope and out of sight. He didn't know what to do.

Should he work his way up to the road and flag down a car? Should he climb up higher and double back to see if he could still save his buddy? He had his doubts. Scott had not stirred during the brief confrontation back at the bike and Brad had enough experience with accidents and bodies to know that there was little hope. Still, that was his best bet. For one thing, he could retrieve the keys. The climb up to the road might take more than an hour, so he followed his instincts, climbed up enough to stay above the path that Randy would be taking farther down along the slope and headed toward the scene of the attack. What had taken twenty minutes running, now took him about an hour, because he stopped and listened every so often to make sure he was still clear of that crazy murderer.

Randy had a different dilemma. He couldn't let the other kid live and take a chance on being identified. Now he was really in deep. He could just hear the prosecutor in front of the judge: "*Violation of Probation. Grand Theft, Murder One and attempted murder.*" He would go up for life for sure. He had to make sure that the other guy didn't leave the forest alive. So… what could he do?

By the time he reached his vehicle, he had formed a plan. What would I do if I were in the kid's shoes? Would he really climb all the way up the slope? That could take a day, so the other possibility was, try to get in their car and outrun Randy. But that was only possible if Randy's truck was gone. So that wouldn't work for the moment. He walked around the other's pickup and tried the doors. Locked. He considered slashing the tires, so the kid would not get very far, but he dropped that thought immediately. No, no. He had to catch that loudmouth youngster and knock him off. He just couldn't let him live.

Back at his truck, the saddlebag containing the shirt with all the nuggets disappeared underneath his seat and he sat for a moment to nurse his busted nose. "That little bastard!" he muttered to himself and cranked the engine. Backing out slowly, dodging little trees and rocks, the finally found a spot where he could turn around. For the next ten minutes he sat and watched to see if the boy would appear and try to race out. Nothing stirred, so he eased forward and headed east.

A half mile down the track, he found what he'd been looking for, a dead tree by the road side. After passing it, he got out and with the help of some broken branches, maneuvered the trunk square across the dirt track. Nothing but a tank could get over that obstacle. Satisfied, he cranked up his machine and a quarter of a mile farther up the slope he moved it between some trees, making it invisible from the path.

Walking back took only a few minutes because he was going downhill. He selected a spot on the left of the path, reasoning that the kid would come out of the left door and move toward the tree. The moment the boy would bend over and start to move the obstacle, he would plunge right into his back, the same way he did the other guy. All he had to do now was wait.

Brad found Scott just the way he had expected. Lifeless, lying on his face in a pool of blood. Quickly he took the keys, his wallet and his money clip. Just as quickly, he surrounded and covered the body with rocks, so that wild animals would be discouraged from getting to him. He felt he should be back here within two hours with help. A lot of help.

Slowly, he worked his way back, stopping from time to time to listen for footsteps or glimpses of a man with a bloody hunting knife. To his surprise, their truck was still there, undamaged. He had expected Randy to bust the engine or slash the tires, rendering the pickup unusable.

First he hid out behind a bush, expecting a trick, but when there was no movement anywhere, he moved slowly to the driver's side. Before inserting the key, he turned around and scanned the area, guarding a sudden attack. His heart was racing but his mind was clear. "I need to defend myself."

Instead of getting in the car, he went to the toolbox in back and extracted a crowbar. It felt good in his hand. Once behind the wheel, he left the door wide open and turned the key real gently, expecting an explosion any second. Nothing happened. He got in,locked the doors and kept the windows up, ready to run over somebody. Backing up until there was room to turn, he kept up his vigilance, ready to swing if attacked. Nothing happened and Brad started to relax when he spotted the tree trunk across the road.

"That's it! That's the trap." Thirty feet before he reached it, he stopped and scanned the woods and the path up ahead. Nothing moved. Not even a rabbit or a squirrel. He wished he was in his own truck, because he could throw a grapple hook from here, catch the tree, back up fast and dash by there in seconds, but he didn't have anything in back but Scott's carpentry tools and ropes.

The hair on the back of his neck warned him of danger, the same as it did when he was looking into a steep ravine or down a perpendicular cliff. Danger was out there! For sure!

What would Randy do? Jump him just when he was bending over to move the stump?

Probably! Brad got out of the truck again and went around back. A long rope was in the bed and the young emergency worker quickly knotted it into a big loop that would encircle the end of the dead tree. Back around the front, he tied the end of the rope onto the bumper and with the crowbar hidden in the coil of heavy rope, he approached the barricade.

Randy wondered, What's keepin' the guy? What's he doin'? He expected the kid to be more anxious to get past the obstacle and he should have become suspicious. Brad was taking too long to make an appearance. His own heart was racing and he had to really bite his tongue to keep from jumping out and running for the boy. Finally there was some progress. "He's got a rope? He's gonna pull that tree out with his truck? That kid's no dope. But… he's gotta come out here just the same to tie the rope around it, so nothin' changes, I'll get him right when he bends over. Get ready, Randy. You got it under control."

Brad could feel the tension as if it was déjà vu. As if he'd seen it in a movie. He knew just when Randy would strike and he also knew just how to clobber him. Calmly uncoiling the rope as he moved forward to the right, the upside of the slope. He was going to the far side, away from Randy. It was logical to him, that you'd take advantage of the incline to roll the tree out of the way. Randy hadn't thought of that. In his mind, Brad would drive right up to the log and get out of the left side of the car. Now he was heading to the right side of the path.

Right on cue, when Brad bent over to put the loop around the end of the stump, Randy ran from his hiding place, but he had four more paces to go than he had intended and just as he lifted the knife in a full sprint, a crowbar came up out of nowhere and cracked his jaw. He yelped as he went down and just as he hit the ground with his face, a second swing of the crowbar hit the back of his skull and Randy was no more.

Young Brad was elated and scared. Elated because he'd pulled it off but scared because he realized that he had just killed a man. Was that murder? Self defense? Hitting him in the back of the head was self defense? It had to be. The knife was still there. It had dropped from his hands, but it was still there. "The man wanted to kill me, right?"

The rope around the tree cleared the path in no time and Brad decided to leave everything the way it was. The body, the knife, the rope and the crowbar, literally, everything.

On the way back up, he spotted Randy's truck, parked off the path. A wicked thought hit him. The gold! He couldn't take it all, because the whole story and the killings were woven around the gold discovery and the motorcycle. He made a decision. From under Randy's seat he took the saddlebag, removed the shirt that had the handkerchief and napkin tied inside and quickly liberated them. He re-tied the shirt, put it back in the leather bag and stuffed it back under Randy's seat and drove off. 100 feet further up the bouncy path, he spotted a big white aspen. The two wraps with the nuggets were buried right behind it and covered with rocks and leaves.

Brad clocked the mileage from the aspen to the road, 1.2 miles, and started to flag down any car that could lend him assistance.

Golden Nuggets
IX
The plot thickens

Keith figured he might as well make a day of it. After crossing over Gore Pass two more times, he continued on to Steamboat Springs for lunch. There was nothing going on at the pass so there was nothing urgent to report. Just a few days ago, he had a new radio/telephone system installed in his trunk and now he could call his boss as soon as he was clear of the mountain peak.

"What will they think of next?" On *Star Trek* they even had hand-held telephones that flipped open and transmitted over thousands of miles. His was a box in the trunk and a wire to his dashboard, complete with a long antenna on the fender. The darn thing had cost him more than 4,000 dollars, but in the mountains it worked much better than a CB or cell phone and besides, his boss would reimburse him… eventually.

Lunch had been delightful and accompanied by two beers, Keith had enjoyed the atmosphere of the old ski resort. Steamboat Springs had more of an old western ambiance than Vail or Aspen and he made up his mind he should spend a long weekend there. Soon!

All those warm fuzzy thoughts were going through his mind as he again motored back up to the Gore Pass, this time from the east. A mile or so before reaching the peak his reminiscing was interrupted by a young man standing in the road, frantically waving with both arms. A white pickup was parked on the shoulder and Keith assumed the boy had engine trouble, so he slowed down and moved over behind the truck.

The young man dashed to the driver's door and as Keith lowered the window, he hollered, "Please help. Can you call Emergency Service and the Sheriff? There's been a murder down here."

"A murder? Where?"

"Down below there." Brad pointed across the car toward the valley.

"And who are you?"

"I'm Brad Brogan, I work with ESU and I don't know if there's a phone in the rest area on the other side of that peak."

"I've got a phone. Just a minute," as he took the instrument from its hook on the dash. "I'll call the State Police and they'll know who to send down here. Come around and sit in my car, so you can tell me all about it while we wait."

Brad was relieved to have found help so fast, but he worried about how much this man would ask and how much he should tell him.

Keith was not as successful with his new phone as he had hoped because the mountain peaks did block some of his transmissions, but he reached the State Troopers in Kremmlin, who would contact the officials in Toponas, to the west and help might be coming from two directions.

"Tell me about the murder, Brad and what is your involvement in this?"

"I, uh, me and my buddy Scott... and who are you?"

Keith explained that he was the security officer for the M.I.C. Investment Group that had an interest in developing the upper corridor of the Gore Pass.

"A couple of years ago, we obtained a lease from the Parks Department, but we haven't done anything with it. So, theoretically, you're sitting on our property..."

"But we're still a coupla miles from the Pass..."

"Maybe so, but you're stalling. Tell me about the murders. What's your involvement?"

Brad stalled a while longer, but bit by bit Keith drug the story out of him, even though the young emergency worker didn't tell him the whole truth about the amount of nuggets there were and the reason for the killings. Matter of fact; he didn't understand the reason for the killing, the reason why Randy had wanted them both dead. There wasn't *that* much gold.

"You see Mr. Keith, I'm pretty sure my buddy is dead, but there's always a chance, right? So I wanna get down there as fast as we can before it gets dark and see if the medics can still do something for him, you understand?"

"How about the other guy, Randy?"

"Oh, he's dead alright. The second blow with that crowbar got him right behind the ear and nobody can survive that. It was a good thing I was ready for him, 'cause he lunged at me with his knife. He musta thought that all I was carrying was that rope and that I was an easy target, but that dead tree across the trail was such an obvious trap, man. He musta thought I was real stupid."

"You could also go up for murder…"

"No way man! It was self defense. You'll see. I left everything the way it was, unless the wolves walked away with him. That's why I'm hoping the ESU people are gonna… there they are…"

Wailing sirens and flashing lights in the distance announced the arrival of at least one emergency vehicle. Brad jumped out of the car and onto the road, waving his arms. When the fire truck stopped, he jumped on the running board and yelled into the window, "Do you have an ATV aboard?"

"No buddy. Who are you and what's the emergency?"

"There's two people down there that may be dead. I think they're dead and you can only get in there a little ways with a pickup. You can't get in there at all with this big thing. Is anyone else coming up with an ATV, maybe?"

"We don't know. We have an ambulance on the way, but I'll get on the horn and see what we can do. We came up from Kremmlin, but there's help on the way from the other direction. Excuse me a moment." The fireman climbed back into his cab and started talking on his radio. When he jumped back down he asked, "How long a walk is it to the bodies?"

"The first one we can reach in my pickup in fifteen minutes or less. The other one is at least another hour's walk, 'cause you can't get through there with a truck. We need an all terrain vehicle."

"What the hell were you guys doing down there?"

Keith butted in, "You won't believe it, but they were digging for gold."

"You're shittin'me."

"No seriously…"

Brad cut him off, "We're wasting time! Is anyone coming up with an ATV?"

"Come off it, man. We don't have a helicopter that can drop one off. I left word and somebody should be here shortly."

"Oh, God! I may never be able to find him if it gets dark." He finally broke down and slumped over the fender of the fire truck. "He was my best buddy. All my life…" Sobbing, he slid down and fell to his knees. "All our lives… Kindergarten and on…"

"Come on buddy. This is not gonna help. Pull yourself together, man. You're gonna have to lead this expedition." The fireman grabbed Brad unceremoniously under the arms and picked him up. "Now pull yourself together, okay?"

At the same moment more sirens came within earshot. "There, you see? Here comes the cavalry!"

It wasn't exactly the cavalry, but there was an ambulance, another fire truck and two pickups, one complete with a four-wheel all-terrain vehicle. From the other direction two Highway Patrol cars joined the racket, followed by a deputy sheriff. When they all turned off their noisemakers, the men could finally hear themselves think. The Fire Chief from Toponas took over, "Who's in charge here?"

"I guess you are, sir." The driver from Kremmlin said with a smirk.

"What's going on? Who called?"

"I called," Keith stepped up, "but Brad here knows what's happening."

"Okay Brad." He motioned for the young man to come out of the crowd that had gathered.

"Sir, we have to hurry. My buddy is severely wounded or dead already…"

"Who's your buddy?"

"Scott Pierce, but we have to hurry. He's down the slope and we can't get there by truck, so we need the ATV and a stretcher. The other one is fifteen minutes down the trail and you can get there with the pickup…"

"Who's the other one?"

"I don't know! All I know is that he called himself Randy or George, but for God's sake we're wasting time. Scott may have…"

"Don't you order me around young fellow! Let's get this organized…"

Brad was getting furious. "I'm going down. Follow me if you want to or stand here and talk." He turned toward his truck in spite of the chief's call, "Come back here!"

"We better get with it!" Another emergency worker shouted and started toward his truck, the one with the four wheeler in its bed. He made a quick u-turn and followed Brad down the trail.

The flabbergasted chief looked around sheepishly and asked, "Who's got a stretcher?"

Stretchers were loaded in the other pickup and four men jumped aboard, while the firefighters stripped off their cumbersome suits.

"No need for all of us to go down there, right chief?'

"You're right, Is there any chance of getting another ATV here, so I can go down and take charge?" The chief felt naked without some people to command.

"Not much. Let's wait. They've got their radios. We'll know soon what's going on."

"And who's that?" The chief noticed Keith for the first time.

"I don't know ," the fireman answered. "Let's ask him."

The twosome walked over to the car that Keith was leaning on. "And who may you be and what brings you here?" The chief had the need to feel important.

"I represent the owner of this property."
"The owner? This is a Federal Park."
"We have a ninety-nine year lease."
"You do?"

Golden Nuggets
X
The Death Trail

Brad, with another Emergency Service man beside him, eased Scott's pickup down the trail, closely followed by the ESU vehicle with the ATV aboard. Within fifteen minutes they came upon Randy's body, just in time to scare off some coyotes, who had started tearing at the body.

Corby, the senior rescue man, took one look at the scene and shouted. "Don't touch anything! Don't move anything. The man is dead. We need some picture takers down here. I'm calling upstairs for the Sheriff or the Highway Patrol to send a man down. Joe?" He addressed one of the other rescuers. "Stay here! George, get the ATV down! Brad, which way do we go from here?"

"Right down that trail for about a mile and then a hundred feet up the slope."

"Okay, John, grab a stretcher and let's go. Joe, don't let anybody move anything until they've taken pictures, okay? Okay, start Humpy and let's roll."

"Humpy?" Brad asked in amazement.

"Yeah man. That's Humpy, our humping four wheeler. Hop on. Point the way."

The ATV with the three rescuers and a stretcher aboard, bumped and hopped its way west according to Brad's direction. Twice, Brad thought they had travelled too far and twice he climbed up the slope a way, only to come back to the vehicle, saying, "Only a little more I guess."

Finally, he yelled, "That's it! I remember that big aspen. Stay here." He jumped off and disappeared into the brush growing up the slope. He was back in six minutes.

"This is it. It's too steep to take Humpy up, so let's take the stretcher and bring him down."

"How is he?" Corby wanted to know.

"I knew he was dead, but I kept hopin' I was wrong, but he's dead alright. Let's go get him."

The three of them climbed and clutched their way up the slope until they came upon a grave of sorts, a body covered and lined with rocks.

"What the hell did you do, Brad? If you thought he might still live, why did you bury him?" Corby couldn't believe what he was seeing.

"You see, with that guy Randy out there, I wasn't sure I'd get out of here alive or when I could get back here with help. I didn't even expect I'd be back here so fast. So I wanted him protected, no matter how long it took."

"Okay, let's get him down. There's certainly no sign of life in him. That stab in the back must have pierced his heart." Corby had moved the rocks from the top of the body and looked at the blood stained shirt and the point of entry just below the shoulder blade. "Did he have a weapon on him?"

"No."

"Then why did the S.O.B. kill him from behind? That's cold blooded murder."

"Yeah! We were talking about divvying up the gold amongst the three of us and then when I wasn't looking, he jumped on Scott and came after me."

"Holy Jeez! How much gold was there?"

"I don't know. All I know is that this guy had a saddlebag full of it and that some of it bounced out as the Harley rolled down the mountain. That's how we got on the trail."

"I don't believe this. How did you stay alive?"

"Well, I can move faster than anybody in these mountains, but he gave me a head start because he had to gather up the gold before he could run after me."

"Great Scott! No pun intended. I've seen and heard many things in my career, but this takes the cake. Let's get him on the stretcher. Tie a rope around your right wrist and your waist. It's steep as hell from here on down. Tie the other end to the stretch. I'll go backwards in front of it so you just give me enough slack so it will slide." He turned to the other paramedic, "George, you stay in front with me. Take it easy, one bush at a time."

With slow precision, the threesome eased the body down the steep slope. One in front, looking forward with the left bar on his right shoulder, the other, walking backward, handling the other pole. Brad trailed with ropes on each bar, tied around one wrist, while the other hand sought support from little trees and sturdy bushes. Inch by inch, foot after foot, they worked their way to the ATV and strapped the stretcher on top at an angle. Corby drove. George rode in back, holding on to the bouncing body, while Brad sat in front, bracing the stretcher against his body on one side and clutching the vehicle's frame with the other. It was rough. Sometimes they had to stop and shift the body so they'd fit between two trees and other times the little buggy wanted to nosedive down the trail.

They were back an hour after they departed the scene with Randy and the wolves and joined the activity. There was an additional four-wheel-drive pickup with Sheriff's markings on its doors and another ATV. The murderer's body was already strapped in the bed of one of the vehicles and within minutes the whole caravan was ready for return to the highway.

The fire trucks had left, but two ambulances patiently awaited their cargo and a decision had to be made as to the destination of the corpses.

"Since this is not within our jurisdiction," a deputy started off,

"I suggest that the State Police decides where they go. I'm sure that the young man..., uh, Scott, should be returned to McCoy, but the nearest coroner is in Steamboat Springs. The other guy..., uh... Randy..., should end up in Boulder, but who's going to handle the investigation? Highway Patrol, or should the Sheriff take that on?"

The senior State Trooper, the one with two chevrons on his sleeve, spoke up, "I'll radio our headquarters. Meanwhile, young man," he turned to Brad, "you keep yourself available. When you get to McCoy, report to the sheriff's office and give them a detailed report. After all, you killed a man, allegedly, so you may not be off the legal hook and you're our only witness to date. So don't go traveling anywhere, you hear?"

"Yes sir, but it was self defense. The guy was comin'..."

"I know, I know. Just get it all in writing, okay?"

Brad sighed a sigh of relief. "Where's Scott's body going? What am I goin' to tell his folks?"

"Have the sheriff go with you. He'll want to do that anyway. He's done it before. Don't worry."

Looking around sheepishly, Brad asked, "Does anybody want a cold beer?"

It broke the tension and all the uniformed men refused, but the ones in civvies gladly took him up on it, including Keith, who had stayed around, learning as much as possible.

***

The caravan left before it got dark. One empty ambulance, two ESU trucks, a sheriff's deputy, Keith and finally Brad in Scott's truck. In Toponas, he turned south toward McCoy, dreading the thought that he had to face Scott's parents.

***

"Say that again, Boy! You did what? And who did what?" Ronald, the sheriff turned and waved Brad to follow him. "Sit in here and wait. I'll be right back. Do you want a coke or something?" The young man just nodded and found a chair at the far side of the table. It was a stark room with a huge mirror on one of the sidewalls and burglar bars all across the window. He got the creepy feeling that he was in jail already. There was nothing in the room but a table and six chairs. No pictures, no file cabinets, nothing but bare walls.

He started to wonder if they would really try to pin a murder charge on him. There was no question that he killed a man, but what could they call that? "Unmeditated murder?" He knew it was self defense, because if he hadn't killed his attacker, Randy sure as hell would've killed him.

The sheriff walked into the front office. "Sonders, call Buffet back in to man the front desk. Then set up the recording equipment and start rolling the moment I walk in."

"Yes sir."

Sheriff Ronald Cobalt picked up the phone and quickly dialed a number. "Did Marge call in?... Damn!... Okay…" and hung up. Walking into the projection room, "I would really have liked Marge to be here, but she's off somewhere. After all it's Saturday and she should be enjoying herself, right Sonders?"

"I wouldn't know. I work Saturdays."

"Don't rub it in. I was just taking the missus to a movie and dinner when you called me, 'Boss, you better come in.' remember?"

"Sounded urgent."

"Y'all set?" Sonders nodded.

"Okay, roll it when I walk in."

"You didn't bring the coke!"

"Sure didn't. Be right back."

This time he not only brought a coke, he brought a legal pad and a pen. He thought that would look more professional.

"Alright boy, I heard only bits and pieces from the deputy who was on the scene, so you just start from the beginning. I mean the very beginning. Don't leave anything out.

"Yes sir."

Brad started with the story about the Harley crash and the rescue mission he was involved in and the sheriff listened without interruption until the gold nugget was mentioned.

"Is that the gold piece that Scott took to the jewelry store?"

"You know about that?"

"I know a lot. Answer me. Was that the nugget you found?"

"No, no, no! That was a piece that he found himself..."

"Scott was in on the rescue?"

"No, he wasn't there. That was the next day when..."

"You went back the next day?"

"Yes, I was getting to that. Can I have another coke, maybe?"

Ronald nearly made a mistake. He started to turn to the one-way mirror and order Sonders to bring a coke, but he caught himself in time. The boy should be under the impression that he was unwatched by outsiders.

"No. Let's wrap this up. Keep talking. We still have to face the Pierce family. Keep going!"

While Brad talked, Ronald made some notes, but didn't interrupt any more. After forty minutes, the sheriff stood. "Do you know where the Pierces live? We better go in my car. They can come and get his truck later. Let's go."

***

Deputy Buffett asked Sonders when he was released from the phone duty, "What was all that about?"

"About a gold find and some murders."

"Gold find? Where?"

"Up on Gore Pass."

"Really?"

Golden Nuggets
XI
Gold in them thar…?

Saturday night.

"What are you trying to tell me Keith? I got your message, but you said so many things. Someone was murdered over a gold discovery and there is no gold and why were two people killed on my property?" The little Indian man nearly shouted into the phone, while pacing back and forth in his office.

"Mr. Samandran, down below where the murders took place is not in the parcel that you petitioned for, it's north of it, down in the ravine…"

"But all the action you described was up on the road, which is my property…"

"Yes, all the rescue vehicles and the police authorities were up on the road, because the way down is nearly impassible…"

"Then where was the gold?"

"Allegedly, the gold was in the saddlebags of the motorcycle that went over the edge last week…"

"Allegedly? Keith, you're starting to sound like a cop. *Was* there gold or was there *no* gold?"

"There was gold…"

"Then why the *allegedly?"*

"Because I didn't see it. I only heard them talking about it."

"Okay, did you hear how much and from where?"

"Nobody knows where it came from but there was enough to kill for."

"Now Keith, here's what we're going to do. You pick me up at six in the morning and take me out there. I have to be back by ten. My children are involved in a religious play and I can't miss that. Be at the gate at six, okay?" He hung up.

Keith stared at the dead instrument. "Religious play? On Sunday? I thought he was a Buddhist."

***

Steamboat Springs, Coroner's office.

The bodies were on a slab, ready to be shoved into the vault, awaiting autopsy on Monday. In their light grey knee-length lab coats, two workers were about to finish for the night, anxious to go home.

"Did you hear what set off these murders?" The older nurse asked but didn't wait for an answer. "A gold find."

The young male assistant was astonished. "Here in Steamboat?"

"No, at the Gore Pass. They must've been fighting over the loot, that's what started it."

"They haven't found gold in Colorado in a hundred years!"

"Yeah, yeah, they're still mining gold, but there haven't been any new finds until now."

"Wow! These two guys got killed? There must've been a lot of it."

"Could be. Let's lock up."

"Gold really? Up in Gore Pass?"

***

Sheriff Cobalt and Brad drove up to the modest home of the Pierce family. The lights were still on down stairs, so they rang the bell.

The door opened within a minute. "Ronald, what brings you here at this hour?"

"May we come in?"

"Sure, sure. Come into the living room. Mabel is still up. We're watching Saturday Night Live. There's nothing wrong with our boy, is there?" Mr. Pierce, a short, balding man, walked backward as he talked and Mabel jumped up as they entered the room.

""Sheriff? Brad? What's wrong? Why are you here?"

"May we sit?"

"Of course, of course. Sit. You can take the couch. I'll sit over here. Greg, turn that thing off." She pointed at the TV and turned back to the duo. "Something's wrong, right? Brad, weren't you and Scott out together?"

"Mrs. Pierce..."

"Call me Mabel."

"You're right Mabel, something's terribly wrong..."

"You had to arrest Scott? What have you guys done now? Scott doesn't live with us anymore and we never know what these kids are up to..."

"Mabel... Mrs. Pierce..." The Sheriff couldn't get two words in edgewise. "Mabel!" He raised his voice. "Mabel, it's worse!"

"Worse? What could be worse?" She got up from her chair and yelled, "He was in an accident, right? He got into a car wreck, right?"

Mr. Pierce had jumped up as well and grabbed a hold of her. "Mabel, sit down. Let Ronald talk. Let's not get hysterical until we know what's going on. Come sit." His voice had a soothing effect on her and she did sit back down.

"Greg, you better keep holding her hand. It's gonna get worse." He lowered his voice and his head. When he lifted it back up, there were tears in his eyes. "It's much worse. Scott is dead."

Mabel screamed, shook off her husband and jumped at Brad. "What have you done to him? How did you kill him? I knew you were no good, you little bastard, you're just like your father..."

"Shut up, Mabel!" Her husband and the law man both had jumped between her and Brad and pushed her back on the couch that Brad and the sheriff had occupied a second before. The sheriff held her down and told Greg, "Get some water or whiskey, we gotta calm her down. Hurry." Turning to the distraught woman, "Mabel, Mabel, calm down, calm down. Brad did not hurt Scott. Brad tried to help him. You gotta believe that!" He firmly held on to her shoulders as her husband tried to get some water into her, but she refused to drink. "I always knew those two were up to no good and now he comes over here with that halo on his head lookin' innocent to tell us how he killed our son." She started screaming again. "Get him outta here before I kill him! Get out! Get out, you no good bastard!"

"Brad, wait in the car." Turning to the father, "Call Doc Kuchs, see if he can come over to give her something to make her sleep through the night. It's gonna be a bitch to deal with her again when she wakes, but maybe the Doc has some answers."

An hour later, Sheriff Ronald Cobalt dropped Brad off at the *Colorado Eagle* at his request.

"There's no way I wanna face my folks tonight. I'll walk home when they're asleep. I already hate the thought of explaining it to them in the morning..."

"I understand Brad. I understand. Be at my office at nine on Monday. We'll go over the report and if you agree with everything, you sign it and we'll send it off to State. You'll be asked to come in for more questioning, you understand?"

"I jus wish I could bring him back."

***

"You never drink no scotch, Brad. What's up with you? You sure you don't want a beer?" Bartender Tracy was very concerned.

"Okay, give me a beer too."

She returned with both drinks. "I can't refuse you a drink, because you're still stone sober, even though it's already eleven o'clock. But tell me, what happened? Did you have to work late?"

"Worse!" He chugalugged his whiskey and nearly choked. Another patron rushed over and beat him on his shoulders. "Drink a bit of beer. What's the matter with you Brad?" Two other regulars walked up and asked Tracy, "What gives? What's with the boy?" She shrugged, "I don't know. I think it's his first drink of the day."

Brad collapsed on the bar. "Scott is dead. My best buddy is dead and it's my fault." He exclaimed between sobs.

"Scott? Scott Pierce? What happened? When did that happen? Where was he killed?"

The questions came from three sides from four different mouths and Brad only lifted his head long enough to say, "It's all my fault. Give me another scotch!"

"No, no. We're not gonna start that. Drink your beer and tell us what happened. You'll feel better when you do." Tracy had been in the bar business a long time and had seen scenes like this a hundred times. "Here, dry your eyes and chug your beer if you want to."

She handed him a towel and reached for a fresh bottle.

"Wanna tell us about it, Brad? Can we help in any way? Where is Scott now?" They were all old time acquaintances.

"Scott? Now? In Steamboat Springs I guess."

"Steamboat Springs? What the hell is he doing all the way over there?"

"That's where the nearest Coroner's office is and they'll have to do an autopsy on him…"

"But why all the way out there? Isn't there anything closer?"

"Yeah, man, but it all happened at Gore Pass and that's in their jurisdiction and that's why…"

"What was he doing at Gore Pass? There's nothing there." The natives knew the area well, apparently.

"We found this gold, you see…"

"You found gold? At Gore Pass?"

"Let me explain. You won't give me another scotch, Tracy? Then I'll drink beer till you have to carry me home."

"Don't worry buddy. We'll get you home. Tell us about the gold.

Golden Nuggets
XII
Gold Rush

When Samandran and his chief security man came over the pass, the little brown Indian man made a sweeping gesture to his left, "Keith, this is where I picture my casino. Look at that view!"

"How far does the property go?"

"On both sides of the road, about a quarter mile. Right to over there, where the pass narrows. Right beyond where those trucks are."

Two pickup trucks were parked on the opposite side of the road.

"Pull on over!" The Indian developer screamed. "What the hell are they doing on my property? Do you have a shotgun in this car?"

"Why? You planning to shoot somebody for trespassing? You don't even have any signs up." Keith Brannon talked as he pulled in front of the first truck.

"I want to fire three warning shots in the air. That ought to tell them to come up."

"Gunga Din?" Keith couldn't help but smile.

"How do I get *No Trespassing* signs up here so I can keep those clowns out of here?"

"*Posted* signs should be easy to get at any hardware store."

"Get on the horn and get a bunch of them up here. Do you know where my property begins and ends?" Samandran was hopping out of the car as he spoke and leaned back in the door, "Do you have a shotgun or not?"

"Yes, I do. I'll pop the trunk. Don't shoot anybody!"

"I might!" He grabbed one of the gun cases in the trunk and unzipped it, finding a rifle instead of a shotgun. "That will do." In a metal ammo case he found a box of 30-06 cartridges and figured, "These have got to be the ones."

In seconds, the fifty year old Indian man had three rounds loaded and lifted the weapon to his shoulder, ready to fire a few rounds in the air. What he didn't realize was that the safety automatically came on when the rifle was loaded and he couldn't budge the trigger. Samandran lowered the rifle and studied the contraption, moving a few levers and when he found the right one, he immediately fired a round because he still had his finger on the trigger. The bullet hit the driver door just as Brannon opened it and went right through the metal, two inches above Keith's hand.

"What the hell?" He dropped down on the seat. "What are you doing? You damn near killed me!"

"I'm sorry, I'm sorry. I couldn't get the safety off." The boss had run to the open door. "Did you get hurt?"

"Give me that thing. Don't you know how to handle a gun?"

"I fired a *Lee-Enfield* when I was in the Indian Army, thirty years ago."

"What are you trying to do?" Keith was holding the rifle and wasn't about to hand it back.

"I wanted to fire three shots in quick succession. Isn't that the sign to come on out or help?"

"How many rounds did you put in?"

"Three, but…"

"Okay, I'll fire three fast rounds and we'll lock the gun back in the trunk before they arrest you for attempted manslaughter." In the trunk, he located the box of cartridges, loaded one more and fired three shots in the air. *Bam-bam-bam.*

"Let's see where these trucks come from and let's take down their tag numbers." Brannon took charge before his boss could do something else stupid.

"Keith? Did you order the signs?"

"Yes, they're looking for them now. It's Sunday, you know."

"Go and call the Highway Patrol. I may have some of these guys arrested. What is that other truck doing here?"

A vehicle had come over the pass from the same westerly direction and pulled up behind the Security man's car. Four guys piled out.

"What's going on? Is this the spot?" A big burley man in a camouflage outfit stepped forward toward Keith, who was still holding the rifle.

Samandran, all five foot two of him, stepped forward and flashing his white even teeth in his brown face, snarled at the man, "You are trespassing on my property and I'm ordering you to leave."

"Your property? Who are you? Cochise? This is federal land buddy and nobody is ordering nobody around. So step aside before I hurt you."

"Nobody's gonna hurt anybody either." Keith stepped forward with the rifle at ready. "Mr. Samandran here has leased this land from the Parks Department and we're bringing up *Posted* signs, so there will be no misunderstanding, so you best leave."

"We heard gold was found here and we aim to look for some. Whaddaya gonna do about it? Shoot us? All of us?"

"Stand by. We're calling the State Police and they'll take charge. Mr. Samandran, why don't you get in the car and start calling? I'll stay here."

The little man agreed and climbed in the driver's seat to manipulate the phone.

Meanwhile, Keith addressed the three burly men and the youngster, "Where'd you hear about the gold?"

"We heard and that's what counts. What do you know about it?

"There's no gold here. An accident with a Harley, right here," he pointed down the slope. "is all there is. The driver had some gold nuggets in his saddle bag and he spilled some, but they've all been recovered by the authorities. That's all there's to it."

"And you want us to believe that?" The big guy laughed out

loud. "You want us to believe that cockamamie story? Hahahaha!" His comrades joined in and at the same time, the camouflaged man jumped forward, quicker than his size would let you believe and grabbed Keith's rifle while two other ones jumped on his back. In seconds he was overpowered and the speaker of the bunch stepped up to the open car door, aimed at the startled Indian, "Out. You skinny weasel, out!"

Just then, another truck drove up from the east and two civilians in coveralls emerged. They walked up to the assembled group and asked, "What's going on?"

"And who might you be?" The burly man holding the rifle was still in control.

"We heard about a gold find and we brought picks and shovels and we're gonna stake us a claim."

"Stake a claim? This is federal land."

"That's the way it works. You stake your claim and you register it the next day with the Department of the Interior and from then on in, it's yours to explore. That's how it works. So if you don't mind, we're gonna go down and explore..."

"But it's my land!" Little Samandran screamed as loud as he could. "and there are people already down there. See those two trucks? And I'm not giving permission ..."

"Oh, shut up!" The burly shouted.

"No, I will not shut up. I have a lease..."

"Put'em back in the car." Turning back to the latest visitor in the blue coverall, "So what you're saying is, you go down there and find a spot you like and then you stake it? With what?"

"We brought wooden stakes with numbers and names, but you can cut and whittle your own and mark your boundaries, but you gotta do some good measuring so you can register it properly..."

"Like how?"

"Like how what?"

"How do you measure where your stake is?"

"You mark where you are on the road here and you keep track of how far down you go..."

"How do you do that?"

"We have 500 foot ropes, so at the end of each rope, we know how far we are from the road."

"Holy shit!" He turned to his buddies, "Did we bring any rope?"

"Some."

"Some? How much is that?"

"Not much."

"Ah, damn. Let the little fart out of the car."

The youngest of the team opened the car to let the property owner out, just as a State Trooper, blue lights flashing, pulled next to the caravan on the shoulder of the road.

"What is going on here?"

Before long, there were two more troopers and a Sheriff's Deputy, plus three more pickups and Samandran missed his children's performance.

Golden Nugget
XIII
Confrontation

"I want these men arrested." Samandran was arguing with the highest ranking State Trooper, the only one who had stripes on his arm. "These men attacked us, took our rifle and imprisoned me against my will."

"Imprisoned? Where?"

"In my own car. They grabbed Keith..."

"Who's Keith?"

"The man over there, he's my security chief."

"Security chief of what? And who are you?"

"I'm A.J. Samandran. I own some hotels and resorts around here and I own this property too. I want..."

"Hold it a minute!" The patrolman was astonished. "You can't own this. This is a Federal Park."

"But I obtained a 99 year lease option three years ago."

"That so? I wasn't aware of that. What are you gonna do with it? Mine for gold?"

"No, I was planning on building a hotel, casino-resort area here at the top. The view is magnificent."

"Alright, alright. Let's go talk to the culprits. The alleged culprits." The trooper started walking.

"That big one over there."

"Let's see what he's got to say." Both of them moseyed over to the group of men around their truck and Patrolman Potter approached the big bully. "Sir, what's your name?"

"Benson, Josh Benson." He didn't appear scared or impressed.

"Mr. Benson, this gentleman over here, Mr. Salamander...

"Samandran!"

"Whatever. He says you attacked him and that you..."

"We attacked him? When we drove up, he and him," he pointed toward Keith, "came at us with a rifle and ordered us off the property. Well, we took the rifle away from..."

"It wasn't loaded." Keith interjected.

Benson went on, "And the little runt here wouldn't shut up, so we put him in his own car. At least we couldn't hear'm anymore."

"You see? I want them arrested. I..."

"Hold it, hold it. We got to sort this out here and now and I'm makin' a decision. All of you!" He waved at the other law enforcement officer and the remainder of the potential miners, "Come here. Come closer. Listen up! Whether Mr. Salamander owns this property or not makes no difference to me. This is a National Forest, a Federal Park and you need a pass to be on the property. So go to the nearest ranger station and get a pass and don't come here without it. Anyone caught here without a pass is subject to arrest. You hear?" He raised his voice. "Do you hear me?"

"But we can be on the road, cain't we?" The burly guy spoke up.

"And then sneak your ass down there when nobody's watching? No way! You stop along here and you'll be arrested. Now pull out! *Now!*"

Muttering among themselves, the group disbanded and headed for their vehicles.

"But I want those men to be arrested!" The little Indian was not about to give up.

"Are you egging me on, so you'll be the first one to be arrested?"

"Yeah man! That's telling him. Arrest his ass." The burly four shouted their support as they eased into their truck.

"Come on sir, let's go." Keith was anxious to get away.

"I know my rights. I'm a citizen and I have my rights and…"

"One more word and I'll lock you up…"

"You can't do that!… I will call the govern…"

"Deputy… Cuff'em and put him in the back of my patrol car."

"But Officer," Keith cut in, "is that really necessary?"

"One more word from you and you'll join your master. Do you understand? Get out of here?"

Keith started to move away, but turned, "May I ask where you're taking him, so I can pick him up when he's released?"

"Highway Patrol Quarters on Route 40 near Kremmlin. Now get."

Keith cranked up the car and headed west. "Might as well be nearby. Maybe I'll go to Steamboat Springs and have some Rocky Mountain Oysters."

All that remained was one pickup and the lawmen with their vehicles.

"Where did all these guys get that stuff about the gold?" Patrolman Burton wanted to know.

"From what I gathered," the deputy spoke up, "in a bar in McCoy someone dropped that info and another deputy over there told his brother, who told another and so…"

"That sounds like the story I heard," a patrolman cut in. "In Steamboat, in a bar, a coroner's aid told about a coupla guys in the morgue that got murdered here at the pass, fighting over gold."

"I'll be damned. The gold rush was started in the bars. I guess that's the way it was in the Old West…" He paused. "Now who in the hell is that? Whaddaya think they're doing?"

He pointed at a pickup that had stopped a couple of hundred yards from them and began unloading things.

"Let's check it out." He cranked up his engine, turned on the blue lights and rushed over to the new arrival.

"State police." He announced on his megaphone. "Stop what you're doing." After getting out, the law officer walked over to the men that were unloading the pickup. "Who are you and what are you doing?"

"We work for Samandran Maintenance and we're putting up *No Trespassing* signs all along his property. You see, there are rumors..."

"We know all about that! Do you have a map that outlines his property?"

"Sure!"

"Well, I'll be... Show me the map."

Hovering over the map and all its markings, Benson told his fellow officer, "Get the Salamander out of my car and get'im over here."

When the little fellow arrived, he was shown the map and asked, "Is this actual? Is this correct?"

"Yes it is and has been for three years, so now you see, you're actually standing on my property." His Indian accent, with the short clipped words, became stronger when he was mad.

"Okay. Give me your card. Here is mine. Tomorrow a full report will be sent to you and... hey fellows?" He addressed the pole diggers. "Are you going back toward McCoy? Mind giving him a ride?"

"No problem."

"Good. Now sir, next time, do not hinder police officers when they're trying to do their job. Understood?" With that he withdrew and took off in his car.

Back at the other patrol car he ordered the other officer, "Stay here until that last guy comes up." He pointed at the remaining pickup. "Write him a citation. I'm sending up your relief in an hour, okay?"

"Okay, sir."

***

Back in McCoy, Mr. Pierce had come over to Brad's home and in the presence of the parents asked the young man to relate the whole story. In the modest but cozy home, the four of them sat around the dining room table, sipping coffee and snacking on blueberry pie. Interrupted by sobs, Brad told the whole story from beginning to the bitter end.

"Didn't you see the attack coming? Didn't you know he was gonna kill you?"

"We had no notion, Mr. Pierce. He seemed like a nice man, about forty, he seemed okay. What can I say? We agreed how we would divide the stuff and all a sudden, he's coming at me and he had already knifed Scott and..." He broke down again. "I couldn't attack a man with a dagger and I was scared shitless. I figured I'd run and then he would run too and I would circle around and help Scott, you see, but when I got back there was no life left in'im and I covered him with rock, so the animals wouldn't get to him before I got back with help..."

This time his mother broke down. "Good God, Brad. How do you always manage to get into trouble? God help me, I've brought you up better..."

"Mary, for God's sake, the boy doesn't do drugs, has never been arrested or nothin'. He's basically a good kid. Don't come down on him so hard, Mary. Pull yourself together."

Scott's father cut in, "Did you mention Pauline, my sister's daughter? Was she in on this?"

"Well, yes. No. No, no. I mean yes. She'd check on the legalities if we found gold and if we could claim it when we did. She told Scott to stay away from it and not do anything stupid. I'm so sorry." He collapsed again.

Mr. Pierce spoke up, "I better go back home. My daughter came over to be with her mother. She's destroyed. I'd better get back. Where is the body now and when can we bury him properly?"

"Oh, I don't know. The sheriff has all that information, but I'm sure they took him to Steamboat Springs for an autopsy."

"All the way out there?"

"All the way out there."

Golden Nuggets
XIV
Guilty or not?

Monday morning.

When District Attorney Hans Bromeyer checked his morning reports, he couldn't believe his eyes. He snatched up the phone and called in his assistant, Anne Morgan-Dubois. Within thirty seconds she breezed through the connecting door, bringing with her a plume of Chanel #5. Her golden hair was piled high on her head and her silver gray pantsuit outlined her body as if she were poured into it.

"Yes, sir." Yellow pad and pencil at ready.

"Sit. Have you read the report on the double murder Saturday?"

"Glanced through it and put it on your desk. Still waiting for an autopsy report from…"

"Did you see where one of the killers went home? Wasn't even arrested. What's going on here? Someone murders someone and goes home? Since when? Who's handling this at the State Police office? Get with the coroner and call the CSP and find out what's behind this. I feel I need to send off an arrest warrant somewhere. Get back with me as soon as you can."

"Will do, sir." She glided out of the room, leaving the D.A. wondering why he never met a dish like that when he was single.

The coroner was nowhere near a final report. He'd just got the paperwork ten minutes ago and he hadn't seen the bodies yet. "Call me back at noon." was his only comment.

The State Troopers weren't much more help because Officer Potter was on the late shift and the patrolman on duty had the same report as she had. "What else?" The pretty Assistant D.A. asked herself. "The sheriff in McCoy maybe?" She picked up the phone.

"Sheriff Cobalt, please."

"Who may I say is calling?"

"The District Attorney's office in Steamboat."

"Really?... Just a minute."

"Cobalt here. That you Hans?"

"No I'm his assistant, Anne Dubois. Just trying to put some pieces together for my boss, Hans, and your name came across our desk. We can't figure out how we ended up with two murders and no murderer."

"Well, like I said, the one guy, Randy, murdered the other one, Scott, and then in self- defense, the third one killed the first one, Randy. So what is your question?"

"That's just about what the report states, but that doesn't make a whole lot of sense. Can you break that down for me in more detail and where is the third one, as you call him? Is he in custody…?

"No. Why should he be?"

"Well, he killed somebody, didn't he?"

"Miss Anne, in case you missed something in law school, in this country, someone is innocent until proven guilty, not the other way around. Unless you and the District Attorney find enough of a flaw in my reasoning, I'm keeping this boy around here, but, Miss Dubois, if you issue a warrant for his arrest, I'll have him picked up in minutes and extradited to your jurisdiction."

"Mr. Cobalt, please. Let's not start on the wrong foot. We're trying to put two and two together, but with the information we have to date, we couldn't even put one and zero together, so please, bear with us and help me any way you can. Do you have a complete report on the whole series of events…"

"I will in an hour. My girl is transcribing it now, as we speak."

"Let me give you my fax number. Can you forward it to me as soon as you can? I would appreciate that. After all, we work for the same justice system, don't we?"

"I sure hope so."

***

"Keith? Where the hell are you?" Samandran sounded edgy.

"I was gonna ask you the same thing. I went to the Highway Patrol station where they were going to take you, but..."

"I never went there..."

"Now I know, you were never taken in and..."

"And I had to bum a ride in a pickup truck to get home and I never saw my kid's performance."

"Why didn't you call me? I would've..."

"Call you where?"

"Remember I have a phone in my car? You even used it to call the State Patrol..."

"But how would I know your number?"

"You have it in your little black book in your back pock..."

"Never mind. Where are you, Keith?"

"I'm leaving McCoy."

"Come to my office. We have a plot plan ready for you, so you can supervise the posting of the signs all around our Gore Pass property. We're lucky nobody got hurt there yesterday 'cause they would be suing us today. What is the appropriate kind of sign that we should be using? *POSTED* or *NO TRESPASSING?* Which one gives us the best legal protection?"

"I believe the *NO TRESPASSING*, but why don't you call your Legal Beagles and I'll call the Sheriff's office and that'll help us decide."

"Okay. Don't spare any money on signs."

***

Monday Noon.

"Miss Dubois? Do you pronounce that Du boys or Du bwah?"

"Du bwah, how can I help?"

"This is the Coroner and…"

"Oh, thanks for calling back. What have you got?"

"Since we have both the murder weapons, it was easy to determine what caused what and obviously number one was knifed right through the heart. Professional killing, I would say, probably military trained, special forces, et cetera. Number two received two blows. The first one right under the chin and then a deadly blow at the base of the cranium, right at top of the vertebra. Was that the one who knifed number one and…"

"Guess so…"

"Then where is the person who killed number two?"

"Somewhere out in McCoy…"

"Where's McCoy?"

"Oh, a little dot on the map between Toponas and Wolcott."

"What's he doing there?"

"He lives there."

"He's not in custody?"

"Nope."

"Why not?"

"Don't ask."

***

Emergency Services Unit # 36.

Chief Korman's office.

"Brad, after hearing your story and the opinion of the sheriff, I have no choice but to suspend you without pay…" He held up his hand. "No, no, no. Don't interrupt. You are not guilty of a crime and I'm not suggesting that, but you did find a gold nugget while on duty and you failed to report that. I don't know what the consequences will be, but we'll leave that to the justice system. Meanwhile, go home and relax. Write everything down in as much detail as you remember. Do you have a computer? No?... Go to the library and type it up. By the way, do you still have that nugget?"

"Nugget? Which one?"

"Which one? How many do you have? I was talking about the one you found when you were bringing up that body out of the ravine."

"Oh, that one? Just a minute." He reached into his left pocket and came up with five little golden rocks. He spread them on his supervisor's desk and said, "I guess it's this one."

"You still have them?" The surprise was written all over his scraggly face.

"Nobody asked for them."

"That's hard to believe. Then again, who should ask for them? The Highway Patrol? The sheriff? What is this worth?"

"I could sell'em for about $2,500."

"Wow! And you just walk around with them?"

"My pocket is the safest place I know."

"That's funny, but I guess you're right. Has anybody said anything about who really has a right to them?"

"No, all we talked about is the killings and all and how it happened."

"Wow again. Well, Brad, don't sell them. If they determine that they're not yours to keep, turn'em back in. Now go and write."

"I refused to take typing in High School..."

"Time to learn. May come in handy some day. I'll call you when we can reinstate you, okay?"

"Thank you sir."

Chief Korman picked up the phone."Sheriff Cobalt please."

"Who may I say is calling?"

"ESU."

"Just a moment."

"Cobalt here."

"Ronald, do you know that this boy Brad is walking around with thousands of dollars worth of gold in his pocket?"

"You're kiddin' me."

"No, I've seen'em. About a half dozen nuggets."
"Boy, that puts a different slant on things, doesn't it?"
"It might."

Golden Nuggets
XV
What's the connection?

Boulder, Monday morning.

"Mr. Johnson?"

"Speaking."

"This is Sergeant Brown at the Sheriff's Office. The sheriff has asked if you can come in as soon as possible. He needs to talk to you."

"Really? Sure! I mean, yes. Let me get my crews on the road. I'm a little shorthanded this morning."

"We know."

"You know?"

"Yes, it pertains to one of your employees and…"

"Not Randy?"

"Yes, Randy, so please come in."

"What's with Randy?"

"Please. He's waiting."

Sheriff's office, Boulder Colorado

"Hi, Ralph. What's going on? What's with Randy? Is he in jail?"

"Sit down, J.J."

The middle aged painting contractor sagged down in the chair alongside the cluttered desk of the local sheriff. His stucco and paint covered overalls could stand some repair and serious washing. He looked exhausted, even though it was only ten in the morning.

"Having a lousy day, J.J.?"

"Jeez, I have plenty of work, but keeping workers in this trade is nearly impossible, 'cause nobody wants to work hard any more. All they want to do is work a few hours, collect their check and go out for beer or wine. It could drive me nuts. I'm even thinking about hiring some illegal Mexicans, but then I take a chance on ending up in court. I just can't win or get ahead. Like I said, it's driving me up the wall. What's new here, Ralph? What's with Randy?"

"Randy is dead."

"Oh shit. Car accident?"

"No, murdered."

"Christ Almighty! Murdered? How? When? By whom?"

"We know all of that, but what we want to know from you is, how did Randy and Jack, the one who got killed on his bike, get hold of a bunch of gold?"

"Gold? They had gold? Where did they get gold? Both of them?"

"Well, at least one of them. Jack went over the edge into the canyon and apparently had a bunch of gold nuggets in his saddlebags and sprayed them all over the mountainside."

"You gotta be kiddin' me? Where the hell could he have gotten that much gold?"

"That's why you're here, J.J. Where did those guys work together where gold nuggets were ready for harvesting?"

"Oh my God!"

"What?"

"They did a job at the old Museum of the Granby Mining Company in Rand a week or two ago. Do you think there might be some loose gold lying around there?"

"That would be pretty stupid, don't you think?"

"Yeah, that would be more than stupid, but nobody has reported a loss that I've heard of. Have you had any reports of gold thefts, Ralph?"

"Not a word."

"That's baffling." J.J. sagged in his chair. "Do you suppose they robbed the place, split the profits and Jack took off for California and crashed on top of the mountain?"

"That's exactly what happened. Randy went out a week later to find the bike and the loot and killed somebody who had discovered the stuff already and then got killed himself in the process."

"Then who killed Randy?"

"According to the report I got, Randy tried to kill the other guy too and then this guy killed Randy in self-defense."

"Which other guy?"

"Apparently two buddies went on a treasure hunt and found it and then Randy surprised them and..."

"How did they tie me into this picture?"

"Well, Jack was brought to you last week for burial and Randy had a paycheck on him with your business address and his driver's license was registered here. So that made it easy."

"Where's Randy... I mean, where's his body now?"

"In Steamboat, in the morgue. Have you ever been to the old museum up in Rand?"

"Sure. I measured the place and made up the estimate and proposal for the ceiling repair."

"Was there any gold in sight?"

"You kiddin'? Only old junk from the gold rush days. Nobody visits that place any more."

"They haven't called you about anything missing?"

"No, as a matter of fact, I just got their check in the mail for the work they did."

"J.J. Do you have their phone number?"

"Not on me, but I can call my office."

"Do that and I'll fix some coffee. How do you drink it?"

"Regular. Which phone can I use?"

Sipping coffee, the two of them talked and listened to a secretary at the Granby Mining Company.

"No, no gold was missing. No, nothing was missing out of the old Museum. No substantial amounts of gold had been mined in years. Just enough out of the old vein to make it worthwhile to keep the company operating. No sizable nuggets had been found in twenty years?

No, the vault had not been broken into. No, nothing out of the ordinary has happened of late."

After they broke off the connection, Sheriff Ralph Comte turned to J.J. Johnson, "They didn't have any nuggets on hand, so where did they come from? I bet you, though, when they hear about these nuggets involved in the accidents and the murders, they'll jump right up and claim that they're the rightful owners, even though they didn't know they had them and didn't realize they lost'em."

"What a mess, Ralph. If it is determined that these guys stole the gold while working for me, am I gonna be held liable?"

"Oh, God, I hope not. You had nothin' to do with it. Right?"

"Hell no. This is the first I heard of it. I have liability insurance of course but that mostly covers accidents and things. I don't think it includes robbery and murder."

"Let's not worry about that yet. You said earlier that they may have split the loot and if that is true, then where is Randy's half?"

"Huh? Randy's half? I know where he lives and he has a little girlfriend, a widow with a coupla kids. Do you wanna check that out?"

"Let's. I need to round up a few deputies and picture takers and you can ride with me." He got up. "And by the way, J.J. I appreciate your time and your help."

"Of course, of course. I just hope I don't get a lot of negative publicity about employees that rob the place while working."

"Oh, come on! Don't worry about that. I doubt it will ever come to that. Come on. Let's go do some police work."

Randy's apartment rendered no gold or any evidence of gold. Judy, his friend was on the job and she broke up when she was informed of Randy's death.

"My girls latched on to him like he was the father they lost three years ago. They're gonna be devastated. What happened?"

After Judy composed herself somewhat, they retreated to a break room in the department store where she worked and settled around a folding table, with cokes and coffee.

"Judy, did Randy tell you anything about the gold that Jack and he discovered?" The sheriff was doing the asking.

"Gold?" She seemed genuinely surprised. "Gold? He never spoke that word. What's with the gold?" The pleasant looking middle aged mother of three sat up straight and asked again. "What gold?"

"He didn't mention gold or nuggets at all?" Ralph remained very patient.

"Not to me he didn't. Where would he get the money to get gold? He barely made enough to pay the bills and his child support. I know. He was embarrassed that he couldn't spend more money on my girls and he worked all the overtime hours he could get, isn't that true Mr. Johnson?"

"That's true, that's true." J.J. concurred.

"Did he give you any secret documents or papers for safekeeping?"

"Why would he do that?"

"We have reasons to believe that he may have had a stash of money and has it hidden someplace. Your place maybe?"

"My place? Are you crazy? We scraped by every weekend, eating pizza and going to the park and the lake. All low cost outings."

"Which park? Which lake?

"The one near Loveland, you know..."

"We know. Anything else you can tell us? We want to figure out why he was killed and so do you, right?"

"Yes."

"Here's my card. Call me when you can think of anything else."

"Where's Randy now?"

"In Steamboat. He'll probably be shipped here in a few days and then we can plan..."

"My girls are gonna be devastated."

Golden Nuggets
XVI
Higher up!

Steamboat Springs, Monday 11 AM.

Anne Morgan-Dubois checked her appearance one last time and approved of herself. At age thirty-one, she still looked like a college student in her senior year. Five years of marriage and one little boy completely agreed with her and she couldn't be happier, except..., she still had not handled a major case in court, with the chance to show off her great judicial abilities. This time, it looked that might happen until someone poured cold water on the whole deal. She stepped out of the ladies room and proceeded to her boss' office. "Enter," resulted from her knock and she swooped in.

"Sir, I hate to say this, but it looks like the whole case is taken out of our hands completely..."

"The murders up at the pass?"

"Yes and it all ends up in the jurisdiction of the CBI in Denver." The DA rolled his eyeballs toward the heavens as Anne continued, "Yes, our famous, or should I say infamous, Colorado Bureau of Investigation.

"Why? For Pete's sake, why?" He couldn't believe it.

"Why? Because the case is in the hands of the sheriff in McCoy where one of the victims lived. You know, that is within the jurisdiction of the CBI Grand Junction office. The crime took place on federal property in the district of the Colorado State Patrol outside of Kremmlin. The other victim was from Boulder, where the sheriff is handling the investigation and the lease/property deal is in the hands of the Federal Authorities in Denver. In other words, it's all outside the limits of our powerful little office here in Steamboat."

"Damn. It sounded like a doozy of a case. Something that you could really put your teeth into. That's too bad."

"Should I inform the coroner to forward his report to Denver?"

"Yes, but have him send you a copy, so you can keep up with things and maybe a twist of events will get you back in the ball-game."

"Oh, sure! Fat chance, but I'll ask for a copy. I'd like to see them screw up, so I can jump back into it."

"That's my girl."

Two hours later.

"Anne, did you get the latest dispatch?... Look at my e-mails. The gold may have been stolen from an old mine in Granby. You might wanna shoot out there and check it out."

"You serious?"

"Damn tootin'. Get in the car and report to me. That's an order." He added with a smile.

"Hoorah for you, boss."

To her secretary, she said, "If anybody asks, I'm off to Rand near Granby."

"Granby? Where's Granby?"

"Do you know where Hot Sulphur Springs is?"

"Never been there, but I know where it is on the map."

"Well, that's it. If it were winter, I'd pick up my son and go skiing, but this is all work, so I'll check in with you later."

Even though the distance was barely eighty miles, it took Anne more than two hours to reach Granby and she was sorry she hadn't planned any better. She would have to call her husband to pick up their son from the nursery school, because there was no way she could be back on time, unless she turned right around. That didn't make much sense, so she proceeded to find the old Granby Mining Company north of the town.

The ancient frame building was right out of an old western movie. Any minute, she expected John Wayne to step out of the front door with a lever-action rifle in hand. The only vehicle in sight was a beat up white Ford pickup without a bed lid. The front door was locked and her knocking produced nothing but a startled cat that had been dozing on a window ledge. Figuring that whoever belonged to the truck had to be around there somewhere, she turned to the north side of the building, where several smaller buildings were located. Just as she turned right at the end of the weathered building, on old man nearly staggered into her.

"Whoa lady! Didn't see you coming. What in the world are you doing here?"

"I'm looking for the owners of the mine…"

"Owners? They're in Denver. It's owned by a company that…"

"Then who manages the property?"

"Manages? Like who runs it?" The old man with a lumpy cowboy hat and brown teeth laughed out loud. "There ain't much running to do. During ski season, we open the museum part, but this time a year, only Mrs. Cornfield comes here in the morning to do paperwork and make bank deposits. You see, we sell a lot of gravel from back there." He pointed over his shoulder toward the creek. "If you'd been a little earlier you could have seen a lot of activity down there, but they get out of here before three, so they can be out of the mountains before dark."

"Where can I find Mrs. Cornfield at this hour?"

"She home by now. What do you want with her?"

"I'm with the District Attorney's office and I want to talk to someone about an alleged robbery."

"Hahahaha!" He laughed out loud, showing his ugly gapped teeth. "The robbery? That was thirty years ago. It got Mr. Connors killed. People still think that his ol' man shot him, but they could never prove it, so he keeps right on livin'."

"Who was Mr. Connors?"

"You're not from this area, are you?"

"No, I'm not, so who was Connors and why was he killed?"

"Let's sit on that bench a minute. My arthritic legs need to rest from time to time. What's your name anyway?"

"My name is Anne and yours?"

"I'm Buck Buckley. I been with this company for fifty years. I started off minin' when there still was a mine." They sauntered over to a wooden bench that leaned against the building, sat down and Buck continued, "Now I play security man a little bit. I work from eight to four and then some young whippersnapper comes in with a pistol on his hip. You'll see him in a bit."

"Tell me about the robbery and who was Connors and why did he kill his son?"

"Oh, he was the owner of the mine then. You wanna talk to ol' Connors?"

"Is he here?" Anne figured she would get more out of the former owner than out of the old guard.

"He lives a ways up the mountain in back of us. Wanna follow me up there?"

"Shouldn't you stay on your post?"

"My Post? This dump and Connors' house is all part of my post. You wanna see him or not?"

Anne glanced at her watch. "Why not? What do I do? Ride with you or follow you?"

"Lady Anne, you wouldn't wanna ride in my deathtrap, believe me. Just follow me." He slowly pushed himself up from the bench and wandered to his truck. "I don't drive fast, so don't worry." With that he opened his door, cranked her up and started backing up on the gravel lot.

Anne quickly made it to her car, just in time to get behind Buck, who turned left onto the road. Less than a mile, going south, the old Ford turned left again, this time onto a paved road that was just wide enough to let two cars pass without knocking each other's mirrors off. The paving deteriorated into a packed gravel surface as it zigzagged its way up the slope. They didn't pass a single dwelling, all the way up until the trees parted and exposed a sizable pasture with a century old mansion at the far end. It looked like the Haunted House of Amityville with a big barn alongside, set back about ten yards.

Buck pulled right up to the front steps and Anne parked right next to him. Both exited and walked up the old creaky steps while the front door swung open and a stooped grey-haired man appeared leaning on a cane.

"Welcome, welcome! What gives me the pleasure of such an elegant visitor?" He extended his hand. Two more steps and Anne gently shook the bony fingers. "Hello, Mr. Connors, I'm Anne Dubois."

"Well, young lady, welcome to my modest abode. Come in, come in. Let's make some tea. What brings you here? Come in, sit here on the couch. It's the only thing in this place that's less than fifty years old. Buck? Where did he go?"

"I'm here boss." He stuck his head around the door from the kitchen. "I'm fixin' tea."

"Oh good, oh good. Tell me Anne, what brings you all the way up here to the dumps of Colorado?"

"I work for the DA and we're investigating a gold robbery…"

"Now? Thirty years later?"

"No, a more recent one and we think the gold nuggets were stolen from your company, or at least what used to be your company."

"There was no gold to be stolen from this company. That was done thirty years ago and it caused me to go bankrupt and I had to sell the mine in order to survive. My sonofabitchin' son was behind all that and they never did find the gold, so in an argument, I shot the spoiled little bastard. I had always given him everything, sent him off to college, where he learned to smoke pot and shoot cocaine and then he came back to beg for more money and I wouldn't give it to him. That's when he broke into the safe and stole all the nuggets. Six months of work. Nearly thirty thousand dollars worth. That was lot of money back then. Here comes the tea."

Buck walked in with an elegant tray, displaying a silver teapot and three hand-painted China cups. With a surprising swiftness, he poured tea and offered one to Anne and Connors.

After presenting cream and sugar, he withdrew and sat at the far end of the room, sipping his fresh brew.

"Enjoy, Anne. Why did you say there was a recent robbery and why did you think it was from our old mine?"

Anne started to slur, "Well, there was an accident way up.... way up..." She dropped her cup. "Oh, I'm sorry... so sorr.." Buck was at her side fast enough to keep her from falling on the floor and he laid her gently on the couch.

"Good work, Buck. Good work. Tie her up gently, she's a beauty. She should bring some good bucks. How'd you get her?"

"She just drove up and started asking questions..."

"Get rid of her car. Pitch it into the ravine. Make sure it doesn't burn, that could attract attention. I better call immediately, so they can pick her up in the dark. This is gonna be a good one Buck."

"She's a beauty. I wanna have my way with her first..."

"You old fart. You think you can still get it up? Go ahead. I'll watch. Maybe I can get myself aroused too. Go for it."

Golden Nuggets
XVII
Towing away

Monday, noon.

"This won't work. There's no way I can turn around. I'll have to back up to the road and come in backwards." Georgy from George's Towing Company realized that the trail to Randy's truck was nearly impassable and there was no way for him to turn around and hook on to the deserted vehicle in order to pull it out.

He was talking to his helper Noah in the right seat. "You stay here and guide me when I come down. Nobody told me there was no road down here. Go north on Federal Road 217, that's all they said. About a half mile. Well, the pickup is here, so we did the right thing, but this is no Federal Road, this ain't even a dirt path, so Noah, stay where you can see my mirrors. Take the flashlight and flash when I'm about to hit a boulder or a tree, okay?"

Noah got out and watched his boss work his way back up the slope. He meandered over to the old vehicle and inspected the truck bed that was laden with five-gallon plastic cans. Must be a painter, he said to himself. Inside the cab was nothing of interest except a folded note behind the visor that read, *"51 paces from the parking lot 6 feet from the tree"* all in lower case.

"What parking lot? There's none around here." He folded it up and stuck it back behind the visor. A black leather bag under the seat caught his attention. All it seemed to hold was a blue shirt, but as he pulled it out by the sleeve, gold nuggets started to tumble across the cluttered floorboard.

"Holy Jeez! I better put them back." As quickly as his fingers could move, he picked up the spilled gold and put them back inside the shirt. He rolled it up, stuffed it in the leather bag and pushed it back under the seat. He was about to get out when he spotted something glistening between the empty beer cans and discarded McDonald cups. It was indeed another nugget and Noah figured that this one was meant for him. He pocketed it and went back onto the trail, just in time to see his boss backing down the treacherous slope. The tow truck was wider than most pickup trucks and was being scraped and scratched on both sides by brush and branches.

"I'm gonna have to charge extra for this trip," Georgy muttered, "I may have to repaint the whole damn truck."

It took them more than a half hour to get Randy's vehicle onto the flatbed and another two hours before he dropped it in the backyard of the State Patrol. A detective and fingerprint expert swarmed over the vehicle immediately and one read a scrap of paper that said, *"51 paces from the parking lot 6 feet from the tree"*

"Wonder if this has any significance?" he said to his co-worker, "I better bag it and have it checked."

***

Anne woke up with the worst headache she had ever experienced and her wrists hurt like hell. When she tried to bring up her hand to her forehead, she realized they were tied and her mouth was taped. "What is this?" she screamed in her mind, "What's happening to me?"

Her legs were also bound together and she felt like she was wrapped in a sheet. She wasn't sure, but it felt like she dirtied her pants, but wasn't sure if she was even wearing any. She tried to jerk herself upright, but couldn't.

A deep male voice, right above her face said, "Easy honey, easy."

A cloth was pushed over her nose and she recognized the smell. "Chloroform," she thought before she passed out again.

The limousine kept humming along, turning from I-25 onto I-40 West, staying just over the speed limit.

***

Denver 7 PM

Bureau Chief Baxter was frustrated, "We've gotta get better equipment in these cars. These mountains interfere with everything; radios, phones, everything. Where is Furmann and when did you last hear from him?" He was ranting and raving, because nothing seemed to come together. The DA in Steamboat reported his assistant missing. The sheriff in McCoy let one of the killers run loose. The sheriff in Granby couldn't find a trace of the missing DA, nor did he know where she was supposed to be heading. The Boulder authorities couldn't figure out where the gold had come from, although they were guessing it came from a mine near Rand, "wherever the hell that is."

His agent Furmann had left for….. *wherever?* and didn't answer his radio. The State Patrol reported a saddlebag with gold and secret instructions. Two bodies were in a morgue and had to be shipped someplace. Where? Anyplace?

"Furmann is supposed to be handling that. Where the hell is Granby? How far is Rand from there? Who do we have up there? The missing ADA is now our priority. Get some men over there. Have there been any accident reports between Steamboat and Granby?"

Baxter's secretary had already left, so one of the junior agents was catching all the flak from the frustrated bureau chief.

"Try raising Furmann again. He wouldn't have gone and turned off his cell, would he?"

"Sir, it's 7:30, he may be at the movies with his wife or he…"

"He better not without checking in with me. I sent him to examine the truck with the gold in it and figure out where it came from. He should be at the State Troopers barracks now and he should be reporting back to me…"

"Sir, if I may? If that's where he went, he couldn't be reached by cell or radio. He's on the other side of the mountains. Shall I call the troopers by landline? That might work, sir."

"Right. Give that a shot and put him through to me immediately if that works, okay?"

"Okay, sir. I'll get right on it."

Baxter, fifty-six and balding, was cursing under his breath. With private industry offering high salaries and great working schedules, it was hard to recruit good agents who were willing to put in long hours with little recognition for all their dedication and time away from home.

Furmann was one of his exceptions. Smart, dedicated, hardworking, he was handed a raw deal a few years ago by the Colorado courts when they overturned the conviction of a serial killer because, allegedly, Furmann had squeezed a confession out of the murderer, by twisting his arm out of his rotator cuff. The killer went free, the agent was reprimanded and his future within the agency was shot to hell.

Yet, Jeff (Herman Furmann to his colleagues) remained with the agency and was determined to redeem himself. That's what worried the tired chief. Normally he would have heard from him and he could have gone home, but when the call came in about the female ADA who was missing and not answering her phone, it became urgent for Furman to get out there and find the lady.

"Why would Hans whatshisname send a woman out by herself to investigate a burglary? Don't they have detectives that do that? Is the DA up there also the chief of police? Couldn't he have assigned some deputy to go with her? And where in the hell is Rand?" Baxter kept fussing. The intercom interrupted him.

"Mr. Baxter, Furmann on line two."

"Herman? Where the hell are you?"

"I'm at the State Police barracks, west of Kremmlin where I'm supposed to be. What's up?"

"The DA in Steamboat sent a female ADA to Rand to investigate a gold robbery and she ended up missing. I need you to go out there and find this woman…"

"Where is Rand?"

"Somewhere north of Granby and…"

"How long has she been missing?"

"Herman, she was supposed to be back at her office by five and it's now 7:30 and they haven't heard a peep from her…"

"Does she have a phone, Mr. Baxter?"

"Yes, but like you, you can't always reach everybody in these mountains. How far are you from Granby?"

"I don't know. Forty miles maybe."

"Head over there. Stay overnight if need be, but find the woman."

"What's her name and what does she look like?"

"Oh, shit. Wait a minute. Call the DA in Steamboat. Copy down the number. Get all the details from them and report to me on a landline. Call me at home when you find something."

"Okay boss."

Jeff Furmann was barely twenty-nine and in his fourth year with the agency. Six years in Air Force Intelligence had prepared him for a career in law enforcement and secret service. The job with the CBI in his hometown was a blessing and allowed him to marry his high school sweetheart and set up household in a neat little home near Boulder. All went well. He liked his job and the staff liked him. Though difficult cases weren't thrown his way immediately, he cracked a case of a serial killer who concentrated on college girls. It brought him a lot of recognition and a conviction, so his future looked rosy.

That was until a conniving lawyer convinced a higher court that the evidence and a confession were obtained illegally. That sprung the killer and made Furmann look like the guilty man in the case. It nearly got him thrown off the force, but a hearing panel sided with him and cleared his name. Big deal! The cloud of suspicion hung over his head at all times. Now he had to convince the world that he was good and that he was honest. He had to prove himself all over again.

Cranking up his car, he said to himself, “I may have to find a motel first and start at dawn. Let’s see what happens.”

Golden Nuggets
XVIII
White Slaves?

Irving, Texas, 8 PM.

Up on his third floor balcony watching the sunset, Jud Judson stroked his pitch black hair while he listened intently on his cell. "Hot damn!" After hanging up, he reached for his drink and pushed a button on his phone. When a male voice answered, the big man spoke quickly, "Get up here Bob."

Jud weighed in excess of three hundred pounds and could barely walk. His knee got shot up in 'Nam just after some nurse gave him herpes and he had been at war ever since. His private war was with the whole civilized world. From the balcony of his three story house he could see the Cowboy Football Stadium and the planes flying in and out of the International Airport. They seemed like toys that King Kong could throw around and Jud dreamed of being powerful enough one day to destroy all of them. He hated planes and all authority and... His thoughts were interrupted by a skinny man with bulging eyes in black pants and T-shirt.

"Yes Jud."

"Bob, that load coming in here from Colorado is welcome in one way and a pain in the ass in the other..."

"Like how?"

"Well, it means business, but the timing is off. The *Bright Ad-*

venture just left Galveston and now we'll have to have him stop in New Orleans to pick up this load. Damn! Why couldn't they have called an hour earlier?"

"Maybe they didn't have her an hour earlier."

"Or maybe the old farts fooled around with her, wasting our time, but anyway, this gives us a chance to look at her. The main problem is, we have no secure place in New Orleans where we can load her. Have we ever had any dealings out there that you know of?"

"No, we've been so successful in Galveston and Padre Island, that we never needed to go that far east."

"Call Vito in New York and see if he knows how New Orleans operates? I know he ships out of there."

"Okay. When do you expect her?"

"Not till early morning."

"Okay, that'll give us a chance to clean her up and get her ready for the trip to N.O."

Jud thought, "The timing may be just right. My herpes are dormant and I'm not sore anymore. I bet she's a good looking piece of ass."

***

Jeff Furmann found a motel and also a gas station, where the attendant remembered a beautiful blond asking for directions to Rand and the old Granby mine.

"What time was that?"

"About three, I guess."

"And you're still working?"

"Yeah! It's a bitch, but my relief didn't show up, but I'm closing in a half hour and I'll crank me a beer."

"Crank two and drink to my health." Jeff gave him a five-spot.

"Oh, thanks, buddy. The mine is just twelve miles up that way."

"Thanks, I wish I could join you. I could stand a beer or two, or three."

In spite of the late hour, Furmann decided to drive to the old mine anyway and indeed, thirty minutes later he walked around the dilapidated buildings hoping to find some clue as to the whereabouts of the young female ADA. His dark eyes and black hair made him look more Hispanic or Jewish, but he was neither. Someone in his background had been an Apache Indian and mingled with the Furmanns, who had come over from Germany at the turn of the century. At that particular moment, none of that was on his mind.

Nobody seemed to be patrolling the complex, but when he returned to his car, a young man in black pants and a white shirt stood by his car door, with a pistol pointed right at Furmann's eyes.

"Put your hands up, buster!"

"I'm a CBI agent..."

"Sure, and I'm Santa Claus. Put those hands up."

"Look at the license tag and you'll see that I'm with a government agency out of Denver..."

"Don't move." The young man with a look of authority on his face kept the gun pointed at the detective while he walked backwards to the rear of the car.

"That tag don't tell me much!"

"Can you tell that it is an official plate?"

"Kinda. Do you have a badge?"

"Right here." Furmann opened his jacket exposing a shiny star like badge. "Well, anyway, I'm a Special Agent with the Denver office of the Colorado Bureau of Investigation and I'm looking for a young woman, who came to this mine this afternoon and hasn't been heard of since."

The young guard lowered his gun and sighed, "Good God, not again!"

"Whaddaya mean? Not again?"

"Every winter young girls disappear from here, mostly from the ski slopes, but never in the summer..."

"Girls disappear...?" Jeff's ears perked up.

"Yeah, mostly snow bunnies, you know. Young party girls..."

"Regularly?"

"Well, two or three, most any year…"

"And they're never found?" He heard about that before, but was never assigned to those cases.

"Never! As if they disappeared in a snowdrift or an avalanche or something, but they never show up anymore."

"Were you here this afternoon when she drove up?"

"No, when I came on at four, there was nobody here, not even the old fart, Buck, who I was supposed to relieve…"

"Where's Buck now?"

"At home, I guess, getting drunk."

"Do you know where he lives?"

"Yeah, in a shack, an old motor home up on the hill." He pointed over his shoulder.

"You wanna show me?"

"Sure. Let's take my truck. I've got four-wheel drive, you need that around here. I'll come around in a sec."

"Okay, I'll lock my car."

The security man didn't look a day over eighteen, but in his white shirt, with black epaulettes and pocket flaps, he looked plenty authoritative. His crew cut resembled that of a Marine recruit and Furmann asked as he hopped in, "Were you in the military?"

"No, but I will be in two years. First I gotta get my degree."

"Good for you. What branch of the service are you aiming for?"

"Air Force. I'm gonna be a fighter pilot."

"Go for it man! Changing the subject, how long has this been going on? Missing girls, I mean?"

"At least four, five years that I remember."

"And they never found a trace of them?"

"Not that I know of. Hold on! We're turning off the road. We'll bounce for about a quarter mile and we're there. Hold on."

"How do you know where this Buck lives?"

"I've driven him home a few times when he was too drunk to even walk."

"Drunk on the job?"

"Drunk any time. He's not a regular alcoholic, but when someone gives him a shot of gin, he goes off the deep end and he don't stop drinking for days. Here we are. He's still up. All the lights are on. Come on."

The twosome, the young man in the black and white uniform and Furmann in a business suit approached the old motor home and knocked on the side door.

"Come on in! What are you standing out there for?" The voice sounded groggy and loud. Jeff opened the door and stepped in.

"Well halleluiah! Who might you be? And Benny? What gives me the pleasure? Let me make some room here." Buck swept a newspaper from a chair. "Sit, sit. What do you gentlemen drink?"

"No, we're alright. I just wanna ask you a question." The lawman did the talking as he sat down. He looked into the squinty eyes of the scraggly old man, who smelled like he could use a bath. "A young lady came by the mine today, right?"

"Today? How young?"

"Yes or no. What time did a blond lady stop by?"

"On my shift?"

"Yes, on your shift, about three o'clock."

"Didn't see no young girl. There's nothing to see or do at that old hole in the ground..."

"Did she ask about a robbery?"

"A robbery? Thirty years ago?"

"What did you tell her?"

"What did I tell her? We haven't had a robbery in thirty years... Whadaya mean? There was no girl." He looked startled and reached for his whiskey glass. "This is good stuff. Kentucky Bourbon. Good sippin' whiskey. Don't drive me crazy like gin does... Want some?"

"No thanks. What time did she leave?"

"What time..." He looked at his watch and hesitated. "I told you there was no girl. I worked till four and..."

"You weren't there when I came in at quarter to four." The watchman interjected.

"Sometimes I leave a little early. I get mighty thirsty sometimes..."

"Was she good looking?"

"You betcherass... what was I saying? There was no girl and I'd wush you leave now." He stood up and pointed his finger at Furmann. "NOW!" He nearly toppled forward. "Now! Out!"

The two investigators bowed out, slowly exiting the way they came in, closing the door behind them.

"When you turn around, shine your lights on that shed. I'm walking over there." The G-man walked to the left of the dwelling and opened one of the big barn doors, just as the truck lights swung around in his direction and he plainly saw a red Volvo convertible, like the one that belonged to Anne Dubois.

He ran to the pickup, "I'm calling for backup. Who's closer? State Police or Sheriff's Department?"

Golden Nuggets
XIX
Assault

While Benny, the security man, spun the truck around in the direction of the road, shotgun pellets peppered the truck, but did little damage. Buck was clearly visible in his doorway, blasting another shot in their direction. They couldn't hear him, but they could very well imagine what he was shouting. Something like, "Stay the hell off my property, you bastards!"

Out of range and out of view of the old motor home, they raced back to the mine where Furmann got on his radio and rounded up two sheriff's deputies and a State Trooper to assist him in getting the old man in custody. They met in thirty minutes and put a plan together to apprehend Buck Buckley without anyone getting hurt. Two cars, containing a deputy and Furmann, the other, a State Patrolman with the other deputy, eased their way up the bumpy path to the old man's residence. The young security man stayed behind, much to his dismay, to watch the other law enforcement vehicle.

The two cars stopped half a mile short of the old R.V., in order not to be detected and the men walked up the rest of the way. At the clearing, two lawmen moved around to the left, Furmann circled to the right and Deputy Jim Coleman waited for them to be in position before he approached Buckley's door. He knocked loudly, resulting in a tirade from inside, "I told you to stay the hell away from me.

Get lost before I blow your head off!"

"Buck, this is Jim Coleman. I heard you had some trouble and I came to help."

"Who?"

"Jim Coleman. Deputy Coleman. Open up, so I can talk to you."

"Who?"

"Jim Coleman. Remember little Jimmy that came to play at the mine a lot?"

"Who?" The door opened an inch, showing the barrel of a shotgun. "Whadaya want at this hour?"

"I heard you had a problem and I came to see if I could help."

Furmann had moved along the front of the old motor home to within a foot of the door, stun-gun at ready. The other deputy had crept up from the other side and was ready to snatch the door. Buck couldn't see either one. Coleman had the outside doorknob in his hand, ready to pull.

"You don't need that gun, Buck. Put it down." With a swift motion, Jim grabbed the barrel that was pointing at him and jerked it down. A shot went off, pellets penetrating the boot on his right foot, while the old man nearly smacked into his face. At the same time, the other deputy on the left grabbed the door and pulled it wide open. Furmann jumped from the other side, caught Buck's left hand and twisted it with such force that the old man fell on his knees, screeching like a banshee. Coleman bounced backward down three steps and Buckley landed on his face in the dirt outside his home. In seconds, his hands were twisted behind his back and handcuffs were slapped on them.

"Let's get him inside." Furmann yelled, grabbing the culprit under his armpits. "And shut up." He screamed in Buckley's ear. To the State Trooper who came running up, "Jack, check that shed and the red Volvo. See if there's any trace of the girl."

When they had Buck inside and forced onto a chair, the G-man addressed Coleman, "Take that boot off and see if the shot did much damage." Turning to the other deputy, "Run down and bring one of the cars up. There ought to be a first-aid kit in there. Take the keys to both of them. The trooper's car is in the lead, but check the other one for a kit if need be."

He finally faced Buckley, who had not stopped screaming and cursing, "Where's the girl?"

"What girl?

"How many teeth have you got left?"

"Huh?"

"I'm gonna knock the rest of'em out with the butt of your shotgun and claim it was an accident. Now where is the lady who's red car is in your shed?"

"I don't know whatcher talkin' about."

"Hand me that gun." Deputy Coleman had untied his boot and was removing a bloody sock, but reached over and picked up the shotgun. Furmann grabbed it and took a stance like a hitter at home-plate.

"No, no, no! I don't know where she went. Connors takes care of that. Don't hit me."

"Who's Connors?" The baffled CBI-man held the gun in midair, both hands on the barrel.

"He's the old guy that used to own the mine." Coleman interjected.

"Where is he?"

"Up in the old mansion on the slope?"

Turning back to Buckley, shotgun still posed to strike, "He takes care of what?"

"He calls and they comes and gets'em. That's all I know."

"They comes and gets'em?" Furmann mimicked the old drunk. "Where do they take 'em?"

"I don't know. I jes gets my thousand dollars and that's it. I don't got nuttin' to do with nuttin' else."

"Holy Jeez! Do you believe that? Jim, where's that mansion, how far out?"

"Fifteen, twenty minutes, maybe."

"Let's go."

Once outside with the old man, "Aim your lights at the shed."

The deputy swung the car around. "There it is."

The lights swung by the open door, revealing a red convertible, while the trooper walked into the barn at the same time. "Not a sign of her."

"Go to your car and call for a forensic team to get up here immediately. There's a life at stake. I don't care if it's the troopers, the sheriff, the CBI or the FBI. As a matter of fact contact the FBI anyway. This smells like one of their projects."

The trooper turned and the other deputy entered with a first-aid kit in hand. Furmann asked him, "Are you good at this?"

"No need to." Coleman interrupted. "Just give me some gauze. I have a coupl'a pellets in my foot and they'll have to come out, but that can wait."

"Not if I can help it. We need you to guide us to Connors' house and then we'll have you rushed to the closest emergency room. Anyway, can you stand on that foot or do you have to hopscotch?"

"I'm okay."

"Alright. You hobble to the car, get in the passenger seat, and Bill," looking at the other deputy, "you and I grab the old fart and he rides between us in the backseat till we get to the other car. Let's heave'em."

The two of them grabbed Buckley and walked him out of the room and down the steps.

Coleman had preceded them and held the back door of the sedan, where Furmann slid in next to the old man who had become extremely quiet.

"Close that door, would you?" Deputy Jim hobbled back to close the door on the old aluminum R.V.

"Did you raise anybody, Jack?"

The Trooper behind the wheel answered while he put the car in gear, "One car with two deputies will meet us at the mine. I couldn't give them proper instructions how to get up here at Buckley's place."

"That's okay. What else?"

"Our headquarters is contacting the FBI and they'll be calling back on this frequency, so you can also get in on it when you get in your car. Here's our other vehicle."

Furmann spoke up again, "Jim, get that car turned around and meet us back at the mine."

After shaking hands with the newcomers, Jeff looked around at the group, "Do any of you, besides Jim, know where old Connors lives?"

"I do." One of the newcomers spoke up.

"Good. You get in the car with me. I'm getting my rifle out. You," he turned to the trooper, " take old Buck to the lock-up and then drop Jim by the emergency room and depending on what the doctors say, bring him back up here or take him home."

"Oh, no! I'm okay!" Coleman wanted to be in on the action.

"Once the pellets are out, the doctor makes the decisions, okay? I'd like to have you in on this, but your health comes first. So, off to the hospital!" The two walked off, slowly.

"Listen fellows. We need this man alive. If I understand this right, they have been absconding with young girls from this area for years and we have to get to the bottom of this besides saving the lady attorney from Steamboat. So we gotta do this swiftly. We all swing up there with our car, lights out if possible. He may have a porch light or safety lights, even motion lights, but anyway, we don't want him to see us and take potshots at us. So… you two drive up to the building, as close as you can get. Get out immediately and circle the house to the left. Break down the first door you come to. You," he pointed at the patrolman, "do the same on the right. There may be side doors and you may have to run all the way around back, I don't know, but I'll hit the front door, where I expect him to come if he sees us coming. Remember, we need that sonofabitch alive. He must be ruthless, so be careful. Let's hit it. You lead. I'm taking my car. Do all of you have tazers or stun-guns? We need him alive."

"Can I come?" The young watchman had stood by all that commotion with his mouth open.

"Sure, come with me. Do you know where he lives?"
"Sure do."
"Come on. We're leading the way."

Golden Nuggets
XX
The Mansion

As Furmann had expected, the mansion was well lit, especially on the outside. Spotlights on three poles and wall mounted lights on both sides of the front door and on the barn.

He quickly spoke into his mike. "There she is fellows, all aglow. Drive right up to the building. Speed is everything."

Acting as he spoke, he stepped on the gas and raced toward the front steps, slammed the car in *PARK* and jumped from his vehicle, not bothering to close the door behind him. He took the steps two at the time and grabbed the doorknob. He pulled his *Glock,* fired into the lock and banged his shoulder into the majestic door. Something splintered, glass shattered, the door swung open and he nearly fell forward into the foyer. He stumbled, regained his balance and ran right into the living room, where a startled Connors jumped from his couch.

"What the hell is this? What do you think you're doing?"

Shifting his pistol to his left hand and extracting his *Taser* with his right, he shouted, "Raise your hands and shut up. This is the CBI. You're under arrest!"

"For what?" The old man started to move backwards, his shiny maroon housecoat opening up, revealing yellow silk pajamas.

"Stand still and raise your hands before I put a bullet through your head." Furmann was ready to use his stun-gun, but that could kill a man of Connors' age. He certainly didn't want to bring him down with a 40 caliber slug. He needed him alive and talking.

"You can't just go barging into people's homes in the middle of the night. I know my rights. I wanna see a warrant and..." He never got to finish his sentence, because the deputy who had gone to the side of the house appeared behind him and in a flash, grabbed one of the old man's arms and spun him around while twisting him face down onto his couch. In seconds the lawman had cuffs on him and Furmann holstered his weapons. "Good work man! We make a good team."

The patrolman and the other deputy also appeared on the scene and two of them pulled Connors back on his feet and asked Jeff, "Where do you want him?"

"Right there is fine." They put him back on his couch, this time, butt first.

"You broke my arm and my shoulder," The gray-haired fellow screamed.

"Go ahead and twist it even harder, until he shuts up!" The G-man ordered. He pulled up a chair right in front of the culprit and with his face within inches from the man's bushy eyebrows, he ordered, "Let's start talking. Every time you scream or lie, we'll twist your arm right out of its socket. So listen. Where is Mrs. Dubois?"

"I don't know what you're talking about..."

"Twist it!"

"Owwww!"

"The blond lady with the red Volvo?"

"I don't know no ladies with red Volvos!"

"Twist it some more."

"Owwwww!"

"Officer," He turned to the patrolman, "find a fire extinguisher." The lawman turned toward the kitchen in the rear. "Now Mister Connors, this is what we're gonna do. We're gonna suspend you from that beam. We'll have the fire extinguisher at ready..."

"I don't see one..." The patrolman reappeared.

"Get one from my trunk." Turning back to the old geezer, "Like I said, we're gonna hang you from that beam, not by the neck, but under your arms, we don't want you to die... yet. Then I'm gonna set fire to your fancy pajamas and anytime you decide to come clean, we'll extinguish the fire. I'll bet when your prick and your balls begin to cook, you'll be ready for cooperation..."

"But I don't know..."

"Don't give me that shit. We found the Volvo in Buck's garage and..."

"That stupid ass! He was supposed to dump it in the ravine, that dumb sonofabitch..."

"Well, he also squealed about the other gals.."

"I'm gonna kill'im..."

"You may get that chance, 'cause you'll end up in the same prison cell..."

The patrolman returned with a small red extinguisher and waved for Furmann to approach him. "Sir," He whispered. "You can't do that. It may cost you your job if you torture..."

"Officer, I don't give a damn about my job. I want to save the life of that girl even if they prosecute me. Now let's get on with this."

"Connors, one last time before we turn you into roast pork. Where is that girl?"

"She's on her way to Dallas."

"To Dallas? Who's taking her and what for?"

"I don't know. I just make the call and they come and get'em."

"Who do you call and what's the number?"

"It's on my desk. I call Jud and then he sends me money."

"How much money?"

"Depends..."

"Depends on what? Wait a minute," He turned around. "Jim find the number, call it in to the FBI, have'em trace it."

"Now back to you? Let me read you your rights, *you have the right to remain silent....*"

"Don't give me that shit. After you made me talk, you tell me I can remain silent? You know what? I don't care. With that last one

I couldn't even get it up anymore and my heart is gonna give out any day now, so there ain't much you can do to me, so I really don't give a shit what you do..."

"But we can torture the hell out of you until you breathe your last breath, or... we can make you as comfortable as possible for the remainder of your life. Your choice. Paul, get a pad and start recording what he tells us, starting with the reading of the rights."

"Connors, what time did they pick her up?"

"Just after dark."

"Just after dark, that means about eight. They have a four hour head start. Do they drive all the way to Dallas or do they have a plane somewhere."

"I don't know. I think they drive all the way. The guy in Denver owns the limousines, but I can't order them. Jud does the ordering."

The patrolman reentered the room. "The FBI is on it."

"Great, You folks take him in. One of you stay behind and have forensic go through all his paperwork. Do any of you know what ravine he's talking about?"

"What ravine?"

"He mentioned that he ordered Buckley to dump it in a canyon. There may be dozens of missing vehicles in there. Get somebody on it. Where's the nearest airport where I can charter a plane. I gotta get to Dallas." Getting up. "Take down everything they say and even the things they imply, record it all. Take the boy, the watchman, back to the mine. I'm racing to the nearest airport. Thanks for all your help. You guys are great and I'll reflect that in my report. Now I'll see if I can save another law officer, Mrs. Dubois."

Furmann was advised by the operator at CBI headquarters to get onto Route 34 and head west to Loveland, where a jet would be waiting to take him to Dallas.

"All the way to Loveland? That'll take me hours. Isn't there any way I can get on a puddle jumper and make it shorter?'

"By the time you find a little airport and a charter pilot who is willing to get you over these mountains at this hour, you'll be spending more than two hours and offhand I don't know what the weather conditions are at this hour. We don't want you to clobber into a mountain somewhere."

"Have you located this guy Jud in Dallas?"

"Actually he is in Irving and we have people on the way to block off the area..."

"Won't he alert the car with the woman and tell them to make some detour?"

"No, we haven't even contacted the limo rental place here in Denver, but we have the Highway Patrol in Colorado and New Mexico looking for a stretch with Denver plates. They have been ordered not to stop them or interfere, just report their position."

"Oh, great."

Colorado Bureau of Investigation agent Furmann felt pretty positive about the whole thing. He felt he had done a good job, a great job even, and his boss had taken the bit and ran with it. Jeff had never been to his boss's house, but he imagined that he had quite an electronics and radio ensemble under his roof, because everything fell in place as if he was operating from his office.

The miles crunched away and when he passed through a little town with an all-night convenience store, he grabbed some coffee and a hotdog. He had been so busy, that he forgot when he had something to eat for the last time.

Motoring down from the mountains toward the flatlands of Central Colorado, his radio crackled again. "Furmann, on board the plane, you'll be communicating with the FBI in Dallas/Fort Worth. You will land right there and they'll be waiting for you. Try to get a little shut-eye on the plane. You haven't run off the road yet, have you?"

"Are you kidding? I'm so hyper, I could stay up for two more days."

"Good boy, Furman. You've earned your laurels today. Keep it up!"

"Will do!" To himself he said. "You bet I will."

Golden Nuggets
XXI
At 35,000 Feet

Once they were at altitude, Furmann was allowed to use his cell phone again and just as he was about to dial his office number, it rang.

"Agent Furmann."

"Furmann, good morning, although it's only three o'clock out your way. This is the FBI in DC. Did we wake you?"

"No, I was just about to call my office..."

"Good, the Director wants to speak to you, hold on." The phone crackled a few times and a sonorous voice came on. "Agent Furmann, this is Lester Jarvis and I understand you've come upon a great discovery, the missing girls from Colorado, is that correct?"

"I believe so, sir. We have two men in custody who are involved in the kidnapping of our assistant DA from Steamboat Springs and they let it slip, that they had been involved in the same practice for years. Once we recover the car wrecks from a ravine, we'll have more definite proof."

"What did they do with these women after they kidnapped them and..."

"Apparently, sir, an outfit in Dallas simply came and picked them up and later on sent them their payment."

"Payment? How much and were the girls also raped, Furmann?"

"About the first question, all I know is that the man, who lured them away initially, got a thousand dollars per catch. How much the main culprit, Connors, received, I don't know. The answer to your second question, yes, I believe they took advantage of them while they were unconscious. The older one, the leader of the team stated that he was disgusted with himself because, quote: 'I can't get it up anymore.' unquote."

"The swine! What do you know about their destination?"

"Your team located the place where the phone calls are received that another victim has been caught and they pinpointed it in Irving, Texas. That's where I'm heading right now. I hope to be there before the young DA arrives, so we can rescue her and get her back home."

"Any ideas what happens to the girls, once they reach Texas?"

"No, I never worked a case like this, but rumors have been abounding for years that there's a healthy trade in white slaves all over this globe..."

"You mean white females, right?"

"Yeah and young boys, ten, twelve years old."

"Those bastards. I'm heading for the office and I want to keep updated, okay?"

"Sir, your best bet may be your Dallas office."

"Right! Thanks Furmann. Good work."

"Thank you sir." He stared at his phone and wondered who he was going to call when he was interrupted, so he called his own office in Denver.

All the operator on duty knew was that the FBI in Irving had an area surrounded and were waiting for him to land at DFW International while another team awaited the arrival of the limousine. It had been spotted on I-40 in New Mexico and again in Texas, doing just a little over the speed limit, so it was easy to calculate their time of arrival, barring accidents or traffic jams on the road. The G-men were confident that Furmann would be in place when the captive arrived. "Just let the pilot transmit the exact time of touchdown."

Jeff relaxed, closed his eyes and reviewed all the events in his mind and actually dozed off. He hadn't slept in twenty-four hours.

***

In Irving, Jud was awakened by a phone call from the limo.

"Sir, sorry to wake you, but this is Jimmy, the driver,..."

"What the hell do you want at this hour?"

"Sir, it may be nothing, but twice a patrol car moved up behind us, followed for a while and then drove off and..."

"He didn't flag you down?"

"No, but I had the feeling that he was taking down our number, you know what I mean, and when he was satisfied that he copied it, he went on, you know what I mean?"

"Well, it may mean nothing, but we can't take any chances. Where are you now?"

"We just turned off of I-40 onto I-27 in Amarillo, you know what I mean and then we'll take 84 to I-20, all the way into Fort Worth."

"Do this. Stay on 20 through Fort Worth/Dallas, turn on 635 North till you hit 80 and 80 will run into I-30. Now you stay on that till you hit Irving, so you'll be coming in from the east instead of the west. If you see anything suspicious again, call me and we'll have to do something different. Okay Jimmy?"

"Okay boss. I was just getting scared, you know what I mean?"

"I know, I know. Just keep your eyes on the road."

"Damn, now I'm wide awake and I was dreaming of a good looking blond. I wonder if she'll come back when I close my eyes." Big Jud was talking to his assistant Bob, who had awakened him with the call. Bob was as skinny as Jud was fat. He chain smoked consistently and never gained an ounce, no matter what he ate or how much. Jud had been his Gunnery Sergeant in Vietnam and Bob adored the man as if he were God.

"Let's have a drink. What's good at this hour? A Napoleon Brandy? Let's do it. I need to fall asleep again, no point in being horny when you have no broads in the house. Can't wait to see that bitch. Connors said she was a beauty. It'll have to wait a few more hours. How long do you figure from Amarillo to Dallas, Bob?"

"It's more than 400 miles, so at 70? I guess five hours, plus."

"That's what I figured. You better make that a double brandy. I need to fall asleep again."

7:40 A.M. Central Time.

"Bob, you heard anything from anybody?"

"No Gunny, I'll run you a bath and then I'll have breakfast ready."

"Don't call me Gunny and why are you making breakfast?"

"Maria got a little snookered last night. She made herself a batch of Sangria and must have drunk too much of it, so I'm letting her sleep."

"You're so generous. Fix me a glass of milk with a raw egg and a shot. That'll perk me up."

"Okay boss."

***

At DFW, the Grumman touched down and immediately after it ramped out, a car drove up and a middle aged gentleman climbed out, dressed in a grey business suit. He warmly welcomed Jeff Furmann with a firm handshake and a "Howdy Partner. We're early, so we can have some breakfast as we talk. Come."

Right outside the airport perimeter, in a blue and white *I-HOP,* they dug into pancakes, eggs and home-fries and a gallon of coffee.

The FBI agent had identified himself as Special Agent Charles Clark, "Charlie to my friends," and took the lead in the conversation.

"Our best guestimate is that the limo will arrive at about 8:30, providing there are no traffic hold-ups, so we have plenty of time. The location is only ten minutes from here. The only puzzling thing is, it's in an industrial complex and there are no units that were occupied last night, so I don't know how anyone could have received a phone call from Colorado at that location…"

"The call was made in the afternoon from Connors' mansion, so there might have been somebody on duty at that time..."

"True, but another thing, we have not located the owner or the lessee of the unit. The complex office is still closed and our computers haven't been able to come up with anything. The phone number is listed in the name of the Judson Corporation, that's all we know."

"Judson? As in Jud Judson maybe?"

"Who's Jud Judson?"

"I don't know, but Jud is the one they called from Colorado to inform them that they had another victim..."

"That might be a connection... Let me call my office, I'm going outside a minute." He whipped out his cell phone as he walked out. Furmann ordered another heap of pancakes.

At the *Airport Industrial Park* things were awkward, to say the least. Unit 25 was just one of many in a long row. Every mini warehouse had an ordinary office entrance with an overhead garage door to the left. In the rear, there was another overhead door and that was it. No one was inside and what made it awkward was the fact that the law enforcement vehicles all stood out like a sore thumb. They were all plain sedans, Chevy's and Fords, but most all the vehicles that started filling the complex were pickup trucks and vans. Special Agent Clark was embarrassed.

"We have to park in between those pickups in order not to attract attention and the way we have to snag'em by covering the entrance and the rear, plus all exits to the park. We should have thought about trucks and old vans before coming out, but we didn't have many people on duty when the call came in the middle of the night. All we can do now is wait. Let me call again."

Talking to his office, "Do we have a good description of the limo? Color and length? Could a chopper be able to pick it up from the sky? Try that out and call me back."

"8:15. An hour to go."

"9:15. Is everybody ready?"

"9:45. Where the hell are they?"

"10:00. Any sightings from above?"

"10:15. We've been snookered, let's break the door down and see what we can find."

Golden Nuggets
XXII
Las Colinas

Irving Texas, 8:42 AM.

"There they are, right on schedule. Open the garage door. I'm coming down."

From his balcony in the elegant subdivision of Las Colinas, Jud had a wide view of the tree lined avenue, fronting the house. He heaved his huge frame off his bench and made for the elevator, arriving in the basement right in time to meet the Denver limo. Jud watched as the two men in black chauffer's outfits lifted a body from the back seat, draped in a big yellow sheet.

"Let me see!" The fat man lifted the sheet off her face and exclaimed. "Wow! She's a beauty, she oughta bring big bucks. Get Maria to clean her up. Has she eaten at all?"

"No, sir, we just kept her sleeping. Less trouble that way."

"Good, take her to the first floor bedroom, the one in back."

"Okay, Jud."

"Did she have any ID's on her? A pocketbook?"

"No, nothing."

"Good."

"Bob, help Maria, take all her clothes off and burn'em. Don't fool with the lady yet. I'm first. You got the casket ready? You gotta be on the road in a half hour if you're gonna meet the *Bright Adventure* in New Orleans."

"Don't worry boss. I'll make it a quickie."

One of the chauffeurs came running out of the bedroom. "Mr. Jud, she's awake. Jimmy's holding her down."

"I'm coming." As fast as his fat frame allowed him, he wobbled toward the back of the house where Jimmy, the driver of the limousine, and an old Mexican woman were holding down the struggling blond.

"Good God, she stinks. Hold her legs, Bob." He walked to the head of the bed and removed her gag.

She screamed immediately, "What are you doing? Who are you? Turn me loose. I need to get back to my boy and my husband..."

Jud covered her mouth with his pudgy hand. "Don't worry little lady, you'll have plenty of husbands and sons where you're going." Turning to Bob. "Put her out. I can't stand screaming bitches. And clean her up. She shit all over herself."

Her screaming subsided as he left the room. The chloroform was very effective.

Fifteen minutes later Bob entered the living room, where the boss was lounging in a huge checkered housecoat. She's ready boss, but Maria got all horny, cleaning the woman and now she wants to shave her..."

"The hell with that. Give her and the chauffeurs a beer and put a porno movie on the big screen. They'll take care of Maria, I'm sure. Come, let's turn this bitch on her belly with her legs dangling down. My pot got so big, I can't do it on top anymore. I gotta do it doggy style."

Twenty minutes later, rolled in a blanket, Anne was put and secured in an oversized casket and placed in a black GMC Yukon. Bob was going to be the lone driver, because the Denver crew insisted, they had to get back and sat down at a hearty breakfast before starting on their return trip.

Jud showered, dressed and joined the twosome in the kitchen where Maria hummed a happy tune, while frying eggs. Everyone seemed well satisfied.

***

At the industrial park, a frustrated Agent Clark ordered the door busted down and, pistols in hand, four G-men dashed inside. Nobody was in the office and on the desk were some scattered papers and a phone, that was all. The warehouse in back was the surprise of the century, dozens of inexpensive caskets.

"Holy God! Caskets? Are they destined to carry live or dead people?" Clark wondered, but Furmann said, "I don't give a damn what they're designed for. Where's Anne, that's what I wanna know."

"Check the line. Call the phone company. The phone may have been forwarded to another line, another number. Remember call-forwarding. Get me the moment you find something." He shook his head. "Jeff, did you ever think that when they called this number it might ring somewhere else? I betcha, that's what happened. Let's look at the caskets. Do they have a manufacturer's plaque on them? Look in here, see these latches? They're designed to tie people down while they're being transported. What a bunch of scum that must be. Maybe the papers on the desk are bills from the casket company..."

"Sir, we have an address in Las Colinas, where the phone..." One of the agents came out of the office space.

"Where's Las Colinas?" Furmann wanted to know.

"A classy neighborhood in Irving! Let's go! Let's go. Two of you stay here, record everything and have forensics come out and dust everything. Let's go!"

Four cars with eight G-men swung into action. Clark was on the phone. "Give me directions... thanks. Get the locals to seal off the area, especially look for a stretch limo with Colorado plates." He turned to Furmann, "It's only a few miles from here." Jeff just nodded. Into the car radio mike, the agent ordered. "Johnson and Potter, go around back. Bust your way in, don't wait for us. Be prepared to fire. These people are animals. Brown and Fellows, check side entrances to the left and Andrews and partner hit the right. Just bust your way in, the more confusion we create, the easier it will be to corner them. Let's hit it."

***

In the kitchen, sipping milk, Jud Judson jumped up. "What the hell was that? Who's in the garage?" Before he reached the garage entrance, the front door shattered and two men stormed in, hollering. "Put your hands against the wall, fatso, and spread your legs!"

"What in the frigging hell do you suppose you're doing?"

"Shut up and against the wall. Furmann, cover the kitchen. Potter, cuff this pig." Clark ran into the living room, looking for more suspects. Fellows and Brown came storming in from his left. "Hit the upstairs, shoot if you must."

Potter reached for Judson's arm, while still holding his Glock in his left hand, but the old Marine was quicker than his size would have indicated and with a swift turn he circled Potter's neck with his right ham hock arm and with his left hand, wrestled the pistol out of the G-man's hand. In the struggle, a shot went off, hitting the big man in his fleshy thigh.

"Damned, you pig." He cursed, while craning the FBI man's neck till it snapped. Potter sagged to the floor and Clark came running back, startled by the shot. The moment he rounded the corner Jud shot at him, nicking his right shoulder, but Clark got a shot off hitting Judson in the middle of his belly. Rushing in from the kitchen, Furmann pressed his barrel against the massive head. "Drop it, or you're dead."

Jud dropped the pistol. Clark crawled forward and picked it up. "Who's in the kitchen?"

"Three people, I need to get back there."

He got there just in time, because the chauffeurs had gotten off their chairs and were heading toward the garage. "Hold it right there. Put your hands up against the wall. You stay here too! He hollered at Maria, who was trying to get out on the porch. She hesitated and turned the doorknob anyway, so Jeff fired a shot at the glass next to her head. "The next one will be in your brain. Stop sniffling and come over here, up against the wall with these two." He could hear Clark's voice in the next room. "Call an ambulance. Fellows, get a first-aid kit out of my car. What was upstairs? "

"All clear, sir." The agent reported while exiting through the front door.

"Brown, help Furmann in the kitchen. I think he's up against three."

10:50 AM.

Ambulances and police cars lined the street in front of the house. Big Jud had been carried out tied to a stretcher. Special Agent Clark refused to go to a hospital, but his shoulder was bandaged and had stopped bleeding.

Sitting at the kitchen table, he was holding court. "Where is the lady that you brought in here in your limousine?"

"I don't know..." Jimmy spoke up.

"I'm warning you. If you do not cooperate, we'll throw the book at you. The lady is an Assistant District Attorney and we'll get your asses in prison for the rest of your life for kidnapping a LEO."

"She was...?"

"What do you mean she was?"

"Are you saying she's dead?"

"No, no, sir, I mean I didn't know who she was. I thought she was just a girl, a snow bunny."

"Like the others?"

"Yeah, I didn't know she was anything important..."

Furmann couldn't stand it any longer. "Quit the bullshit. Where is she, before I shoot you in the balls."

"She left with Bob."

"Who's Bob and what did they leave in?"

"Bob lives here and we put the casket in the SUV."

"What brand and what color?"

"What brand? A Chevy I think and it's all black."

"Charlie, we better get an FPB out. Black SUV leaving Irving."

"How long ago?" He turned to the chauffeur.

"Half hour, maybe."

"Fellows, get on it." Back to the suspects, "Where were they taking her?"

"I don't know. Maybe Maria knows."

"Maria, where did they take the girl?" He was hoping the Mexican would understand English.

She did and she whispered. "To zee sheep."

"To the ship? What ship? Where?"

"Galveston, I theenk."

"What's the name of the ship?"

"I no know. *Adventure*, I theenk."

"The *ADVENTURE?"* Furmann dragged out the word.

"I theenk."

Golden Nuggets
XXIII
Lost at sea?

"I'm flying to Galveston immediately," Jeff Furmann informed the Dallas Special Agent.

"I trust I can use the same plane I came in and if your office can pinpoint the location of the *Adventurer* in Galveston, I'll be waiting there when Anne Dubois arrives in the SUV. Of course, your troops may locate and intercept them on the highway somewhere, but if that's the case, I'll simply turn around and come back. Okay, Charley?"

"Go for it. We have things under control here and we'll grill the hell out of this threesome and we'll comb this house for records about past disappearances and the tactics of this lugubrious bunch. I'll talk to you on the phone while you're up there. So, Godspeed Jeff. I'm proud of you." They shook hands and Furmann was off, being driven back to the International Airport.

An ambulance rushed Judson to a nearby hospital where he would receive emergency surgery. The chauffeurs and Maria were taken to the local FBI building for further interrogation.

When at cruising altitude, Jeff got through to the FBI office in Houston, where they had obtained the latest information from the Galveston Port Authority and their own computers.

"Sir, could the name of the vessel be *Bright Adventure?"*

"*Bright Adventure?* The Mexican woman said *Adventure,* but she might just have picked up parts of a conversation. What about it?"

"Well, we have no *Adventure* in port, but the *Bright Adventure* sailed yesterday."

"Yesterday?" Jeff was shocked. "For where? Is it turning around, maybe?"

"We have no such communication, sir."

"Damn! Who owns the *Bright Adventure* and where is it registered?"

"We'll be back with you in a few minutes."

Jeff walked up to the pilot and asked, "Is it feasible to cruise the nearby Gulf looking for a ship, once I have the description?"

"Not in this plane. Let me put you through to the Coast Guard."

"Wait just a few minutes until I have more particulars about this vessel. I should have some input momentarily."

"Whenever you're ready, sir."

Back in his seat with a fresh cup of coffee, Jeff impatiently waited for the call from the Houston office. It came after twelve minutes.

"Mr. Furmann?"... "Speaking."... "The ship is a 266 foot luxury cruiser, owned by Sheik Ahmad Al-Akadan from Dubai, owner of huge oil holdings."

"Oh shit!"

"Pardon?"

"Forget it. Where is it registered?"

"Registration Panama, crew nearly all German."

"Destination?"

"Aden, stopover in San Juan, Peurto Rico and the Canaries."

"Holy Moses. How do we catch up with that S.O.B.?" The frustration came through in Furmann's voice. "Thank you so much." He disconnected.

Next call was Charlie Clark's cell. "Charlie?... Jeff... The ship, if we are tracking the right one, left port yesterday, so why would they still try to catch it in Galveston?"

"Well, maybe Maria didn't know that. Maybe the Dubois girl appeared on the scene after the Adventure already sailed."

"Then where the hell would they be taking the girl?"

"What would be the next logical port? Beaumont? New Orleans? I don't know."

"If I have your permission, I'll have the pilot divert to New Orleans and if your office there can pinpoint a possible docking space, I'll at least be there. Meanwhile, can the Coast Guard scan the Gulf and maybe locate her?"

"We'll get the satellite in action and alert the Guard. Once we have her on the scope, it'll be easy to track her. Have you found out who owns the ship?'

"Yeah, and it may make you throw up. An oil sheik in Dubai."

"God help us. I'll call you back."

Sitting on the jump seat behind the pilots, Jeff got to watch the GPS in action and studied an old fashioned aerial chart at the same time. It gave him some perception of where they were and where they were moving to.

A Coast Guard commander called twenty minutes later. "Sir, we have some data for you. The *Bright Adventure* would probably cruise at about twenty, twenty-two knots, so she's already 160 miles or so off our coast. We may have a satellite bearing on her in another minute or so. Now if she received a call last night to return to port or the nearest port, New Orleans would be the most logical destination. On the east bank of the Mississippi, halfway between the Gulf and New Orleans, there's a G*etty Oil Company Cargo Dock.* Do you have writing material available?"

"Just a moment… go ahead,"

"The location is at 29-52 North and 89-57 West. We have the area under surveillance because of suspicious activities there and specifically at the *Braithwaite Ammo Dock*. If any shady dealings go on, it's usually at that facility. We are betting that your ship is heading there if they are to pick up anything that's contraband. The location also allows them to be back at sea in a minimum of time. So sir, our recommendation is that you speed over there. A Coast Guard Chopper will meet you at N.O. International if so desired. Call me back with your decision, a.s.a.p."

"Will do and thank you Commander." Jeff turned to the pilot in the left seat, "I guess it's now New Orleans International. Go change your heading. I'll call Agent Clark for clearance, 'cause I'm hopping you guys all over creation, okay?"

"Changing course to one-one-zero."

"Clark? Charley?... Okay, now I got you. It's Jeff at thirty thousand. The Coast Guard just gave me a lot of input about the potential destination of the *Bright Adventure*. They'll confirm the exact location in a while via satellite, and if they're in doubt, they'll send a plane up. I was advised to fly into New Orleans where their chopper would pick me up and get me to the river. Now we're gonna need a lot of help and back-up. Will you call your counterpart in the Big Easy or shall I coordinate things from up here?"

"Yeah man, why don't you handle it? Call Special Agent Gneuff, he's a good man. I'll call the chief in D.C. and make sure that you get all the help you need. Just take charge, Jeff. You're on top of it. Who knows what other captives they have on board? Save'em all boy, save'em all."

"Agent Guneuff? Is that the proper way to pronounce that, sir?"

"Nuff, like you had e-nough, nuff is fine."

"Sir, as you may already know, we're expecting a 266 foot ship to pull into port with possible white slaves aboard. When she docks, we're going to have a boat box'em in, so they can't move back out, possibly have para-jumpers rappel down onto the deck from a chopper and agents ready to board from land. We don't know how much of a crew we'll have to deal with, but we know they're German. I don't know if that means much. Caught red-handed in American waters should tell'em that resistance is foolish, but you never know. Not knowing how many victims they may be carrying, we need several ambulances standing by. I can..."

"Furmann, I'll see to all that. What's the exact location?"

"We suspect the Braithwaite Ammo Dock at the Getty..."

"I know where that is..."

"We'll have a Coast Guard or Navy plane shadow her in, in case we're mistaken about their docking space."

"Good man, Furmann. I spoke with Mr. Jarvis earlier..."

"Who?"

"Lester Jarvis, our bureau chief in Washington and he's all excited that you may have found the trail of the missing girls. It has been a thorn in his side for years, not being able to crack the case. He's rooting for you."

"Well, that's good to know. I'm getting back to the Coast Guard and I'll keep you posted."

"Please do. Out."

"Coast Guard, Galveston? I spoke earlier with a commander, but his name escapes me...'

"Commander Green, I'm sure. Just a minute. I'll get'im."

"Green here."

"Oh, hi Commander, Agent Furmann again. We have things rolling in New Orleans and we may be calling on you people to come in with one of your boats and block in the Adventure after it docks, but the local FBI office will probably be coordinating that."

"No problem. We have a bearing on the Adventure. She's a hundred and eleven miles off the coast, heading zero one five, straight for the Mississippi. Should dock at about five o'clock."

"Great! That will give us all the time we need to be prepared. Good show, Commander. With all the magnificent modern equipment that you folks have at your finger tips, it might even be safe for me to take sailing lessons."

"Go for it. We'll save you wherever you sink."

"Thanks a lot. That's encouraging. Furmann out."

"Captain, how much longer?" Jeff was standing behind the pilot's seat.

"Hour and a half."

"I'll take a cat-nap. I'm dozing on my feet."

"Sleep well. We'll make a hard landing and that way, you'll know we're there.

Golden Nuggets
XXIV
OOPS!

When the Gulfstream touched down in New Orleans, it was too early to proceed to the dock, too early for the Coast Guard chopper to arrive, but not too early for lunch. The FBI pilots seemed to have all the time in the world and didn't have to rush off to some other hotspot in the U.S. or the rest of the world.

The captain assured him, "Mr. Furmann, we'll stand by as long as you need us. We're assigned to you and your mission, so, yes, we'll stay here and hopefully bring you and the young lady back to Colorado."

"Great, guys! The SUV with their captive left this morning about nine, nine-thirty, so it should have covered about two hundred miles by now. How far is it from Dallas to New Orleans by car?" The three of them were having a leisurely meal in the airport terminal which gave them a chance to mull things over.

"By car? Averaging sixty miles or better? Most interstates now allow 70 miles an hour, so I would guess about eight hours, which should put it at the pier at about the same time as when the ship is expected."

"Ah, damn."

"What's the problem with that, Mr. Furmann?"

"Call me Jeff, and the problem with that is that two actions are taking place at the same time and I'd like to be involved in both of them."

"Like what?"

"Capturing the SUV and liberating the girl at the same time as we're boarding or assaulting the ship. I'd like to get the liberation over with and then hit the ship. I wonder if the Highway Patrol could locate the car on the highway somewhere between Dallas and New Orleans and force it off the road or into some rest area? From which major town would they be approaching New Orleans?"

"On the last stretch? On I-10 from Baton Rouge which is about eighty miles northwest of here. It may be a hell of a job, locating a black SUV, possibly a Chevy with Texas plates. You may be better off waiting till one turns off onto the road that follows the river on the east bank. That would narrow it down considerably. When you get hold of a roadmap, you'll be able to find a route number and select a good spot to corner the culprit. You'll be right off Naval Air Station Orleans, so that might be a good place to operate from."

"Good thinking, Captain, I'm just too eager to grab that S.O.B. and free that girl. I'll have the chopper pilot search for a good spot. I'm gonna need a car or cars in order to pull it off. I better get back with the FBI boys."

"Right on and there's your bird. All red and white and it's a big one. We'll be taking a nap aboard the plane, so you just call us on our cell when you need us."

"Good going guys. I'll see you later." With that, Jeff was off and out the door.

His phone rang just as he hit the tarmac. "Furmann here."

"Mr. Furmann? Lieutenant Odom. We're on the ground with our chopper at your service."

"Got you in my sights, I'm at your five o'clock, a hundred yards away and closing fast."

"Good show, come aboard."

Two hours later at the Naval Air Station, a plan was finalized. In the little village of Dalcourt, on the east bank of the Mississippi, the rescue would take place. A plain car was in place along Route 39, six miles north, to report the early sighting of a Black Chevy SUV. In Dalcourt, at an intersection, a local police officer controlled the traffic light and four cars and vans were staged strategically to block in the Texas car as it rolled to a stop at the light. An ambulance was parked around the corner, ready to go into action.

The helicopter had taken off again, this time to meet the incoming ship, loaded with ten Navy Para-Jumpers in flak vests, armed with sub-machineguns and 45 caliber pistols. They would shadow the incoming ship on radar from a distance and attack as soon as it docked.

Little could be done but wait. As they had feared, no positive ID of a suspect's car had been made on the crowded interstates, so the only thing left to do was wait.

Special Agent Gneuff had a team waiting near the Braithwaite Ammo dock, doing the same as the other teams, waiting and drinking coffee.

Jeffrey Harold Furmann sat in a black Buick sedan, thinking about chewing his nails. He had been in many difficult and dangerous situations before, but none that had him so on edge as this one. He had seen pictures of Anne Dubois, that had been e-mailed to the FBI office and he felt like she was his own sister. She was a very pretty lady, but one picture of her and her two year old son nearly melted his heart. The look of love on her face was so genuine, he got choked up. He turned to his fellow G-man,

"I'm personally gonna strangle those bastards that have done that to her. What makes animals like that tick? Don't they have any human feelings? Tearing a mother away from her family as if she were a stray animal? I..."

"Take it easy Jeff. It's worse for her husband and kid than it is for you, but you must stay calm. You can't go into action with anger and frustration blinding your judgment. That might prove dangerous. Is this case closer to you than other cases in the past?" Agent Baylor, in his black windbreaker with FBI emblazoned on the back, sat behind the wheel, the engine idling and the air-conditioning humming.

"No, not really... well, yes, damnit! From the moment I heard about the disappearance of the Assistant DA, I was as possessed with the idea that I had to find her fast and when I found out she had been kidnapped, I couldn't focus on anything else. Gotta find her, gotta find her... was all I could think about. You're right. It has nearly become an obsession. I am going to rescue that gal. That's all there's to it. Besides that she's from my home state and..."

"Hold, hold it..." The radio crackled. "Outpost one, a black GMC Yukon with Texas plates just passed by me. I'm following at a distance, speed 43 miles an hour, over."

"Got you. Outpost two, three and four...get ready. Four minutes. Flash the light operator. Have him turn to red in three and a half minutes. So it's a GMC Yukon, not a Chevy."

"They're practically identical."

"Right."

From their position, they would pull up to the north as if they were running the light, then cross the yellow lines and stop smack in front of the SUV, bumper to bumper. The seconds ticked away and it was nail biting time again.

In the distance they could spot the black vehicle moving along with the traffic. The light switched to amber and then to red. The oncoming cars came to a stop, but there were two cars ahead of the Yukon.

"Go for it." Baylor called into his mike and gunned the car into the other lane, nearly crashing into the first one at the light. Both Furman and Baylor dashed out and ran for the van, pistols drawn, while two cars nudged up to the side of the GMC and one pulled right up to his rear bumper.

"Out! Out!" Furman hollered as he yanked the door handle. It was locked solid. "Out! Now!"

The driver was on the phone. Jeff fired a shot through the driver's window, shattering it in a thousand pieces. "The next one is in your brain. Drop that phone, raise your hands." He reached in, unlocked the door and pulled it open!

"Out! On your face! On the ground. Hands above your head!" He grabbed Bob's collar and yanked him out and down. In no time other agents were on the scene and had him handcuffed and frisked so fast, that it didn't even cause a traffic jam. The FBI cars pulled onto the sidewalks, Taylor pulled his vehicle out of its blocking position and one G-man got behind the wheel of the SUV and drove it behind the ambulance on the side street, where anxious hands pulled open the back doors.

"Holy Maria!" they gasped as they stared at a coffin, a plain looking casket.

"Pull it out, pull it out!" Jeff had dashed around the corner. "She's in there. Pull it out." He reached over to give the medics a hand and the moment they put it down, he lifted the lid and there she was, gagged and unconscious.

"Get the gurney." One of the nurses shouted and reached inside to remove the gag. Two fingers on the victims throat and she sighed.

"She's alive. Let's get her out." A dozen hands reached in , undid the straps that held her down and gingerly lifted the woman's body, wrapped in a yellow sheet. They deposited her on the gurney that had been put in position. It took just a few strides to the back of the ambulance and when she was strapped in, Furman jumped aboard and shouted at the nearest G-man,

"Tell Baylor, I'm going with her. I'll call him..." The doors slammed shut, the sirens started wailing and the ambulance shot into the street, throwing the CBI man around the interior. "Hold on buddy." One of the medics laughed. "We do things quickly."

"Where're we going?" Jeff found a strap.

"We're going to West Jefferson Hospital in Marrero, which is the nearest and after they stabilize her, we may have to take her to another center, but that may not be necessary, she seems to have had minor trauma, her pulse and breathing are normal. They just put her out for a long time. I hope you don't mind me asking, but what in the hell happened here? Who moves live people in a coffin?"

"You'll read about it in the papers, but basically, they transport white slaves."

"Good God! You've gotta be kiddin' me."

"I wish I were. I really do."

"What is this world coming... here's the hospital. Stand aside buddy."

The ambulance stopped underneath the overhang at the emergency entrance and all Jeff could do was walk in and watch Anne disappear behind some swinging doors.

"Where do I find a cup of coffee?" He asked the elderly volunteer at the desk.

"At the far end," She pointed to her left, "there's an alcove with machines of all sorts. Coffee, cookies, sodas, anything you want." Furmann was not even listening anymore. He dialed a number. "Charlie? Charlie Clark? Jeff. I got her. Call my office for me please and have them inform the family in Steamboat, will you?"

"Wow! Great! How is she?"

"She's in a hospital, still out of it, but breathing. Call'em please."

"Sure thing. Nice going ..." but the phone had gone dead.

After sipping some hot, but lousy coffee, he called Agent Gneuff and repeated that Anne was in good hands in Jefferson and asked, "Do you have the ship?"

"No damn-it! She's turning around and is steaming south. Somebody must have alerted them."

"Good God." Jeff sank into a chair.

Golden Nuggets
XXV
Golden Nuggets?

Jeff Furman was assured by the attending physicians, that Anne Dubois was terrified, but healthy, had been raped, but showed no physical trauma. Because she had been sedated for more than eight hours, she had to be kept overnight for observation and would probably be released in the morning for her trip back home.

A check with the Gulfstream pilots indicated that it was no problem. They would remain in an airport hotel and await instructions in the early hours of the next day.

"Yes, they would ask for clearance from the FBI as well as the FAA if they could fly directly into Steamboat Springs."

They were confident it would all work out okay.

The young CBI agent, all of a sudden, had the whole evening to himself, but no transportation. He called his wife and apologized for not talking to her any sooner, but she knew her husband and she understood his intense dedication to duty. He wasn't always easy to live with, but she remembered his passion for his job.

A local motel was easily located and they had razors and toothpaste for sale. An attendant from the hospital had dropped him off and was nice enough to stop by a liquor store, where Jeff loaded up with a six-pack and a pint of scotch. He figured, he'd get a good night's sleep.

Wrong!

His cell phone rang, the moment he took his tie off. Agent Baylor on the horn.

"Jeff, Gneuff is out chasing the *Adventure* back into the Gulf, two cutters are in on the pursuit and I'd love to see how they're gonna handle that. Twice, the chopper has fired across their bow because we're afraid they might kill their victims and throw them over board to get rid of any evidence. So far, so good. They should have them cornered momentarily. Anyway, that's not why I'm calling you. I'm downtown with our friendly SUV driver Bob and I'm about to put him through the wringer. Do you wanna be in on this?"

"Sure, but I have no transportation. Should I grab a cab or would you pick me up? Where are you guys?"

"Call a cab. Take this down." He dictated the address of the FBI Headquarters in downtown New Orleans and Jeff finally poured himself a tall scotch. He hadn't had a chance to get ice cubes from the dispenser, so he sipped his *Dewars* straight and it felt good going down. The front desk promised they'd have a taxi in ten minutes, so young Furman put his jacket back on, chucked the tie and walked to the lobby, drink in hand.

The cabby didn't flinch when the G-man got in with an obvious open alcoholic container but rolled his eyeballs heaven bound, when he heard the delivery address. Jeff couldn't care less. He was beyond mellow. The actions of the last two days caught up with him, and he actually dozed off in the back seat. He didn't spill a drop.

At FBI headquarters, he was asked to check his gun and that surprised him. Was that overdoing security checks? Once inside, Baylor dashed out to meet him. "Howya doin', buddy?"

"I was about to conk out when you called, but I wouldn't miss this for the world. Where do you have the sonofabitch?"

"He's in regular lockup, but we're ready to grill him. Do you wanna go first Jeff? Watch what you say, though. We're gonna record every word."

"I promise I'll behave, although I might strangle the bastard, right then and there."

"I'll jump in and restrain you if you do, but I fully appreciate your feelings. I'd like to get four horses and quarter him. You smell like booze. Let me get you a cup of coffee. Take it in with you, but don't offer him any. We're letting him rot. This way."

Agent Andrew Baylor, fiftyish and well built, led Jeff to the little kitchen and poured a cup of black java, handed it to Jeff and guided him to the interrogation room.

"He's been read his rights and we recorded it, so just go in and talk to him, any which way you want." He opened the door.

The room was stark. An aluminum table and two folding chairs. That was it. No windows, no decoration, just ivory white walls, a mirror high on the left side and a steel door on the opposite side.

Jeff put his hot brew on the table and made himself comfortable on the near side of the room. Five minutes passed and two strapping G-men led Bob into the room, chained and cuffed. His feet couldn't move but six inches at the time. His hands were on his belly, but he could move them a millimeter each way because the cuffs were secured to a belt of steel around the man's waist. The big guys deposited him on the chair on the opposite side of the table.

Jeff picked up his cup and slurped loudly, but didn't look at the criminal. He regretted he hadn't asked for a yellow pad to look more impressive, but he found a little note pad in his outside jacket pocket. Before he could take down the first word, Bob spoke up.

"What do you want from me? I'm just a chauffeur." He was a balding, pudge little man with bulging eyes.

"Shut up!" Furmann snapped and started to scribble a few words. He entered the time, the place, the hour, but didn't look at the culprit. A minute passed.

"You can't keep me here. I know my rights and..."

"And you know the rights of the girls you've transported, right?" He bent over the table and shouted into the face of the surprised kidnapper. "How many have you screwed and how many have you killed?"

"I never killed nobody! You cain't pin that on me!" He shouted back and tried to stand, which resulted in two guards rushing back in the little room, pushing him back onto his chair.

"You sit and stay put, or otherwise, we'll nail your feet to the floor, you bastard!" Jeff had risen and shouted down at the haggard figure in front of him. "We're gonna put you in a cell with hardnosed criminals, that haven't seen daylight in years and who'd love to rape you through the night. Just think of how much fun you'll have."

"You cain't do that. This is the..."

"We can't? But you and Jud can? You can attack all these young girls you've brought in and you're saying our hardened criminals are not allowed?" He gave the last few words a bit of a feminine twist. "By morning you're gonna wish you were dead."

"You cain't do that to me. I'm just a flunky, a chauffeur. I just work for Gunny and...."

"Gunny?"

"Yeah, Jud was my Gunnery Sergeant in 'Nam and I jus work for him. Can I have a cigarette?"

"Sure, in a minute. Are you willing to testify against him and save your own neck?"

"Testify against him? Against Gunny? Never!" His eyes seemed to bulge even more.

"Guards!" The two G-men reappeared. Take him to his cell, the one with the four murderers."

Bob screamed, "No, no! I'll talk, I'll talk. I'm never gonna see him again, anyway. right?"

"He was shot twice, once in the gut and once in the thigh. He may be dead by now."

"You're not jivin', are you? How did you find me anyway? Did he tell you where I..."

"How else do you figure we found you here in New Orleans, while normally you export from Galveston?"

"He told you? He ratted on me? What's he trying to do, save his own fat neck, by screwing me?"

"Yep."

"That bastard. That's how come you were right at the intersection when I got there? There was no way anybody could've known..."

"We were expecting you and now you're gonna fry..."

"Wait a minute, wait a friggin' minute! What can I do to save my own neck?"

"Tell us about the operation. The more you help us, the more you help yourself. We already have Maria, the chauffeurs from Denver, Connors and Buck in Colorado, so now we're grabbing the ship and the crew and we'll need to roll up the whole operation and you're gonna help, right?"

"I don't believe this. It was all goin' so smoothly. We'd get the girls, snow bunnies, from Colorado and..." He hesitated and actually grinned, "that's why Gunny called'em his *Golden Nuggets,* because they brought a lot of gold in from the mountains and he..."

"How much did they bring in ? In dollars?"

"How much?" Bob raised his big eyes to the ceiling. "Depends. Looks, figures, hair..., They were crazy about blondes. This last one would probably bring in a million bucks, she's a looker. Most of'em..."

"How were you paid? In dollars or..."

"Dollars of course. The guy in New York would get the money through an Island account and then Jud would get his share and I would..."

"Who's the guy in New York?"

"The big honcho? You don't know? Vito Machetti or Marketti or something. He always came through with the cash and..."

"Did he also ship girls out through Galveston, like you guys did?" Furmann had a hard time remaining calm, because the criminal talked like he was dealing in sacks of potatoes or coffee. Not human beings at all.

"Sometimes. New Orleans and Galveston, the sheik would schedule the ship and we would just deliver."

"Did you rape all the girls as they came in?'

"Rape? I never thought of it that way. I kinda used to think, they'd enjoy it too, but if they screamed and carried on we just put'em out and..."

"I'm getting sick." Jeff got up. To the guards, who had remained in the room after the last outburst, "I hope you castrate him, without anesthesia." He got up and walked out.

"What about me?" The criminal screamed at the top of lungs.

"Go to hell." Jeff turned the knob.

To Baylor he said. "Golden Nuggets? Those bastards. How do people sink so low? Can you get me back to the motel or shall I take a cab again?"

"I'll drive you back and we're gonna stop for a drink on the way."

Golden Nuggets
XXVI
Aboard the Bright Adventure

"Herr Kapitan, wir müssen sofort umdrehen!"

"Mr. Captain, we have to turn around immediately!"

"Wieso denn?"

"Why?"

The first mate had run into the captain's lounge without knocking, hollering, "Mr. Captain, we have to turn around immediately!"

"Der Bob wurde arrested und die Amerikaner wissen das wir die Mädchen an bord haben."

"Bob has been arrested and the Americans know that we have the girls aboard."

"Verdamt nochmal! Gehe nach plan B."

"Damnit! Go to plan B." He ran up to the bridge.

Before the ship had completed half a turn, a Coast Guard helicopter swooped down on them, with the haler blaring loudly; "Continue on course! Continue to your destination. We're preparing to board."

The vessel stopped turning, lay still for a moment and reversed its direction. While the stern slowly moved to the east, the chopper moved over the bow and two paramedics rappelled down in quick succession carrying automatic rifles.

"Plan C." The captain shouted into his mike, being heard all over the ship and in every stateroom.

Two American sailors ran swiftly to the bridge and the down staircase. Two more rappelled down and took up shooting positions on each side of the ship in case anyone jumped overboard. Up in the helicopter, a machine gunner sat in the open door with his finger on the trigger.

A four engine *Midnight Express* boat of the US Custom and Border Protection came racing out of nowhere and bumped into the starboard side of the *Adventure,* while a grappling hook was thrown up and secured itself on the railing. Two armed men in flight suits scaled the side of the ship and disappeared below deck.

The *coasty* on the bridge, shouted, "Hands above your heads, except you," poking the man at the wheel in his ribs with his rifle, "Steer upriver."

"Vat are you doink?" the captain hollered back.

"Shut up before I punch you full of holes."

"Ve are protected by international law…"

"So are we and shut up. You'll have plenty of time to talk while we let you rot in *Dachau* or *Bergen-Belsen.*" Into his shoulder mike he said, "I need more men on the bridge and down below, over."

"Coming up. Cutter on the way."

"Wait a minute." An elderly man with a black skipper's cap spoke up. "I'm the pilot who came aboard at the three mile sea buoy and I just guide the ships upriver until the river pilot takes over and…"

"Okay, so you're innocent, so now shut up and raise your hands."

The Coast Guard vessel that had been lying in wait was running at full speed downriver and was already visible on the horizon.

"Stop all engines." Crackled through the instrument on the coasty's shoulder."Stop all engines." He repeated to the helmsman. The yacht had regained its upriver direction and now began to slowly ease backwards with the river flow. A second helicopter appeared overhead and landed gingerly on the bow deck. G-men spilled out of both sides, dressed in black windbreakers with FBI emblazoned across their backs in big white letters, pistols at ready. Two ran down the main stairs, two down the side entrances and two more onto the bridge.

"Hello there! You've got things under control, I see." Agent Forest called out.

"I'd feel better if you cuffed them..."

"Will do. All of you put your hands behind your backs." He addressed the three crew members.

"I must protest..." The captain started out.

"You can protest all you want, buddy, but you're going to jail for the rest of your life. Now put them back there."

"I know my rights..." The captain was not about to shut up.

"Too bad you forgot the rights of your prisoners, but don't worry. We don't use Nazi techniques in this country. "You'll get a fair trial and *then* we'll kill you. We're more human and civilized. Now on the floor!"

With the help of the Coast Guard man and the other agent, they got the two Germans and the pilot to lie flat on the floor.

"By the way, I'm Special Agent Mel Forest. What's your name?"

"I'm Petty Officer Josh Garrett." They shook hands.

"I'm heading down. Shoot them if they move. One of your buddies will be up here momentarily to steer the ship to the Navy dock. Now, don't kill'em. Just shoot them where it hurts the most." He was gone and his teammate followed.

Down below, in the galley, nearly a dozen sailors were lined up against the far wall, while two coasties kept their automatics trained at their backs. Forest took one look and satisfied that things were under control, he turned to one of the Americans, "Where are the women?"

"Down below, forward cabin."

"Thanks." The G-man dashed toward the bow through the narrow passage ways.

Two German sailors were hand cuffed to the railing along the hallway and three FBI agents were hovering over four women on a set of bunk beds.

"How are they?" Forest wanted to know.

"Only one is coherent. They must have put them out when they heard that they were being boarded. The chloroform rags are still on the floor. Other than that, they seem okay, but we need a doctor fast."

"Coming up. He's on the cutter. I'm going up on deck to see if we can get a few men down here to bring them up. Are there more Krauts hidden down here somewhere?"

"I don't know Mel. I've only been in this cabin, that's it."

"Okay. I'll be back." He raced down the hall and up the stairs, just as the cutter was tying up on port side. "A doctor? A doctor aboard? Good. That's what I thought." He waved at a uniformed officer who was scampering across the railing.

"Follow me Doc." Turning to a sailor, "Hey guys, get some stretchers."

Three of them made it down the stairs as fast as their feet would carry them and the doctor took charge the minute he landed in the prisoners' cabin.

"Which one is coherent?" He asked from no one in particular.

"Over here, Doc." The voice came from the far end of the cabin and the young doctor ran over, immediately checking the young woman's pulse. "You're fine, ma'am. Say ahhh."

"Ahahhh!"

He seemed satisfied. Get her upstairs. Is there a med-e-vac helicopter on the way?"

"Will be here in minutes, sir." An agent answered.

"Good, we need these women in a hospital as soon as possible. Let me look at the others. Is this the way you found them? In gowns and no underwear?"

"Just like you see'em, Doc."

"The bastards!"

"Pardon?"

"I mean *Schweinhunden.*"

At the helm, the petty officer had taken over the wheel and

the marine pilot had convinced agent Forest that he had nothing to do with the ship or its operations, that he just came aboard to guide the vessel into the lower end of the Mississippi, where another pilot would come aboard in order to steer it into dock in New Orleans.

Indeed, as the victims were loaded in choppers for the trip to the nearest hospitals and the all German crew was transferred to the Coast Guard cutter, a pilot boat showed up and traded a younger pilot for the older one, who was thoroughly shook up and glad to get off the *Bright Adventure*.

Mel Forest decided to stay aboard and study the layout and the procedures that had brought so many women to their unknown destiny in some foreign land. He learned from a Filipino cook, who spoke German and Spanish, but very little English, that they were all trained in emergency codes. Plan A meant, the prisoners went overboard in weighted coffins. Plan B called for knocking them out and hiding them underneath the floorboards in the engine room.

Plan C was the most inhumane; the women would be killed and then hidden under the boards.

All the FBI agent could do was shake his head. He headed for the deck.

He whipped out his cell phone and called Gneuff. "All's under control here, sir. Do you want me to come ashore and get involved in the interrogation?"

"Negative, Mel. Go through the ship's logs and find out how many of these trips they've made over the years and how many ports they've sailed in and out of. We have a chance here to really show a pattern of behavior in this ungodly trade. Get off at the Navy yard and I'll see you in the morning. I'm gonna browbeat some of that scum."

"Have fun, sir."

"You bet I will."

"Do we have photographers on the team?" Forest asked no one in particular.

"Yes, sir. He's in the hole, taking pictures of engine and escape hatches."

"Thanks, I'll find him." He headed back down the stairs again, preparing to do the only thing he hated about his job; paperwork. When he encountered the picture taker, he touched his arm and asked, "Can you also take close-ups of documents, sailor?"

"Of course. All I do is change lenses."

"Okay, come to the captain's quarters when you're done here."

"Sure thing."

While nosing around the luxurious cabin, Mel was surprised to see a family picture of the captain, his wife and two teenage daughters. "How could he? How could he possibly transport girls slightly older than his own, knowing what their destiny would be?"

His thoughts were interrupted by his cell phone. "Mel? Would you believe that the State Department already received a call from the United Arab Emirates Embassy in Washington, to immediately release the ship and free the crew?"

"Already? That was quick. What are you gonna do?"

"Miss Rice already told them to go to hell, but in nicer terms."

"Hoorah for Condoleezza."

Golden Nuggets
XXVII
Going Home

Even though the doctors in New Orleans wanted to keep Anne a few more days for observation, the pressure was on to get her back to Steamboat Springs. The DA was embarrassed as hell by the turn of events. Anne's husband had been on national television expressing his concerns and the director of the Colorado Bureau of Investigation wanted to cash in on all the positive publicity his office was getting for solving the case so quickly and bringing it to fruition within forty-eight hours.

So, early in the morning, Jeff met the ambulance at the emergency exit and hopped aboard for the short ride to the waiting FBI Gulfstream. All the clearances with the FBI and the FAA had been made and the ride to Steamboat wouldn't take but two and a half hours.

Anne should be back in the arms of her husband and young son and the chief of the CBI should be standing on the tarmac, gloating about the expedient rescue operation.

Anne was still groggy, but she relayed her experience to Agent Furmann in great detail.

"So, as I understand it, you went to the mansion and received a warm friendly reception?"

"Yes, they were as nice as could be. Mr. Connors told me about the disappearance of the gold and how he shot his son in anger, but never was convicted of it. Everything was nice and cozy and then… wham! I was out."

"How'd they knock you out?" Furman was taking notes.

"I don't know. Buck went into the kitchen and made some tea. He served it on a most elegant tray with tiny china cups and we all sat there and drank it and… and… I must have passed out. When I came to, I was in a car and a guy put a rag on my face and I went under again."

"Holy cow. Do you remember if they attacked you? Physically, I mean."

"No, later in the big room in a big house, a fat slob started to play with me. My private parts… you know what I mean…, and I screamed and passed out again. I don't know what they did to me. I didn't regain consciousness until I was in the hospital where you picked me up."

"Well, courageous lady, you survived a hell of an ordeal and you helped solve a long outstanding kidnap and slavery case so a lot of lives will be saved in the future because of your tenacity."

"Me? What did I do?"

"You did enough. Lay back and rest. You'll be back with your husband and child within a few hours. So relax. They'll be waiting when we land. So, relax and sleep as much as you can, okay?"

"Okay." She reclined her seat as far as it would go and dozed off.

Furmann tried to catch a few zzzzzs, but his phone interfered.

"Agent Furmann? Mr. Taylor, CIA. Can you hear me?"

"Yes sir!" He nearly snapped to attention.

"First let me compliment you on an outstanding job in solving this crime and..,"

"What did I do?"

"And second," The voice on the other end of the line continued as if he hadn't heard a word Jeff said. "We need your information and expertise to roll up this gangster activity once and for all."

"But sir…"

"So as soon as you land and deliver the ADA to the Steamboat operation, we want you to turn around and stop in Denver to pick up some personal items and clothing and proceed to Langley AFB on the double. You're going to be an integral part of the expediential force that will bring this crime wave to a stop. You've been cleared by your bureau chief and the FBI and you will be working closely with the CIA and Homeland Security. We'll see you in a few hours."

"But sir..." The phone was dead.

Jeff collapsed back in his chair as if he had just lived through a bad dream. CIA? Langley, Virginia? Headquarters? He wasn't sure he had heard right. What did he know and what had he done to be asked to get in the midst of the action?

His attempts at sleep didn't work, so he dug out his notepad and decided to call Dallas and find out what they had learned from Jud, Maria and the chauffeurs. He needed all the input he could find if he were going to be grilled by the masters.

Next he called Special Agent Gneuff in New Orleans and noted down what they had learned from the kidnapper, driver Bob and the German crew. He scribbled as fast as he could and decided he'd take his laptop on the flight from Denver to Virginia, so he could type it all out.

The most surprising thing that they had learned was that a talent agency in Texas lured good looking blond co-eds into the modeling business and then shipped them off to Galveston and the Near East.

"How'd they get away with that? Didn't they leave a trail?"

"We're on the trail now, Jeff. We may have them before the day is out." Gneuff assured him.

"How long has this been going on?" Furmann was flabbergasted.

"Too long. Three or four years already."

"Good God."

"Hang in there Jeff. You're doing great. See ya."

FBI officials from the Colorado office were awaiting them in Steamboat and Jeff was transferred to a smaller jet for his trip to Denver. He didn't get a chance to meet Anne's husband or her immediate boss, the DA.

The two FBI pilots who had become near personal friends in the last two days were relieved from flying duty because of the many hours they had spent in the plane and now flew as passengers back to their home base.

"My car is still at Loveland, you know and..." Jeff informed one of the G-men.

"It'll be there when you get back. Anything of value in it that we have to worry about?"

"Guns in the trunk, that's all."

"We'll pick it up and get it to your house or your office. Do you have the keys on you?"

"Sure do." He reached into his back pocket and handed over a set of keys.

"Jeff, I'm Jerry Stubach and this is Pete Booth. We have been on the case of the missing girls for two years and you have finally provided the break we needed. We're going to pump you for details all the way from here to Langley. We're going to record everything and forgive us if we become a little overbearing. You are not in the hot seat. As a matter of fact, you're sitting on the throne. We just want to be as prepared as possible when we meet the CIA, you understand?"

Jeff just nodded.

"Have you ever dealt with the CIA?"

"I can't say I have."

"They don't like to be upstaged. They will use every scrap of information that you give'em and make it look like they discovered it, so they can take all the credit. Right now they have egg on their faces, because, you, as a lowly agent have accomplished more in two days, than they have in the two years, so be prepared."

The co-pilot up front motioned to them to get strapped in. "Ready for take- off."

"We'll continue when we're up there."

Jeff's head was spinning as he watched the runway lights rush by and then disappear below them. Maybe it was a good thing to get all his thoughts and information in proper order.

After all, he had gone through a rollercoaster of events and this way he didn't need his laptop, everything would be recorded for him.

In Denver, he was rushed home. He barely had time to explain to his wife what was happening, grabbed the necessary changes of clothes, some suits and windbreakers and was out the door again to the waiting plane that would take him to the lions' den of intelligence, Langley Air Force Base, Virginia.

The hours flew by rapidly and Jeff thanked God that someone had brought food aboard and there was plenty of coffee. The two G-men were very efficient and took some of Jeff's answers apart in order to get the whole picture straight in their minds and on record.

One statement surprised them. "Did you say Vito Marchetti?"

"Yes, I'm not sure of the spelling, but it sounded like Marketti from New..."

"What did he say about him?" Stubach was doing the asking.

"Let me see. I was asking about shipments of golden nuggets out of New Orleans..."

"Golden nuggets?"

"Well, that's what they called the girls that came out of Colorado, so we referred to all the slaves as golden nuggets and I believe he said that the Dallas operation mostly shipped through Galveston, and New York through New Orleans and that's when the name Marketti was mentioned. It sounded like he's the head honcho in the big city, like Jud was in Dallas. Why do you ask?"

"Well, he's been a thorn in the side of authorities for years, but they've never been able to pin him down. He's been in court for conspiracy to murder, money laundering and a dozen other offences, but his witnesses either disappear or clam up and can't remember anything. He laughs in the face of the law and now you offer a spark in this dim picture. Let's go over this once more. As close as you can remember, what exactly did he say?"

They hashed and rehashed everything Jeff could remember and the things he had heard from Gneuff in New Orleans and Clark in

Dallas. The notes he made on the plane to Steamboat came in very handy and he learned an awful lot about interrogation from the older investigators.

By the time they landed, Jeff was worn out as if he had gone through a wringer. He was grateful, that their first stop was a comfortable suite and a bottle of scotch. He was assured that they wouldn't be briefed or debriefed till the morning, so it seemed okay to pour a stiff drink.

They were dead wrong. He'd learn fast about the workings of the CIA!

Golden Nuggets
XXVIII
The Penthouse.

"Jeff, this is Jerry. Meeting in the penthouse at seven sharp. Tie and jacket."

"At seven? Where do we get a bite to eat? Besides that, I'm bushed. Where's the penthouse?" Jeff was startled right out of his socks. He was nearly undressed and ready to take a nap before dinner.

"Don't worry. There'll be a car to take us over there. Grab a sandwich downstairs in the snack bar. Be out front at six forty five." His newfound FBI buddies apparently knew the score.

Agent Jeff Furmann was dragging his butt and was getting a first taste of the panic driven CIA activities. He barely had time to inhale half a turkey sandwich before he was rushed into a waiting sedan that sped to the towering CIA building on the sprawling Langley Air Force Base.

At five minutes to seven, he was seated with two dozen other men and women in a theater style conference room. At exactly seven, a hush fell over the room when a door opened behind the podium admitting four men who strutted on stage and seated themselves, facing the audience. The tallest and skinniest of them stepped up to the microphone and without introducing himself started his address.

"This morning at the PDB, the President demanded immediate action on this international incident and follow-up on the kidnapping scheme," Jeff wrote 'PDB?' on his notepad. "which is the reason for this late meeting. Tomorrow morning we're going to swoop down on New York and Texas and round up the culprits once and for all. The FBI," he turned and pointed at a middle aged gentlemen with a golden brown bald head and a ring of white hair, "and the local authorities have pooled all their resources and information and we hope to make a clean sweep. The whereabouts of some of the key figures in this plot are still in question, but we should be able to smoke that information out of the first captives of the day."

Jeff stood up. "Sir, the German captain of the *Bright Adventure* should be your best source of information, because he had to deal with all the big honchos on both sides of the globe. He should..."

"And who are you?"

"I'm Agent Furmann, Colorado..."

"Oh yes." The tall, skinny man looked annoyed. "And where might this captain be?"

"He's in FBI custody in New Orleans, sir."

"Very well." He turned to the FBI man again. "Lester? Take heed." Facing the crowd again, "Thanks Furmann. I want to talk to you later."

Jeff sat down, wondering if he had spoken out of turn.

"Ladies and gentlemen, I realize that many of you are working on important cases, but if any of them can be postponed, we'd appreciate your immediate involvement in this chase. This case of exporting young women has gone on too long and we've had egg on our faces for too many years. We're gonna break this wide open and we're gonna do it *NOW!*" He hammered the podium with his fist. "The President wants results *NOW!*" He banged again for emphasis. "We're breaking into four groups in the adjacent briefing rooms and regroup here in an hour with workable and positive plans of action." He turned back to the door and stopped. Grabbing the mike once more, he spoke just one word, "Furmann!" and signaled for Jeff to come up front.

"What's a PDB?" The Colorado agent asked his neighbor as they moved on.

"A PDB? That's a Presidential Daily Brief that the CIA prepares every morning."

"Oh!"

In the adjacent office, Jeff was introduced to Jed Taylor, the CIA spokesman and Lester Jarvis, the famous FBI director.

"Coffee, Furmann?" Taylor asked, "or water maybe?"

'Beer' Jeff thought, but he answered, "Water would be great, sir."

"Come sit." They gathered around a large oval table along with three other men and a woman who were not introduced.

"How long have you been working this case, Furmann?" The CIA head was still doing the talking.

"This is my third day, sir."

"Third day? How much do you really know about this organization?"

"All I know is that they operated out of Colorado, mostly capturing attractive snow bunnies and that they had an organization of modeling studios in Texas and that a man named Vito Marchetti operated in New York. New York shipped mostly out of New Orleans and Texas shipped mainly out of Galveston. That's about all I know." He unscrewed the bottle cap, but before he could take a swig, another question was fired in his direction.

"How did you learn all that so fast?"

"Well, we captured two suspects in Colorado and four more in Dallas… actually Irving and I questioned the man who was transporting Anne to the New Orleans dock. He…"

"Was he the German captain you referred to?"

"No, I personally never even saw that man, but he transported the victims coming from Texas as well as New York and he delivered them to Dubai, to the Sheik, and he must have been involved in the distribution of money, so I think, the kraut has more inside information than anyone."

"Good thinking, good thinking." Taylor turned to his left and directed one of the gents, "Contact the FBI in New Orleans..." Turning to his right, "That okay with you Lester?" All he got was a nod. "And get all the info you can get, especially about the New York operation, okay?" A young man stood up, nodded as well and walked out.

"How'd you get involved so suddenly, Furmann?"

"Sir, I followed up on a missing Assistant D.A. out of Steamboat Springs and I lucked upon the kidnappers, just hours, maybe minutes, after they shipped her off to Irving, Texas."

"You lucked upon them? Aren't you a little overly modest?" That brought a chuckle to the small circle.

"Well, what should I say? That I did some outstanding detective work and some exquisite interrogation?" He chuckled himself. "Well, I did."

"How long have you been on the force, Furmann?"

"With the CBI four years and six years with Air Force Intelligence, where I got most of my training."

"You guys make a note. Air Force Intelligence may be a great recruiting source." Now everyone laughed, not just chuckles, but hearty laughs.

"How did a lady ADA get involved in this, Jeff?" This time is was the FBI boss asking. "Was she sent off by herself?"

"Sir, that's the most baffling question. I have no idea why they sent a lady prosecutor out to investigate a gold robbery, rather than a sheriff's detective or a team of troopers? A woman by herself? I don't know."

"Is that what started this? A gold robbery?" Taylor took the lead again.

"Yes, a robbery and then a subsequent double murder."

"Where's the connection, Furmann? I mean the connection between a robbery and the kidnapping?" Taylor kept calling him by his last name.

"Apparently, the snow bunnies that visited the gold mine and museum were invited up to the owner's Mansion, where a cup of tea knocked them out, just like Anne..."

"So the mine or the museum was their bait?"

"Apparently. Many girls have disappeared from there over the years and we should have complete records on those and the cars that are being lifted out of a ravine right now will further identify the victims." Jeff remained very sure of himself and was not at all intimidated by the high ranking officials he was dealing with.

"Good God. That scum! And were they all shipped to Dubai?"

"Sir, I don't know that. The ship's records will tell that tale. All I know is that the ship, the *Bright Adventure* is owned by a wealthy sheik over there."

"Do we have the name of that sheik?"

"The Coast Guard has all the details about the ship's ownership and registration, sir."

"Did anyone give you any hint as to the value of these gals? How much they would pay?"

"The guy in Texas, Jud Judson called them 'his golden nuggets' and expected at least a million for Anne Dubois because she was so pretty and the lowest flunky in Colorado, the one who lured them up to the Mansion, expected a thousand dollars."

"Wow! Can you fathom the figures they were dealing with, if you add in the cost of the delivery by luxury yacht? They must want blond girls very badly. Who would wanna pay such sums?"

"Sir," the sole lady agent in the group spoke up. "Just think about Osama bin Laden, who allegedly receives twelve million a month from their oil business, he alone could afford a couple of them a week."

"God help me. I hope there's some justice in this world somewhere. It makes me sick thinking about it. Anyway, let's reconvene to the meeting room and see what plans our agents came up with. Furmann, you'll be working with Agent Jacobi over there. You'll be heading for Manhattan. I hope your nose will work there as well as it did in the fresh air of the Rockies."

Golden Nuggets
XXIX
The Big Apple

When Agent Jeff Furmann finally got back to his bedroom, he poured a scotch on the rocks, but never got to finish it. He conked out, thoroughly exhausted. That was probably the best thing for him, because he slept fitfully for eight straight hours. When persistent ringing woke him, it was 6:45 in the morning and he spoke into the mouthpiece, "Yes sir... fine sir... okay sir... will be there sir."

And he was. Right at the front door at 7:05, shaven and dressed. He carried his overnight bag, not really knowing if they would get back to Langley or not. He had guessed right. They would probably stay in Manhattan according to CIA agent Jacobi, who would be his mentor and his partner during the upcoming chase. Jeff hoped it wouldn't become a *wild goose chase*.

The Air Force Base was already a beehive of activity. Fighter jets roared into the sky in twos and fours and little passenger jets were flying in and out. The former airman shivered with excitement, reminding him of the action packed years in the Air Force. He had enjoyed the thrill of the afterburner many a time in many different parts of the world, but had never flown out of Langley before. It was an impressive base, to say the least.

On the Gulfstream jet, in the company of another dozen agents, the details of the day's plans were explained and it seemed that

Jacobi, Jeff and two more agents would team up in one vehicle and drive across the Washington Bridge from Teterboro and head for Upper Manhattan, where Vito Marchetti had a penthouse, overlooking the Hudson River. Search warrants would be waiting for them on arrival and bulletproof vests and maps would be provided as well. Each agent was expected to carry his own weapon already, but additional ammo would be available if needed. Jeff carried his *Glock* with fourteen rounds, but he would welcome another clip or two.

When the initial briefing was completed, sandwiches and coffee were handed out and Jeff reclined his seat and leaned back as far as he could. He had spent more time in the air in the last three days than he normally spent in a year and he felt totally relaxed. This mission was completely out of his hands and he was ready to enjoy that luxury. He closed his eyes and dreamt of mountains, clouds and valleys.

The announcement, *fasten your seatbelts, store your tray table,* woke him up just in time to take in that magnificent view of the New York skyline and the Hudson river with Miss Liberty proudly raising the flame of freedom. Within minutes the Gulfstream touched the runway and the contingent from Virginia was welcomed by a half dozen agents from the New York, New Jersey area.

Contrary to the original briefing, Jeff and Jacobi went with a team of FBI agents from the Manhattan office and disappeared in a powerful black Buick. On the way across the Washington Bridge, maps and sketches were explained and rehearsed in their minds, so they would be able to execute their mission without a flaw. Their target was the luxury suite of the infamous Vito Marchetti. Two elevators ran up and down the twenty story building, but just one could reach the top floor and only if it were operated with a special key, which they didn't have. So two men would get off on the nineteenth floor, pick the lock on the staircase door, climb to the twentieth and push the button on that floor, which should bring up the other two. One G-man would stay at the elevator, gun drawn, guarding the stairwell as well. There were no other exits anywhere, except if someone jumped out the window with a parachute.

All went well. Jeff and Jacobi waited at the nineteenth floor until the elevator light indicated *UP* and the doors closed. In seconds, all four were at the imposing front door of the penthouse. One FBI man with a fistful of gadgets quietly turned two invisible bolts and turned the knob. Without a sound, two men in black FBI blazers and Jeff in a business suit rushed into the apartment, guns at ready. The lead man waved at the other two to spread out and Jeff headed to his left toward the huge living room. A whirring sound caught his attention and he glanced to his left into the open door of a private office. The thick carpet muffled all sound and Furmann was inside in three steps. The whirring sound, on and off, came from a shredder and two people were working diligently at moving stacks of sheets into the machine.

"Stop that! Raise your hands." Jeff shouted as loud as he could. "Stop that!" One of the men startled, recovered and continued to feed paper into the gadget. "BAMM" Jeff fired a round into the shredder, hollering, "The next one is in your head. Raise those hands. Up against the wall. Start walking backwards. No, no! Keep those hands on the wall and move your feet backwards. That's better."

Startled by the shot, both FBI men appeared in the door. "You alright?"

"I'm fine. Keep searching the rest of the place, I've got control here."

Another shot ran out, this one came from the hall. "Check it out! I'll shoot these bastards if they move."

The G-men disappeared and raced back to the front door. Right in front laid a bleeding body, with his arms outstretched, a pistol clenched in the right hand.

"He wouldn't stop." Jacobi explained from his position at the elevator door. "He raised his gun to shoot, but I was quicker."

"Good, call on your radio and have an ambulance sent up. Push the button for them to be able to get all the way up here. We better check the rest of the place." The twosome in their black windbreakers turned around again and reentered the suite, still ready to fire.

Three turned out to be the total number of occupants, all male. None of them were Marchetti. The wounded man in the hallway was whisked away, but was not expected to live.

The other two were disarmed, cuffed and sat on the couch in the living room, viewing the magnificent expanse of the Palisades on the Jersey side of the river. Neither seemed to enjoy it though.

Jacobi started to ask questions, but Furmann took him aside and said, "Let's not question them together. Let's separate them. We need to pump them before they're taken downtown, where their lawyer will spring them before we have a chance to interrogate them. I'll take the older one to the kitchen. Take notes."

Jacobi was not used to being ordered, but he relented and Jeff took the older man by the arm and said, "Come," and led him away.

"Whatcha doing with me?" the white haired man protested.

"We're going to throw you off the balcony and label it as suicide unless you shut up and listen." In the kitchen, Furmann dumped him on a chair, hauled another one to within inches of it and sat down so close to the criminal, that he could smell his breath.

"You were caught destroying federal evidence and that will get you at least fifteen years in Sing Sing..."

"But I just work here...."

"Shut up until I ask you something. Ever been to Sing Sing? Same nice view of the river. Are you married?"

"Yeah, but..."

"Kids?"

"Yeah, but..."

"Grandkids?"

"Four and..."

"If you ever want to see them again, you play ball with me, you hear? If you lie or screw up, I turn you over to the parents of the girls you kidnapped and then we'll send the rest of your body up to the river to the big house. Do you understand?"

"But I never..."

"You didn't understand, did you? I told you not to lie."

Jeff got up and walked around the old man's chair and lifted both his arms behind his back, nearly raising him off his seat. They could nearly hear the rotor cuffs tearing.

"AWWWWW!"

"Just checking your handcuffs." He sat back down and went nose to nose again with the sweating man. Jacobi came running in. "Everything alright?"

"Just mad at the thought of going to Sing Sing." To the old man he whispered, "Do we now understand one another?"

"I want my lawyer…"

"Your lawyer and your priest will arrive at the same time, so they can write your will and give you the Last Rites. So now talk. Where's Vito?"

"He left."

"When?"

"Yesterday."

"Let's try this again or I'll have to check your cuffs again. Where's Vito?"

"He's in the Bahamas."

"That's a big place. Which island?"

"Caicos."

"What's he doing there?"

"A plane is gonna pick him up."

"Whose plane and where's he going?"

"I don't know, he didn't tell …"

"I'm gonna check those handcuffs again." Jeff started to get up.

"No, no! He's going to Abu Dahbi, the sheik is having him picked up…"

"Abu Dahbi? The Emirates? Mister, you have a right to remain silent. Anything you say may be…"

"Now you tell me that crap?" The old man got feisty again.

Jeff got up. "I hope you will burn in hell for your involvement in this sickening affair. The devil is already waiting for you and we'll hurry you along. Start thinking of your granddaughters that we're gonna use as bargaining chips, trading them for the girls that you've shipped over there over the years. Your wife is also gonna love that." He walked out.

"What's the direct line to Taylor?" He asked Jacobi. "We've got to hurry."

Golden Nuggets
XXX
Goose Chase

CIA Chief Jed Taylor, fussed a bit about the disappearance of Marchetti, but was pleased that no blood was spilled by the law enforcement officers and loads of incriminating documents had been captured. He did give immediate permission to fly to the Bahamas and put the international spy agency in action to trace the bandit and supply the details to the agents while in the air over the Atlantic.

Jacobi and Furmann dashed out and left the cleanup and transportation of the culprits to the remaining GBI men. The pilots were briefed by phone and a twenty minute ride by Jacobi and Jeff across the river to Teterboro gave them enough time to get all the proper clearances and off they were. Airborne just thirty minutes after Taylor's okay. Great going.

Jacobi was used to being in charge of action details, but even though he was twenty years older than Furmann, he didn't resent the initiative by the exuberant young Colorado G-man.

Jeff consulted the pilots about the different airports on the island and which one was big enough to land a jet, large enough for intercontinental flight.

"More than likely, *Grand Turk International,* but a good pilot could get his plane down in two other fields when the weather is right, *Provinciales* and *South Caicos.*"

"Holy smoke. Which one do we decide on?"

"Have the agency check departures from the different airports around New York and find out if the guy booked a flight or chartered a plane. I bet on the latter. Call'em now, so we can determine where we're going to land. Right now we're cleared into *Grand Turk,* but we can change that in midair."

"Okay, thanks." Jeff made it back to his seat next the CIA man and showed him the choices they had once they arrived over the Turks and Caicos.

"Let's call Taylor."

Langley advised them to contact the FBI's Manhattan office and provided a number. All personnel in New York were hard at work, scanning all reported departures and passport records. Nothing yet. But fifteen minutes later a call came in on Jeff's cell that a twin turbo-prop had been chartered at Westchester County Airport, destination Fort Lauderdale. The name Marchetti was not used for payment, but a charge was made to a Visa card issued to VMC Corporation, one of Vito's companies. They were on the right track. Fort Lauderdale Executive Airport was being contacted for arrival and departure details.

Another ten minutes went by before a report came in that the plane had not landed in Lauderdale, nor anywhere else in the U.S..

"They flew on to Caicos, without clearances. They're lucky they didn't get shot down." Jacobi commented. "Now how do we find out which airport. It looks like each airport is on a different island."

"Back to Manhattan." Jeff punched the numbers again. "Do you folks have connections with the FAA in the Bahamas? Can you find out if the twin landed in the Caicos?"

"Stand by. Rather… we'll call you right back." They walked up to the cockpit.

"According to this chart, every one of the airfields could handle a good size jet, but the one at Grand Turk has the longest runway. Which would you choose if you were a pilot?" Jacobi wanted to know.

"I know what I would choose, the longest one possible. If that plane has to make it all the way across the Atlantic, it couldn't be a small twin. A big twin maybe. I would guess they'd refuel in the Canaries and then hop over to the UAE, the Emirates." The captain looked up, "You been there?"

Jeff chuckled. "In there? No! All around there? Yes. Kuwait, Iraq, Iran, Aden, Saudi. Yep, I've been there. Not anxious to go back… there goes my phone… Furmann here."

"Mr. Furmann, there's no record of any landing by that charter yesterday at any of the Caicos-Turks airports."

"You're kiddin' me."

"No sir, I'm not."

"Then where could he have flown to?"

"Any of twenty different fields in the Bahamas? Maybe?"

"Holy hell! Where do we go now? Have you called the charter company and looked in the plane's logbook? He must have recorded his take-offs and landings. Call Westchester and find out where he landed."

"Yes, sir." Click.

"Good thinking." Jacobi added. To himself he thought; that boy is on the ball.

It didn't take five minutes before the same operative from New York called back, "Mr. Furmann, the plane is flying, the logbook is up in the…"

"For God's sake, let them radio the pilot and read the log entry. Should take a whole second." To Jacobi he said, "Can't these people think for themselves? Are they underpaid or something?"

This time it took longer for the return call, but when it came it was all good news. "Mr. Furmann, the plane landed in Georgetown and off-loaded three passengers, two females and a male, resembling Mr. Marchetti."

"Where in the hell is Georgetown?"

"I don't know sir. I'm assuming it's in the Bahamas."

"Good God! Thanks." Turning to his right, "Mr. Jacobi, let's see if there's a Georgetown on the map."

The aerial chart was unfolded again and indeed, smack in the middle of the Bahama Islands was one called Great Exuma, sporting a city called Georgetown.

"Exuma? Then why did the SOB tell me Caicos?"

"Was he protecting his boss or was he just confused? Maybe they told everybody Caicos to throw us off the trail, in case we got onto him. Marchetti must have heard about the capture of the *Bright Adventure*, so he may have figured 'they're coming after me next'. That's why these guys were so busy shredding papers back there. They must have known we'd be out there any minute. So what do we do Jeff? Go to Exuma?"

"What else? We got to get the guy somehow, right. Let's talk to the pilot." He moved by Jacobi and walked up front.

"Captain, we just learned that the little charter landed at Georgetown on Great Exuma, not in the Caicos. Does it look hard to get in there?"

"Let me take a look." The pilot dug into his big black bag next to him and extracted a two inch thick ring binder with flip cards, about 6 by 9. He fingered through them, examined one and said, "Piece of cake. Is that our new destination?"

"Yes sir, it is. I'll inform Langley."

Furmann felt like he had egg on his face when he walked back to his seat. He had made sure that he sounded very convincing when he told Taylor, that Vito was in the Caicos and now he had to admit, he wasn't. Not far off, but not there either.

The Director was not available, but the agent in Virginia took down the information without a comment and Jeff felt somewhat relieved. He walked back to the pilot. "Captain? Can a trans-atlantic jet get into that airport?"

"I doubt it."

"Then he may not be fleeing to Dubai, right?"

"Or he may have jumped on a puddle jumper and flown to another airport or taken a boat to another island with a longer runway."

"Holy Jeez! What do we do now?" He started to turn back to the CIA man, but changed his mind."

"I'll tell you what we'll do. We'll land in Georgetown and ask the

FBO or the authorities where he went after landing. Simple enough?"

When he told Jacobi, he was hit with another surprise. "Didn't Manhattan tell you that the Bahamas reported no landings by that twin yesterday?" Furmann frowned. "Didn't they?" Jacobi persisted. "Do you know what that means? It means that someone on that airport, someone in charge, lied to the authorities and will lie to us as well when we question him."

"Oh shit! I'll tell you what, Jacobi. When you're not looking, I'll squeeze the sonofabitch and I'll get the truth out of him. The reason that I tell you not to look is so you can deny seeing anything inappropriate going on. That way, you can't be called on the carpet in the future and..."

"You better think about what you're gonna do buddy. You're not on American soil. They can hold you there for a long time. I don't think they like Americans, but they'll gladly take our dollars. Have you dealt with them before?"

"Can't say I have."

"They'll charge each one of us landing and take-off fees and they'll only accept cash. I hope you brought enough, or else they'll impound the plane."

"I hope you're kiddin' me."

"I'm dead serious."

The CIA man was right. It was like being back in a third world country. Everyone smiled. Everyone volunteered their services, everybody was willing to do something for them in exchange for money, but nobody knew a thing and no one was on duty when the little twin landed. They received offers for taxi rides, boat trips, cheap hotels, snorkeling, good restaurants, but not a single person had seen Marchetti. The people in the FBO (Field Operations Office) had no records of refueling or parking such a plane.

Furmann finally got a little official looking pickup truck to drive him to the control tower, where he insisted on talking to the man in charge.

Finally, after denials that he was on duty, a very dark skinned man with a most pleasant face and a bright smile came out of the back office and introduced himself. "My name is Malcolm Stone, how may I assist you?"

"May we speak in private?" Jeff pointed to the door which had just produced Mr. Stone.

"Well, of course, follow me." He reentered his domain and pointed to a chair.

"Again," he pronounced it *a gain,* "How can I be of service?"

"I'm Agent Furmann, working for the CIA and yesterday a small twin prop landed here and your people deny…"

"My people?"

"Is the FBO under your control?"

"Not really." It sounded like *not rally.*

"Are you the top authority on this field?"

"Of course, I am, of course."

"Then can you order your people to answer honestly that the airplane landed here and where the passengers went."

"Mr. Farman, you are out of place. You can not order me or anyone else…"

"I can call the Island Police and…"

"And I can arrest you, because you probably have a weapon on you and that's against our laws…"

"And I can file a charge with your and our authorities, that you have falsified official records of planes landing and taking off from your field and that would not only cost you your cushy job, but will land you in jail…"

"Oh ya?"

"Yes, and I'll have you extradited to the United States, so you can find out…"

"Mr. Farman, what is it that you want to know?" He wasn't smiling anymore.

"What time did that plane land and where did the passengers go?"

"Just a moment Mr. Farman." He pushed a button on his phone. "Johnston? In here please."

An older black man knocked and walked in. He remained standing.

"Johnston, remember that twin engine private plane yesterday?"

Johnston looked startled and stuttered for a moment, "Yessa, yessa."

"Where did the passengers go?"

The older man stared at his boss in disbelief. "The passengers?"

"Yes, answer me! Where did they go?"

"They rented a single engine plane and left."

"Rented? From the FBO?"

"Yessa."

"You go with Mr. Farman and find out where they went."

"Now?" He looked positively scared.

"Yes! Now!" Johnston turned and Malcolm Stone rose from his seat and asked, "Mr. Farman? May I ask? Anything serious?"

"White slavery. Young girls."

"God Almighty." He collapsed back in his chair.

Golden Nuggets
XXXI
More Geese?

Johnston and Furmann were driven back to the FBO, where the surprised manager looked at Johnston, his eyeballs white with fear. "I told the mahn no airplane…"

"Tell'im. Tell'im *NOW!"*

"But sir…!"

"Now!"

The trembling man reached for a logbook in a drawer, flipped back one page and read, "Piper GN327 landed at 14:30 yesterday and took off at 14:52, after paying 1200 dollars American in landing fees."

"Twelve hundred bucks?" Furmann caught himself asking a dumb question. "Where did the passengers go?"

"Passengers flew out at 15:05 in Cessna G4484." The man was actually shaking as he read the log.

Someone must have thrown the fear of God into these people, Furmann thought.

"Destination?"

"Just a moment." He turned a page or two. "Flight plan called for Grand Turk, but we know they diverted to South Caicos."

"How do you know?"

"The pilot logged touchdown and take-off in South Caicos." He closed the book as to indicate that was all there was to know.

"How much did they pay you to deny that they were here?" Jeff was peeved.

"Uh, uh, uh,… sir… uh…"

"What did they tell you would happen if you talked?"

"Sir? Can you jus go and leave us alone?"

Johnston cut in, "Mr. Farman, you have all you need to know. Why don't you go catch them?"

"Damn right I will." He turned and stormed out of the building, back to the airplane.

To Jacobi and the captain, he hissed, "Those sonsabitches! They changed to a small puddle jumper and landed in South Caicos."

"Captain, let's go." Jacobi took over.

"Wait, wait!" A pickup raced toward them, with a uniformed man standing in the bed, waving frantically. The co-pilot was about to lift the door that doubled as a ramp, but stopped long enough to watch the waving man jump off, with a piece of paper in his hand.

"Your dues! Your landing fees!" he hollered as he ran to the open cockpit door.

Furmann had nearly strapped himself in when he heard the commotion and rushed back to the entrance.

"What's he want?" He asked the co-pilot.

"He wants landing fees."

"I'll handle this." Jeff pushed the crewmember out of the way.

"Tell Stone and Johnston and everyone else, I might still get your asses locked up in prison and I may put a bullet through your head right now if you don't get the hell out of here!" He pulled his Glock out. "Now!" He pulled up the door and told the pilot, "Go!"

"I don't know if we can do that…"

"Orders from Taylor. Go!"

He walked to his seat as the pilot gave it the gun and sped down the taxiway toward the end of the runway. To the tower he said. "Gulfstream GGH11, emergency take off runway 3-6."

"You have some balls!" Jacobi said as Jeff sat down again.

"You may be right, but if it takes balls over brains, then that's what we're gonna use today. I want that murdering bastard. I want him so bad as if he had kidnapped and raped my own wife. Results is what I'm after. Diplomacy and tact hasn't worked very well in this case and I'm leaving that to the higher-ups. I just wanna catch and torture the SOB."

"Let's hope for results." Jacobi leaned back as the jet roared down the runway and into the blue Bahamian sky.

They didn't even go to 10,000 feet before they started a letdown onto a most luscious tropical island, South Caicos. The view was spectacular. The sea was perfectly green with edges of blue and it seemed like there were a thousand islands scattered all over the place. Thank God, some of them seemed long enough to accommodate an airport and a harbor.

The pilot must have had the same thought, "Thank God for prevailing winds, or we wouldn't be able to get in here."

The experienced crew had no problem, but had to make a U-turn at the end of the runway in order to taxi back to the ramp.

Furmann and Jacobi couldn't figure out if the people on this island were just nicer or if they had received a call from Georgetown telling them what was in store for them.

"Yes sir. G4484 landed here at 15:55, paid his dues and left at 16:30 without refueling, which we discouraged, but the…"

"Where did the passengers go?"

"A private limousine was waiting for them and they left. They did not give us a destination."

"I know." A dark skinned teenager spoke up.

"You know what?" Jeff addressed him.

"I know the car. It belongs to the big house."

"Can you show us?" He whipped out a ten dollar bill.

"Sure. I'll get a taxi." He reached for the greenback, but Furmann pulled it back. "Get us a car." To Jacobi; "Tell the pilots to stand by and inform Langley, we're on the ground pursuing the bastards." He followed the young fellow outside of the terminal and watched him hail a taxi. The two climbed in, but waited for the CIA man to hurry back and join them.

"How far from here..."

"How far? Not far. On the far side of the island in the big house."

"Who owns the big house?"

"Some rich Arab. Much money and many wives. Comes over twice a year for a few weeks. Rest of year, Americans come and go. Much money, many girlfriends, small bikinis, sometimes no bikinis. They swim and drink and..."

"How many people, I mean personnel live in the big house year around?"

"Workers? Servants?"

"Yes, how many?"

"All year?"

"Yes. All year. Steady employees?"

"All year? Five, maybe six. My uncle work there for seven years already. Nice job, no problems."

"How much further is it?"

"Five more minutes, maybe."

"Driver, pull over. Pull over there." A dirt road turned off to the right and the cab stopped. Jacobi and Furmann got out and walked a few steps to be out of earshot.

"Aren't you afraid they're gonna take off and warn them?" Jacobi didn't trust the situation.

"I haven't paid them, have I?" Jeff smirked. "No, they'll stay until they get their hands on our money. But what I want to ask you; Do we walk in there like John Wayne or Billy the Kid and just take over? There are five or six fulltime employees and then Marchetti and some women and God knows who else and Heaven knows if they're armed and with what? We wouldn't have a chance. Could we call for back-up? Our cell phones don't work here. So what do you propose we do?"

"Now you ask me? Now that we're in the middle of nowhere? Shouldn't we have engaged the local authorities? Gotten ten law enforcement people to back us up?"

"You're right, you're right. I get too damn impetuous sometimes.. I'll tell you what I'll do. We drive up to the mansion, ring the bell, ask for Mr. Vito Marchetti and present him with a warrant…"

"Which we don't have."

"He doesn't know that and ask him to escort us to the plane."

"Oh sure! And you think he'll go for that?"

"Maybe if I tell him that fourteen more lawmen are encroaching on the house?"

"Christ! You have more imagination than my grandson." Jacobi scratched his head.

"Do you have any better ideas? Let's have them."

"No, I don't."

"Okay, we can't afford to waste more time, so I'm taking a chance. I'm walkin' up to the front door…"

"What if they have a gate?"

"Oh, Christ, can we get away from all the negatives? Let's go." He turned back to the car.

Jacobi shook his head and followed. He had never dealt with such a single minded idiot before.

To the driver Furmann said, "Drive up to the door and wait. We'll be going back with you in a few minutes." Jacobi rolled his eyes toward the sky.

There was a gate. Wide open. The driver took the right fork and stopped in front of the majestic entrance to a building that reminded Furmann of Mussolini's mansion on Capri.

"Well. Kiss my wife for me." Jeff smiled at the G-man as he got out and walked up the marble steps.

He rang the bell twice and a stately looking colored man opened the door on the second ring.

"Yes?" He was immaculately dressed in a white shirt and perfectly pressed black pants.

"Mr. Marchetti, please?"

"Master Marchetti is not here." He pronounced 'here' like 'hair'.

Furmann felt his temperature rising. "I know he arrived here yesterday from New York, now would you please announce me?"

"Like I just told you sir, he's not here."

"I work for the CIA, you may be subject to arrest."

"For what? For telling the truth?"

"If he's not here, then where is he?"

"He took a boat to Grand Turk in order to catch a plane." The servant remained very composed.

"A plane? When and where?"

"An Airbus was to land an hour ago and he is probably on it now."

"Where? What airport?"

"Grand Turk of course."

"Goodgodalmighty. May I use your phone?"

"Certainly. Come on in."

Four minutes later Furman ran out the door to the waiting cab and screamed at no one in particular, "They took off twenty minutes ago. They're over the Atlantic. Jacobi, can we get them shot down, somehow?"

"I wouldn't know how Jeff. I wouldn't know how."

Golden Nuggets
XXXII
Caribbean Vacation.

"Let's calmly talk about this. Do they have a landline in that big house that could get us through to Langley?" Jacobi was taking the initiative.

"Yeah, I just used it to converse with the tower at Grand Turk airport."

"Come on. We're going to use that again." He got out of the cab.

"Can I come too? That was my uncle at the door." The teenager was anxious to get involved.

"Sure kid. Follow me."

"Can I have my ten dollars now?"

"Furmann, give'im the money." Jeff did and followed the other two up the grand staircase. The same well dressed black man opened and just as politely let the G-men use the phone again in the elaborate office.

"Uncle Dom? Can I stay?"

"Sure, but you may have to walk home."

"That's okay. I can walk and I can run and…"

"Go jump in the pool and be quiet."

Getting through to Langley was a cinch. Getting Director Taylor was not. He might have been on a golf course and wouldn't admit it. Twenty minutes went by before he came in, loud and clear.

"That you Furmann?"

"No, this is Jacobi."

"Is Furmann there?"

"Yes sir."

"Put him on."

"Agent Furmann here." Jacobi looked as if he had just been insulted.

"Furmann, did you catch the bastard?"

"No, we were within twenty minutes, but he took off before we could get to the Grand Turk airport and he's over the Atlantic now. Can we get a fighter up to force'em back or shoot'em down?"

"No Furmann, that's out of the question. Where are you now?"

"We're in the home, palace, I should say of the sheik in little Caicos."

"Good. Stay there. I'll get with the Bahamian authorities, they'll confiscate the house and you two wait for further orders. Do you have access to e-mail?"

"I'm not sure..." Taylor cut him off.

"Good, make up a report a.s.a.p. and mail it. We'll be back in touch within the hour." And he was gone.

"He said wait here." He looked at Jacobi a little sheepishly, "and he wants us to e-mail a report."

"Let's check with the uncle." They got up and found the uncle in the kitchen.

"Would you gentlemen like a beer or a glass of wine? Something to eat maybe?"

"Speaking for myself, I'm ready for a beer."

"Me too." Jacobi joined in.

"Sir, what's your name?" Jeff addressed the servant as he filled two chilled glasses with Heineken beer.

"Dominic, but call me Dom. Everyone does."

"Okay Dom, come pull up a chair." They seated themselves around the kitchen table.

"This is agent Jacobi and I'm Jeff Furmann. Call me Jeff." He sipped the ice cold beer and made a smacking sound, an obvious sign of approval.

"We have some news. Some good and some bad. First; we've been asked to stay here and wait for orders and..."

"You better send the cab back to the airport..." Dom was being helpful.

"But we have to get back there..."

"I can drive you when the time comes."

"I'll pay the driver." Jacobi got up and walked out the front door.

"Dom, "Jeff hesitated, wondering how he should put it. "Dom, there may be some big changes here and some might affect you."

"What changes, sir?"

"Jeff, call me Jeff. The sheik will probably lose this property. The Bahamian Government will probably take it over. Depending on what they're gonna do with it, you may lose your job or they may keep you. I don't know."

"Why is that sir? Uh...Jeff?"

"The sheik and Mr. Marchetti have been involved in criminal activity and may end up in jail. As far as I'm concerned they'll end up in prison and be hanged, but I'm not the final judge and jury..."

"But why?"

"They have been dealing in white slavery, maybe even black slavery, I don't know, but when they're caught ..." He stopped talking. He wondered if he should use an expression, like "They'll have their balls cut off." But he decided not to use it. Instead, "They'll have to defend their actions in several different countries I fear, and I wouldn't give you two pennies for their lives."

"Oh, goodness. Slavery? Not here in the Caicos?"

"We don't know the whole scope. Right now we have his ship and a dozen of his operatives in custody and agents are running all over America, capturing co-conspirators, just like we were chasing Vito Marchetti all over the map."

"Oh, goodness. How long has this been going on?" Dom looked shaken. He might have turned pale if his skin weren't so dark.

"Don't know for sure, but too long, that's for sure. The slimy bastards."

"Are you talking about me?" Jacobi joined them again in the kitchen.

"Now do we have any reason to call you names?" They all chuckled and it broke the ice somewhat in the chilly atmosphere that hung over the trio.

"Dom, we're waiting for a call within a few minutes and then we'll know what the near future holds. Meanwhile, you just continue with your work as usual. I'm sure the government will continue paying you and the rest of the staff and maybe forever, so don't worry yet. The time may come that..." He perked up. "There goes the phone. I'll get it." He dashed to the office, Jacobi on his heels. He didn't forget his beer glass. Jeff did. Dom ran after them, glass in hand.

He picked up the receiver. "Furmann!"

"Mr. Furmann, Special Agent Gerald Glass, assistant to the director. These are your orders." He hesitated. "For now. You remain in the palace. Retrieve your personal belongings from the aircraft. The director will join you there tomorrow. Your wife and son will fly in tomorrow as well...."

"My wife?"

"You're going to have a brief vacation. You will expose yourself to the sun as much as possible. Get a healthy tan without burning. With your dark complexion, that shouldn't be difficult. You need to be as dark skinned as an Arab in a few days. So now just relax, enjoy yourselves and we'll see you tomorrow." Click.

Jeff stared at the dead instrument in disbelief.

"What did Taylor say?"

"That wasn't Taylor. That was his assistant, I forgot his name..."

"Glass?"

"Yeah, that was him. We're staying here and my wife and kid are flying in too. Dom..."

Dom had put the glass down and was about to walk out of the study. "Dom, we're staying for a few days. Keep track of all expenses, so we'll make sure that you will get properly reimbursed."

"A few days? I'll have to get more beer." Dom was on the ball.

"Now you're talking. We'll pick some up on the way back from the plane." Jeff was all enthused.

"We haven't made up a report yet." Jacobi was more practical.

"We'll do that when we have the beer and we'll do it at poolside. I have to get a tan."

"A tan? For what?"

"I'll tell you later. I better call my wife and tell her what's up, she might be worried. What time would it be in Colorado?"

"I don't know what time zone we're in."

"She's still at work, I'm sure. Let's get our stuff and then I'll call her."

"Alright. Dom, are you ready to travel?"

"In just five minutes, sir."

"Jeff."

"Jeff!" He flashed a brilliant smile.

An hour later Jeff called home, but got no answer. By the pool, cold Heineken within reach, they put their report together and managed to e-mail it to Langley. It took several tries, because the computer was different and exceedingly slow.

Jeff called home again, but no answer. He wondered if she had gone to her mother's for supper. He left the number of the sheik's palace and didn't worry about it anymore. She would call when she got in, he was sure.

When the phone finally rang it was nearly ten o'clock in the evening and it was her alright.

"Honey, I'm in Grand Turk, how do I get to you?"

"Grand Turk? How the hell did you get to Grand Turk?"

"Honey, when they told me they would pay for my flight over tomorrow, I decided, the hell with them. I'm going today. Are you kiddin' me? A vacation in the Bahamas? I can't believe it. How do we get to where you are?"

"You stay there. Go to the restaurant and stay there. I'll come get you. I'm on a different island."

"You are?"

"Don't worry. I'll come get you." He hung up.

"Dom, Dom! Get me to the airport. Jacobi, get on the phone and charter me a four passenger puddle jumper with a pilot. My wife is in Grand Turk at the airport and I'm gonna get her. With my son? I forgot to ask her. Of course, she'll have my son. Dom? Are we ready to roll?"

He ran after the black man to the garage.

"I can't believe that." Jacobi said to himself. "The agency is going nuts."

Golden Nuggets
XXXIII
Under the Bahamas Sun

The CIA Gulfstream had long departed and the only choice Jeff had was to rent a little single engine four-seater in order to retrieve his wife Julie and son. As it turned out there was a six-seater, a low wing Cherokee-six available, but that might even be better in case she brought a lot of luggage.

He should have known his wife better. All she had with her was a tote bag.

"Luggage? I brought no luggage. I have two bathing suits for Joey and three bikinis. What else do I need here? You have towels, I'm sure." She was overly exuberant and giggled like a little schoolgirl, while she kept kissing and hugging her husband. "This is fantastic. How did you swing a deal like this, Jeff? Did they promote you to chief detective or something like Special Agent? This is great."

She kept on babbling as they walked from the restaurant to the little low-wing plane for the return flight. Furmann just grinned from ear to ear, holding his right arm around her waist and his left hand firmly enveloping Joey's. He was on cloud nine.

The pilot insisted that Jeff rode up front, because of 'weight and balance' and Joey was disappointed as well. He wanted to steer the aircraft and Jeff wanted to nuzzle with his wife in the backseat. Tough luck. It was a good thing the flight only took twenty minutes and the view of the night sky and the glimmering sea took up all of their attention.

Dom was still waiting with the limousine and made the visitors feel very welcome, by opening the doors and saluting little Joey.

"This is where we're staying? Is this the Taj Mahal?" There was no end to Julie's enthusiasm.

"Yep, your palace for a day or two. Come on Joey. First stop the pool. A bit warm, but well lit." Turning to Dom, "Where do we bed down the young fella?"

"Follow me, sir, uh, gents, uh, Jeff."

It didn't take but five minutes for everyone to be in bathing suits and in the water. Dom's energy was also amazing. He served margaritas in beautiful plastic glasses that changed colors as they drank. Joey immediately wanted to take one apart to figure out what made it tick.

Julie warned; "Don't drink that Joey, that's got..."

"Don't worry ma'am, it's a virgin one."

"Oh! Thank you."

An hour later, the boy safely tucked in bed, the three of them sat around a poolside table, bringing Julie somewhat up to date. Dom had excused himself, but left word that there was still a pitcher of the golden green liquid in the fridge.

"This is really paradise. How long do you suppose we'll be here?" She seemed ready for a week.

"We'll know more tomorrow, but I'll be here long enough to get a good suntan." Jeff answered.

"A suntan? What for?"

"So I'll look cuter when I'm naked with a white hiney."

"Talking about that, let's hit the sack. I wanna see that body while it's still white. Come on! Good night Mr. Jacobi."

"I wish you guys would call me Sol."

"Okay, goodnight Sol. See ya in the morn."

In the morning, when Jeff asked Dom how far it would be to

the nearest store so he could buy his wife some summer dresses, the middle aged servant answered, "Follow me sir, bring the Missus." He led them to the far wing of the mansion and turned into a huge bedroom with an equally huge walk in closet. "Help yourself, Ma'am, they'll never be back."

"Are you kiddin'? Look at it Jeff. A hundred dresses, two hundred pairs of shoes, fifteen sunhats. Where do I start?"

"Start by finding your size and take what you need or fancy." Dom was grinning from ear to ear at her overwhelming enthusiasm.

"Wow! I will. If you gentlemen leave, I'll try on a few."

"Ahhh!"

"Leave!"

Dom convinced Jeff to start wearing *speedo* briefs for a more complete tan. "I haven't worn those since I was ten." He commented. Sol approved.

"You're in good shape. You can wear those. With my gut, I'd rather wear something more conservative."

"Well, you won't need as much of a tan. What time do you figure the brass will be here?"

"Not before noon." Jacobi felt relaxed. "Dom, any chance to go snorkeling somewhere?"

"I'll call for my nephew to come and take you to the best spot. There's plenty of snorkel gear in the pool shed. Just find the right sizes."

"Alright, Joey? Joey?"

"He's already in the pool, sir. Jeff."

"We might as well make the most of this. What do you say, Jac...Sol?"

"I say, let's go conch and lobster diving."

By two-thirty, two taxies arrived and seven G-men and a woman piled out.

"Good God! Look at that! They must need a sunny vacation pretty badly. Look at'em. And see the suit cases? Let's go help'em."

Furmann, Jacobi, Dom and the nephew all ran down the steps in order to bring the luggage into the house. "Dom? Is there room for all of these folks?"

"Plenty, sir, plenty. Don't worry."

Jeff stepped up to Director Taylor, because he was the only one he knew. "Welcome to paradise, sir."

Taylor actually smiled. "We sometimes need to change briefing rooms in order not to grow stale. This seemed like a great planning platform. Show me around." He only carried his attaché case and Dom must have gathered that he was the head honcho. "Mr. Furmann, does this gentleman require a special suite?"

"That would be nice, thank you." Taylor answered before Jeff could get a word out. "Is there a meeting room in the building as well?"

"Yes sir. The cinema."

"Cinema? Not a room with a big oval table?"

"With a round table. Will that do?"

"Show me."

At four, everyone sat by the poolside with a drink, beer or water, when Dom announced; "Food is on the table in the dining room."

All but Joey and Julie, filed into the stately dining room where Taylor announced, "After chow, we'll meet in the room at the end of the hall, we'll lay out some initial plans and by seven, we gather again in the cinema, where we'll show you some intriguing shots of some of the progress we have made. At nine, you're off till seven in the morning." Someone groaned and Taylor smiled, "Alright you rascals, breakfast at eight. Enjoy your meals."

The meeting around the big table involved mainly Furmann and an agent called Achmed Askari. The two would be flying to the Middle East with the specific purpose of assassinating or capturing Marchetti and the sheik. Capturing would prove to be difficult, because of the logistics involved. How do you capture a man and get him in a car and then into an airplane, without anybody noticing? It might take as many as four men and they didn't have that many available without being noticed in a foreign country.

The cinema proved to be exciting. There were live shots of the ship, the *Bright Adventure,* inside and out. Lingering views of documents spread on the floor. A picture of the captain, who tried to keep hiding his face by turning around, until someone grabbed his head and held it right in front of the camera. He was obviously handcuffed.

His crew was shown as a group in a prison setting. None looked particularly happy.

Next came shots from Texas. Jud was chained to a bed, looking very pale, with tubes dripping into his veins. The drivers and Maria were familiar to Jeff as well, "But where is Bob?"

"Hold your questions till later."

A store front of a modeling agency in Bryan Texas and Dallas, was shown with three handcuffed individuals in front of one of them.

"A woman got into this as well?" Jeff couldn't believe his eyes.

Pictures followed of the interior of Marchetti's penthouse, again with a close-up of lots of papers on the dining room table.

Several more faces and names were highlighted, none of whom were familiar to Furmann.

The ones, he was most anxious to see were not there. Driver Bob must have been in a different facility in New Orleans and Buck Buckley and Mr. Connors were in custody of the sheriff's department in Colorado. Either they weren't contacted, or the mighty arm of the CIA didn't reach that far.

All in all, the size of the smuggling organization as well as the scope of the CIA operation were breathtaking.

"I need a stiff drink after this." Jeff whispered to Sol.

"I'm with you buddy."

Golden Nuggets
XXXIV
The assignment

"Furmann," Taylor began, sitting in swim shorts and a t-shirt on the patio, "We have cleared this with your boss, what's his name in Denver, so you are assigned to the CIA for the time being. You have to trust me that the contracts that are being drawn up by our legal staff are very favorable."

"Favorable for me?"

"Yes of course YOU!" He poked Jeff in the chest with his right index finger. "You have shown a keen perception for this business and most of the faces you saw on the film clips last night are in custody because of your doing and we appreciate that, the President included. The embassy of the UAE is giving us some fits, but we're turning it around and rubbing their faces in the dirt for letting that type of despicable trade to take place on their soil." He sipped some black, very black coffee and continued, "Anyhow, you and our Egyptian are going to the Middle East as soon as you're dark enough to look Arabian and by the way, grow a mustache. We'll have complete details about Dubai, Abu Dhabi and surroundings by this afternoon and we want both of those bastards taken out. It may involve a few more of their henchmen, but by the time you arrive there will be a letter perfect plan in place, something that will be right up your alley." He sipped from his coffee cup again, making slurping noises. It was the blackest coffee Jeff had seen since leaving Saudi five years ago.

"You will probably be gone for two to three weeks, which is why we invited your wife and son here, so you have some time together before you leave. Do you speak any foreign languages?"

"Not really. I picked up some Arabic and some Japanese while in the Air Force, but I'm not fluent in any of them. And of course I speak a lot of pig-Latin, street Spanish from the Mexican neighborhoods in Colorado. Not something you'd learn in college."

"Well, don't talk when you don't have to. Achmed speaks Arabic, Farsi and some local dialects. You just play dumb when you have to."

"That should come easy."

"What?"

"Acting dumb. It comes natural to me."

"You are too modest Furmann. By the way, we have combined a record of missing females over the last few years and the documents obtained from the ship and Marchetti's place. We hope to start tracing them in the Near East and maybe bring some of them home. That won't be easy, unless you can capture detailed records from the sheik's domain. If we can't find any, we may never have a clue as to whatever happened to those girls."

"Why do I need that tan and mustache?"

"So you'll blend in better. You may be dressed out in a *jalaba* or a *dishdash* or whatever they call it in the Gulf States. With your complexion, you won't arouse suspicion."

Furmann inadvertently stroked his chin, grateful he didn't shave yet that morning.

"Now go and snorkel or swim, whatever gets you tan without burning. Plan on being ready for briefing at 1400. Have fun."

"Have fun, he said. That's the first time he showed a human side to him." Jeff talked to himself as he went looking for Joey to take him snorkeling. He found the boys, his son and Dom's nephew in the shed, trying different masks and snorkel gear.

"Good show. We're gonna wear life jackets. It's easier to float."

"Life jackets? How can you dive down and grab a conch?" That was the nephew talking.

"We'll float and you dive, okay?"

"We'll bring a tube with a net so we can save a lot of conch."

"What's conch?" Joey wanted to know.

"They're a little bigger than Colorado snails." His father laughed. "You'll see."

A package had been flown in and in the cinema, the contents were revealed. Mostly slides and DVD's. While most everyone enjoyed a leisurely lunch, two of the operatives put a presentation together. Jeff showed up in shorts and T-shirt, and that seemed acceptable. He had shaved, but not under his nose. He was hoping that the first semblance of a mustache would show, but he was thoroughly disappointed. One day was not really giving it a chance, he thought. Patience, boy, patience!

With pad and pen in hand, he established himself on the first row. His instructions were to make notes of the items he wanted to see more often. He listed items as the scenes flashed by him. "Vito, the sheik, Dubai, Abu Dhabi, the Trucial Coast, the whole of the Persian Gulf, locations of airports, military bases, palaces and mosques."

He also wanted to see more of the general dress of the men in the street and in restaurants. He was surprised that in the airports, just about everyone was in western dress, even though the percentage of women in those facilities was minimal. In the streets and market places plenty of women were visible, but nearly all in long dresses, some even veiled. It seemed like a mix of what he had seen in Egypt and what was still the norm in Iraq.

The young Colorado investigation agent tried to absorb as much as he could, but realized that he should sit in that same room many more times in order to commit all the details to memory. Especially, more close up shots of the sheik and Marchetti, so there would be no confusion when he came upon them face-to-face. His pad was full of scribbles when the lights went on and he turned to Taylor to ask what the follow up would be, while he and his staff were still present and after they had gone.

"We're meeting in the big room. Be there." Was all the director had to say.

Jeff took the time to run by the poolside and tell his wife, "We're still in meetings. Put Joey to bed. I'll be back. Love you!"

He wanted to give his kid a hug, but he was in the far end of the pool, having the time of his life. Oh, well!

Seated around the oval table, Jeff wished he had brought a beer. Some of the others had but he was guzzling a bottle of water. Well, he was young and new to this organization. He would learn.

"Lady and Gentlemen, the presentation tonight showed how much we know about the unknown, but also how much we have to learn as yet. Each one of you, introduce yourself to Agent Furmann and explain your expertise. Ask him, in what field he needs the most intense training in and then schedule your time with him. Just remember that he needs to be out in the sun in the daytime. This leaves you time for some leisure during the day as well, but will ask you to work long hours at night. Achmed and this boy, Furmann, will be our eyes, ears and hands overseas and their expertise and knowhow will determine how successful we will be in this operation. So, go to work. Furmann, what's the first point on your list?"

That was the beginning of a long but instructive evening.

All in all it was a fantastic vacation. Snorkeling, deep sea fishing and shopping, strolling the wide beaches and eating exotic food was a thrill beyond belief for the little Colorado family.

Five days of it and the CIA staff left. One more day and Jeff took Julie and Joey back to Grand Turk Airport, this time by boat. The tearful farewell was based on the knowledge that their father and husband was going into some possible imminent danger.

For the first time, Jeff felt doubts when he waved at the departing plane. So far, he had taken the initiative and had good success. Now the whole operation ahead was one big question mark. There was no solid plan in place. Most of the next few weeks were going to be a crap game. Roll the dice and see what comes up. He didn't doubt his ability, but this time he was going into hell or paradise or both. He walked back to the boat very slowly and sat quietly all the way back to Little Caicos, without noticing the silvery sea and the brilliant blue sky.

Achmed and Jeff spent two more days, reviewing maps, satellite pictures, mug shots, busy marketplaces, crowded mosques and underground entrances to elaborate palaces.

New clothes and passports were issued. Furmann became Jeffrey Morgano, born in California of Mexican parents. His mustache was barely visible, but his image was pretty much perfect. He had become a representative of the Boeing Corporation, an accountant concerned with the financial problems of the newest helicopter. Not for long.

"A Mister Taylor on the phone!" Dom hollered across the pool to the stretched-out Furmann.

"Don't they have remote phones here?" Jeff fussed as he sprinted to the other side.

"Yes, sir. Furmann here."

"Yes, we have a small change in plans. The U.S. Ambassador in Abu Dahbi is being a real ass. You were to operate out of the embassy, but he doesn't want a part of it and he doesn't want you to be a Boeing rep. Too much at stake. The Emeritus are considering the purchase of three big planes and the bidding is fierce between the Airbus from France and the 767 from Boeing. He wants nothing to happen that can smear the good ol' name of Boeing, so you're going to be a leather buyer for a Puerto Rican shoe manufacturing plant. They actually do business there. You'll get new papers. You'll fly into Oman and Achmed will leave you there until he has a cab that will transport you around. The fifteen percent labor force consists mostly of foreigners with a lot of Egyptian cab drivers, so that'll fit right in. You'll be operating out of Dubai instead, which is actually better. The capital, Abu Dhabi is on an island you know, so that might prove to be too constrictive anyway. So it will all work out. How's the tan and the mustache?"

"I look like an Arabian prince."

"Good. Get some of their money while you're at it."
"Thanks... I'll try."

"Achmed? Do you want to hear the good news? You're going in first. You're going to be a cabdriver and I wait in Oman until you're all set. Isn't that gonna be fun. We won't be conspicuous. American businessman being driven by an Egyptian slave. Make sure you learn where we can buy beer. By the way, have you seen how many sheikdoms there are over there? How are we ever gonna find the right one and did you know that the one we're supposed to knock out is a second cousin of the premier of that country?"
"Jeff, don't you ever get tired of talkin'?"
"Who? Me?"

Golden Nuggets
XXXV
Salaam, Welcome

Instead of flying them over on a CIA plane, the two co-conspirators flew commercially to the Azores and spent the night. From there Achmed flew to Cairo, where he changed to Egyptian clothes and booked separately to *Seeb International* in Oman. Furman caught a flight to Athens and connected to the same airport at Masqat, the capitol of Oman. They booked in separate hotels, Jeff in a luxury hotel in the center of the city, Achmed in a neighborhood joint. They met in a local restaurant and compared notes for the last time. Thereafter, the Egyptian caught a bus to Dubai with a number of other laborers and Furmann (Morgano) stayed in town till Achmed had bought a suitable taxi and a convenient place to stay.

Jeff spent his time visiting leather merchants and enjoyed the bickering in the different market places. Most of the local places and people reminded him of biblical times, they were so colorful and romantic. Some of the merchandise he bought, he shipped home to Denver including some nice gifts and souvenirs. He didn't really know what he was going to do with the leather, but he figured it made him seem legitimate. He walked around with shipping and purchasing receipts. What could make him look more authentic?

After five days, Achmed called. He had clothes, pistols, an AK-47 and a perfect place to stay, a two bedroom condo near the harbor.

"Come on, baby. Time to go to work. I'll pick you up at Dubai International at 4:45, UAE flight 119. Be on it."

Achmed and his cab looked so genuinely local, that Jeff hardly recognized him. The white garb and the headpiece made him look Jordanian or Arabian, but his smile was the same as always, broad as the avenue. It took more than an hour to get from the airport to the flat and it seemed like a miracle that they made it without putting additional scratches on the yellow Mercedes. The traffic was unbelievable and everybody seemed to be speeding and leaning on the horn. What a spectacle!

Once inside, new clothes were tried on and pistols and ammo checked and cleaned. Wearing a Glock holster inside the folds of the white gown was simple. Getting it out in a hurry was more complicated. It took practice.

The Egyptian had been in touch with the American Consul in Dubai and done some checking on his own.

"We have a colleague in the consulate. A Harry Knowles, k.n.o.w.l.e.s. Good man. Speaks the languages and he'll come by here at about seven. He'll bring beer. That stuff is hard to come by in this country. They're very Muslim in spite of some of their modern dress, like you saw in the airport. I heard that some of the bigger hotels have booze, but I couldn't go in there asking for a six pack, could I?"

"We used to buy booze from a cabby in Iraq and Jordan. What's the matter with you? Still new on the job?" They had a hearty laugh over that remark.

Harry arrived a little after seven. "Damn traffic! It's a good thing they don't have women drivers here. It would be even worse. Hi, I'm Harry Knowles."

Contrary to the other two, Harry was blond and blue eyed, which caused Jeff to remark, "How do you get to do any undercover work with that pale skin and blue eyes?"

"I just do the organizing and I let others do the fighting. That way I never get shot."

"Thanks a lot! Let me at that beer. That's all you brought? Two six-packs?"

"Right, so be frugal with it. This is the situation, as I know it. We will not get any cooperation from the local law enforcement officials as far as the sheik is concerned. As you may already know, there are dozens of sheikdoms and they're all cousins. They all got rich all of a sudden when they discovered oil here and kicked out the English some forty, maybe fifty years ago. The natives all make a good living and all the hard labor and dirty work is done by foreigners."

"Like taxi drivers from Egypt?" Achmed thought he was funny.

"Yes, like taxi drivers from Egypt. They work hard and are frugal. They send a lot of money home to Mom and Pop and children. How much have you sent so far?"

"I haven't made a dime yet. Furmann is a lousy tipper."

"Anyway. Your hopes of getting Marchetti out alive are slim to none. I have no idea how you would accomplish that. Facing justice in the U.S. sounds idealistic, but I don't think it'll work."

"So we'll kill'im." Jeff was ready.

"Okay, but let's not lose sight of our most important goal, liberating the girls. In order to find out what they've done with them and where they are may be a near impossible task and our honorable asshole, the ambassador, is not giving us any assistance whatsoever."

"How about if I ask Taylor to ask the President to put heat on him?" Furmann felt his blood pressure rise. "The President himself approved this mission."

"Great, get on it. Stop by the consulate tomorrow morning to use the phone. Meanwhile, Marchetti lives in a mansion on the coast outside of Dubai. The sheik lent it to him, but the scuttlebutt is that the sheik considers him a liability, and would love to get rid of him. That's beautiful. We'll do it for him. He has no access to local trade records in this region anyway, so we don't really need him alive. If he's killed by a local tribesman, it'll look like the hit was ordered by his former friend, the sheik. Jeff, I think you would look good as a local tribesman, what do you think?"

"How do I get a silencer and what are Vito's daily habits, does he go to the market or out to eat?"

"So far, we have a gardener on his property and he'll have some of those details in the morning. We're also trying to slip a maid into his household. Thank God, most of his servants resent him. That helps."

"Where's the sheik?"

"He lives outside of Abu Dhabi and that's more difficult. Have you looked at that city? It's on an island and very hard to get in or out of undetected. If you knocked him off at home, they'd seal off the bridges and have you caught within an instant."

"I'm a good swimmer. Are there many sharks in these waters?"

"You may be kiddin' Jeff, but that's one possibility. Getting a speedboat off the coast and speeding you to Kuwait before their fighters get up to take you out, is one possibility. The other is, his shipping offices are right here in Dubai and he does come out here by helicopter every so often and he does attend the services at the local Mosque on occasion. Our best bet is probably breaking into his office and getting hold of his records before he panics. And panic may be caused by a foiled attempt on his life."

"So what should we do first? What do you recommend?" Jeff was itching to go.

"If we raid his office first, he'll know that we're here. He'll realize fast that we have operatives in the country and that might make him more cagey. If we kill Marchetti first, it might have the same result. What do you think?"

"Well, in my book, locating the girls is of the utmost importance, so let's raid his office first. Then we knock off Marchetti and work on a plan to get the sheik. If we don't get him now, we'll get him in the future, as long as we get the lowdown on where the girls are."

"Sounds good." Harry acknowledged. "What about you, Achmed?"

"Sounds good to me too. When do we do it?"

"How about tonight?" Furmann had been on inactive long enough. Vacation in the Bahamas and buying leather in Oman was not his idea of excitement.

"No, no, no.!" Harry waved his hand. "We know the address of the place, but we know nothing of the layout, the security system or people on the job after hours. We don't have a clue. We're going to scan it all tomorrow. First you're coming by the consulate. Your cabdriver knows where it is." He smirked in the direction of the Egyptian. "We'll have the input of the gardener and then we'll go and case the area around the office. We may also drive by Vito's place and get a feel for the scenery. No, we're not rushing anywhere tonight."

"What if he gets suspicious after losing his ship and his palace in Caicos and starts destroying or hiding records..."

"He could have started that two weeks ago if he wanted to. No, tomorrow night we hope to be ready. I know you're ready, Jeff and..."

"I'm just not used to doing nothin'. It drives me batty."

"I understand, believe me. I understand, but we're not gonna do anything in haste, something we may regret. So, have a beer, get some sleep. Make notes of anything that enters your mind about the operation and we'll see ya in the morning. Salaam!"

After a half hour, Jeff couldn't stand it anymore. "Achmed, do you suppose there is a nice pub or restaurant near the harbor?"

"You mean near the office?"

"Well, if the office is near the harbor, that would be a happy coincidence, wouldn't you think?"

"I don't know, Jeff. I don't wanna go against their instru...."

"I don't either. I just like to get a feel for the surroundings in the dark, you know what I mean?"

"I tell you what. I'll drive, but I may not stop. Is that okay?"

"I can live with that."

"Are you going as a westerner or a local, Sahib?"

"Local is the call."

Golden Nuggets
XXXVI
Ali Baba?

The harbor area and the adjacent market were even more lively than the capitol of Oman. The taxi moved at a snail's pace through the throng of shoppers and sightseers. It looked like every nationality from all over the world was represented and even the long garbs had such a wide variety of color schemes, that it resembled a Renoir painting. The older generation seemed to dress very modestly, but the teenage boys and girls in blue jeans and tank tops could have come straight from Brooklyn or Spanish Harlem.

The taxi ride was so slow, that Jeff decided it wasn't worth it. He started to direct Achmed to turn around when the driver looked back at him and said, "It's the second building on the right."

"His office is here? In this mess?"

"Now you understand why he has a helicopter pad on top of the building. He doesn't wanna deal with this mess anymore than we do."

"Is there any place where you can pull over?"

"If there is, I'm not stopping. Look at all the details. I'll go even more slowly if I can and you memorize all you can. It may help in the planning."

"Do I see that right? Does that hotel have a beer sign over the basement door?"

"Looks like it, but again, we're not stopping. You don't want to be seen anywhere around here."

"What if I can get some lowdown from some of the locals? Some of them may even work for the sheik."

"Forget it brother. We're outa here. I'll see if we can swing by Vito's place. At least there should be less traffic out there." To prove his point, he started to speed up once they passed the drab five story building that was supposedly the sheik's office.

"That didn't particularly look opulent, did it?" Jeff was disappointed. "It probably has fire escapes on the back of the building. Is there an alley we can get into?"

"Not tonight. I'm driving by Marchetti's place and that is it for tonight. Tomorrow we hit'em with both barrels."

"Spoil sport."

The consulate was a surprise. It was a private business, where the Honorary Consul conducted some affairs that pertained to American citizens in his region. Jeff had been in many an embassy when working for Air Force Intelligence, but this was entirely different. No Marine guards at a gate, no x-ray surveillance upon entry, none of that security and secrecy stuff. Just an ordinary office with a pretty secretary at the front desk. She was a dark-haired beauty who rattled on the phone in a foreign language and then approached her two visitors in perfect English, or maybe perfect American. "Good morning gentlemen. Mr. Knowles is expecting you. Follow me." She got up from behind her desk and led the two G-men through the backdoor of the room.

In her modern dress, Jeff wondered if she was a local girl or if she had been imported from the U.S.

"Where are you from, miss?" He asked as they proceeded through a long hallway.

"Cincinnati." She threw him a smile over her shoulder as they stopped at a large double door. Before Furmann had a chance to comment, she opened the door and announced, "Mr. Knowles, your guests are here." She stepped aside and Jeff threw her a last glance as they passed her. "Wow!" He thought, but he said, "Morning Harry. Nice day again."

"Yes, no doubt. It's gonna be only 110 degrees. Nice day." He pointed to some chairs around a mahogany table. "Sit. Coffee? Tea? Juice? Anything?"

"Coffee for me." Achmed answered.

"Same here."

Harry put a pot of steaming brew on the table, plus a tray with an assortment of sugars, substitutes and cream. "Help yourselves."

A screen was set up at the far end of the room and Knowles walked over to close the heavy curtains on the other side. A corner lamp and the reflections of a laptop on the table provided the only light. Harry took a seat at the computer and clicked a button. On the screen an aerial view of the city appeared. With an electric pointer, Harry circled the north western sector of the city.

"This is where we are and this is where we're going to operate." Another click zoomed in on the harbor section. "Here's where both our targets are. The office is here," His pointer rested on a cluster of roofs, one with a white cross on top. "That's the sheik's place. This is how we may have to get in. You notice that the surrounding buildings all have the same height, so you'll have to find your way to the roof of one of the adjacent offices and somehow get on top and walk over to the entrance of the sheik's helo-pad. Any ideas?"

"Can you zoom in on the alley behind those buildings?" The picture on the screen enlarged the immediate surrounding structures and showed a network of connecting alleys.

"Swing to the left a little." The edge of the landing-cross highlighted the scene and the maze of narrow passageways between the offices and adjacent stores became like a *lego* puzzle.

"If we can enter that maze from the east and simply wind our way to the back of this building," Jeff got up and pointed at the screen. "Then we work our way up and over to that shed, which must be the entrance to the sheik's place and we ease our way down. What do you know about security and alarms, Harry?"

"Very little, or rather… nothing."

"Damn! If an alarm goes off, we're stuck on top of a building without a parachute."

"How about a long rope?" Achmed was serious, but the other two thought he was kidding.

"A jump rope?" Jeff though he was funny.

"No, a long rope to the ground, so we can slide down fast instead of running across more roofs and down stairs, while the security men step out in the alley and wait for us. A rope will get us down in seconds."

"I think you're the smartest cab driver in Egypt."

"Remember, we're in the Emirates."

"Okay, so you're..."

"Gentlemen, may we remain serious. What will happen if an alarm does go off?"

"We have to kill it before we hit that door."

"Great! How?" Knowles remained on the trail.

"Can we get hold of floor plans and electrical layouts?"

"In time for tonight's operation? I wouldn't know how."

"I could go in during the day and scout the place." Achmed stayed serious as well.

"Go in as what?" Harry was anxious to hear what he had in mind.

"I deliver a package from the consul addressed to the sheik."

"Sure. Like what kinda package?"

"The consul has received info about the whereabouts of his ship and the fact that the U.S. Government wants to confiscate it and sell it."

"Confiscate it? We already got it!" Jeff was being critical.

"Well, whatever term you use and whatever the message is, something that looks official. I take a cab over, not my own, go up to the office and insist on personal delivery, which should stall them for a while, right? And...."

"Dressed as what?"

"As a courier from the consulate or the embassy. How else?"

Knowles cut in, "He has a good point, but let me finish with this part. We think we know what the layout of his office is, but we don't know if he would keep secret papers in a vault or in a file cabinet. If they're in a vault we may be up the creek. Do either of you know how to crack a safe?" Both shook their heads. "I was afraid of that."

"When you deliver the package from the consulate, see if you can get into the inner sanctum and spot the location of a safe. It doesn't sound probable, but do the best you can."

"In other words, you're going along with his plan?" Jeff sounded incredulous.

"Can you think of something better?" Knowles let them feel that he was in charge.

"Well, uh..."

"Let's plan on it. Achmed, we have proper clothes here, I think. Otherwise, we'll go out and buy some. Jeff, you had wanted to call headquarters from here, but we're twelve hours ahead of them. So' it's ten at night. Do you wanna call now or wait till it's eight in the morning over there?"

"I'll call now, if I may."

"Sure. Come with me to the secure phone. Meanwhile, George will come in and load you up with local cell phones and silencers."

"Who's George?"

"Don't ask. George is our specialist. Just George, okay?"

"Okay, okay. Where's that phone?"

"Whom am I speaking with? Agent who?"

"Agent Blank? Okay, connect me with Director Taylor, please."

"Who is this?"

"Agent Furmann, calling from Dubai. Please put me through."

"Sir, I can't do that."

"Wait till I tell Taylor that you said that. What time is it out your way?"

"It's eleven at night and I can't reach the director at this hour."

"I hope you like your job. You may not have it much longer." Jeff was getting mad. "Take down this message. To the President of the United States and the Director of the CIA; the Ambassador will not, I repeat, will NOT cooperate. Period." And he hung up.

"Boy, you have a temper." Harry said.
"Sometimes that helps."

Golden Nuggets
XXXVII
Oops!

A pistol with a silencer attached was difficult to hide in western clothes, so Achmed carried his Glock in a regular shoulder holster with the silencer forming a bulge in his sports jacket on the other side. By not buttoning his jacket, it was not too obvious. A very impressive package was organized with real official looking stamps on two sides. Inside were quasi formal papers, requesting the transfer of ownership papers of the *Motor Vessel Bright Adventure*.

Furmann was supposed to stand by his cell phone within the consulate, but he was too restless, too eager to go, so, dressed in a long hooded garb, he set out and walked in the direction of the target building. He was afraid to take a cab, because who wouldn't be suspicious of an Arabic looking man, who couldn't speak the language.

They figured it would take him half an hour, so he set off at 12:30 and Achmed took a cab at 12:45. That should get them to the office address at the exact same time. Jeff would wait for a call from Achmed before entering the building. So far, so good.

The Egyptian arrived at the front door and was surprised that there was no guard or any kind of security. No signs at the elevator to indicate what floor he should go to, but he surmised that the top floor would be most logical, because of the heli-pad on the roof. He was right as well as a bit surprised. In the rangy looking building, he had not expected huge ornate bronze and silver doors, but there they were. They reminded him of some of Saddam Hussein's palaces.

A silver button was his only choice, other than knocking, so he pushed it while at the same time trying to turn the doorknob. No dice, it was locked of course, but within a minute, a tall brown skinned man in the traditional local frock opened the door. "Salaam Aleichem!" He bowed slightly, "How can I help?"

"Sheik Ahmad al-Akadan, please."

"He's not here. How can I help?" The tall man's English was pretty good, although heavily accented.

"I have to deliver this in person," He held up the package. "Is he in his palace in Abu Dhabu?"

"I cannot say, but I can deliver it to him." The servant held out his hand.

"No, no. I have to deliver it in person."

"A package from who?"

"American Consulate, very important."

"Step in a moment." He stepped aside and Achmed was guided into an elaborate reception area.

"Sit please." The tall man left through another ornate door and the Egyptian walked around the room studying beautiful paintings, while really looking for signs of a security device.

He reasoned, it had to be there, because someone would set it on the way out.

He had worked himself halfway around the room, when the tall man reappeared with a phone in his hand. "His Excellency himself." He extended the instrument to Achmed.

"Excellency, Salaam Aleichem."

"Aleichem Salaam, how can I help?"

The G-man switched to Arabic. "Emir, I have to hand you this message from the U.S. government and receive your signed receipt. If you are at your home right now, I will arrive there later this afternoon, no problem."

"No, I shall come there. How come you speak our language so well?"

"I'm of Egyptian birth, Emir."

"Very well. I'll be there within forty-five minutes. Salaam."

"He's coming here." Achmed was a little befuddled as he handed back the phone.

"Very well, you can wait in his suite. Follow me."

Two women in the inner office hastily covered their faces when the stranger entered and the tall man told them in a rapid dialect, that they were excused for the remainder of the day. Though Achmed didn't speak that particular slang, he grasped the meaning and he thought to himself, "Two fewer to deal with."

The huge windows faced the waterfront in the distance and the view was panoramic.

"You can rest here." The servant commented. "The sheik will see you here. What can I get you to drink and eat?"

"Coffee would be fine, sir."

"Call me Oban, please."

"Okay Oban, coffee please." He left the room.

The Egyptian walked to the window, punched a few numbers on his cell. "Jeff, I'm on the top floor. The sheik is flying here in forty-five minutes."

"Jeez. How many people are up there?"

"I don't know. One for sure. I gotta hang up." He pocketed his phone just in time and Oban found him staring at the harbor scene.

"Your coffee, sir. Anything to eat?" He put down a silver tray with a beautifully carved little silver coffee pot and a tiny china cup. A matching sugar bowl, but no cream.

"No thank you. I just finished lunch."

"Anything to read? The magazines are all in Arabic, but you master that language, no?"

"Yes, I'll be fine." He seated himself on a large poof next to a low wooden table covered with white lace. The tall man sat down as well and watched as Achmed poured himself some coffee and added a spoonful of sugar. He stood as the visitor started to sip the thick black liquid, then turned and left.

As soon as the man was gone, Achmed took the coffee pot and his cup to the wet-bar in the far corner and poured out more than half. He returned to his window view, carrying his cup, but not drinking. "I'm not about to let them knock me out." He said to himself.

Making sure there were no obvious cameras observing him, he took out his phone again, but Furmann didn't answer.

***

Jeff had taken his own initiative. He felt he couldn't just keep walking the street in front of the building for another half hour and he couldn't be walking into the basement bar that flashed a beer sign. Not in his Arabian outfit. So he rode the elevator to the top floor, pushed the same little bell and when the tall man opened and leaned forward a little, saying, "Salaam."

Furmann whipped out his pistol and shot him right in his brown forehead. He plopped forward without a sound.

Jeff opened the door as wide as he could and pulled the man inside by his ankles. He hid him behind a sofa along the wall. Whatever had spilled out of the man's forehead looked kinda messy and the G-man pulled the doormat over it and figured, 'that'll do for the moment.' He closed the gigantic door and shuffled toward the inner sanctum, his pistol out in front. No one was at their desk inside the secretarial office. A check of the rooms to his right didn't result in any surprises and the staircase to the roof was deserted also. The sizable kitchen was clean, but deserted, so that left just one door, another palatial entrance.

Furmann gently, very gently, turned the knob and eased the door open, an inch at a time. It showed a great expanse, a suite fit for a king. This is where Achmed had to be. He could feel it, but he couldn't see him. He pushed the door open further and saw nobody. Before entering, he thought it wiser to call first. It took a few seconds for the phone to get energized again, but when it rung, it seemed the ringtone came from the other side of the door he held open with his foot.

"Achmed?"

"Jeff?"

"Where are you?"

"Hahahaha! I'm on the other side of the door." Achmed had heard some commotion and dashed next to the door, pistol in hand, so he could catch anybody sneaking up on him. He stepped up, grinning from ear to ear.

"So you thought you could sneak up on me buddy? No such luck. Anybody else would have caught a bullet in the base of their skull. By the way, what are you doing up here?'

"You didn't expect me to stand out front for fifty minutes waiting for something to happen, did you?"

"Where's Oban?"

"Who?"

"Oban, the tall dark skinned servant who..."

"Oh, him? He's behind the couch."

"What's he doing there?"

"Allah put him there, while he's checking out seventy-two virgins."

"You shot him?"

"You could say that. We have another thirty minutes before the big honcho arrives, so let's look for records. Why don't we start here in his main domain."

They busted desk drawers, file locks, scanned through dozens of ledgers, but couldn't find what they were looking for, addresses of purchasers of *Golden Nuggets.*

The secretarial area had several steel cabinets and it took a while to bust them, but it's amazing what a 45 caliber bullet can do to a little lock. Thank heaven for silencers. They found some files, all in Arabic, which showed imports from the U.S. and they laid them in a neat pile near the door, along with Achmed's package that still awaited delivery. But... no sales receipts from potential buyers, the very things they needed to trace the whereabouts of the girls.

"Did you see any sign of a safe?" Jeff was getting impatient.

"Let's go back to his office. Let's check behind large paintings."

"Good thinking. There are also some big paintings in the reception area."

"Right! Let's start here."

The suite with the view received a thorough going over, but no wall safe was detected.

"Let's check the hall. But wait." Jeff hesitated. "There comes the chopper. Let's catch him when he opens the door from the roof."

"Let's."

Golden Nuggets
XXXVIII
The Trucial Coast

The two stationed themselves on each side of the door that led to the roof, pistols at ready. There were two simple locks, which Jeff turned, so the sheik could just turn the knob and walk in. No bolts or any other security measure. They must have felt pretty safe up there. The copter landed, the engine slowed and shut off. The G-men held their breath.

Footsteps were audible on the stairs and it sounded like just one person was descending. "No guards?" Jeff wondered, but he couldn't worry about it very long, because the door opened and a grey bearded man walked in, dressed in the long popular dress of the Middle East. Achmed was hidden behind the open door and Jeff was flat against the wall on the other side. The sheik stepped into the room and immediately felt a pistol in his ribs. "Hands up! Up. High!" Jeff hissed in his ear. "Up and keep'em up." while he kicked the door shut with his heel, exposing the Egyptian in his western dress.

"What is this?" the sheik cried out in English.

"Shut up. Achmed, search him." While one hand poked at the little sheik's ribs, the others turned the locks, so no one could come in and surprise them.

To their amazement, al-Alkadan carried no weapons.

"Keep those hands up and start walking to your suite."

"Who are you?" He turned to Furmann, surprised that the man in local garb spoke like an American.

"Shut up and keep walking." Achmed repeated the same command in Arabic, which puzzled the native even more. A native looking man, who sounded like a Yankee and a western dressed man who spoke like a local.

Once inside, Jeff ordered him to sit on a straight chair, yanked his belt out of his pants and told his partner, "Tie his hands behind his back. Real tight. Let him suffer."

"Who are you and what do you want?" The little Emir remained defiant.

"I'll tell you what we want, you little shit. We want the addresses of the buyers who bought the young women from you that you imported from America. Where are those documents?"

"I don't know what you're talking about."

"I'll refresh your memory." Jeff walked behind him and shot him through his right hand.

"Oww!" He screamed as he stood up, lifting the chair with him.

Both attackers pushed him back down. "Now do you remember?" Furmann held the smoking pistol right under his nose. "If not, the next one goes into your balls, understand? Where are those papers? Do you have a safe here?"

The little man turned to Achmed, his face twisted with pain. "Why is he doing that to me?" he asked in Arabic.

The CIA man answered in the same tongue, "You bought and sold his sister and he'll torture you until you die unless you provide him with the addresses." He felt a little lie might help.

"But I have no safe here and… "

"Then where are the papers?"

"At my house." He was actually crying.

"Where in your house? We'll send someone by there to pick them up."

"They're in my safe. Nobody can open it, but me." He tried to pull his arm out from the noose around his wrists, but couldn't.

"What's he saying?" Furmann was frustrated that he didn't understand what was going on.

"He says the papers are at his home in a safe."

"Do you believe him?" Jeff was hot under the collar. He moved his nose nearly into the little man's eyes, "I'm goin' with you in the helicopter and we're going to retrieve those papers"

"No, no!"

"Oh no?" He stepped behind the crying man and with his gun-butt smacked the hell out of his bleeding hand. Another shriek echoed through the room while Jeff calmly wiped the blood off his pistol with the flowing folds of the sheiks gown. "Next I smack your other hand, but you may need that to open your safe. So I'll squash your nuts instead. Now tell me, where are those addresses?"

"In my safe. Please, torture me no more and come with me and I'll give them to you."

"Fly with you? I might just do that, but you understand that I'll kill you instantly when you pull a fast one on me."

Achmed quickly translated and the sheik nodded. "Yes, yes. You come. But I bleed. I may die."

"No you won't. Buddy, rip his dress to shreds and bandage his hand."

Just as his partner bent over to tear at the dress, a shot rang out from the direction of the door. Jeff dove behind the sheik and fired three quick shots at the man in the doorway. Looking up, he saw the man fall forward and another round in the top of his head finished him off.

"Where the hell did he come from? Achmed, you okay? Oh, good God, he got you. Let me see, take off that jacket. Jeez, two holes, in and out of your shoulder. Let me help you."

Tearing the sheik's tunic to threads, he had the Egyptian bandaged up pretty fast. Next Jeff whipped out his cell phone and dialed Harry's number at the consulate.

"Harry, Achmed is hurt. Get'im out of here. There are also some dead people up here, but don't call the authorities until you get my buddy outta here. I'm flying to Abu Dhabi, get the marines to pick me up at the front door of the palace. Out."

He turned to the sheik, who had become very quiet. "That guy over there, is that your pilot?"

"No, my bodyguard."

"Some stupid bodyguard. Is the pilot still up there?"

"I think so."

"We're going traveling, you bastard. Get up. You make one wrong move and you are dead. My gun is right at your spine. One shot and you're done, do you understand? When we're in the plane, tell him to fly straight to your palace. One wrong move and he's dead too. Then I'll fly the chopper."

Turning to his fellow G-man. "Harry will be here in minutes. He'll take care of you. I'm taking your gun and your ammo. Never know who I'll meet on the way."

"But you're sticking your neck out…"

"I know, but that's what I've been doing for a long time. I'll get those papers, pal."

Grabbing the little sheik by the arm, he said. "Now no false moves if you want to live. You saw I'm a pretty good shot, so easy boy, easy."

The two moved slowly out the door, stepping over the sprawled body of the would-be hero, who came to the rescue of his boss. Jeff kept the sheik in front of him, figuring if someone else shot at them they would hit their boss first.

The door to the stairway was open and Furmamn figured that the bodyguard had let himself in with a set of keys. "Damn, how stupid can we get? I've gotta start thinking straight."

He was cursing himself under his breath. The door to the roof was closed, so Jeff shoved his prisoner forward and said, "Open the door and walk to the helicopter as naturally as possible. I would hate to have to shoot the pilot. Let's go."

With the nozzle firmly planted in the small of his back, the multi-billionaire walked to the waiting helicopter and the moment the pilot spotted him, he jumped out of his left seat, ran around the front of the craft and opened the co-pilot's door. When they were real close, Jeff showed the man his pistol and said, "That won't be necessary. We'll ride in the back. We're flying straight to the palace. If you make one wrong move, the sheik is dead and you'll be next."

Prodding the little man with his silencer, "Tell him to fly straight over, so we'll all continue living. If I die, it will be after you two are facing Allah to pay for your sins. Tell him. Have him open the back door. Easy now."

Some rapid fire Arabic resulted in the back door being opened and before the two of them climbed in, Furmann ordered the pilot."Get into your seat and start the engines. I'll close this door. Remember; no funny stuff."

The sheik rode backwards and Jeff buckled him in, all the time with his hands tied behind his back. He shrieked with pain, when he leaned against his wounded hand. The startled pilot looked around. "Just keep your eyes on your instruments. Your boss will survive."

Facing forward, he could see both the little man in the opposite seat and the back of the pilot's head, who had put on a headset and started the engine. The whoosh-whoosh of the rotor blades increased and before long they were up and away.

The Persian Gulf looked beautiful from up there and didn't reflect all the bloodshed that had gushed all around it for ages and probably for many more ages to come. Inland was a glob of desert sand, but the Trucial Coast was charming with lots of palms, ports, palatial homes and green golf courses. If the mission wasn't so damn serious, Jeff could really have enjoyed the ride. He had bluffed when he told his prisoner that he would fly the helicopter, but in spite of the fact that he had flown many a mission in one, he didn't have a clue as to how to fly one. He hoped it wouldn't get to that point.

His thinking was, he would get the papers, walk out of the front door, where an armored U.S. Marine vehicle would be waiting for him and speed him to safety in the Embassy.

He took for granted that his call earlier today would have stirred the Director and the President into shaping up the 'Honorable Asshole' and forcing him into full cooperation.

If that didn't happen, he wasn't sure what he would do, but he was confident, he'd think of something.

Finally, as the miles churned away, his thoughts returned to Achmed. The bullet had hit his shoulder, just as he bent down to tear at the hem of the sheik's robe. One second earlier and he might have caught it right in his heart.

"How careless and stupid can we get?" He heaved a deep sigh.

Golden Nuggets
XXXVIII
Pay dirt, finally.

Abu Dhabi looked magnificent from the air. In the middle of a wild array of islands, the Capital city was built on the largest one, with bridges spanning to other islands and the mainland. As in most Middle Eastern cities, most buildings were brilliantly white, including the rooftops. The lavish homes, scattered around the perimeter, had red roofs and manicured green lawns. It was a site to behold. Compared to Abu Dhabi, Dubai was nothing but a dump.

The sheik's domain was a virtual palace, Disneyworld style. On the north side was a large extension, three stories high with a flat roof and a giant red cross in the middle. The heli-pad, Jeff thought.

Indeed. The pilot brought the copper down gently and turned off the engine. On the side of the landing pad, a beautiful blue waterway stretched toward the Gulf, intertwining with other rivers and bays as far as the eye could see. On the south side, a massive glass wall turned out to be the window of the sheik's boudoir and that's where the trio entered. The room was immense, with gorgeous couches and leather poufs strewn throughout the room. Along the far wall was a big round bed with angled mirrors overhead.

"You pervert." Jeff hissed between his teeth, but out loud he said. "The safe?"

"Over there, behind the painting. But you have to untie my hands, so I can open it."

"Forget that. Your lackey here can do that. Just tell'im how" They walked over to the six-by-four foot painting of a younger sheik in an outlandish uniform. "Must have stolen that from the Czars.", The American muttered. The pilot walked ahead of them, while Furmann kept the nozzle firmly at the bandit's spine.

"Tell him how to open it."

"You know I can't do that. It's a secret code."

Jeff hit the wounded hand with his gun and the little man yelped.

"Open it!"

The pilot grabbed the edge of the painting... "The other side." The old man was actually sobbing. The right side of the frame moved easily on its quiet hinges and revealed a three-by-three foot steel door, with a dial in the middle.

"Give him the code."

"I can't..."

"Tell'im or I'll shoot up your other hand."

"Allah il Allah!"

"Stop praying and start talking." He hit the sore hand again.

"Right, two times, stop at eleven. Good, turn left, go past eleven and stop at three. Now turn to seven, our holy number. Pull it open."

The heavy door swung open noiselessly and exposed two steel drawers on the right and a stack of documents and envelopes on the left.

"Where's the file I want?"

"Bottom drawer."

"Go ahead, pull it out." Jeff pulled the sheik back a step or two and ordered, "Put it on that chair and open it."

The pilot duly took four steps toward the velvet covered seat and deposited the drawer, which resembled a safe-deposit box.

"Show me what's in there." Two manila envelopes came out. "Open one up and show me the contents. Don't come too close to me. I would hate to shoot you. I need you to fly me back."

The aviator took out some sheets and showed them to the CIA man.

"Read me what it says."

"It's in Arabic."

"Translate, damnit!" His patience was running out.

"One blond female, age twenty, sold to the Emir of Bagdad for the sum of two million dirham. And then some delivery instructions and..."

"The name of the girl? Is there a name?"

"No, just *one blonde female.*"

"You bunch of bastards. Put it back in that box and hand it to me. Do you have any of them here ? I mean right here in the house?"

"Just one." The sheik answered.

"Just one? Where is she?"

"Down stairs, with my wives."

"In the same harem, you little bastard?"

"Down stairs."

Furmann made up his mind. "Mr. Pilot, you go downstairs and get the girl. Have her take just a few personal items and a large bag. And bring something to drink. Cans of soda or something. Unopened cans. Don't say a word to anyone about me or what we're doing. If anything goes wrong, I first shoot your boss. Immediately! Then I shoot everyone else in sight, including you. You understand? I have two of these, look." He took the other Glock out of his waist band. "I can take twenty of you with me, to heaven or hell, wherever Allah wants you. Now get her and be back here in ten minutes. In the eleventh minute I shoot your boss in the back of his neck. You hear? You understand? Go!"

In eight minutes, the pilot was back in the company of a veiled woman in a loose burkah, who was obviously very pregnant.

"Come over here, take off that veil. What's your name?"

"Karen Van Doren."

"Karen, you're going home, but be careful. These people are vicious."

"I know. I've been here nearly two years. And who are you?"

"Just call me Jeff." To the two natives he said, "Okay, we're doing things in reverse. We're calmly walking out to the chopper. We three sit in the back and..."

"Sir, that's not possible, the balance, you know. We need one up front with me."

"Okay, you buckle in the little lady next to you and the shrimp and I will ride in the back. First though, load up that lady's bag with all the money from the safe."

"It has bottles in it."

"Okay, cover the bottles with money, we'll dig'em out later. Now quit stallin'."

The pilot started loading bundles of cash in the tote-bag and started talking again, "But sir, we don't have enough fuel for a return flight."

"That's alright, we'll find fuel somehow. Let's go."

The little procession left the giant room and walked back onto the landing pad. The pilot in front, followed by the young mother-to-be and the sheik with Jeff right on his heels, gun firmly pushed against the spine, metal box under his arm.

Like a good flight attendant, the aviator opened the door for the lady, buckled her in and opened the rear door for his other passengers.

"That's good. I'll take it from here. You just climb and start the engine. Just keep thinking about your boss's life when you do something stupid."

"But sir, the gas..."

"I'll worry about the gas. You just fly."

The starter engaged, the rotors began to turn slowly, then all of a sudden, something caught in the engine and the windmill on top started churning rapidly. The chopper lifted off gently and turned to the east as it gained altitude. The man up front was talking rapidly in Arabic and Jeff was hoping he was simply asking for clearances.

"Karen, can you understand what he's saying?" He had to shout in order to be heard.

"Mostly."

"Let me know if he says anything he shouldn't, like alerting the authorities."

"So far, he asked for clearance to Dubai."

"Good girl." He leaned over in order to see if there was a Marine vehicle in front of the palace, but there wasn't. "Dumb schmuck!" He muttered under his breath, thinking about the U.S. Ambassador.

Flying east at 90mph, they soon were again over a desolate stretch of desert. Furmann figured this was his chance. He would have loved to throw the old sex freak out of the chopper alive from 1,000 feet and hear him scream all the way down. Wrestling with the door against the wind and heaving the sheik at the same time, might be dangerous for his own health, so instead he shot him through his forehead. The soft *plop* of the silencer couldn't even be heard above the engine noise, so nobody noticed. After undoing his own buckle, he freed up the old man, strapped his left leg against the rear seat and pulled the body down on the floor. Pushing the door as hard as he could with his shoulder, he slowly got the head through the crevice and little by little shoved the whole body out. He latched the door again and sat down, exhausted.

The pilot heard the commotion, but couldn't see what was happening, because he couldn't really look behind him. Jeff leaned forward and lifted the man's headset and hollered, "How's the gas?"

"We can't make it to Dubai. There's an Air Force base not far from here, I think I can reach that."

"How far is Dubai?" Furmann had to shout to be heard.

"About forty miles."

"I'll tell you what. See that abandoned house up ahead? That ruin out there along the road? Land there and we'll get out and hitchhike and you can fly back. Land behind the building so they can't see us from the road."

The pilot was not entirely stupid. "But sir, the land may not be suitable..."

"Don't worry about it. Put it down. Retard the throttle. *NOW!*" For emphasis, he shoved his pistol against the aviator's temple. "I said *NOW!* If you want to live, do it now, very carefully."

The aircraft slowed down and descended slowly toward a sandy spot behind a dilapidated building. There was no sign of life, only a lot of dust created by the rotor blades. He nearly had to land on instruments, his visibility became nearly nil. The chopper landed a bit hard, but safely.

"Turn the key off." The pilot obeyed, the engine stopped and so did his breathing as a bullet exploded in the back of his neck.

Jeff waited for the dust to settle a little before he opened his door and walked forward to help Karen out of the craft.

"We'll have a short walk and then we'll get a lift into town. Are you up to it?" She nodded. "Okay, I'll carry the box and that bag. Just don't have a baby yet, okay?"

Golden Nuggets
XXXX
The Hitchhikers

It was a rough hike over the rocky, sandy surface, especially since the sun beat down on them at 110 degrees. They stopped and Jeff unloaded all the money from the bag in order to uncover the bottles from the bottom. It contained four plastic containers of *Fanta,* an orangey kinda drink. They had gotten warm, but they quenched their thirst and that was the important part. He restacked the money in the bottom and the drinks on top, it looked like they'd been grocery shopping.

The total distance to the road was only like the length of a football field, but for the pregnant Karen, it seemed like a mile. Looking over his shoulder, the chopper couldn't be seen from the highway and that was good. There would not be an early discovery unless it was from the air. To the best of Furmann's knowledge, the pilot didn't have time to hit an emergency transmittal button, so he felt confident they wouldn't be chased in the very near future.

There was a fair amount of traffic and it didn't take long before a panel truck stopped for the local looking couple, a man in a hooded gown and a veiled pregnant woman.

"Tell'im Dubai and ask for a map." Jeff whispered as he helped Karen up the steep steps into the cab. Jeff ended up in the window seat. The air conditioning was a blessing and Karen sighed with relief. The trucker asked for their destination and the young woman answered in rapid Arabic that they were headed for a business in Dubai and did he have a street map of the city? The G-man couldn't understand a word, but when Karen reached into the glove box for a chart, he whispered the street name in her ear, which was a good thing because the index was in their native language. In other words, the street names were all funny scribbles that he could never have figured out. Karen did, though and within a half hour they were caught in the typical madhouse city traffic that slowed them to a crawl. What should have taken them five minutes took them twenty, but they arrived at the consulate without incident.

"Tell'em to wait a minute after you get out."

"Okay!"

After a dozen *thank you's* and *salaam's*, Jeff helped her down, reached in the bag and handed the driver a handful of money. When he slammed the door, Karen commented, "You gave him at least ten thousand dollars."

"Good. He earned it. Come on." He helped her up the steps leading to the front door of the consulate and relative safety.

***

"How the hell did you get here?" Harry nearly fell over as the twosome appeared at his office.

"The question is, how do we get out?"

"Christ Almighty, you're alive and who is this?"

"Let me introduce you to one of *the golden nuggets*, Karen Van Doren and she's going home, which brings me back to my question, how do we get out?"

"Man, you won't believe your luck. In ten minutes, an ambulance will be at our front door to take Achmed..."

"How is he?"

"Don't interrupt. We're taking Achmed to the hospital, not to admit him, but a U.S. Navy helicopter will land on their pad and we'll shove Achmed aboard for a trip to a Navy destroyer in the

Gulf, where they have surgical facilities aboard and…"

"And how is he?"

"You insist on interrupting, don't you? You're going on the same trip and then you can ask him in person. Anyway, Karen, can we make you more comfortable? Sit down…"

"May I see the ladies room first?"

"Oh sure, oh sure, follow me."

After he showed the young woman where the facilities were, he rushed back to the front room and urged the secretary to join Karen and see if she could be of help.

Back in his office he faced Furmann, who had found a cold beer in the little fridge and was stretched out on the couch, savoring the cold *Budweiser.*

"What have you got? We only have a few minutes."

"I have the names of the buyers, not the names of the girls, but that's alright. We should storm everyone of those locations and free them…"

"Jeff, we're storming nothing. The Agency will follow up from here and you are…"

"You mean screwing up from here, right? They haven't accomplished a damn thing in four years and…"

"And you're going home. Orders from the boss…"

"From Taylor? He's not really my…"

"Orders from the President."

"Where the hell does he come in?"

"The Ambassador and the Whitehouse have been in touch…"

"At this early hour? What time is it out there? Five in the morning? Where did this message come from? The Whitehouse or the embassy?"

"Well…"

"I thought so. You tell the honorable asshole, as you called him, that he can go and…"

"Jeff, there's gonna be a lot of political upheaval about this…"

"I hope so, so the whole world can see what kind of sick bastards these people are and... Oh, here's our lady"

Karen walked back in the room, looking refreshed. She had taken her head piece off and for the first time, Furman had a look at her golden hair that cascaded down to her shoulders.

"Wow, baby! You look good. How do you feel?"

"I couldn't feel better. I still can't believe I'm out of there. What a nightmare."

Harry grabbed her hand. "It's about over. In a few minutes you'll be on a U.S. helicopter and you'll be on your way home. Where's home by the way?"

"Phoenix, Arizona."

"Is that where they captured you?"

"No. In Colorado, where I was ski-ing."

"Here's the ambulance. Sit, while I put your partner in and then I'll come and get you. So sit. It'll be just a few minutes."

"I'll help. I want to see Achmed."

"No you don't. You stay here. I don't want the driver to see you." He pushed Furmann back and closed the door.

"Then who the hell is gonna drive that thing?"

They got their answer within a few minutes. Harry walked back in. "Okay, we paid off the driver. He's gonna go shopping for a few hours. Come on, you two. You alright?" He asked Karen as he grabbed her arm to help her up and led her through the front door. Jeff followed with the metal drawer and the money laden bag. Both of them were loaded in the back of the ambulance, while Harry got behind the wheel and slowly moved into traffic.

Jeff finally had a chance to look at his Egyptian partner. He didn't look so well.

"Are you in pain, Buddy?"

"No, I'm just weak. I lost a lot of blood. It took forty minutes before Harry came up there and they didn't have the right band aids or anything else, but they stopped the bleeding. Then it took'em an hour to get here, but in another hour I'll be on a Navy ship and they'll take good care of me. I'm just so tired. How did you make out?"

"Look at her! I snatched her away from the little fart and she's going home too. What a beauty. Very pregnant though."

"What happened to the sheik?"

"The sheik? Oh, the sheik? He fell out of the plane and I don't think he could fly with his hands tied behind his back."

"You didn't!"

"Did what?" He grinned from ear to ear. "And I got the list of the buyers of blond cuties. We're gonna rescue a few." He looked up. "Why is he stopping?" Through the back window he could orientate himself somewhat. "I guess this is the hospital."

He was right. Harry opened the back door and said, "The chopper should be here within fifteen to twenty minutes, so keep still. The hospital thinks there's only one man back here. When he arrives, I'll help Achmed into the back seat, Karen follows and you jump in the front and he's off."

"Like hell! I've got work to do. This box with names and addresses needs to get out to our Air Force Base in Kuwait a.s.a.p. We'll have our guys assimilate the info immediately, so Langley can act on it. Karen also needs to get to Kuwait and then to Germany to our base hospital, before she can return home. She maybe quaranti..."

"Wait a minute!" Harry interrupted. "Who's giving the orders here?"

"I am, it's my case. Karen, you keep the bag with the money. That's yours."

"That's a lot of money, sir."

"That's good. You need to buy new baby clothes..."

"But I think, it's more than $100,000..."

"That's good. Consider it back pay. You need some clothes too... Here's the chopper."

"Let's go! " Harry called out. "Jeff, help me with Achmed."

The two of them half carried the wounded man to the plane and belted him in the back seat. Jeff closed that door and opened the co-pilot's seat and started to help Karen in the front seat.

"No, no!" Harry yelped. "You're going too.

"Like hell I will." Jeff shouted at the pilot, "This lady and this box need to get to Kuwait immediately if not sooner. Pass it on. Have a good flight."

"Jeff, get on. Your life isn't worth two cents over here."

"Move back. I gotta job to do!" as he sprinted toward the ambulance.

The helicopter left, blowing dust.

Golden Nuggets
XXXXI
Revenge

"Jeff, I can't go around protecting your ass all the time. You gotta understand, a consul has very little immunity and I have none."

"Did you report the bodies in the sheik's office yet?"

"No, and I may not be going to. So far there's nothing to link us Americans to anything that went on there and I hope to keep it that way. Did anybody see you up there? I mean, other than the dead people?"

"No, the women that may have gotten a glance at me were so busy putting on their veils and the tall geek excused them immediately, so I don't think that they saw anything but some Arab in a pretty gown. By the way, take me by Marchetti's place."

"Are you crazy? In this ambulance?"

"What could be safer? Picture the surprise on Vito's face when he sees you pulling up in his driveway."

"They may get this license plate and trace it back to me."

"Dead men don't read."

"You're incorrigible, you know?"

"I'll knock him off, get out of these clothes and fly away from Dubai International and you can return to your peaceful life."

"No, when they find out at the embassy what happened, the shit is gonna hit the fan."

"What happened? They don't have a clue."

"What happened to the sheik?"

"Oh, he went flying. He believed that Allah would give him wings."

"You're shittin' me. Did anybody in Abu Dhabu indentify you?"

"Nobody saw me. All they know is that the pilot went downstairs to get the little lady and that's all they know. When they find the sheik and the chopper, they may wonder what happened, but it shouldn't connect me or the American Embassy to the flight of the pregnant maiden."

"Nobody saw you?"

"If they got a glimpse of me, all they saw was some Arab in a wrinkled dress. That's all. You just deny you ever saw me. Just practice saying, 'Furmann who? Never heard of him.' It's that easy. I'll send you a postcard from Denver and tell how it all ended."

"Have you always been this crazy, Jeff."

"I've always been this normal. Do you remember Vito's house. It's gotta be somewhere here around the corner."

"I remember. What are you gonna do when you get there?"

"I ring the bell, ask for Mr. Marchetti. When he shows, I shoot him and leave."

"I still think you're crazy, but at least, you're imaginative. There's the house."

"Pull right up to the front door, keep the engine running. Do you know how to get to the airport from here?"

"Sure do!"

"Okay brother, here goes." Jeff climbed out of the passenger seat and walked up twelve steps to the ornate front door. An old fashioned copper, or gold, half moon acted as a knocker and Furmann knocked twice. Fortunately, a Caucasian looking man opened the door, because Jeff wouldn't have known what to say in Arabic.

"Meester Markeetee, pleeze."

"Won't you come in?" Jeff took one step inside and the lackey closed the door. "Come in the parlor, please."

"No, I churry. I wait heer."

"Just a moment."

After a minute and a half, the doorman reappeared with Marchetti, unmistakably. Furmann had his visage engrained in his mind. Apparently, they were not at all suspicious of a neat looking native.

Vito walked up to five feet from the G-man and asked politely. "How can we be of help?"

All of a sudden dropping his phony accent, Furmann yelled, "I'm helping you to go to hell." And with that pulled his Glock from the folds of his gown and fired three rounds point blank, turned to the lackey and fired two more. The gun clicked. Out of bullets. He smiled as he looked at the surprised look on Vito's face as he crumbled up, while the other man fell forward. Jeff reached behind his back, retrieved Achmed's gun and fired a few more rounds into both of them for good measure. "That's from my buddy. Say hello to the sheik."

He calmly turned around and walked out the door. The *plop-plop-plop* of the silencer was barely audible and nobody else appeared on the scene.

Back in the ambulance. "Can you drive by a creek or a river? I gotta dump these guns. Can you put on your flashers and go faster?"

"And attract attention to myself? No way." Harry was very precise in his actions.

"Suit yourself. I'm getting out of this garb. I'll be glad to look like an ordinary American boy again."

"You? Ordinary? You're kiddin'. How did it go in there?

"It's a very quiet place. Nobody knows there are a coupla bodies in the foyer."

"I must say. I've been with the CIA twenty years, but I've never seen a hard-balled character like you."

"Just think, Harry. The fact that they stole wholesome American girls for their own weird fantasies made me very, very mad and when I'm mad, I think clearly, that's all."

"Sure."

Jeff worked himself out of his oriental clothes and Harry maneuvered them onto an expressway, that showed signs in Arabic and English, *Dubai International.*

"I just hope they serve beer on these flights or are they all Muslim controlled?"

"It depends, if they're flying from one Muslim City to another, they don't serve liquor, but if they fly, like say, from here to Athens, then you can get a cold beer."

"In other words, I'm screwed."

"Why? Where are you going?"

"Kuwait of course. I'm catching up to that ledger with names and addresses of those kinky bastards and I plan to plug me a few."

"Jeff, I told you, you have to report back to Langley, post haste. As fast as you can get there."

"I never saw you. I never heard those orders, besides I wanna hear that from the President himself."

"Sure."

"Just forget you saw me today. When I get back, I'm gonna put some heat on that sissy Ambassador's ass. His job is to work for America and Americans, not some shyster pervert Arabian bastard. You just drop me off and I'll be alright. How do I get rid of these guns? I didn't see any bridges."

"I'll dump them. Don't worry about them."

"Remember, they have your and my prints on them and Achmed's too. You better dump'em deep. What airline should I fly?"

"I don't know. Pick a European or American line, you'll feel more at home."

"And they may have beer."

"True, they may have beer. Go to the information desk and ask who flies to Kuwait, buy your ticket and a good murder mystery. You oughta enjoy that." He laughed at his own joke. "Here you are. Jeff, it's been an unusual pleasure!" He reached over and shook his hand.

"Same here, Harry. I'll let them know, I couldn't have done it without you." He was gone.

"What's the earliest I can get into Kuwait? Four hours? Can't do that. My girl may run off with another man. What other choices do I have?"

"If you hurry, Air France is leaving for Bagdad in twenty minutes."

"Bagdad? They fly commercial liners into Bagdad? I didn't know that. Where do I go?"

Jeffrey Morgano had no problem buying a ticket on his credit card and he passed through security without a problem. In spite of his cocky attitude, he was starting to get nervous. He had a tendency to look over every security officer and everyone who could be under cover. He started to get hold of himself. "Harry said, buy a book. Good idea." He talked to himself as he walked to the kiosk, but just then his flight was announced and he turned back to the gate.

Mr. Jeffrey Furmann, Morgano didn't relax until the wheels came up on the Airbus and the Persian Gulf appeared beneath them. From his window seat he watched the magnificent development of *Palm Jumeirah,* five fingers sticking out from the coast, more than a mile long . Each finger was a straight road, with big houses on each side, all with their own private beach and most of them with swimming pools. Some of them were actual palaces and the whole project must have cost billions of dollars.

"That's what my gas bought for them." Jeff told his neighbor. "What do you figure this paradise cost?"

"Think trillions, brother." Was the answer.

"It's unbelievable how much these clowns must be making." The man next to him just nodded.

As they flew away from all that glamour, Furmann tried to spot an American destroyer off the coast where the copter might have landed or a carrier, from which Karen could be flown to Kuwait after being transferred. He could just picture a very pregnant young woman being hauled from one ship to the other in a swinging basket. Oh boy! Then he realized, they would transfer her by helicopter from one ship to the other. That sounded better.

The hostess asked him in Arabic what he wanted to drink and

it flattered him, because he felt his mustache and suntan really worked for him.

"How about a beer?" He answered in English.

"Heineken alright?"

"Yeah Ma'am, that'll be perfect." He was asleep within five minutes.

Golden Nuggets
XXXXII
The Ancient City, Bagdad

Letting down into the airspace of the historical city of Bagdad was a disappointment. Much of the ancient splendor had been replaced by modern buildings and an obvious amount of war damage was still relevant. Agent Furmann was grateful that nobody fired *SAM* missiles at them on the way in and the landing was as smooth as it would have been on any other runway in the world.

The terminal was practically undamaged and if it weren't for the fact that a lot of armed military personnel were obvious everywhere, Bagdad International would have seemed as normal as JFK or LaGuardia.

A friendly Marine sergeant arranged for a ride to the military compound after Jeff had identified himself as a CIA agent. That hadn't been too easy, because his passport, his driver's license and credit cards all carried the name Jeffrey Montano. A call to headquarters, which resulted in a call to Langley and that in turn lead to the proper identification of Agent Jeff Furmann.

He had a tough time convincing anybody of the importance of getting him to Kuwait in a hurry. A very patient Air Force major made call after call and Jeff started to boil.

"Major, I can not reveal the importance of my mission so call the director of the FBI or the CIA and they'll personally clear me."

"Sir, they're all in bed at this hour...."

"Call the Whitehouse, someone is bound to be awake."

"Stand by, sir." He dialed another number. After a minute, he handed Furmann the phone, "Colonel Davis, Adjutant to General McCormick. Talk to him."

"Colonel, put me through to the general please. It's of the utmost importance, but we can't get anybody on the line in Washington or Langley..."

"Mr. Furmann, hang on a minute. Why do you have to be in Kuwait in such a hurry?"

"Two people, a wounded agent and a former hostage are being flown in there off a carrier and they're carrying classified documents that I, in turn, have to transmit to the U.S. I have to be there when they arrive."

"Stand by." Jeff looked at the dead instrument and said to himself, "If I had memorized the name and the location of that Emir here in Bagdad, I could make myself useful, chasing another *golden nugget* and maybe killing a few more...." The voice on the other end of the line interrupted his thoughts.

"Mr. Furmann, arrangements are being made to fly you over. Let me speak to the major..." Jeff handed over the phone.

"Yes, sir! Okay sir!" Was all the airman said and hung up.

"An F-18 from the Marine Corps is being cranked up and you'll be on your way in minutes."

"An F-18 no less?"

"Yes, sir."

"Well, Semper Fi."

While in Air Force Intelligence, Jeff had been in many a plane, but never in anything as fast and modern as an F-18 Hornet.

"Don't you have any luggage, sir?" The major walked out onto the tarmac with the G-man.

"No, I left my guns in Dubai."

The sleek Marine jet taxied to the tower and turned around. A pickup raced over and attached a ladder to the cockpit as soon as the canopy raised to its maximum extend.

"Sir, do you know how to handle a parachute?" The Marine corporal asked as he helped the civilian into the backseat.

"Yep, although I never used it yet."

"Today won't be the first time either, sir. Have fun."

"Thanks." His helmet was plugged in and his mask adjusted. The young mechanic verified that the oxygen indicator was blinking and removed the ladder.

"How do you read, sir?" A female voice sounded in his earphones.

He pushed the radio button on the stick. "Read you loud and clear."

"Tighten your straps. We're leaving."

When the afterburners kicked in, Jeff was pressed hard against his backrest and when the lady pilot pulled the stick back, he felt crunched against his dingy, which also functioned as his seat cushion. The airfield disappeared so fast beneath him that he had to swallow and pop his ears as they climbed at 10,000 feet per minute.

After all the chitchat with ground control and the tower had subsided, he pressed the intercom button and asked, "Ma'am, which airport are we flying into?"

"Sir, we have no choice. I've been cleared into *Ali Al Salem Air Base,* that's where we're going."

"Will the plane off the carrier land there also?"

"Sir, I have no knowledge of that. I just drop you off and return." She hesitated. "But sir, all U.S. military activity is conducted at that base, so I don't see why a Navy plane coming off a carrier would land anywhere else."

"Okay. Thanks."

At 40,000 feet, the view of the region was just plain dismal. The whole area consisted of desert and rocks, as far as Furmann was concerned with just a long streak of green right down the middle. He pushed the button again, "Who the hell wants to live here?"

The Marine pilot chuckled, "Not me, sir. That's for sure."

Jeff relaxed as he was sucking 100% oxygen and thought back on the days when he had helped establish the various bases in Kuwait, when the air was still soggy with smoke from the oil well fires. *Al Mubarak* and *Ahmed Al Jaber* were a couple of other airfields with which he was familiar. He had spent many a night sleeping in a tent without heat while during the day, he interrogated Iraqi prisoners. He shuddered involuntarily when he thought about the mentality of the POW's. As far as he was concerned, most of them were cowards who grew huge mustaches to look more heroic. Their mentality toward women stood out foremost in his mind and it didn't surprise him that they traded in white females as if they were cattle. "Bunch of animals." He thought.

Reflecting on his trip from Bagdad, he had to be grateful that he didn't have the address of the local Emir with the *golden nugget,* because he would have had a hell of a time going after him. He had no guns, no local money, no connections, no maps, no knowledge of the layout, nothing at all. No, he was better off being in an F-18 on his way to meet his partner and the documents.

Jeff took for granted, that once on the ground, he would thoroughly familiarize himself with all the locations where the girls were being held and that he would go after their captors with a vengeance. Of course, he would see to it that Karen and Achmed were properly transported back to the U.S. and then he'd go on his rampage, making like a modern day Robin Hood.

He couldn't have been more wrong.

The Hornet sped across the Middle Eastern country, following the river Tigress and descended into Kuwait airspace. The country was so small, Furmann could see both borders at the same time. Iran on one side, Saudi on the other. What a hotspot! Had been that way through the ages. He shook his head and wondered if there would ever be peace throughout that region. Before long, his attention was drawn to a fast approaching runway and the way the lady pilot handled her machine. It all seemed so smooth and effortless while the speed bled down from 400 knots to two hundred, then to one fifty and screeeeech, they were on the runway with the nose way up in the air. Slowly, the front of the plane came down and another screech, a shorter one, told him all three wheels were safely on the ground.

The air base bustled with activity. C-17's, C-5's, C-130's either taxied back and forth or were clustered together in the far reaches of the field. F-15's and F-16's took off in pairs and many others were ramped out in front of the distant hangars. Jeff couldn't twist his head around fast enough to absorb all that hustle and bustle, but before he realized it, they came to a stop in front of a building, that blazed the word 'OPERATIONS' across its façade.

"Here's where you get off. I have to check in a moment, so you'll be on your own. Sorry I couldn't serve tea and crumpets, but I was kinda busy up there."

"Thanks for the ride." The switches had been turned off and she probably did not hear that last communication.

Jeff unbuckled and with the help of a crew chief undid his parachute and worked his way down the ladder.

"Hello, young warrior!" A familiar voice greeted him.

"What the hell?" He turned and exclaimed in total surprise, "Mr. Jacobi! Sol! What the hell are you doing here?"

"Rolling out the red carpet. What else?"

"How the hell did you know I would be coming in on that incredible speed monster?"

"I'm with the CIA, remember? We're supposed to know everything, right?"

"Sure! I've noticed. Is Achmed here yet?" Jeff was eager to learn how his partner was doing.

"Come with me. I have a car waiting on the other side of this building. I'll clue you in."

Golden Nuggets
XXXXIII
Mission accomplished?

The CIA complex was surprisingly big and modern. Things had changed an awful lot since Jeff was last here after the first Gulf War. Big satellite disks were in the front yard of the complex and on the roof. Air-conditioning hummed softly and the temperature was more than comfortable.

"Better than in my day." Jeff commented.

"You been here before?" Sol Jacobi was surprised.

"Yep. First Gulf War."

"What were you doing here? Army?"

"Nope, Air Force Intelligence."

"I didn't know that."

"How do you think we won that war in a hundred hours? All because of superior intelligence by the Air Force."

"I'm sure that did it. And you personally handled that, right?" Agent Jacobi was having fun.

"Of course, of course!"

They settled down in a comfortable office with half a dozen TV and computer screens.

"There's tea, coffee, sodas and water at the wet-bar in the corner. Help yourself and make yourself at ease." Sol seemed at home.

"Thanks." Jeff found a bottle of cold water and settled in at the far end of the oval table that dominated the room. "Now you're gonna tell me how Achmed is doing?"

"You're right, Jeff. That's what I'm gonna do." The senior agent set down next to the anxious young CBI agent.

"Achmed is still on the cruiser in the Gulf…"

"Why?"

"Can you wait a second?" Jacobi didn't like to be interrupted. "I'll tell you why. The doctors on the ship performed surgery and stitched him back together and he's doing fine. They decided that there was no hurry to fly him here…"

"Who decided that?"

"Langley and the doctors advised them that it was better to keep him in observation for a few days, just in case of complications."

"How bad were his wounds?" Jeff wasn't entirely happy with the answers he got.

"Mostly flesh wounds. Bullet in and out, but they always worry about infections…"

"That's why I wanted him out of there on the double, because, you know, they always pick up infections in the hospitals and…"

"Whatever you say, Jeff, Achmed is on the cruiser for a few more days and nothing is gonna change that."

"Damn doctors. Anyway, how about Karen?"

"Who?"

"Karen Van Doren, the *golden nugget* that I liberated, the pregnant blond…"

"Oh. I didn't know her name. She's on her way from a carrier. She was coptered from the cruiser to the carrier and she's in the air now, as we speak. She should be here momentarily. She'll come directly here and doctors are standing by to examine her…"

"She's young and she's healthy. She'll be okay and we should be able to ship her home just about immediately…"

"Not so fast, Furmann. She will be quarantined in Rahmstein, in the Army hospital and the good news is…'

"Why? She's fine…"

"Would you quit interrupting me? As I was saying, her folks will be notified and they'll be flown into Germany to be with her, but nobody enters the U.S. immediately after captivity in any of these barbaric lands and she is no exception."

"Okay, okay. How about the documents?"

"She has those with her."

"Oh, good! Than we can start planning our liberation plan and get those girls away from those damn perverts..."

"That's another thing, Jeff. You won't be liberating anybody...."

"I what? You what? This is my operation and..."

"Wrong pal! This is a CIA operation and the agency is gonna handle it..."

"The CIA had it for a dozen years and accomplished nothing. I had it for two weeks and sprung one and got all the inside scoop as to the location of the others. What do you want to do? Get all the other ones impregnated, tortured or even killed? I..."

"I know how you feel, but orders have come down from..."

"I don't give a shit about orders. I wanna save those girls from the perverts that bought them..."

"Jeff! Jeff! Let's not get excited! Let's see what the girl brings in and analyze it. I'm calling the tower to see what her ETA is. Excuse me a minute." Jacobi got up and walked over to a corner desk and picked up a phone.

"She'll be here in twenty minutes. Are you hungry? Let's go to the cafeteria and grab a fast hamburger or something. Let's go." Sol didn't wait for any reaction and started walking to the door. Jeff couldn't do anything but follow.

After a good cheese burger and a coke, the twosome drove to the operations building and walked through the complex to the flight line.

Within minutes, a twin-engine prop plane appeared in the pattern and prepared for landing. An Air Force ambulance drove up and medics quickly jumped out and opened the rear doors. It dawned on Jeff that Karen might be hustled out of there immediately and he wanted to make sure he had a chance to talk to her, so he walked over to the emergency vehicle.

“”You can't walk out there!” Sol screamed, but Furmann kept right on walking.

“Where are you taking her?” The G-man asked the nurse who had captain's bars on her lapel.

“Base hospital! Who are you?” She wasn't bashful.

“I'm the guy that liberated her and...”

“Liberated?” She sounded incredulous.

“Yes. She was held captive for years and I need to talk to her and...”

“Follow us to the hospital. Who is she and how is she?”

“She's okay, but very pregnant. She also has some papers for me and I need those immediately.”

“Shouldn't be a problem, sir. Here she comes.”

Karen appeared in the doorway of the twin-engine craft and with the help of an attendant made it slowly down the steps.

“Oh, I thought she would come down on a stretcher!” The nurse exclaimed.

“No, she's fine.” Jeff started to walk toward her, but was stopped briskly by a rifle toting airman. “No farther, please.”

“But I...”

“Stay right here!” He raised his rifle.

“Good God, do I look like a terrorist?” Jeff was annoyed.

“Yes, you do.” The nurse chuckled as Karen reached the ambulance. His tan face and black mustache made him look very Arabic.

“Hello Karen. How was the trip?” He smiled as he grabbed both her hands.

“I wouldn't mind if I didn't see another aircraft for a year.” Her smile was dazzling.

The nurse interrupted, “Let me help you up here.” She lifted the young woman under her arm and a male nurse helped from the other side and within seconds Karen was seated in the vehicle.

“I'll come see you in the hospital. Where are the papers?” Jeff was anxious, but the former hostage obviously didn't have them.

"The pilot does. There he comes. I have the bag though. I'll see you later." The doors were being closed after the nurses climbed aboard.

The soldier with the rifle kept Jeff from approaching the young man in the flight suit and he had to wait patiently for the pilot to reach them.

"Agent Jacobi?" He asked Jeff.

"Negative, I'm agent Furmann, may I please have that package?"

"No sir. Not unless you're Jacobi."

"Good grief. That's Jacobi." He pointed to the man behind him. "Sol, he wants you to have it."

"That's fine. Thank you Lieutenant." He returned the man's salute and accepted the tightly wrapped documents.

"How did he know your name?" Jeff wanted to know.

"Langley instructed them to hand those over to me, because no one was sure when you would appear."

"Bunch of pessimists! Of course I would be here."

"We didn't know until an hour ago if you were dead or alive. Not 'til you contacted that general in Bagdad."

"Well, surprise! Surprise! I'm alive and well. What do we do first? Go to the hospital or go over these papers first?"

"Papers first."

"Halleluiah."

Golden Nuggets
XXXXIV
O O 7 ?

"How are you holding up, Jeff? Do you need some rest or can you go on for a few more hours?" Jacobi and Furmann were on the way back to the CIA building.

"I can go on for hours, but what are we gonna do first? I really wanna dig into these files and see where the young girls are hidden and how widespread this is. That okay by you?"

"Fine by me. We'll go through them and make up some sort of a synopsis that we can fax to headquarters and then discuss it on the phone with the powers that be."

"Okay. I'm dying to find out more details. Here we go." They exited the car and rode the elevator to the fourth floor of a brand spanking new building.

"Nice digs." Jeff commented.

"It's amazing what a few oil dollars can do for you." Sol snickered as they made themselves comfortable around a conference table.

"How is the bundle organized?" Furmann couldn't wait.

"Let's see. Let's put them in stacks of countries first and log them. Grab that yellow pad and then we'll break them down by cities." Jacoby unwrapped the plastic covering and produced a yellow folder. "The Navy made it waterproof apparently."

"Good boys, good boys. Hand me the first one. *Russia?"* He

was flabbergasted. "The Russians even got into this lugubrious business?"

"Next... Kuwait." The folder ended up next to the Russian one.

"Iran... Emirates... Iraq... Oman... Saudi... nine countries total!" The stacks added up to eight. Duplicates were added and the total became twenty four, with Saudi in the lead with four.

"Read me the names of the cities, slowly, so I can copy them correctly"

They worked diligently and worked up a summary until Sol announced, "It's eight thirty in the morning in D. C., so let's see who's in."

It took just a few minutes to get a satellite connection on their secure phone and very soon there was the familiar voice of Jed Taylor, the big boss, head of the CIA.

"How are you Furmann?"

"Just a moment, sir. This is Jacobi. Here's Agent Furmann."

"Furmann, you rascal. You've been busy I hear. Where are you now?"

"Ali Al Salem..."

"Good! How's the girl?"

"She seemed well. She's in the base hospital right now, but mainly for observation and..."

"Good. She'll be able to travel, right?"

"Looks that way..."

"Did you get the records with the address of the other victims?"

"We're ready to fax them to you right now..." Taylor kept interrupting.

"Good, do that. How many total?"

"Twenty four sir, I should say, twenty three to go. One's here obviously..."

"Good, fax it and we'll get right on it..."

"Mr. Taylor, I can get right on it, right here. One of them is right here in Kuwait, I can have her liberated within hours..."

"Who do you think you are? Double-O-Seven? " The director

sounded serious. "No, No! You travel home and from here on in our diplomats take over..."

"Diplomats? Those asses? You think they'll accomplish anything? No, they'll get snowed and the girls will continue to suffer! No, sir! I'm going after them..."

"You will do no such thing. You did all you could do and now you're coming home. You'll accompany the girl.... whatshername...? to Rahmstein and then you report back to Langley on the double."

"You gotta be kiddin'..."

"No, no.! Word will get around and the girls will be hidden or worse..., done away with. No, from here on in the State Department will take action..."

"The State Department? They'll screw up everything and it will cost some of the girls their lives..." Jeff was getting furious.

"It is out of your hands..."

"Nobody even knows that I spirited this girl Karen away from the sheik in Abu Dhabi and his body won't be found for weeks or maybe never. He's being devoured by hyenas as we speak....'

"You listen to me..." Mr. Taylor started to shout.

"No you listen to me. Even if they find his corpse, there's no way they'll connect that to the CIA and girl smuggling. We have plenty of time to get the others out before anyone gets wise..."

"The answer is *NO!* You're job is done and you did well, but..."

"Drop dead!" Furmann slammed down the phone. He turned to Jacobi, "I'm going after the chick in Kuwait right now. I can have her here within the hour..."

"Jeff! JEFF! You're not doing any such thing. You're of more value working on the rescue of ALL of them, not just one. You can't infiltrate countries like Russia or Saudi. They'll be on your tail in no time and they'll kill off the evidence. They'll destroy the girls. Stay here where you're most valuable..." The phone rang, disturbing his lecture. "Jacobi,... yes sir... yes... sir... I'm doing that right now... yes... right now... He's right here.... No problem, sir... Yes, sir!... No problem... Will do, sir..."

Sol turned to Furmann, “Let’s get these sheets faxed out. I think your notes are legible although yellow paper is not the best way to transmit something by fax, but you’ll be carrying the originals anyway. Let’s do it and then we go look up Karen.”

While working and driving, Jacobi slowly convinced Jeff that he would be of more value to the operation from a supervisory and advisory standpoint, because the operation was too massive for one man to execute. He had a calming effect on the Colorado G-man.

“He called me Double-O-Seven. I may adopt that nickname. It sounded good. I hope you give me a little more respect from here on in.” He had to laugh at his own joke. It broke the ice. Jeff started to relax and when they came face to face with Miss Van Doren, he melted some more. She was indeed a beauty and the nurses had done a good job, sprucing her up. She felt ready to travel and the baby was not due for another three weeks, so she was okay.

Her face lit up when she heard that her folks would be notified and flown into Germany, but she wasn’t happy with the thought that she might have to remain there for at least a month before returning to the U.S.

“The military facilities are really great in Europe and they’ll take good care of you. They’ll have luxury quarters for your folks and the food is outstanding.” Jeff wanted to add, “and the beer is great.” But he decided to skip that part. “Do you know yet if you’re expecting a boy or a girl?”

She smiled broadly, “It’s a boy alright. The sheik was all excited, but what he doesn’t know is that it’s probably not his kid.”

“It isnt’?”

“No, it could be from any one of his sons…”

“Really? How many sons?”

“At least six.”

“Six? You gotta be kiddin’ me.”

“No, they all came over regularly to try out the buxom blond.”

“Without the knowledge of the father, the sheik?”

"Oh, yeah. If he had found out, he would've killed me."

"Killed you? Not the sons?" Jeff was dumbfounded.

"Oh no! He may have scolded them some, but he would have killed me. That's the way they reason. They rape a girl and then she is stoned for committing a sin. That's the way it goes, so I let the old man believe that it's his baby."

"Is that unbelievable Sol? Can you fathom that? And five or six of his sons? How old were they?"

"The youngest was about fourteen and the oldest one about fifty." Karen didn't even blush as she spoke.

"Fourteen?"

"Yeah, one of his older brothers first taught him. He was clumsy at first, but he was gentle. I didn't mind him."

"Jeez! How many kids does he have? The sheik I mean."

"Who knows? He had four wives at one given time, but had divorced a few, one died and right now he has four again and a couple of concubines like myself. So he probably has twenty-five or thirty kids."

"Had, you mean. He doesn't have anything anymore. He's deader than a doornail."

"Doesn't he have some seventy-two virgins up in Heaven?"

"No, that's a misunderstanding. They get greeted by seventy-two Virginians like George Washington, Thomas Jefferson et cetera and they clobber the hell out of'em." He chuckled at the dumb look on Karen's face.

"Anyhow, Miss Van Doren," Jacobi cut in. "We'll be picking you up in the morning when we have a flight scheduled, so meanwhile rest, girl, rest."

"What am I going to do with all that money?" She looked puzzled.

"What money?" Sol wanted to know.

"Never mind." Jeff interrupted. "You just hold on to that okay? That's yours. Consider it payment due for services rendered. Go sleep." He kissed her on the forehead and turned away.

"What money?" Sol asked when they walked out the door.

"A little gift from the sheik. I have no local money, so you're buying the drinks tonight, right?"

"What drinks? Where?"

Golden Nuggets
XXXXV
From Tigris to Rhine and Potomac

Early morning in the desert is usually the best time of the day before the cold air turns to intense heat. The cool temperature was an open invitation for Jeff to go jogging, although he didn't have the right garments for it. Luckily, the Base Exchange was open at seven and with the American dollars that Sol had advanced him, he bought the minimum; shorts, socks and sneakers. Later he would have to come back and obtain some traveling clothes that would get him across the ocean and a stopover in Germany.

Running around the parked aircraft and all the maintenance activity reminded him of his earlier career in the Air Force, where this type of activity was a daily routine for him.

He had slept very fitfully, once he resigned himself to the fact that it was inevitable for him to return to the U.S. and that he would not personally chase any other *golden nuggets*. Nine hours of sound sleep was just what he needed and he felt like he could take on the whole world. He breathed deeply and remembered the last time he had jogged around the field while the oil wells were burning out of control, set aflame by that Iraqi maniac, Saddam Hussein.

His thoughts were interrupted by a pickup with an amber flashing light on top that came racing after him and stopped right in front of the early jogger. An airman jumped out and asked,

"Mr. Furmann, Morgano?"

"Yes to both of those."

"Please come with me." They climbed aboard.

"How did you find me?" Jeff was surprised.

"The receipt on your bed in the B.O.Q.'s, sir."

"Receipt?"

"Yes sir. A receipt from the BX for shorts and sneakers, telling us you'd gone jogging. Next time you should take your money and I.D.'s with you. We don't have very reliable help on this base."

"Whadayaknow? Why the hurry?" Furmann was catching his breath.

"You have a breakfast meeting and a take-off at o-nine-forty." The airman was well briefed apparently.

"Oh, great. Is the girl scheduled on the same flight?"

"Girl? I have no knowledge of any girls, sir. I've been instructed to get you and that's it. I brought toothpaste and razors, and I'll run to the BX for anything else you might need while you shower."

"Beautiful. I need a clean shirt and underwear, that's all. I'll give you the money."

Breakfast was with Sol Jacobi, who presented him with a brand spanking new briefcase.

"The originals are all in there. We have copied everything and faxed it ahead. Here's the code to the locks on the case. Memorize and destroy. The contents are again waterproofed and sealed. What will probably happen is that you drop off Karen in Germany and that you'll immediately board a military jet or an airliner for Dover or D.C. . They wanna go over all the details with you in a hurry. By the way, the luggage you had in Dubai has been shipped to Langley, so you'll have some clothes to wear when you get there."

"They want me to wear an Arabian tunic?"

"Well, whatever you brought with you from Oman. Your stuff from the Bahamas will also be waiting for you." Jacobi seemed to be well informed.

"Great. Do you know something Sol?"

"What?"

"Now that I won't be chasing any more perverts, I've lost my ambition for the whole deal and I wanna go back to Colorado."

"Come on, Jeff. You're still an integral part of the operation and..."

"And I'll end up doing what most of you guys do all the time; paperwork! Working in an office. That's not my cup of tea. I..."

"Jeff, you'll find yourself planning and overseeing the operations to free the girls..."

"Without blowing some S.O.B.'s brains out. What will happen Sol, they may free most of the girls through diplomatic negotiations, but the perverts that bought them and raped them will go unpunished and will go looking for another source of young females. It makes me wanna puke."

"I know how you feel... excuse me..." Jacobi addressed a young female first lieutenant who approached their table. "Yes Ma'am?"

"Miss Van Doren is out front and would Mr. Furmann please join us? We're boarding in ten."

"Well, Jeff, this is kinda the end of the line. I don't know when I'll be working with you again, if ever, but it has been an experience."

"A good experience, I hope?"

"An inspiration, to say the least."

"Well Sol, I know men don't hug in the CIA, I'm sure, so I'll just shake your hand..."

"Let's hug."

"Thanks for all your help. Stay safe."

The C-17 *Globemaster* revved up its powerful engines shortly after Karen, the Air Force nurse, Dotty and Jeff were settled in. The remaining passengers on the plane were mostly soldiers in various stages of discomfort. Twenty or so were on stretchers and the rest were buckled in along the walls of the flying monster. This was the biggest airplane that Jeff had ever been on and he regretted that it didn't have any window seats. He would have loved to see what they were overflying.

His chance came later. A young airman came around, asking what they would like to drink and Jeff stopped him and asked, "Can you tell the pilot, that I'm former Air Force, now with the CIA and that I'd like to come up front."

"Do you have an I.D. I can show him?"

"Sure." The only identification that seemed valid was a passport in the name of Jeffrey Morgano, but the airman gladly took it.

After ten minutes he returned the document and said, "Captain Morgan will gladly welcome you up front when we're out of Iraqi airspace. We should be over Turkey in another fifteen. I'll come get you sir."

The young G-man was so flabbergasted that he forgot to thank the soldier.

"Karen, Dotty, I'm going up front in a while. Keep a close eye on this briefcase, will ya? I don't wanna carry that up there. Okay?"

"Sure thing. We'll sit on it." The young nurse had a great sense of humor.

The view from thirty-eight thousand feet was spectacular. The brown of the Turkish landscape gave way to the blue of the Mediterranean and before long the Greek isles loaned their sparkle to the scenery. From the jump seat in the cockpit, Jeff had a panoramic view, a thousand times better than looking through a little window of a passenger jet.

They chatted amiably about his time on the Force and his present duties.

"So you're part of the team that's our precious cargo?" The pilot asked.

"Who me? And the girl?"

"I guess so…"

"I think those wounded soldiers are pretty precious too." Jeff was very sincere.

"True. But we got word 'expedite!' Get you to Rahmstein fast."

"Really? I haven't felt that important in my life." It got a chuckle out of both the men at the controls.

Greece disappeared from under the wings and the Adriatic loomed on the horizon. The snow clad mountains of Switzerland and northern Italy on the far horizon came into view and before long, the pilot spoke, "Sir, food is being served and by the time you finish, we'll be letting down into German airspace, but it has been a pleasure having you up here. We hope you have a nice continuation of your trip."

"Thank you guys. Thank you." He gave a hand salute and retreated to his original seat.

"Wow! That was fantastic!" He was about to belabor that point when it dawned on him that Karen didn't look well. "Karen, are you okay?" He grabbed her hand.

"Just a little airsick. Over land it got a little bumpy, but she's fine." Dotty seemed to have the situation well in hand.

"No early labor pains?" Jeff's frown indicated that he was serious.

"No, not for another three weeks, I hope." The blonde mother to be, smiled in spite of her misery.

"We'll be on the ground soon. Less than an hour, I think." He squeezed her hand and she squeezed back, gratefully.

Indeed, within the hour, the giant machine started its slow descent and unfortunately, the turbulence increased, so Karen had to use another barf bag.

Mercifully, the C-17 finally rolled to a stop and the passengers were guided out of the huge barn door under the tail section. It drizzled outside and before Furmann had a chance to say goodbye to the girls, a man in tan raincoat, holding an umbrella, worked his way through the throng and said, "Agent Furmann, come with me please." He grabbed Jeff by the arm and passed by a half dozen injured soldiers into the rain and across the tarmac to a waiting limousine.

"Furmann, I'm Special Agent Jack Forestall and you and I are flying to D.C. together. We're catching a *Lufthansa* flight out of Frankfort and a small plane will get us into Langley."

They settled back in the cushions of the backseat and Forestall continued, "I'm sorry, I didn't even ask you if you needed a potty break, but we'll be in the terminal in twenty minutes. Just in case."

He actually smiled. Like Jacobi, Jack was a middle-aged man, but with full head of dark hair and a neatly trimmed mustache.

Jeff sighed, "Whatever! I don't seem to make my own decisions anymore, but that's alright. I also don't have to think much and that's relaxing."

Golden Nuggets
XXXXVI
The firing squad?

In the first class cabin of the *747,* they enjoyed considerable privacy and Jack Forestall took the initiative.

"Jeff, we have pitifully little information of what you did in the Emirates or where. All we have is the account that Harry wired us from Dubai, but he was not present at your rescue of the girl and neither was he in on the flight back and forth on the sheik's helicopter. So as we fly along, tell me your story in detail on what transpired. I'll record it as we go and we'll transcribe when we arrive at headquarters."

"And then you can nail me for any transgressions I've committed, right?"

The older CIA agent chuckled, "Transgressions? You? I can't imagine such a thing." He produced a little gadget from his side pocket. "Let me rewind this thing and then it will record up to seven hours. How long is your story?"

"Ten minutes, maybe." Now it was time for Furmann to grin.

"Oh come off it. Here we go. Start with your arrival in the Bahamas."

"You know all that! Taylor was there himself."

"We need details as to how you traced Marchetti, especially since there was no FAA record of his plane landing in those islands."

"Okay, okay, but wait till I get another cold beer."

Jeff talked endlessly, interrupted only by food or drink services, during which Forestall shut off the equipment. Every so often, Jack would ask him to clarify or repeat a statement, but generally he listened patiently. Up to a point, like, "You shot the sheik and threw him from his own helicopter?"

"Yeah, I would have liked to throw him overboard alive and heard him screaming all the way down, but I couldn't afford to unbuckle myself, then unbuckle him and try to wrestle with the door against the wind while trying to wrangle the old man out of the chopper; he might have grabbed on to me and we both might have gone overboard. I couldn't take that chance. So I killed him first and that made things a lot easier."

"If you say so. Where were you at this point?"

"Over desolate desert. They may not have found him yet."

"Good grief. Go on."

The story continued and Jack didn't interrupt again until they came to the scene at Marchetti's house.

"The doorman, or whoever he was, just walked back to get Vito? He didn't question who you were and what you wanted?"

"You forget that I was dressed like a local and looked like one. Dark skin, mustache, everything." He grinned and added, "And don't forget I put on a beautiful local accent, 'Meester Marketti, pleeze'." He laughed at his own performance.

"It must have been very convincing, 'cause Marchetti just walked up to you and what did you say?"

"I'm not sure I said anything. I had Achmed's pistol and mine and I just let'em have it."

"Them?"

"Yeah. I killed both of them for good measure. The other guy was probably as guilty as Vito, otherwise, why would he have been there?"

"Interesting point, Jeff. Interesting point."

They talked and listened until they had to prep for letdown into Dulles International, where a two-engine propeller plane was already standing by at the far end of the field. A uniformed security man hustled both of them out of the plane, through the backdoor of the building onto the tarmac where a sedan with a yellow blinking light was waiting for them. It took only minutes to cut across the airport and board the smaller plane and off they were to Langley. They had flown for ten hours, but gained six hours since Frankfurt so some folks were still at the office.

Thank God, Taylor wasn't, so Jeff was excused to find some food and a bed with the assurance he wouldn't be woken till seven in the morning.

A sixteen ounce prime-rib and some red wine did wonders for his stomach and a long phone conversation with his wife and son was equally soothing for his mind.

He slept like a baby.

At eight, after coffee and eggs, he fingered through a *True Crime* magazine in the penthouse waiting room, until he was called into the director's office.

The chief didn't get up, but waived at Jeff, "Come in, sit." He pointed to a seat next to his desk, while Jack sat on the other side.

"I haven't had time to read your transcript yet, but Agent Forestall briefed me and it seems that you did one hell of a job. At ten this morning I have to brief the President and I would like to give him your evaluation of the whole situation. Go ahead."

"Are you recording this?" Furmann was being cagey.

"Of course. Why do you ask?" Taylor didn't like being questioned.

"Because, if you play it back for the President just like I told you, he'll get the unadulterated truth and not some watered down version." Forestall snickered but caught himself.

"He'll hear, what I want him to hear and…"

"In that case, I'm not talking to you. I'll go with you in…"

"There's no way…"

"In that case I'm leaving." Jeff got up.

"Sit down. This is not the way we work around here and..."

"I noticed. That is why you had fewer results in six years than I had in two weeks. So you tell your President... my President, that I'll be glad to tell him all about it."

"In a ten minute briefing?"

"That's all the time he allots? That's all this means to him?"

"You don't understand..."

"Yes I do. Dozens of our women may be murdered before they're rescued and I laid my life on the line for them and you're gonna play footsie?" He got up again. "Tell the President, I'll talk to him any time he feels that this is an important matter." He turned to the door.

"Furmann, come back." The director rose up himself. "Tell me in five minutes what you feel I should tell the President in ten minutes."

Jeff turned, but remained standing. "Tell him, we now have the conclusive evidence of at least one, just one, organization of perverted arch criminals that deal in kidnapped American slaves and that at least twenty-four of our girls may be in imminent danger of getting killed when word leaks out that we're on their trail. Immediate and decisive action alone can save those citizens. We need action now. *NOW!"* He hollered as he slammed the door behind him.

"Forestall, go after him. Make sure he stays here. He may have to appear before the President. Tell'em that." Jack disappeared and Taylor said to the other two agents in the room, "At least that'll keep'em here for a while."

Forestall caught up with him at the elevator.

"Jeff, hold it. I'm riding down with you. Take it easy. Let me buy you a cup of coffee." Because there were other people in the lift, they did not exchange another word until they were all the way down.

"I hate that! I hate that! It has 'screw-up' written all over it. I hate it." Jeff was still fuming.

"You forget how valuable you are to this operation..."

"I just found out upstairs. Two weeks of laying my life on the line is worth ten minutes. That's how valuable I am."

"The planning and briefing of the other agents in order to get a twenty-four prong action launched at one time will have to be very precise. You will have to tell the whole team what to expect, based on what you have experienced, and the President may very well need to hear you before giving it his stamp of approval."

Jeff's face lit up a little as they pushed through the cafeteria line. With coffee in hand, they found a vacant table, just as Jack's cell phone rang.

"Yes, he's with me. Yes, I'll tell him. I'll come along." He clicked off.

"You're going to be before the senate sub-committee at two. I'll take you there."

"Sub-committee? And then the real committee? See what I mean? It'll be Christmas before anything gets done and by then these charming senators will have blood on their hands. Do they really give a shit?"

"Let's hope so, Jeff. Let's hope so."

"What do you do before a senate committee?"

"You sit at a table before them, with a microphone in front of you and you…"

"Like they sit on a podium or a bench like a judge and I sit below them, so they can impress me with their importance?"

"Something like that."

"Jeez. Can I just get back into the field and solve some crimes? I have little or no respect for those clowns who seem to have one obsession…"

"Like what?"

"Like getting rich off taxpayer's money."

"There are some honest, dedic…",

"There are? Boy, I may be in for a surprise."

Golden Nuggets
XXXXVII
The Sub-Committee

Agent Jeff Furmann, in all his twenty-nine years, had never been inside the capitol building. The mere size of the structure surprised him, but the interior of the rotunda nearly overwhelmed him.

"Wow! So this is where some of our money goes, Jack."

"Not some! A whole lot. Here's where they decide whether I'll get paid next year."

"You? Not me?"

"No Jeff, you're being paid by the State of Colorado."

"Oh, yeah. That's right. Maybe I'm lucky."

"Like how?"

"Like they can't cut my pay this afternoon, no matter what I say."

Jack chuckled, "No, they may cut your balls off at the rate you've been going, but they won't be able to cut your pay." They stepped into the elevator. "Here we go. We're twenty minutes early, do you wanna take a tour?"

"Right on, man. Show me around."

At 2PM they were seated in the gallery of the hearing room. In front of them on the main floor was a table, outfitted with three microphones and along the opposing wall was an imposing bench, resembling a courthouse structure. Behind the bench were nine equally imposing chairs, each one fit for the Queen of England. The nameplates indicated that eight males and one female were expected to ascend their thrones, but by 2:10, nobody was in the room, except the two agents and a technician.

At 2:16 PM, six Senators filed in, five men and one woman and Jeff whispered at Jack, "Where are the rest? Playing golf?"

"Maybe they're out campaigning."

The man in the middle of the bench banged his gavel; "The hearing will now come to order."

"What order?" Jeff whispered again. "I thought we were pretty orderly."

"Shush."

A lady appeared through a side door and took a seat a few rows behind the table on the floor.

"Recorder!" Jack whispered.

The man with the gavel spoke up, "Is Agent Jeffrey Furmann present?"

Jeff stood up. "Present." He made a mock salute.

"Will you please come forward and take a seat at the center mike on the table."

"Sure." He got up and asked, "Jack are you coming?"

"I haven't been asked."

Furmann approached the table, made himself comfortable and pulled the mike closer to him. He spoke into the instrument, "Is this thing on?" He could hear his voice on the speaker system and the obvious leader of the panel, said, "Yes, you're on." He looked to both sides, checking if his fellow panelists were ready and spoke up.

"The Senate sub-committee on National Security is now in session. Sir," He looked directly at Furmann and said, "Will you please rise, raise your right hand and swear that you will tell the truth, the whole truth and nothing but the truth, so help you God?"

"I will if all of you rise and swear right along with me."

A murmur rose from behind the bench, but the man with the gavel, the Honorable Jason Goldfarb, wasn't amused. "Mr. Furmann, will you please adhere to the rules of this committee hearing and swear as requested."

"Like I said, I'll swear to tell the truth, if you people swear the same thing..." The gavel interrupted, bang, bang, bang... "Mr. Furmann, you either cooperate or we'll hold you in contempt."

"In other words, you folks behind that beautiful desk can lie all you want, while I'm being held to the truth? No way! You're sitting here, stalling the rescue of a number of American Citizens instead of giving orders to initiate the operation..."

Bang, bang, bang... "Mr. Furmann..."

"In case you don't know yet! Twenty-four American women are held in captivity and when word gets out that we're on their trail and that I already have liberated one of them, these girls will be murdered on the spot, as to get rid of the evidence...."

Bang, bang, bang, "Mr. Furmann, one last time..."

"Mrs. Kellogg?" He addressed the sole lady on the panel, the Honorable Estelle Kellogg, "Do you have a daughter? What would you do if your daughter was kidnapped by an old perverted Arab and raped daily on a huge bed underneath dozens of slanted mirrors? Would you take action or sit here and talk?"

"I... I, I don't know what..." She stuttered.

"What if you knew that five of the sons of the esteemed sheik, gang raped her as well, teaching their youngest one, fourteen, the finer tricks of sex on your daughter's body?"

The lady gagged and pulled a tissue from her pocketbook.

"And what would you do if you knew she was eight months pregnant, but didn't know by whom?" Jeff kept shouting while she got up. "And if the sheik finds out that he might not be the father, he'll kill your daughter, not his sons, no, he'd kill you daughter for being unfaithful..."

Mrs. Kellogg threw up before she reached the door.

The Honorable Mr. Goldfarb must have pushed a hidden button, because two armed bailiffs rushed in and approached Furmann as he stood behind the witness table. It didn't keep him from carrying on. "I hope you are recording this and rush it to the President, so he'll be inspired to take action before you have the blood of our American women on your hands."

"Arrest that man!" Goldfarb shouted, but two of his colleagues rose and urged the chairman to hold off a minute.

"I want to hear what this man has to say." One of them spoke up loudly. "Can we have some order and have Mr. Furmann calmly state his case?"

"Okay, okay!" Goldbarb calmed down and pointed at Forestall in the gallery, "Sir, can you come down to the floor a moment?"

"Sure thing!" Jack got up and joined Jeff and the deputies at the witness table.

"Sir? What is your name?" Goldfarb was still standing.

"Special Agent Jack Forestall, CIA, sir."

"Are you familiar with this case and…"

"Very much so…, I…"

"Now you're helping them stall even longer while there are twenty four innocent lives on the …"

"Bailiff, take him out! Now!"

The uniformed men grabbed Jeff by the arms and started to pull him away from the table, but the G-man didn't stop. "The whole country will know when one of these women dies because of your dilly dallying, that your senseless stalling is responsible for their death…"

"Hold it a minute!" One of the other Senators spoke up again. "Mr. Furmann? Can you summarize in five minutes what is going on, so we can indeed jump into action?"

"Five minutes? Okay. I walk out in five minutes." The bailiffs turned him loose. Jeff picked up a mike and spoke rapidly, "For years, good looking blonde girls have been kidnapped and sold to rich foreign perverts who added them to their harem. I have freed one of them and have obtained the list of twenty-four other ones, surviving in slavery in eight different countries. Some authorities want to free these girls through diplomatic negotiations, and have the culprits punished by their own governments." He took a deep breath. "Well, you know what that means. The first thing they'll do is get rid of the evidence and in this case, these are our girls. They'll be murdered and disposed of. This is a stupid way to go about this. We need immediate covert action to save their lives and I hope you will now contact our President and initiate that action."

"Mr. Furmann, you said you liberated one. Who is she and where is she?"

"Her name is Karen Van Doren, she's eight months pregnant and in a military hospital in Rahmstein , Germany. Her parents are on their way to meet her."

Jeff put down the mike and shouted, "My five minutes are up. Now it's up to you to save these lives or contribute to their murders." He turned and for a moment it seemed the deputies would grab him again, but a shake of the head from the chairman negated that.

"Mr. Forestall, would you kindly stay a moment?" Jack had gotten up, but sat back down.

Furmann turned one more time, "IF I'm ever called back here, I'll bring a camera crew to show America how much you really care!" With that, he opened the door and was gone.

Twenty minutes later, Jack found his protégée staring at one of the many beautiful paintings in the rotunda.

"Jack? Has this country really become the greatest nation on earth because of jackasses like that on that committee, or did we really have some tough decision makers in the past?"

"Jeff, one comes to mind. Truman had to make a tough decision; kill thousands, including women and children in order to potentially save a million American lives. He did."

"The atom bomb?"

"Yep. I could give you a thousand other examples of men… and women, who did what they had to do for our country, including you."

"Me? What did I do?"

"What did you do Jeff? You laid your life on the line to save just one of our citizens and you would do it again and again, wouldn't you?"

"Damn right I would."

"Jeff, there are hundreds, even thousands of Americans that would do the same. That's what makes us the greatest nation."

"Oops."

Golden Nuggets
XXXXVIII
Interpol?

On the drive back, Jeff tried to convince Jack that he should go directly to his hotel, grab his stuff and fly off to Colorado.

"All I do here is I get more aggravated, because I'm not doing anything. My hands are tied. I turned over all the data pertaining to the *golden nuggets* and there's nothing I can do here."

"Do you have your papers back?"

"Papers? You mean the documents?"

"No, I mean your driver's license, your passport? Your own identity?"

"Oh, no!"

"You also have to register your hours with Admin and get paid. You've got a buncha money coming, so let's take care of all that and say goodbye to the director..."

"You mean Taylor? Do you suppose, he'll even talk to me? He must've heard about my antics with the sub-committee. I doubt if he'll even see me, but I don't give a damn.... , all I wanted to do is shake this bureaucracy into action, any kind of action instead of just talking and negotiating and maybe I did some good. That lady Kellogg might be the key. She got really shook up when she imagined what really happens in those boudoirs. She may ..."

"Scuse me, my phone." Jack whipped out his cell phone and

flipped it open. "We're on I-95, just south of Alexandria." He listened for a while and spoke again, "Sure thing. That sounds great! Will do!" and he clicked off.

"What was that?" Jeff couldn't control his curiosity.

"We're going to Ferry Farms."

"What's Ferry Farms?"

"A little town just above Fredericksburg and there's a great steakhouse called *Foxfire*, where we'll meet the brass for dinner."

"Really? Why there?"

"Like us, they have to eat sometime and we have a private room there that's electronically safe, so we can talk freely and eat prime rib at the same time."

"That part sounds good. What's the occasion?"

"You'll love this. Some action has been undertaken. You'll meet with a team from Interpol..."

"Interpol?"

"Yep, they've just flown in from London, including two chaps from Scotland Yard..."

"Hoorah! We're going international!"

"Yes and promise me something. Be at your cooperative best. Don't blow your cool at them. They'll pump you for every episode of your action overseas and they may be repetitious. All they want to know is every little detail that may help them to spring the girls. You'll..."

"All this was told you in a ten second phone call?"

Jack had to chuckle in spite of himself. "No, no. I've worked with them before and picture this; they already have a man in Russia, several in Saudi, in Bagdad, Oman and many other places. They may spring into action tonight based on whatever information you already brought and other data that you may fill them in on."

"Now you're talking! I tell you what. I'm going to behave like a gentleman, no, like a Colorado Agent. You'll be proud of me."

"Good, I'm counting on you. I hope they give you time to eat."

"Me too. I hope it's Rocky Mountain beef."

The *Foxfire* was already crowded and Jack had a hard time finding a parking spot. The business has been known for years for its quality food and its proximity to Langley Air Force Base made it a popular spot for Military and CIA personnel alike.

Jack led them to a backdoor, where a numbered lock allowed them entrance after a few pushes on the code pad. The interior was all dark mahogany and chrome trim. Very impressive. Jack made a few turns down the carpeted halls and Jeff trailed along until they encountered another controlled door. When it opened, they were met instantly by Mr. Jeb Taylor, who gloriously called out, "And... here's our hero of the hour. Mr. Jeff Furmann."

Jeff was so flabbergasted they could've knocked him over with a feather. Taylor seemed almost jubilant. The surprised agent turned to Jack, wanting to ask, "What happened?" But didn't get the chance. Taylor grabbed him by the arm and introduced him around to the gathering of intelligence agents, standing around with drinks in their hands. That was highly unfair, because Jeff could certainly use one by now.

Jack must've known, because he pressed a cold Heineken in Jeff's hand and that way, the introductions went off without a break. Jeff forgot the names of everyone he met as soon as he turned to the next one, except for one. A chubby round faced Britisher with a purple nose, who was introduced as Inspector, Johnston-Jones, Scotland Yard.

After everyone was acquainted, Taylor rang for silence by hitting a wine glass with a fork.

"Gentlemen... excuse me, ladies, (there were two ladies in the room.) in half an hour the salads will be served and I'd like to take that time to have Mr. Furmann (that's the first time he called me 'mister', Jeff thought.) tell us briefly what transpired between the time he received a call that an Assistant DA was missing until today."

"Briefly? I could write a book." Everyone laughed out loud.

"Come over here Jeff." (That's the first time he's called me Jeff.) The director led him to the head of the table. "And please... don't interrupt him. Make actual or mental notes about anything you want to ask, but I'd like this boy to tell us in thirty minutes what he has accomplished."

Jeff started off slowly. The phone call in the mountains, the arrest of Buck and Connors, the frustrating flight to Dallas, then New Orleans. The arrest of Bob and the recovery of Anne Dubois. He was on a roll and indeed, no one interrupted him. He relayed what he knew about the capture of the *Bright Enterprise* , since he was not personally involved in that action.

The involvement of the CIA, the trip to Upper Manhattan and the frustration, that Vito had escaped the net. The trip to the islands and again the disappointment that they were just minutes behind the criminal.

He was interrupted by a chuckle when he told them about his mustache and suntan, which still made him look like a Mid-Easterner. His story in Oman and meeting up with Achmed in Dubai was interrupted by the food and he was asked to continue after the salad.

Thankfully, they served a hearty red wine in anticipation of the steaks and it helped lubricate his tongue.

After the salad plates were removed, he was asked to continue the story and he summarized his experience with the sheik and the helicopter trip in just a few minutes, including the rescue of Karen Van Doren.

Food delayed his speech again and he was glad to devour a sixteen ounce piece of prime-rib. After desert was served plus an after dinner drink and coffee, Jeff again continued, but didn't mention the money from the sheik's safe that Karen still had in her possession. The shooting of Vito Marchetti and his aide, ended his story. The rest would have been just window dressing.

"Do I understand that no one in the Emirates has any idea that an American or America was involved in the kidnapping of the 'copter and the sheik?" One Englishman asked.

"Not unless the chopper pilot mentioned it to other members of the staff downstairs when he went to get the pregnant girl, but I doubt he would have spoken to anyone."

"So as far as Abu Dhabi is concerned it may have been a competitor or enemy of the sheik who..." Johnston-Jones asked the question.

"Yes, they have no clue that the consulate or any Americans were involved at all."

"Brilliant. Let them believe that it may have been ordinary bandits that were involved. Is there a chance that the downed helicopter or the body of the sheik would reveal any kind of identification of you or the girl?"

"No, only the shells I left behind, but they were from a Glock and that kinda pistol is available all over the world. They could even suspect the Austrians or the Germans, wherever that gun is fabricated."

That evoked a lot of laughter. "Yeah, Jeff! Blame it on the Germans."

"I have a question for you. The ambassador in the capitol was most uncooperative. He is lovingly known as the Honorable Asshole..." He was interrupted by laughter. "Could he have contacted the authorities to arrange for a peaceful extraction of the girl and could the initial contact with their embassy from New Orleans about the slave ship have alerted them to our attack and thus warned them that this was an American action?"

"Good point, Jeff. Something we'll have to look into." Director Taylor had taken over the discussion. "The Interpol people and Mr. Furmann will stay right here for further debriefing and planning. All who are also involved in this process will be asked to remain, everyone else is excused if you so desire. We'll clear the far end of the table and why don't you Interpol people take the lead?"

Jeff stepped back and let himself be led to the far end of the table, where English, French and German foreign agents settled all around him. They produced a detailed photograph of the Emirates capitol and asked Jeff to pinpoint the sheik's palace. That part was simple. The satellite picture was so clear it could have been taken from a thousand feet up.

"See here, facing the water on the north, this is a third story landing pad on top of the rear structure. Here on the south side is the all-glass wall and entrance to his boudoir with the round bed and the mirrors. Here is where his wall safe is located, so we never left the third floor and nobody saw us. That I know of!" He added hastily. "So we walked back to the chopper for the return flight, but this time in the company of the girl."

"Didn't the sheik try to resist?"

"You forget that I shot him through his hand and tied his arms behind his back. All I had to do was grab his wrists, lift his arms and he would scream in agony."

"And his pilot?"

"He knew I would shoot his boss first and then him. He wasn't that stupid."

"Mr. Furmann, would you ever consider coming to work for Interpol?"

"That's funny!" He laughed out loud. "I should ask, 'how's the money?' but instead, is there any action?"

"You better believe it! Furmann, you better believe it."

Golden Nuggets
XXXXIX
Homebound?

Jeff's head was spinning when he woke up. So much had happened in the last forty eight hours that he wondered if it were all real? His watch told him it was 9:25 AM, but his head felt as if it were two in the morning. With a start he sat up in bed. Wasn't he supposed to be somewhere at eight this morning? He couldn't remember. Thank God, the little fridge near the door had orange juice and the room provided him with his own coffee maker.

The Interpol people were on a different time clock and had talked and drunk last night until two in the morning. First at the restaurant, and then in the hotel room of one of the agents. That's what did him in. They had fixed Martini's with Tanqueray gin, flavored with Stock vermouth and that, on top of the wine and the beer he had at the *Foxfire,* had knocked him for a loop.

The shower helped, but he still couldn't remember where he was supposed to be at this hour. He decided to call Jack Forestall on his cell, but all he got was a recorder.

"The hell with them. I need some food." He always felt better when he talked to himself. The breakfast nook was still functioning on the first floor and that did the trick. Two servings of scrambled eggs and plenty of biscuits and gravy and he felt like himself again. Just as he considered calling the penthouse to find out if he were scheduled to be anyplace at a given time, a waitress walked up to him with a phone in hand, "Mr, Furmann? Call for you." She handed him the instrument.

"Furmann here!"

"Jack here. How are you feeling?"

"Me? I feel great. Just finished a hearty breakfast and I'm ready to go jogging."

"You're kiddin'!"

"No. How about you and am I supposed to be anywhere at this moment? Somewhere important?"

"Not that I know of. We're meeting at one with the chief and I was going to ask you if you wanna meet for lunch?'

"Lunch? I just finished a huge breakfast. Where are you?"

"I went home and I'm on my way back in. I have some stuff to do, but why don't you come by my office at twelve-thirty and we'll meet the boss at one."

"Where's your office?"

"On the eighth floor. Eight-two-four."

"Okay!"

A workout in the weight room and another nap did wonders for Jeff's brain and his physique. He had calmed down considerably, knowing that action was being taken by a mass of intelligence officers in different parts of the world.

Jack smiled at him when he walked in. "I've got your I.D.'s for you, but you still have to give an accounting of all your hours and expenses, so they can cut you a check before you leave."

"I'm leaving? Where am I going?"

"Home, I guess. We'll find out in a few minutes."

Find out they did. The meeting room was half full of agents, some of whom Jeff knew and some he didn't recognize. When they were all supplied with coffee or water, Taylor walked in and as usual, didn't offer much of a greeting.

"Gentlemen, ladies, Furmann," He nodded in Jeff's direction.

"There's much to be done." He looked at his notepad. "Jackson, you get with the Marshalls in New Orleans and execute the sale of the ship. What's its name again?"

"*The Bright Adventure*." Someone offered.

"Right! Samuels, you get with the FBI in Dallas. Arrange for the sale of the house and storage, confiscate all his assets after all the data is collected." He looked at his notes. "Klose, you're handling the details in Manhattan about Marchetti's condo and bank accounts. Fenster, you foreclose on the Bahamas' properties and you…," He pointed at Furmann. "you handle the operation in Colorado. We're raising as much money as possible to compensate the victims as they're returned to this country. Find the rest of the gold, sell the criminals' properties, oversee their prosecution and wrap it all up. Details will be provided. Forestall is your contact man."

He looked around the room. "Good hunting, men. This is a proud day for the agency."

With that he walked out.

"Just like that? I'm in charge of the Colorado mop-up? Wipe it all up, he said. On who's payroll? Federal or State?" Jeff felt as if he had just been dismissed.

"You're executing CIA orders, so I guess you remain on the Federal payroll a little longer." Jack seemed content. "That means that we communicate a lot and coordinate your activities. Let's start by getting your paycheck and get you outta here and on your way home. The first thing you do is, take a few days off with your family and…"

"You're my boss now, Jack?"

"Your coordinator, remember? And the first thing I'm coordinating is your get-together with your wife and son. Meanwhile, I'll review all the events in Colorado that led to the kidnapping of the Assistant DA and I'll e-mail that info to you and we'll decide what happens first. The two kidnappers have to be tried, their properties sold and the canyon has to be cleared of all crashed vehicles, so we can identify their owners…"

"Okay, okay! I got the picture. Let's do it. Where do I go for my check?"

"Come on, I'll take you."

The credit card in name of *Jeffrey Morgana* and the matching passport were turned in and a new CIA I.D. was issued along with a Federal credit card in name of Jeffrey Furmann. He was urged to charge all expenses on that card, rather than saving bills and submitting them for re-imbursement. Jeff collected the few leftover clothes he possessed plus the ones that had been shipped back from the Bahamas. While packing everything in a new suitcase that Jack had provided, he felt as if it had been years since he first flew into Langley on orders from Director Taylor. His head was spinning with all the newly acquired knowledge and memories and he decided to write a book about his experiences and call it *The Golden Nuggets*

A company plane brought him to *Ronald Reagan International* where he connected with a direct flight to Denver. His wife was at work when he reached her on his new cell phone but she would meet him at the terminal by the time he landed.

Being home again was a blessing. It seemed his son grew two inches every month and his computer skill doubled every two weeks. It was amazing to Jeff what that kid could show him. Music programs that helped with his guitar lessons, aerial photographs of Bagdad and Afghanistan, the house numbers on the homes across the street… it was fabulous.

"You're gonna be able to help me a lot in my work, my boy. I can study the places right here at home."

"What places, Dad?"

"Places that I need to go to, like a deep canyon in the Rockies and a pass on top of a 9,000 foot mountain."

"Okay, tell me what co-ordinates and…"

"Not now. Now you're heading for bed and your mother and I will talk about where we wanna go for a few days."

"Like back to the Bahamas?"

"Yeah! Maybe. Go brush your teeth."

Going away was not as simple as he thought. School was in the middle of FCAT tests, his wife's job company couldn't spare her right now, but Jeff could go fishing and relax for a few days.

None of that appealed to him, so by the time they hit the bed, he was determined to go to work the following morning. Maybe by going to the CBI office and shooting the breeze with the guys and the chief and maybe shoot some pool in the afternoon. In other words; start off slowly.

It was good to be home again and by the time they snuggled together in the big king sized bed, he forgot all about golden nuggets and nasty old Arabs.

His visit with good ol' Baxter was a pleasure. The Denver office had heard nothing but positives about their wayward agent and his extraordinary exploits. While sharing lunch, the bureau chief had the staff compile all the info they had on the gold theft case and Jeff could take it home and reflect on it at his leisure. That suited him fine.

He picked up his son from school and the two of them got on the computer to locate first; the canyon where the cars were dumped by Buck Buckley and then concentrated on the pass where a motorcycle had started the entire event.

"I betcha Dad, that there's still gold hidden out there. I betcha these guys didn't turn in everything, what do you think?"

"You may have a good point there. Let's look at my reports a moment and acquaint ourselves with the people involved. By the way, can you look up where McCoy is?"

"What's a McCoy?"

"It's a town in the middle of Colorado. Capital M, small c, capital C, o,y."

"I'll find it Dad. Don't worry."

"You're a good man, Charlie Brown!"

Golden Nuggets
XXXXX
Lost Gold

"Let's try this, son. There's a scrap of paper found in this guy Randy's truck that reads; *51 paces from the parking lot 6 feet from the tree*. No punctuation, no capital letters, just *51 paces from the parking lot 6 feet from the tree*. What parking lot? Where did this guy live? Wait a minute... He was from Boulder... Parking lot? Park? Let's zoom in on Boulder while I call the sheriff out there."

"The sheriff, please."

"Who may I say is calling?"

"Furmann, CBI." He wondered if he should have said, CIA?

"Just a moment."

"Sheriff Ralph Koontz here."

"Good afternoon, sir, this is Jeff Furmann, CBI. I'd like to ask you something."

"Shoot."

"A week or two ago, you investigated the theft of some gold nuggets, right?"

"Right, and the guy who stole'em got killed."

"Right! Did you ever locate the stolen nuggets?"

"No, the State Police have the saddle bag that was in his pickup, but we suspect that it was only part of the loot. We believe that this guy Randy had already hidden his half somewhere."

"Is there a park in Boulder that I'm not aware of? A park he may have frequented?"

"No, the biggest one near here is at Loveland, but you might ask his girlfriend, I mean his former girlfriend, 'cause she and her girls spent weekends together a lot with this Randy..."

"Do you have a name and number for her?"

"Just a moment." The phone went dead.

He came back on. "Her name is Judy and I have two numbers for her. Her work and home."

"Great."

"Ms. Judy?" He had forgotten to ask if she had a last name. "My name is Furmann with the CBI and I hope you don't mind if I ask you something."

"No sir, go ahead."

"Did you and your friend Randy go camping or fishing sometimes and where?"

"No camping, but he loved, Randy that is, he loved to teach my girls how to fish."

"Where'd you go?"

"Loveland, usually."

"Thank you so much."

"Any problems, sir?"

"No problems, thank you." He felt funny about not saying things like, "I'm sorry for your loss." Or something else appropriate. After all Randy was not a fiancée or a husband, was he?

Turning to his son, "Joey. How would you like to go fishing tomorrow? We can bring a lunch and picnic in the park. Whaddaya say?"

"Where are we gonna get bait?"

Being that the next day was Saturday, that worked out well. Before eight in the morning, they were on their way.

"Are we going to Boyd State Park or to Carter Lake Reservoir?" The young mother wanted to know.

"To Boyd State, if I'm not mistaken. I don't know if there's any fishing allowed in the reservoir, but we'll find out. Maybe we'll go to both."

Instead of fixing lunch, they decided to get a bucket of Kentucky Fried Chicken legs and muffins, so all they carried with them was a cooler with Coors and Pepsi. Joey had been forewarned, "Don't say 'are we there yet?' Not even once!"

The trip took about an hour and a half and the weather cooperated beautifully, partially cloudy, but no chance of rain. When they reached the park, Jeff drove to the far end, hoping that the measurements started from the very end of the parking lot. They put out their folding chairs and baited their hooks with frozen shrimp, that they bought at the park entrance. Joey was too much on edge to go fishing.

"Shouldn't we look for the treasure first, Dad?"

"Don't you wanna catch some fish first?"

"Let's find the gold first."

"Okay. Let me bait them up and then your mother can haul in anything that bites on any of the rods."

"What are you boys up to?" The hush-hush conversation made Julie suspicious.

"We're just checking out some leads about the gold robbery. You never know."

"Gold along this pond?"

"You'll never know. You just keep hauling in the fish."

"Fifty-one paces from the parking lot. Here we go, buddy." Jeff had produced a slip of paper from his windbreaker and started pacing north along the lake. At approximately 50 yards, there was indeed a sizable tree.

"This has gotta be it. Now six feet from the tree. Six feet? Which way? There's nothing within six feet except a pile of rocks along the water."

"That's where it's gotta be, Dad."

"Okay, let's start diggin'"

One by one, they removed the rocks that surrounded a little tree. Actually just a twig that had been planted a year ago. Most of the rocks were small enough for Joey to handle and Jeff took care of the bigger ones.

"There's nothin' here, Dad. Did you bring a shovel? We may have to go deep."

"Wait a minute, wait a minute! Do you see that wire? Move the dirt away from the tree. See? A wire is tied around it. Stainless steel. Good thinking. Won't rust through in a hurry. Let's see where it goes." He lifted the cable and exposed it all the way to the water's edge.

"There you go, Joey! He dumped it in the water and tied a string to the little tree, so he could haul it up later. Let's bring it in."

Both of them bent over the water's edge and started pulling up the suspected treasure. Once the five gallon bucket broke the water line, the contraption became quite heavy and Jeff said, "Step back, Joey, this damn thing weighs a ton."

"Wow! A ton of gold, Dad? How much is that worth?"

"I don't think it's all gold." He had to laugh at his son's enthusiasm, while heaving the heavy bucket onto the shore.

"I think he weighed it down with rocks, so it wouldn't float to the surface. Let's see." He undid the cable from the tree and the can handle. "Nice quality. Might have lasted twenty years. This guy was no dummy."

Next they removed the layers of tape, electrical, covered by layers of duct tape and finally the lid came off.

"Like I thought. Rocks. Let's get them out."

Small rocks and gravel were tossed out and a plastic bag that was sealed in another bag appeared on the bottom and Jeff stopped at that point.

"Ain't we gonna look at the gold, Dad?"

"Not yet. I want witnesses."

"Whaddaya mean?"

"Just a second." He whipped out his cell phone and dialed 9-1-1. "Operator, this is not an emergency, I repeat, this is NOT an emergency. Connect me with the Loveland Police or Sheriff's Department please."

"Who's calling?"

"Special Agent Furmann, please connect me, it's urgent."

"I thought you said it was not an emergency?"

"Would you kindly connect me?" He started to shout.

"Just a moment."

"Loveland Police, Sergeant Wallace."

"Sergeant this is Agent Furmann, CBI, please send a forensic team to the north end of the parking lot at Boyd Park. No sirens or flashing lights please, but hurry."

"What's the nature of your call?"

"Federal and State business. Please have them hurry."

"What's your cell number?"

Jeff felt like saying, "Isn't it on the screen in front of you, but realized that the sergeant was not looking at the same computer as the 9-1-1 operator, so he gave him his number.

"404 area code?"

"Yes. CIA. Now hurry and get some guys over here."

He turned to Joey, "Let's get back to our fishing poles until those white coats get here."

"White coats?"

"Yeah, you know those lab-coats that the technicians wear?"

"What do we need them for, Dad?"

"Fingerprints, registration, paperwork and so on. Let's go fishing."

Twenty minutes later a team of three 'white coats' that weren't in white coats at all, followed by two local policemen appeared on the scene. Furmann had them take pictures and measurements of the recovery area and the bucket itself. They didn't open the plastic bags, much to Joey's disappointment. They would do that later in the lab.

Forms were filled out and signed and the forensic people left the three fishermen behind.

The spirit for fishing had totally disappeared.

"Man, why couldn't I see the gold, Dad?"

"They have their own way of doing things. They open one bag and record that. Then the next one and again they take pictures and write it down, all the while testing for fingerprints."

"Why Dad?"

"So they have proof of all sorts when they go to court and..."

"How dull. I don't wanna fish any more." The look on Julie's face reflected the same sentiment.

Jeff's face lit up. How would you like to go and spend the night in Estes Park or Steamboat?"

"Yeah man!"

"Can we, really?"

"Let's go!"

Golden Nuggets
XXXXXI
Steamboat beauty

It barely took one hour to bring them to one of the most scenic parts of Estes Park, and the Kentucky fries were great in a roadside rest stop.

"We oughta come up here and ski sometimes, Dad."

""Yeah, it's not as high as Arapahoe and Breckenridge, but they seem to have nice slopes. The snow doesn't last here as long either."

"How's Steamboat? Have you ever skied that?"

"I have." Julie jumped in. What I like there is that you ski right to your hotel room door. You don't have to unload and unpack and drive back and forth. You walk to the lift from your hotel and ski right down to your back entrance."

"Oh, Dad, can we go see it? How far is it from here, Mom?"

"I guess a coupla hours, maybe less. What do you think Jeff?"

"Wanna go?"

"Can we Dad? Can we?"

"After you wash up a little, you've got chicken crust all over your chin."

Steamboat Springs.

"Which hotel did you stay in? Mom? Can we stay there too?"

"Ask your Dad. There, that's the one." She pointed to the far right of the city panorama unfolding before them. "The high rise. You look right onto the ski slopes if you have a room on the north side. What do you say Jeff?"

"Let's do it. Let's spend some of that money I earned on my last trip."

"How much did you make, Dad?"

"A bunch. They must have paid me overtime for every hour I was away. I didn't question it, I didn't try to figure it out, I just took the check and deposited it in the bank. So let's do it. I may even make this a business trip if I can include some business in my trip. How does that sound?"

"You're evil or you're a genius, I don't know which?"

"I prefer genius."

"Me too, Dad. The way you figured out where that gold was, was pure genius."

"That's my boy. Here's the hotel. How will it look if we have no luggage?"

"If we didn't have Joey with us it might look a bit shady, but with a kid? What can they think?"

"Let's get the highest available room on the north side. What do you say?"

"I say 'amen' to that."

The CIA credit card did wonders and the weather contributed to the success of the adventure by racing clouds around the mountain tops, exposing them from time to time and hiding them in veils of white in the intervals.

Joey was ecstatic. Julie was more practical, she studied the menu for the evening meal. Jeff was more businesslike, he studied the phonebook looking for Anne Dubois, but didn't locate her until a sergeant on duty with the Sheriff Department clued him in.

When he reached her, she was all enthused about hearing from Jeff again, but she was still very upset about the whole affair. She had not gone back to work and didn't plan to in the near future or ever. When she found out he was in town she insisted on him coming over to meet her husband and son. They decided on an after dinner drink at her house at seven. "Yes, of course. Bring your wife and son. Of course."

Anne's townhouse was in an elegant part of town and the Furmanns had no trouble finding it. They were welcomed by bear hugs, but the boys of either family didn't get into that. They just waved at one another when introduced. The seven and five year olds were off to some video game in seconds, conveniently leaving the parents by themselves.

"What's with the mustache?" The former DA couldn't believe her eyes.

"The CIA made me grow it, so I could pass for an Arab."

"Don't shave it off. It becomes you."

Once they settled down in the den with their drinks, the conversation rapidly went back to Anne's horrifying experience.

"I just couldn't go back to that office. I was terrified and besides, my boss resigned..."

"He did? Why?"

"The publicity and pressure from every source..."

"Like what?"

"Headlines, 'How could he send a woman out by herself to investigate a robbery? Isn't that a job for a pair of experienced detectives?' and so on."

"Holy Moses? And he resigned over that?" Jeff was a bit surprised.

"Yes, that and the same kind of pressure he received from the higher ups and other authorities."

"So who's running the show now?"

"One of the senior ADA's."

"Could you have gotten the job, Anne?"

"No, I'm just a new kid on the block, but I'm still disgusted with the whole setup. I don't know what I'm going to do." She looked distraught and her husband cut in, "She can relax for a while. She doesn't have to work..."

"Yes," She interrupted him. "I don't have to from a financial standpoint, but I do want to get back into the business world. I just don't want to go back to that office."

Jeff perked up. "How would you like to help with the repatriation of the golden nuggets?"

"The what?"

"I mean, helping the kidnapped girls back into society. We're accumulating a vast sum of money that will be dedicated to resettling the girls in society...."

"How many are there and where is all that money coming from?"

"How many? So far... the four from the ship, the *Bright Adventure* and one, a pregnant one, who I rescued out of Abu Dhabi, who's in Germany right now. All others will also be quarantined and hospitalized in Germany before returning them to the States. They're being liberated as we speak, I hope." He crossed his fingers as he talked. "The money? The properties on the mountain near the mine, the ship and assets in Dallas and New York have been confiscated and will be sold to support that effort. I don't know who is supposed to coordinate that effort, but I would nominate a certain Anne Dubois to head up that department..."

"You're kidding?"

"No. Who would be better suited? You have the education, the experience, pardon the expression, and you have the time. It's going to take a concerted effort to get all these pieces into the puzzle and the CIA may not have a more qualified person on hand than you."

"I don't know what to say."

"Let me make a call and we'll see if we can stir things up a bit." He took out his cell phone and pushed a few buttons. "Jack? How are you?... I'm fine. I'm sitting in the home of Anne Dubois... yes... that Anne Dubois... I AM on vacation. I'm here with my wife and son... Yes... We're in Steamboat Springs, planning our ski trips for this winter... but listen, Jack... Anne doesn't want to go back to the DA's office and the agency needs someone to coordinate the repatriation of the girls, their medical attention, their legal right, their subsidies and this is an educated lady, right here, who can handle all that, so bring it up to the brass and see what they say… Okay…. Okay… Same to you fellow!"

"What did he say?" Anne was all ears.

"He said, I'm supposed to be on vacation and enjoying myself. Well, do I look like I'm not enjoying myself?" That provoked a hearty laugh from everyone in the room. "He'll bring it up to big shots on Monday and they may get in touch with you or they may not. If you get the job, it might involve some travel, like to Germany and Washington, but I guess you could handle a lot of things by phone and computer, right?"

"I guess so. What do you think honey?" She turned to her husband, a nice looking man of about thirty, thirty-three.

"It certainly sounds like something you could put your teeth into. So far, all your cases as an Assistant DA have been jobs that an ordinary legal clerk could have handled, so this smells like a lot of excitement for you."

"If I would make trips out of the country, could I take my family?" She became more enthusiastic by the minute.

"Probably. At best, the government would pick up the tab, at worst, you would have to pay for their travel expenses, but that wouldn't be too bad."

"I always wanted to go to Europe." The husband chimed in.

Another burst of laughter, but Jeff cooled things a bit. "Don't start packing yet. Right now, it's only a suggestion, so don't hold your breath. I'll get back with you on Monday after I talk to the yoyos at Langley."

"What's at Langley?"

"CIA headquarters are on Langley Air Force Base in Virginia and that's where all the top level decisions are made. Some good, some bad. One of their good decisions was to send me to the Middle East, because that really got the ball rolling."

"How so?" Anne wanted to know.

"Well, for one thing I freed one of the girls, but more importantly, I obtained the whole list of kidnapped gals and their destinations and that is what Interpol is working with right now. You see, for years they've been working in the dark without any results, but ever since you got involved, six girls have already been liberated and many more should follow. So, Anne, if it hadn't been for you and your stupid boss sending you on that mission, things might still be at a status quo, but thanks to you, the ball got rolling."

"I think that deserves a toast."

"I'll drink to that!"

"Jeff, you'll drink to anything." Julie smiled as she said that.

"You're right and here's to some of the most beautiful women in the world."

"I hope he's talking 'bout us."

"Me too!"

Golden Nuggets
XXXXXII
View From The Pass

Sunday mornings in Steamboat Springs are magnificent, especially on sunny days in summer. The winter hustle and bustle of skiers rushing in and out of restaurants and making for the slopes was non-existent, and the Furmanns had the sidewalks to themselves. A leisurely breakfast and a morning stroll quickly turned into boredom for little Joey and he wanted to see more action or get back to his TV game.

"Are we just gonna walk, Dad?"

"Isn't that nice?"

"All these buildings look like they're from an old Western Movie..."

"That's the idea."

"But Dad, I've seen enough of them."

"Whaddaya say Julie? Wanna go home?" Jeff was enjoying the scenery.

"Can't we go see more of the mountains and the canyons while we're way out here?" Julie wasn't in any rush to get back to the flat part of Colorado.

"We could take a look at the old mine where all this started..."

"Yeah Dad! Let's. I could go mining for gold." Joey had had visions of vast fortunes.

"Okay, let's check out. Did we leave anything up in the room?"

"We didn't bring anything, remember?"

"Let's check anyway."

***

The rambling clapboard buildings looked as rustic as they did a week or so ago when Jeff first drove up to them. The same guard, Benny, appeared from behind the main structure, but this time without drawing his pistol.

"Hi, sir!" He had forgotten Furmann's name. "Welcome back. I read you found the lady lawyer and got her back. Good work."

"Thanks. These are my wife Julie and son Joey, and folks; this is Benny, the superior guard."

"Superior?" Julie laughed.

"If he hadn't been on the ball and guided me up these slopes to the culprits, the whole chase wouldn't have taken place and those girls could have been in captivity for many more years. So, it was his superior intellect and his exceptional detective nose that made all this possible."

Benny grinned from ear to ear. "That's quite a…"

"It's true. Is there still any trace of gold anywhere? In a creek or cave?"

"Sorry sir, not an ounce has been recovered in twenty years. Now they just mine gravel… over there." He pointed over his shoulder.

Jeff turned to his kid, "Sorry Joey. Maybe we can buy a Nintendo somewhere. Bummer, son. Bummer." Turning back to the guard, "Is the canyon where they dumped the cars far from here and would it be worth my while going there?"

"I only know the approximate location, but the Highway Patrol on the other side of Kremmlin has been hauling them out, so you could see the wrecks in their compound and they could direct you if you wanted to."

"Which would mean coming back in this direction, right?"

"I guess so." The young man shrugged as he smiled at the little group.

"Before we go, is the museum worth a visit and do you have access to it?"

"I have the keys. Be my guest."

Julie got excited, "Come Joey, let's see how they mined that stuff way back when."

"But I can't have any of it, right?"

"I'm afraid so. Let's go."

CHP barracks. 1PM.

"The inspectors aren't here on Sunday, but we do have the nuggets in our vault. I can show'em to you, but I have no authority to transfer possession, if that..."

"No Sergeant, I just want to look at them and weigh them if I can or at least guess at their weight."

"Oh, that'll work. The weight is marked on the bag."

"That'll be great."

Back on the road.

"Just as I thought. What the Highway Patrol has is only part of the partial loot."

"What are you saying, Jeff?"

"What they have in their safe is about one third of what we found yesterday in the lake, so what I'm saying is; there's a lot more gold somewhere else."

"How do you figure?"

"Well, the guys that stole the loot divided it, right?"

"How do we know?" Feminine intuition made her question every detail.

"If we pulled off a robbery wouldn't we want an even split?"

"Not if one of them felt she was the boss. I could demand more."

"He obviously didn't work with his wife, because it was a guy who went over the edge on his motorcycle. Anyway, I'm assuming they made an even split, so each bunch should weigh the same, right?"

"I guess so." She still wasn't happy that her theory was dismissed.

"Well, the CHP found the saddlebag from the bike in the pickup truck of the murderer, Randy, I believe. The amount was one third the weight of Randy's half in the lake and the guys divvied it up in threes before the killing started, right?"

"I don't know."

"Well, I'm tellin' you they did, so that means that two thirds is still missing or hidden on the mountain. The only living survivor is this kid in McCoy and he may be playing footsie with us."

"Where's McCoy?"

"I'm not sure, but I understand it's some hole in the ground about two hours from here, somewhere north of Frisco."

"Are we going there today?" Her tone of voice reflected that McCoy was not her favorite destination.

"No, today, we'll go up on the pass and enjoy the view and snoop around a little and then we go home, Okay? We oughta be home by six or so. Okay by you?"

"That sounds good."

Other than a majestic view on either side of the pass, there wasn't much to see. A bunch of *No Trespassing* signs were the only indication that some event might have taken place around there, but that was it. Mom and son stared at the valley and the mountains to the west, while Dad was calling the Sheriff's Department in McCoy, after which they turned around to take in the view to the east.

On the way back, Joey slept and Julie hummed popular tunes along with a radio station that reached that side of the mountains. Jeff's mind was working. It might have been a day off, but his brain didn't rest. He knew what he was going to do next. It all depended on a return call from the sheriff in McCoy. After a while, he relaxed and started to hum along with his wife, who was wholeheartedly enjoying the scenery.

"I'm a lucky guy." He mused.

8 PM Boulder suburb.

"Yes Sheriff… Sheriff who?... Cobalt?... Thanks for calling back on a Sunday night. I'm Jeff Furman with the CBI and I've been put in charge of cleaning up the details of this messy operation...." He listened for a minute. "Yes, yes, she's fine, we saw her last night, but the reason for my call was, the boy who discovered the gold... what's his name?... Brad?... Can you get him to come into your office in the morning... Shouldn't be any sweat?... Good... How long would it take me to drive from Boulder to McCoy in the mornin'?... So can you have him there at eleven?... Great, don't panic him, so he would take off on us... Beautiful... I'll see you at eleven. Thanks Sheriff.... Yeah, you too. Thanks."

"What was that all about?" Julie had only heard the one-sided part of the conversation.

"Remember I said that... let me see... two thirds of one half equals one third, right?" He counted something on his fingers, "Yeah, I'm right. One third of the gold is still missing and I think I know who's got it and I intend to find it tomorrow. Don't worry. We'll get up at regular hours and I drive off when you and Joey leave the house. Remember I'm off for a few days?"

"You're off for a few days? All you've done was work. Your mind hasn't stopped for a minute."

"But didn't we have a lovely weekend? Come over here, the weekend isn't over yet."

Golden Nuggets
XXXXXIII
More Golden Nuggets

Just after seven in the morning, CBI Agent Jeff Furmann was on I-70, roaring west. He would be in McCoy well ahead of time, but it would allow him time to confer with Sheriff Cobalt. At first he was puzzled why rescue units from as far away as that little town would respond to distress calls all the way up on the Pass, but then he realized there wasn't much else around to support an emergency outfit.

Breezing along the Interstate at that hour, going away from Denver was a cinch. He was itching to call Langley and find out if any other young women had been liberated and what the CIA's reaction would be to his recommendation of Anne Dubois for project director. Patience was not his greatest virtue, but he diverted his thinking to the problem at hand. How would he persuade the young man in McCoy to cough up the rest of the treasure trove, without getting violent. So far, his emotional outbursts hadn't hurt him or the case, but he knew he couldn't continue that and get away with it. Although he felt very justified in pulling some of the stunts he had gotten away with in the past few weeks, he was smart enough to know that career-wise, he was better off becoming a bit more subtle and sticking within the guidelines of the Agency.

All in all, he felt good. He would have liked to run around the Mid East some more, knocking off a few more slave traders, but that was out of his hands for now, so he relaxed.

Exit 157 told him to turn north on SR 131 and before long he was in McCoy, looking for the Sheriff's office because it wasn't on the main drag. Obviously, everyone in town knew how to direct him.

Sergeant Roper was at the front desk, surprised to see a man in a suit and a tie, not the typical neighbor. "Sir, can I help you?"

"I'm a bit early, but I'm expected by Sheriff Cobalt."

"Your name, sir?"

"Agent Furmann, CBI."

"The sheriff just stepped out, but I'll call him right now."

"If he's having breakfast, tell him to finish. I'm way early."

Roper chuckled, "How'd you know?"

"Been around, I guess. I'll grab some coffee if I may."

"Go into the break room on your left. Help yourself."

Ten minutes later the sheriff breezed in. "Hiya, Mr. Furmann, you sure are early."

"I hardly ever travel this way, except in winter when we go skiing and I expect long delays all the time. Not now though."

"Come into my office. The boy will be here within the hour, Mr. Furmann…"

"Jeff, please."

"Okay Jeff, if you call me Ronald."

"Okay," as he followed the lawman to his back office.

When seated, Cobalt addressed the G-man, "What gives us the honor of your presence all the way out here?"

"Mathematics."

"Mathematics? Like in arithmetic?"

"Exactly. We recovered some of the gold that was stolen from the old mining museum and we figure that some of it is still missing, like one third."

"And you think Brad knows?"

"I know Brad knows, but Brad doesn't know that I know, and I don't know where it's at, so that's what we'll find out in the next hour."

"Really? I had some suspicion, because he walks around with half a dozen nuggets in his pockets, but he's such a fine young boy..." He cleared his throat. "I've known him and his folks all his life and..."

"I don't doubt that he's a fine young fellow, but more than half of the prison population weren't criminals until a chance to a crime presented itself and all of a sudden, they're criminals. What I wanna do Sheriff..."

"Ronald."

"Uh, Ronald. I'm gonna scare him into telling me where the gold is. You follow us there. We'll officially arrest him and you bring him back here. I continue east to Denver with the loot and you arrange bail for the kid with your local judge. I have a feeling that he may get off with probation if he cooperates, but that is up to the judge. My concern is to raise a barrel full of money for the slave girls that will be repatriated shortly and need to be able to start a new life. So don't get startled when I put the screws on him. I'm not half as bad as I look."

"What's with those girls that you're talking about?"

"You don't know?"

"Remember we're way out in the sticks, Jeff. We barely hear rumors."

"Let's refresh our coffee, while I tell you. It'll make your hair stand on end."

The interrogation room, 11 A.M.

Brad was surprised when the desk sergeant took him directly into that bare room with the huge mirror on the wall. A plain wooden picnic table and benches was all the furniture in the place and it had no decorations whatsoever. After sitting still for about twenty seconds, he became fidgety and started staring at the mirror. One minute later he got up and tried to walk out, but the door was locked. Another door on the opposite side of the room was also inaccessible because there was no door knob.

"Can I have some coffee?" He hollered at the ceiling, but nothing happened. Sitting down again, his head kept swiveling from right to left as if an apparition was due there any minute.

Furmann and Cobalt were standing on the other side of the mirror, coffee cups in hand while Sergeant Roper was fine-tuning the camcorder.

"He's getting ripe!" Jeff whispered.

"I'll say."

"Get ready to burst in if he gets violent, although I doubt that. He looks fairly docile." He put his cup down and picked up a yellow pad and a pencil. "I'm ready. Give me ten minutes and we'll be going on a hike in the mountains." He walked away and opened the door.

Brad jumped, but didn't say anything. Neither did Jeff. He sat down at the opposite side of the table and started writing. It was quiet for half a minute.

"Who are you and what do want with me?"

Furmann leaned across the table and yelled; "*SHUT UP!*"

Brad nearly choked. Another long pause... Finally...

"Where'd you hide the rest of the gold?"

"I don't know what you're talking about."

Jeff stared at him for a long moment and said very softly, "Let me tell you something, boy. We're going to find that gold. It's halfway between the point where you murdered that guy..."

"It was self-defense..."

"SHUT UP!' Like I was saying; it's halfway between the point where you murdered the guy and the road. Probably near a protruding rock or a very noticeable tree. Our dogs will find it in minutes, but let me tell you something. Have you ever been in prison?"

"No sir, I've never even seen one."

"Prison isn't too bad, it's the people in them. Hardened criminals, murderers, thieves, rapists and stalkers. That would be your company for a while. Not very nice company. They'll steal the money your Mom sent you to buy an ice cream bar, they'll knife you if you squeal or resist and the guards won't do anything about it, because they're afraid of the bums. If you don't cooperate with us, I guess you'll get five to ten in State Prison. You'll be branded for life. You won't get your job back, because you're a felon. No girl will date you because you're an ex-con. Her father would rather shoot you. Your best chances will be that you'll commit another crime, so you can go up the road again, maybe for life." He stopped and wrote something on the pad, letting his words sink in.

"But sir..." Furmann didn't look up.

"Sir! I didn't steal those nuggets, we found them!" He raised his voice.

"But you knew they weren't yours, right?"

"But we found them, sir and..."

"I'll tell you what. You take us to the gold and we'll testify in your behalf. You keep lying to me and I'll testify against you in court, making sure that the judge will hit you with the maximum including cold blooded murder."

"But sir, he was coming at me with his knife and I hit him with the crowbar..."

"Behind the ears? From behind? That's self defense?"

"But I hit him under the chin first..."

"Are you gonna show us where the gold is or not?"

"Yes! Yes!" He stood up. "I'll show you. It's one point one miles off the road behind a big aspen..."

Jeff stood up. "Come on. We're going prospecting."

Opening the door, he faced Cobalt, "Do you have a four wheel drive in your fleet?"

"Sure do, a Jeep Wagoneer."

"Good, cuff this boy in your backseat and you lead the way. I'll get into the jeep with you when we get to the dirt road. Do you have another deputy to ride with us? I don't wanna get lonely."

"No problem. Let's roll. Come on Brad. You're coming with me."

Golden Nuggets
XXXXXIV
Buckling Up

The female deputy was pleasant company for Furmann, but she also had additional assets. She took shorthand. All the way to Gore Pass, Jeff was driving and the young lawwoman took notes. He rattled off some of the things he should be doing as yet in Colorado to tie all the loose ends together and she scribbled without asking too many questions.

She was fascinated though, when the CBI agent started into the slavery part of his experience and hung onto every word about the mine, the mansion and the disappearance of the cars into the ravine.

"Make a separate note for me to check how many cars they have retrieved and how many more there may be in that canyon. That'll give me an exact count how many girls they kidnapped through their organization."

"Will they get the chair?" The deputy wanted to know.

"If they don't, I may be tempted to go to their prison and personally execute the bastards. Can you imagine the anguish they have put these gals through? Don't get me started on that. I might personally choke'em after I did some more damaging things to their family jewels..." He shook his head. "Let's change the subject. Would any girl go to that mine while being out here on a skiing trip or would they go in pairs?"

"Girls always go in pairs, at least."

"That means that we multiply the wrecks found in the ravine by at least two and we know how many women they captured right here under our noses. Do you realize that the CIA and the FBI have been working on that problem for at least ten years without any discernable results? Is that unbelievable? And I happened to stumble on it, because of this minor gold theft. In this law enforcement business, you never know what will happen next, no matter how well you plan. Anyway, I'm having a great time at it, how about you?"

"Are you kidding? In our county, I mainly act as a secretary and phone operator. I've never even drawn a gun on anybody."

"How long have you been at it?" Jeff smiled at her briefly as the curving road straightened out for a while.

"Four years. That's it."

"Married?"

"Just a year ago."

"Don't knock it. The excitement comes in spurts and it's not always pleasant, so enjoy it while you can." He pushed on the brakes. "Oh, they're slowing and pulling over, so this must be it. You get in the front with Cobalt and I'll ride in the back with our young prospector. Here goes."

"How far down, Brad?" The sheriff was easing down the dirt road.

"One point one mile, exactly. You'll see a big aspen on your left. Very white bark."

"Okay. They call this a county road? It's just a pair of tracks."

"Officially, it's Federal Road 277, but it's more of a road on the north side."

"Federal Road? You must have done your homework."

"Oh, we studied the layout and the aerial photographs, otherwise we would never… there it is!" He pointed at a tall white skinned aspen that stood out amongst the shrub and the pines. "That's it Sheriff."

The jeep slid to a stop and all four piled out.

"Take his cuffs off, would you." Jeff ordered. "Did we bring a shovel?"

"We don't need one. I didn't bury them very deep." Brad walked behind the tree, moved some rocks, scraped some dirt with a twig and... "There you go." He held up a bundle, consisting of a piece of cloth and a McDonald napkin. "This was to be Greg's and my share. It's his handkerchief." He choked as he handed it over. "But the sonofabitch must've wanted it all for himself, so he knifed Greg..." He broke up.

"Come on. Let's go. Deputy, put this in a plastic bag and give it to Mr. Furmann. I've got to find a way to turn around. No way can I back up all the way to the road."

"Just a little further down," Brad volunteered. "There's a wide spot, just a coupl'a hundred yards."

"Okay, hop in. Do you want the cuffs back on him? Mr. Furmann?"

"No, that is, if he hands over the gold he still has in his pockets."

Sheepishly, Brad reached inside his pants and produced six more nuggets.

"Thanks. Turn around and pick me up on the way back. I wanna make some notes here."

"Okay." Three of them drove off while Jeff walked up and down a bit, got a feel of the scene and did some scribbling. Within minutes the Jeep returned, facing uphill this time and Jeff climbed aboard for the drive back to the road.

They shook hands and Jeff thanked them for their cooperation and added, "Deputy, when you have all these notes typed up can you fax or E-mail them to me? Here's my card. I'd really appreciate that."

"Sure thing, Mr. Furmann."

The Highway Patrol compound revealed six busted up cars that had been recovered from the ravine and they had neatly typed up the registrations info that matched the vehicles. Jeff kept a copy for himself and faxed another to Anne Dubois, figuring it would be up to her to inform the parents of the owners and their passengers who had disappeared with the cars. He shuddered at the thought of having to do that, and he hoped that the former Assistant DA was up to the task, if she was appointed by the CIA.

The newfound nuggets were added to the saddlebag and transport was arranged to CBI headquarters.

At the Kremmlin town jail, he arranged for the transfer of Connors and Buckley to Denver and visited briefly with Buckley in his cell.

"Are they feeding you alright, Buckley?"

"I hate them sonsabitches. Cain't get one simple drink."

"Talking about drinking. What did you give those girls to make'em pass out?"

"I don't know. I jes fixed the tea and put two drops in the cups for the girls and that knocked'em out in seconds."

"What were those drops?"

"Oh, I don't know. Connors bought them someplace."

"You lousy lowdown bastards!" He turned around and started to leave.

Buck Buckley cried after him, "When will I get out of this dump?"

"When we send you straight to hell!" Jeff slammed the door.

By mid afternoon, Agent Furmann was back in his office and found a message to call Forestall at Langley.

"Hiya Jeff. Have you checked your e-mail?"

"No, I just walked in. What does it say?"

"Briefly, sixteen girls have arrived in Frankfurt and two more are underway."

"That's great. What about the others?"

"That's the bad news. The one in Russia is dead. We expect she was poisoned, but have no proof so far. Two in Saudi are yet unaccounted for, because it's near impossible to get into those castles of the filthy rich Arabs. But we haven't given up hope."

"That was fast. How'd you pull it off?"

"Unofficially, Jeff, Interpol has agents all over the place. You won't believe the scope of that operation. They're fantastic. They might be a great job for you."

"Nah! I like being home with my wife and kid."

"Really? Well good for you. How's things out there?"

"I've got it pretty much wrapped up, but by the way, did Anne Dubois get accepted?"

"Oh, you don't know? She'll be arriving in Langley within the hour. We'll see what she's made of, but she sounds good so far."

"Well, good for you. You guys do something right sometimes."

"Sure we do, all the time. Did you see the note that the President wants to see you?"

"Tell'im, I'm busy."

"Sure."

The End

The following are some excerpts from Frits Forrer's other books

Excerpt from:

Five Years Under The Swastika

Pappa has preceded him down and is warming milk on the electric stove. Mama and Jopie file into the kitchen too and Mama begins again: "You should…"

"HUSH!" Pappa interrupts softly, but sternly. Mamma gets cups down from the cupboard and puts cocoa mix in them, waiting for the milk to get warm.

"Why Pappa? Why? What have they done? And that little girl, what's her name? The granddaughter? They hurt her Pappa! Why Pappy, why? What did SHE do?"

Pappa stirs the chocolate milk. "Come sit at the table."

Frits turns, Joop and Mama are deadly quiet.

"Drink your cocoa! Watch it, it's hot. Hold it…. let me add some cold… here you go. Stir it! Okay, okay."

"Why Pappa, why? I know what you're gonna say: They're JEWISH right? But what did they do? They're not rich Jews that ruin the world and all that garbage. They're poor working people. He's been working for the County-Water-Department for as long as we've known him. He goes to work on his bike at four in the morning, every morning, I know Pappa, he's not rich, I know! Why then Pappa, why? They'll never come back, I know it. They're gonna kill'em!"

Tears are running down his cheeks, Mama is not doing much better and Jopie is staring in his chocolate milk as if there's something fascinating in it.

Mama hands Frits a handkerchief: "Here, dry your tears. Drink your cocoa."

"There's nothing I can say, Frits... nothing! Goddamnit!"

Pappa's last word shoots out with such vengeance that all three of them look up at him, startled.

"Sit down, Herman, drink your cocoa too!"

She's worried that his ulcer will flare up. "Why don't we all drink up-up-up and go to bed. It's too cold in here. Take your cocoa if it's too hot and let's go. Come boys."

Frits is still crying uncontrollably.

"Come in bed with us."

For the first time in years, he's in bed between his father and his mother, his skinny body shaking with the sobs that won't stop.

Finally, with his head against his father's chest, he falls asleep, blissfully.

The WOHLSTEINS were the first.

Excerpt from:

Smack Between The Eyes

"Now comes the hard part!" Frank walked away from Joey, who looked like a businessman on his way home. Nice suit, white shirt and a very conservative tie. His brown briefcase and a laptop bag swung over his shoulder completed his disguise.

Several detectives, including a cleaning lady, were posted near the arrival spot and two were at the end of the ramp, in case anyone wanted to escape from the rear door.

The large bus slowly rolled to a stop. The door opened and Frank stepped up to give the folks a hand, exiting the bus. Some refused his hand, some gratefully grabbed it.

Frank looked at each face as they unloaded and tried to match it with the pictures he had received on the fax and the e-mail.

The only one who bore the least bit of resemblance was an elegant gentleman in a light suit, blue shirt and white tie. His white fedora and his goatee gave him the look of a Caribbean planter.

After the last passenger descended, Frank boarded the bus, scanned it quickly and jumped off.

"Joey! That's the one! The guy with the white hat!" He mouthed it, rather than holler it, but Joey got the message. He ran after the disappearing figure in the crowd. Frank followed. Luck was with them. The elegant planter stopped to look around.

"Probably looking for Nita." Frank thought.

The man reached into his coat pocket and Frank as well as Joey pulled out there guns. The man's hand came out with a cell phone that he flipped open in order to dial, so he never saw the two officers rushing toward him until he heard: "Hands up! You're under arrest!"

His reaction was swift. With his left hand, he threw the cell phone at Frank and with his right hand he reached in his pocket and fired a shot at Joey, hitting him in the hip.

Frank ducked and the phone hit him in his bus driver's hat. In that very second, Hotta Hotta fired off one more shot, turned and disappeared in the crowd.

PANDEMONIUM!

People falling to the floor, officers shouting orders, women screaming and Frank jumping over bodies, trying to get to the fleeing man. An off-duty policeman tackled Frank, thinking he was the culprit and the gunman escaped.

All the police ended up with was a white hat and a cell phone.

Frank was soooooo mad, he could have spit bullets.

ISBN 0-9714490-6-6

Excerpt from:

The Fun Of Flying

Pieter drove around, looking for a quiet spot and settled for a corner lot, surrounded by trees. From the debris on the lot, they built a campfire and concentrated on the task of opening up their beer bottles without the benefit of a bottle opener. That was an interesting challenge!

Two guys would take a bottle each, hook the 'crown-caps' together and pulled till one of them came off, while the other guy got sprayed with beer. Harm was soaked in no time flat and took off his beautiful jacket and threw it someplace. Soon, his shirt was soaked as well and inasmuch as he couldn't handle the buttons in his inebriate state, he tore the shirt to threads.

Meanwhile, some 'serious' singing was being done by the campfire and everybody was in 'excellent' voice that night.

Somewhere during the evening, it was decided that throwing beer bottles all over the place was not very civilized, so they improved the situation by organizing a 'trapshoot'! One guy would throw his bottle in the air, while others threw theirs after it, trying to hit it in mid-air.

Their 'hit' averages stunk, but it felt like a refined kinda way to discard the empties.

Just as the averages were improving by the light of a bigger and improved campfire, sirens started screaming in their direction and soon two police cars ran onto the sidewalk, spitting out four bulky policemen.

"Hands up over your heads!" They meant business!

The boys didn't.

"So nice of you to come! Find a seat and we'll see if we can find you a beer."

"Shut up and raise those hands!"

"In our country, we are more polite than that!"

"We don't give a shit about your country! UP! Up! Now! Put your hands on top of the cars! Now!"

"That won't be necessary, Mr. Policeman. We believe that they're your cars."

"Shut up, I said. Put those hands on the cars!" They were getting mad and rough and started pushing.

"After you, sir!"

"Like hell! Up! Up!"

"Officer, all we were doing was singing a few songs. Is that so bad?"

"You're all under arrest for 'Disturbance of the peace'"

"Officers, if you ever came to visit in our country, we would treat you a lot nicer, I'm sure."

Meanwhile the cops felt them down, but other than 'hiccups' they had nothing on them.

"Get in the cars!"

"After you, sir. After you!"

"Negative. Get the hell in!"

On the way to the station they asked the cops if they had any special requests and they would gladly perform them for'em.

The total ride took only five minutes and they were put in a big cage with just one more occupant; a dead-down drunk who stared at them with wide eyes and a dumb look on his face. He had probably never seen a spectacle like that before in his entire life.

Seven guys, profusely thanking the cops for the ride and offering to pay the cab fare.

Once left alone, the songs started up again and at the stroke of midnight, they stood at attention and sang the American and Dutch National Anthems.

The policeman on duty thought it was very funny and kept supplying them with ice water. Nice touch.

ISBN 0-9714490-3-1

Excerpt from:

Tampa Justice
No Money, No Justice.

Your Honor, I was not informed of all the things that are involved in probation and I want to change my plea to Not Guilty, so I can have a trial and that will clear me for sure."

Well 'Fisheyes' objected vehemently. He had his 'conviction' and he was not about to take a chance on losing it.

"Mr. Fernon?"

"Your Honor, I do not want to represent Mr. Forrer in a trial, because I told Mr. Forrer that I don't do criminal work."

"Then why the hell did you take my case?"

"Mr. Forrer, you will maintain order!"

"Yeah, but Judge, I hired him to...."

"Mr. Fernon, raise your right hand. Is the testimony you're about to give, the truth, the whole truth and nothing but the truth, so help you God?"

"I do."

"Go ahead Mr. Fernon, state your case."

"Your Honor, I told Mr. Forrer, I don't do criminal work and I can not represent him in a trial."

THAT LYING BASTARD! I presented him with two CRIMINAL summonses and he took my thousand dollars to represent me.

"Very well, the motion to change plea is denied and we'll schedule a restitution hearing. Case dismissed."

The bastards! Just like that, in a matter of seconds I'm stuck with a verdict and there's not a damn thing I can do about it. I'm on a five year probation and I'm stuck with it.

To make matters worse, I received a notice from the Department of Professional Regulation that because of my "Nolo Contendere" plea, my Contractors License was revoked.

Apparently, when someone pleads "No Contest" in a construction case, it is assumed by the Department that the person is Guilty and it calls for an automatic revocation.

In other words: I was put out of business.

ISBN 0-9714490-5-8

Excerpt from:

To Judge Or Not To Judge

Pandemonium

J.F.K.
1:30 PM

Three people down! Two shot and one knocked unconscious. Two on the outside of the X-Ray check-in, one on the inside. For a minute or two there was so much confusion, that undercover security police nearly tangled with undercover FBI agents. The problem was everyone was incognito. Nobody was in uniform, not even a jacket with FBI on it or an I.D. card around their necks or pinned to their chests. Bongers' loud voice finally restored order and had the law enforcement officers holster their pistols again without any more friendly casualties.

Peter was the only one so far and Bruce wanted to make sure it stayed that way. It took a little while to convince the locals that Peter was NOT with the FBI and NOT a suspect, but he DID work with them and shouldn't have been shot in the first place. Ambulances roared up to the entrance, EMS personnel raced in with stretchers, I.V. bottles and medicine bags. City police officers tried to take control, than backed off and offered help and cooperation and ten minutes later, all there was left to do was clean the blood off the floors and get the passenger lines moving again.

The Feds had cuffed the captives and moved them into the Rembrandt room temporarily, much to the frustration of the KLM personnel, who had to transfer their cherished first class customers to other, less luxurious quarters. Bruce had everything under control again except; *what to do with the two terrorists?* If the CIA snatched them from his possession, which was certainly within their rights, he might be limited in his access to them. If the New York City police took over, defense lawyers would immediately be informed according to the law and of course, they would tell their clients to zip their mouths.

He called his New York counterpart and got some good advice. The City police would just hold them in *protective* custody in their maximum security prison at Rikers Island and that way, the FBI and CIA could interrogate them while awaiting transportation to Guantanamo Bay where all the Taliban and al-Qaida prisoners were being held. Federal laws provided them with that loophole and Bongers would have at least a few days to put their noses to the grindstone and find out what that whole plot was all about.

A police paddy wagon was provided and while the city cops transported the culprits, Bruce had a chance to track his shooting victims, Peter and Sahira, to the Queens Hospital where emergency surgery was scheduled to take place any minute.

In Washington, Travis washed his hands of the transactions, 'cause he would have to inform the CIA immediately and Bongers had begged him for patience.

"I gotta have some time with them, Lester. If the CIA big shots get involved, the Arabs may clam up altogether and I need to find out what this is all about. I'll get it out of them. I know these clowns, I've worked in the Middle East long enough to know how to deal with them. I'll play one against the other. Just buy me some time

Lester. Stall them by saying ; *'There is an operation in progress, details will be released as soon as they become available.'*"

"Okay, Bruce. I have to trust you on that, but keep me posted immediately, okay?"

"Will do. Thanks."

The New Jersey Bureau Chief knew he was walking a thin line, but he had seen it too often, that when too many different agencies or individuals get involved, the suspects tend to draw into a shell and that wouldn't really help anybody.

"Bruno," he asked his sidekick, "get me a ride to Queens Hospital and hold it for a trip to Rikers Island. Preferably a local cop who knows the territory. Thanks."

He reached for the coffee pot that was ready to serve some first class customers and filled a tall mug. "Good God, I'm hungry. Forgot to eat. Well, it'll have to wait a little longer." He finished the hot tasty liquid. "Good stuff. Must be Dutch."

Rikers Island was originally purchased by the Rykers family in 1683. It's located in the East River between the Bronx and Queens and had many different uses over the years. Most memorable was the training of African-American soldiers during the civil war and the conversion to a prison in the 1930's. The facility houses over 15,000 inmates and is now connected to Queens by a bridge. With the cooperation of the Warden, Bongers should be able to keep his culprits secluded and hidden from the press and over-ambitious lawyers.

"So far, so good!" He said to himself as he climbed into a patrol car for the trip to Queens Hospitals and his innocent victims. "Let's hope they're alright."

ISBN 0-9714490-7-4

Excerpt from:

The Golden Pig
(El Cochino de Oro)

The sharpshooters unpacked their rifles, mounted their scopes and loaded the magazines. One shot with a Remington 30 odd o6 and the other had an H&H 222. Bongers admired the weapons and after putting on the safety, the shooter handed him the H&H and Bruce balanced the weapon in his hand as if he were guessing the weight, He shouldered it, pointing out the window and said: "Nice weapon, very light."

"Love it. Very flat trajectory. I bag groundhogs at three hundred yards.'

"Really? That's great." He handed back the rifle. Ten more minutes and they should be there. The silver snake in the distance grew larger by the minute and soon became a brownish band of muddy water.

"Target to our right at one o'clock." the pilot announced on the intercom, turning about ten degrees. He was looking directly at the mansion, but his passengers couldn't see it from the passenger compartment. Bongers undid his safety belt and got up in order to look over the pilot's shoulder. The captain in the left seat pointed straight ahead with his left hand while keeping his right on the joystick.

"Got it" He stared at the beautiful layout of an antebellum plantation with a massive lawn in front of the two-story colonial. "The plane's moving!" he shouted suddenly and indeed, although it was barely as big as a flea from this far out, they could detect movement. The yellow and black flea was drifting away from the dock.

"Get'em," Bongers ordered.

"Sir, please sit down and buckle in." The pilot spoke without looking up, both hands busy on his throttle and his control stick.

"Right." But he didn't budge. "They're gonna take off down river." He turned around and hollered: "Get ready. Secure that window. Hand me the hailer." That last order was directed to the co-pilot who handed him a mike that was connected to a bullhorn. The chopper nosed down and the throttle had the engine screaming. Their speed went up by forty knots.

Below and ahead, the yellow and black bug had turned with the bend of the river and after it passed two tugs with multiple barges in front of them, its wake became longer and wider, leaving two silver streaks in the water behind it.

"Get next to them." Bongers remained upright, holding on for dear life.

At that point the chopper was doing at least one hundred and thirty knots, while the little seaplane was struggling to pick up a take-off speed of sixty, so they closed fast. The helicopter pilot had to bank steeply to the left in order to end up in the same direction of the seaplane and Bongers was thrown into the side of the craft.

"Told you to buckle." The pilot said calmly as the G-man struggled to get back up. It didn't take long. "Fly alongside him, same speed."

The copter lurched back, its nose pitching up fast, but this time Bongers held on. Their speed bled off from 140 to 70 in no time, but Bruce lost sight of the plane. Thank God, the pilot didn't because all of a sudden, the little seaplane and the helicopter were flying formation, just fifty feet apart.

The man in the little bug wasn't aware of anything except his rate of climb and his speed. He was doing a good job. The plane was climbing at 400 feet a minute and his speed was slowly creeping up to ninety. Then, all of a sudden, he had the shock of his life. Over the noise of his engine, he could hear the drone of another motor, much bigger and louder than his. He looked to his left and there was a copter, fifty feet back and a loudspeaker bellowed: "Throttle back and land. This is the FBI."

His reaction was instinctive. In a second, he turned the plane on its right wing, dove to the ground and gave it full throttle. It was a case of desperation of the worst kind. There was no way he could outrun a helicopter that size, but his nerves were shot by the events of the last twenty four hours. He realized that his maneuver didn't work very well. Within minutes the helicopter was back in position off his left wing. By now, he was skimming the sea grass and flying between the cypress trees. He figured if he could stay on this heading and at this altitude, he'd be over the swamps of Texas and before long he'd be over the Gulf of Mexico, where he would have an advantage. He'd have more fuel than the chopper and they would have to land somewhere and he could possibly make Mexico without refueling. He concentrated on staying as low as he dared and he even throttled back a little in order to conserve gas. He was cruising at 110 and that was not bad. The annoying load speaker came on again: "Throttle back and land or we'll shoot you down."

Henry was gaining more confidence. He said to his wife, who was crying: "Shoot me down with what? They don't have rockets or a Gatlin gun. Who are they kidding? Mow me down with a pea-shooter?"

At that same moment, his side window shattered. "What the hell was that?"

Inside the copter, the window of the passenger compartment was lowered and two rifles were sticking out in the slipstream.

"Can you hit the gas tank or the engine?" Bongers was still very much in control, but also buckled in. Flying formation on the left of the plane gave him a front row view. Both guns fired. Both gunners aimed again. "Go.!"

This time, fuel streamed from the left wing and the cockpit disappeared in a fog of vapor. Henry banked sharp right, but he didn't have a chance of losing the chopper. It was nearly too easy. When the plane leveled without any attempt to slow down or land, the Jersey director ordered: "Take him out."

The shooters aimed for his head, but the buffeting of the chopper as well as the aircraft made them miss, still the 30-06 hit Robinson in the left shoulder and he inadvertently pulled on the stick with his right hand and the plane went straight up.

"Watch it!" Bruce hollered, because for a moment it seemed that the seaplane would land on top of the helicopter. The captain banked sharply and threw the coal to the engine and in seconds they were at three hundred feet, making a steep right turn and looking down on a spectacular sight. The seaplane had been yanked up so steeply, that it stalled and slid back momentarily, then it nosed over and glided down toward the swamp below it as if it were going to dive into the murky waters. The plane behaved as if someone was still at the controls, but Henry's body was slumped backwards and against the door, so the plane handled itself and just before hitting the water and sea grass, it nosed up again while the floats hit the surface and the plane glided along.

Up in the helicopter, they wondered if Mrs. Robinson was an accomplished pilot, but Bongers wasn't taking any chances. "Hit the pontoons. Shatter them if you can." Below them the throttle was still wide open and it looked as if it could take off again. Four shots apiece rang out and the floats started to settle a little deeper in the water, while the gas from the left wing still made for an impressive spray. From up above they watched a scene, reminiscent of a movie. With the motor running full blast, the plane sank deeper into the water until the propeller hit and at first just churned, but then seemed to be grabbed by a magic hand that pulled it under water and the plane dove, rolled on it's back, went under momentarily and floated back to the surface, upside down, the floats sticking up out of the water.

ISBN 0-9714490-8-2

Excerpt from:

Brothers, FOREVER!

His chance came the following day. They were introduced to remote-control explosives. Each one learned to attach a bomb to a tree or a car, run for safety and detonate the device by pushing a button on the remote-control.

In a flash, Yousef switched controls with Amwar and watched as the older man ran downfield and tied his bomb to the rear wheel of an old truck and Yousef quickly pressed the button. Nobody noticed his thumb on the control, but everyone did see the Egyptian explode into a dozen fragments of human flesh. Screams of agony roared from a dozen mouths as they ran toward the victim, and Yousef ran right with them, dropping the remote in the dirt.

All bombs were inspected and reset, making sure there would not be any more accidental deaths. Training was suspended for the rest of the day and a proper funeral was arranged for the bits and pieces that had once been the Ugly Egyptian.

In bed, the young undercover man tried to feel remorse or any other emotion about the fact that he had killed a human being, but all he felt was satisfaction that he had done it so cleverly and aroused no suspicion. Everyone felt that it was the grey bearded Egyptian's own fault or maybe faulty equipment.

Joe slept like a baby. No nightmares.

ISBN 0-9714490-9-0

Excerpt from

The Curse Of The Black Mamba

For a moment she considered putting the diamonds back in the safe, "What could be a safer place?" but she quickly changed her mind. Slowly she walked out of the den, through the spacious living room and into her 'green room'. Burying them with the orchids seemed like a good idea at first, but when she spotted the Water Buffalo on her workbench, she hesitated. The trophy was nearly ready for mounting. It was the biggest buffalo her son Eric had ever bagged and she had single-handedly cleaned it, prepped it and all she had to do was mount it. She had become an expert taxidermist over the years.

"Brilliant!"

Quickly, she unscrewed the wooden back plate and it immediately exposed the hollow of the animal's head and the unusual horns. In seconds, the treasures disappeared into that vacuum and just as she was about to screw the plate back on, a vicious thought hit her, "If they find it, I'll make sure it'll kill'em."

Off the side of the greenhouse was the shed with her trophy snakes. She caught them, she bred them and she milked them. Mieke had a knack for getting venom out of the fangs of vipers and the Black Mamba was her favorite.

She put on her rubber gloves, grabbed a bottle of Mamba venom and in seconds she was back in the other room, ready to pour poison on the box with the golden coins and to soak the leather pouch holding the diamonds. A thought interrupted her, "How long will the poison last when it dries out and how effective will it be a year from now?"

From her desk in the 'snake room', she extracted a pamphlet and quickly scanned to the Black Mamba. The instructions about poison preservation used a lot of expensive and confusing words, like localized necrosis, enzymes, toxins, envenomation, etc., but she got the drift of it. All she had to do was mix the contents of a small bottle, showing a skull and bones on the label, with the poison and that would perpetuate the life of the potion through the development of protein. She didn't understand all of it, only that the venom would remain potent for a long time.

Careful not to spill any of the liquids, she poured them in a larger bottle over the sink and returned to the water buffalo in the next room. She poured the mixture over the cigar box holding the gold coins and into the leather pouch until the Eland skin was soaked, through and through.

Next, the board was screwed back on and the real task began.

The buffalo head weighed a ton, or so it seemed. She had planned to hang it in the den, but there was no way to get it over there by herself. In desperation she decided to hang it in the greenhouse right where it was, even though it would be terribly out of place.

"What the heck!"

A rope around a rafter helped her get it up and a chair on top of her workbench held it in place until she got some big screws through the board and into the wall. She stood back and looked at her handy work with satisfaction.

"Wait till I tell Eric."

She never got to tell him.

She was brutally murdered that night.

ISBN # 978-0-9822207-0-2

About the Author

Born in Belgium of Dutch parentage, Frits grew up along the German Border in Eastern Holland, enduring five years of German occupation and relentless bombing by the Allies.

This led to his first book, ***Five Years Under The Swastika.***

At age twenty, the Royal Netherlands Air Force shipped him to the U.S. for training with the U.S.A.F., earning his wings in October of '53. After completing 'gunnery' in Arizona, the young pilots returned to their home country flying the F-84 Thunderjet. Result; ***The Fun Of Flying***.

Upon completion of his military duty, Frits came back to America, this time as an Immigrant. After twenty years in the New York Metropolitan Area, Frits and his young family, (one girl, one boy,) moved to Tampa, Florida, where he became a General Contractor, which was the basis for; ***Tampa Justice, No Money, No Justice***.

He stayed active in the flying business, maintaining a Commercial and Instructors' rating, flying with many Flying Clubs and the Civil Air Patrol.

On a trip to Arizona, he met his present wife Katy whom he married in 2000.

During Hurricane Ivan, they lost their home and most of their possessions and decided to spend the rest of their lives on a boat. They now live on a 51 foot Cruiser, where Frits hammers out his novels and they sing their hearts out with several choirs and entertainment groups. He visits his old Squadron and his many relatives in Holland on a yearly basis and lives a happy and active life, speaking, singing, boating and writing.

LaVergne, TN USA
18 October 2009

161167LV00003B/1/P

9 780982 220719